Children's books by Evelyn Coleman

To Be a Drum

White Socks Only

The Glass Bottle Tree

The Foot Warmer and the Crow

WHAT A WOMAN'S GOTTA DO

Evelyn Coleman

SIMON & SCHUSTER

SIMON & SCHUSTER
Rockefeller Center
1230 Avenue of the Americas
New York, NY 10020

Designed by Sam Potts
Manufactured in the United States of America

1 3 5 7 9 10 8 6 4 2

Library of Congress Cataloging-in-Publication Data

Coleman, Evelyn, 1948–
What a woman's gotta do / Evelyn Coleman.
p.   cm.
1. Afro-Americans—Fiction. I. Title.
PS3553.047395W48 1998
813'.54—dc21   97-40257
CIP

ISBN 0-684-83175-9

This book is dedicated
to those who freely share so much of me:

Talib Din who married me knowing I didn't have
pots and pans and refused to cook even an egg.
You, my linguist, taught me that angels are on earth.
Soul mate, "you're the man the world should clone."

My mother, Annie S. Coleman,
my brother, Edward Joel Coleman,
my two daughters, Travara (Ty) and Latrayan (Sankofa),
who have always believed in me.
And to my granddaughter, Taylor Parker,
who didn't disturb me when I was on a writing roll.
And her father who remains in her life against all odds,
you're my son, Gamelin Parker.
And to Naphtali Selassie and Chris Speck
who love my daughters.

My father, Edward Jeffrey Coleman,
who taught me "the way of the mystic warrior."
And to all my relatives and friends
who've left this plane already.

And to Indy Choice, I love you.
You are in my memories forever.

PROLOGUE

Kenneth Lawson dreaded waking up. He squeezed his eyes tighter. His head burst with pain. The pain was like a computer virus eating up all his thoughts. Lately it seemed every inch of his face was an open sore, the pulsing ache radiating even from his eyeballs. The sunlight. It had to be the sunlight.

Keith had also noticed the same symptoms earlier, among them, a lowered libido and sperm count. Death for any man. What was life without children? Children to carry on your seed. But Kenneth had reasoned, What's wrong with dying? Until he met Patricia Conley.

He glanced over at his briefcase. The lock was still secure. Inside was the Glaser Safety Slug, sporting pellets of shot suspended in liquid Teflon for detonation on impact. "Glasers don't ricochet or drill through doors and walls—only men," Keith had told him proudly, last year after he'd purchased the gun for protection.

Damn gun. It sure as hell didn't protect you. We're both going to die soon either way, aren't we? But I don't want protection. I want something quite different.

He wished he could go on with his life, but it wasn't that simple. *Don't worry. I won't let them get away with it. Whoever did this to us is going down. And if it does have something to do with the diamond, well, you win. I'll get rid of it, just like you wanted. Sell it to the highest bidder. You were right. Kai is dead, it didn't matter what she'd left us. I should have listened.*

Today he was meeting the French-speaking woman, taking a risk that he'd catch up with Patricia too late. But this woman was his only lead. What she told him was crazy and he knew it. He'd gone to meet her many times before, still not wanting to believe everything she told him. Someone trying to kill her. Not only her but the others. Why kill people who were doomed to die soon anyway? Nothing she said made any damn sense. Plain crazy. Or was it? Either way, the meeting was too close for comfort to Patricia's office, even if it was in a back alley.

Yet, today this woman had given him no choice, once she'd said, in her accented voice, sounding words like they were a part of a sultry blues song, "You must come. I found out who killed your mother."

CHAPTER ONE

If a man shot me in the gut I couldn't feel sicker. I stood outside the door, mortified. My upper lip glistened, my palms itched and I was on the verge of crying. A woman motioned me in but I didn't move. Okay, I told myself. Patricia Conley, don't be such a wimp. Go on in and ask for it. All right. Pretend you're doing the equivalent. "I'd like to purchase a Beretta 950BS-N, twenty-five caliber." No, no. "I'd like a purse full of grenades, please." No, how about, "I'm interested in a vial of nitroglycerin and some fertilizer. See, I need it because I'm about to commit the most daring act of my life."

A man brushed by me, his shoulder grazing my arm. I checked my watch. I would be late if I didn't make my move now. Right now. I took a few breaths and walked in and up to the counter with my head down. This was not me. It couldn't be me doing this. I felt like I would die if the words came from my mouth. Okay. Enough of this bullshit. Either you're going to do this or you're not.

"I'd like to buy a corsage," I blurted out, never once looking up from the floor.

When I walked out with the orchid pinned to my dress I didn't even allow myself a smile. I knew the flower looked silly. Actually stupid. But I often dreamed of a whole row of photos. You know, the ones that everyone showed the next day in school. They're standing in long dresses grinning, a corsage on their front, beside their mother or father or both. That corsage became the symbol that made me aware of where I stood in the world. I didn't go to the prom or any other social activity in high school. I wasn't the ugly duckling; I was the tiger who spends its life alone. Now all that was about to change.

I glanced at myself in the storefront glass. A new me. All primped, a corsage on my chest and somewhere to go. I'd taken the final step when I'd toned down my cursing for this man. I, Patricia Conley, always tried to do the opposite of what any man wanted since Cripple Cooney. I was a brother's worst nightmare. Finally, I could let my guard down completely and share the scared-of-being-abandoned me with someone. I am finally free after thirty-one years of protecting, defending and fighting myself to stay alone. I checked my watch. Oh God. I was late.

At exactly 4 P.M., breathless and frantic, I raced to the counter of the Fulton County Probate Court at 136 Pryor Street. Kenneth Lawson was to meet me in front of the building at 3:30 P.M., and together we were going to Room C230. Knowing his usual penchant for promptness, I felt a tight knot in my throat when I didn't see him out front or in the waiting area.

Gasping for air and vowing to start jogging again I asked at the desk, "Have you seen a tall black man with a mustache and beard in here in the last thirty minutes?"

The woman gave me the kind of stare reserved for monkeys doing their business from trees, and then dramatically rolled her eyes slowly around the room.

I couldn't resist turning. I saw her point. Four tall black men with mustaches and beards were hunched over in earnest conversation with their ladies. I continued undaunted, "What I mean is, I was supposed to meet him outside and I thought—"

She shrugged before I could finish my sentence. So I shut up.

I collapsed on one of the plastic black and chrome chairs, crossed my legs and groped in my purse for a pen. Damn, everything but a pen. A journalist's nightmare.

I walked back to the counter, where a friendlier-looking woman stood. "I'm supposed to get married at the four-thirty ceremony today," I whispered. "You know, in the group thing, but we haven't bought the license yet because of a little glitch with my fiancé's ID. But he's getting it straightened out today and I, uh, suppose it took longer than he thought. So, I, uh, was wondering if I, uh, could maybe start filling out the form since our time is sort of running short."

She smiled warmly and handed me a clipboard with a pen on a string attached to it. I sat back down and read over it. My name, last name first. I ought to be able to handle that, unless of course my name was really "I, uh." Who the hell was that up there talking like some idiot barely able to speak?

Get a grip, Patricia Conley. You're losing it. You're only getting married for the first time. I continued comforting myself. Patricia, people do it every day. Some people do it more than one time if they're scamming. Get serious. Okay. Calm down.

Balancing the clipboard on my knee, I checked in my purse for the umpteenth time to make sure I had the proper ID. To be on the safe side, I'd brought it all. It's the one thing you learn quickly when you hit Atlanta. You can call up an agency as many times as you like, but once you're there, not a damn thing they told you will be right. Georgia Driver's License. Check. My newspaper ID. Check. My passport. Check.

While I ran through my checklist my mind marched on: Think about it. For the first time in your whole miserable life, you, Patricia Conley, will have the great American dream. A family. A real family. And all for the measly price of twenty-nine bucks.

The woman who sat next to me squirmed, her short jet-black hair sprouting blond roots. She had walked in with black manicured nails with white pelicans painted in the center. But at the rate she was chewing on them, the lower halves of the pelicans were surely crippled by now. And she would leave with not only varying sizes of silver and turquoise rings on each finger, but bloody nubs.

The tattooed man with her, his shoulder-length hair also dyed jet black, kept saying, "Damn, you gone bite your hand off before we even get in there."

The engagement ring on her finger made me wonder if Tattoo Man might have a pocket full of bubble gum, since I was reasonably sure the ring didn't pop out on the first try.

By 4:10 P.M. when Kenneth still hadn't shown, I asked Tattoo Man and Biting Nails, "Excuse me. Got any chewing gum?" Despite the tears stinging the corners of my eyes, I almost burst into laughter when he pulled out a handful of colorful balls.

"Look, don't take the red ones. They're mine," he said.

I don't suppose he noticed that his sweating hands and funked-up pockets had turned the red ones pink and speckled gray. I shook my head and said, "Thanks anyway, I can't chew bubble gum." I pointed to my top teeth—"Dentures"—hoping that this small lie would gross him out and he'd move back.

No such luck. Instead, he began describing in graphic detail how his own dentures almost popped out when he and Biting Nails got engaged at a piercing party. Then he lifted his T-shirt and showed off his ear-ringed nipple.

I wanted to throw up.

"You got any pierced parts?" he asked me, as if this was normal conversation. "Hey, if you want a tattoo, man, go to the place in Candler Park, you know, down beside Suzy's Hard Times Cafe. Shit, they're the best."

"You know where that is?" Biting Nails asked me.

"Yes, I know where it is and *if* I decide on piercing, I'll remember that's a good place," I said, wondering if they had a clue how crazy they seemed.

I went to Suzy's often. Her restaurant was located in a one-block strip in the Candler Park community and attracted an eclectic clientele. Suzy's was a borderline greasy spoon serving unquestionably the best Southern breakfast in town. Facing it was a tony bakery/cafe with great French cuisine named The Flying Biscuit.

Suzy had declared a silent war on the Biscuit's upscale customers, who on weekends insisted on sitting in front of her restaurant while waiting to go across the street. The last time I was there, Suzy's daughter had coated the outside window seat with honey, so if any fashion-conscious customer sat on it, all she had to do was sit her honey butt on a biscuit when she waltzed across the street.

But on the other hand, if you were one of Suzy's loyal customers, she'd clear a seat for you even as she cursed. I liked her a lot. If she wasn't white, she would be the kind of woman I suspected might have birthed me. Hard on the outside, but somewhere deep down under the layers of hard times and hurt, another story altogether.

In the parking lot, which had designated shared spaces with other businesses, she had signs that said it all, like: HONEY PIE, SWEET THING, IF YOU'RE STUPID ENOUGH TO PARK HERE THEN I'M STUPID ENOUGH TO HAVE YOU TOWED.

A clerk, unaware she was interrupting our piercing conversation, announced with the calloused tone of a welfare worker calling a recipient's number that we could go into the courtroom.

Everyone herded out the door, straining their necks to see who would go to the gallows with them. One gray-haired man said loudly, "I don't like this; it's too much like the Moonie stuff."

"Excuse me," I said to Biting Nails. "I'll be right back. If a black man, tall, six-six, beard and mustache comes in with a great apologetic, I'm-sorry-I'm-late smile, would you come get me from the rest room?"

"You got it," Tattoo Man answered as if I were talking to him. "His old lady is in the john. And LuAnn here will come git you."

He said it so loud the clerks looked up from what they were doing.

"Yeah. Right," I said.

"Miss," called the rolling-eyed woman before I could escape out the door, "do you want to turn your form in?"

I froze. I was hoping they'd forgotten the clipboard that I'd carefully placed on the chair when I'd gotten up. I snatched the clipboard off the chair and walked back over to the desk. I leaned in and whispered to her in a conspiratorial tone, "Oh. Sure, I'll leave it with you in case he comes rushing in here at the last minute like he always does," cursing inside my head for lying to her and myself. As I moved toward the door, the sound of her tearing up the form filled my ears. Okay, so maybe I *was* the only one believing the lie.

I saw LuAnn staring at me—water in her eyes. She knew the deal. I dropped my head. She came over and hugged me. I wished I could have let go and hugged her back, but instead I pushed her away and said, "Hey. You want to hold on to this for me?" I took the corsage off and pinned it to her sequined biker jacket.

I heard her saying thank you as I rushed to the bathroom. I wanted to get there before anyone could see my streaked face. I fished tissue from my purse with my ringless hand. Kenneth and I had decided no frills and no rings, at least for now. Kenneth said he couldn't afford a diamond ring.

I could hear my heels clanking loudly on the shiny tile floor and I felt all eyes on me—the jilted one.

The bathroom is where I was when I heard LuAnn Biting Nails stick her head in and whisper her own apology: "Sorry. He no showed. And I love the flower. How did you know I always wanted a corsage?"

And the bathroom is where I still was at 6:30 P.M. when the guard banged on the door and then stuck his head in, looking startled to find me there. I know I must have been a sight, crying for hours like that. He looked like he felt sorry for me when he told me it was past closing time and I'd have to leave the building. But it didn't stop his ass from whistling "Rainy Night in Georgia" while he waited for me to come out.

When I did emerge, I held my head down. Crying was not my usual bag, in public or private. Damn, this shit hurt.

Hey, I told myself, this is better than being stood up at the altar; at least you don't know the witnesses. And I can thank Kenneth Lawson, the dog, for insisting I not tell anyone.

I walked slowly up Pryor Street. It began drizzling so I picked up my stone feet as best I could. I hesitated when I needed to turn right to go to the newspaper. It was getting late, but the paper is open twenty-four hours. So I headed toward Macy's. The rain pricked my face, and I thought of the words to the song "Tears of a Clown" by Smokey Robinson. I walked hugging myself and merely trying not to collapse on the sidewalk. The balls of my feet were burning from walking in high heels. The sidewalks were some kind of brick inlay since the Olympics, but they felt like plain cement to me. The stores became a blur, my mind shut down and I understood why zombies move the way they do in movies.

I passed a French restaurant called Le Chef. I'd asked Kenneth to take me there recently but he'd declined. I slowed, mostly because of the tables placed on the sidewalk, like the owners believed they were still in France.

Out of habit I scanned the restaurant, always unconsciously looking for a new angle on a story. And that's when I saw him. Kenneth. Kenneth Lawson. Sitting in a booth toward the back of the restaurant near the kitchen entrance. He was leaning over the table, his hand entwined with . . . another's hands.

I blinked. Searing pain rippled through my eyes. It was a woman. Another woman. While I was waiting at the goddamn probate court, he was working on his ID, all right.

I could feel a blazing wave swoop down over me darker than the flock from the old Alfred Hitchcock movie. My stomach cramped and I staggered in the direction of the doorway. My nostrils flared. I wanted to go in and smash both their faces.

Instead, I moved toward the street, bumping into a blur of a coated man who smelled of garlic. He quickly sidestepped and lowered his head. My mind unconsciously noted, A vagrant. Only an alcoholic vagrant wears a thick coat like that in this hot weather.

Then, I made a mistake anyway, by hopping into a cab waiting for the light to change. I headed for the dojo.

CHAPTER TWO

I spit in my palms and watched Jake Fuller's six-feet-five, 280 pounds of steel muscle bow low at the waist, his rippled bald head glistening sweat.

"Come on, Patricia Conley, you lowlife bitch reporter," he murmured, breaking the rule of silence while sparring on the mat. "You want some of this?" he asked, putting his hand over his crotch and jerking it up and down.

I could see his contempt for any woman daring to join his dojo dancing on his face. As far as Jake Fuller was concerned, this wasn't any run-of-the-mill martial arts school; this was a men's-only party. No women invited.

"Hey, no rules. Full contact," he continued. "Until we're caught. What do you say?"

With a grin fit for a gargoyle, he spread his thick legs, twisting his feet back and forth as if he were squashing a cockroach with each foot. "You're dead meat, baby."

I didn't say a word but bowed only slightly at my waist, hoping the shihans were too busy to watch our sparring or interrupt us in this unsportsmanlike battle.

Jake lifted his heavy-hooded green eyes squinched in the middle of his freckled face and met mine in a blazing inferno.

I wish I could kill him. The bastard dog. I would rip his head from his neck, dislocate his shoulder, stomp him in the gut and paralyze his manhood permanently. I would disembowel him in the same honorable fashion he'd attempted to humiliate me all these months.

Before I could complete my bow, clasping my hands in front to signal I was ready, his right foot caught me solid in the stomach. The breath whooshed from me as I went down on one knee. Flashes of color jumped into my eyes. Then red fire. I stood up, heart pounding, short breaths escaping my lips, pain radiating through my stomach like a burning flame. A quick glance at the shihans. They had not seen him.

I bent over, crouched low to the ground and immediately dropped onto my hands, stretched out my right leg and made contact with his feet, executing an illegal sweep.

In the second it takes a fly to buzz past your ear, he was falling. I continued the spiraling arc with my body, let my right foot make contact with his big head, opening the side of his lip. His mouth guard flew out, hurling blood that spattered his clothes like an abstract painting. Then doing a two-hand stand, I let my feet jut out sideways into his abdomen as he fought to stand. I jumped into a fighting stance, body still low, and moved in for the kill.

"Hold it. Stop. Now, right now," came the shouts. The shihans raced toward Jake. At the same time, gesturing wildly to me, "You, back. Back. *Back*, Patricia, now, this minute."

The high-yellow baldy slumped over, like the snail he was, and crawled on hands and knees to the opposite side of the mat.

I felt powerful hands grab my waist. I did not resist. One of the men roughly lifted my body to the other side of the mat.

"Down on your knees, now," Shihan Scott yelled. "No, Patricia. Do not face the center of the ring. The other way. Your back to the ring. You know the posture. Yes, that way. Bow—bow your head."

I did *not* move. I would *not* bow my head, the memory of what had happened to me earlier poisoning my thoughts.

Shihan Ted walked over, employing his trademark quick, long strides. He leaned down and whispered, "Patricia, bow your head now or *I'll* bow it for you."

I bowed my head, my hair hiding the tears of hot anger flowing down my dark face while my excess adrenaline pumped blood through the veins in my forehead.

I knew they were attending Jake. And I listened to his moans and groans with mixed pleasure, only a tinge of guilt pushing at my conscience.

I had asked him to spar with me for specific reasons. He hated me and all his "sistahs," as he called us. He also hated *The Atlanta Guardian*, where I worked, ever since they busted a scam his law firm had been operating while he was a city politician. And after I'd turned him down for a date, every chance he got, he sought to bring me to my knees, verbally and physically.

First he broke my foot, pretending the weight slipped from his hands. After that, he continued sneaking in illegal punches, then denying it when I complained. He finally attempted to overpower me in the locker room for a kiss, or I suspect more, if Scott had not thrown him into the lockers.

Jake had argued it was their fault. I should not have been allowed a place in the locker room. How was a curtain supposed to provide the men privacy?

Scott banned him from the dojo for a month, but in my view that wasn't long enough.

I hated him for all of those reasons. But I especially despised him for being an ignorant black man who couldn't figure out he was being watched and was sooner or later going to be busted if his shit wasn't clean. And tonight, when my vision was blurred with tears, he looked a lot like Kenneth Lawson.

It had occurred to me when I waved him to join me on the mat that all the men in the room at that moment looked like Kenneth Lawson. And the only thing I wanted to see, more than Jake's butt maimed, was all Kenneth Lawsons dead.

When the shihans were sure he was all right, I knew I would be able to get up and face the others. I quickly wiped tears away with a towel. I swore to myself, *So, throw me out. I don't give a shit.*

In the office, my two friends (or should I say ex-friends) and shihans sat opposite me behind the steel-gray desk. The army-green walls of the spartanly decorated room held only three intricately carved swords, a Bruce Lee calendar and a black-and-white portrait of Kusanku, the grandfather of karate. On the desk, sandwiched between two Chinese dragon bookends, were five books: *The Art of War* by Sun Tzu, translated by Thomas Cleary; *The Art of Peace: Teachings of the Founder of Aikido: Morihei Ueshiba*, compiled and translated by John Stevens; *The Samurai Legacy & Modern Practice* by Robin L. Rielly; and *Shaolin Chin Na*, by Dr. Yang Jwing-Ming. Lying open, facedown on the desk, was *The Bible of Karate: The Bubishi*, a classic Chinese work, treasured for decades by karate's top masters.

Ted Maverick and Scott Brooks stared at me as if a Martian would be more familiar to them, and more welcome.

Finally Ted, an old friend from one of the foster homes I'd existed in, spoke. "You've lost it, little sister. This time we cannot save you. You're outta here. What were you doing . . . trying to kill him?"

I bit my lip and brushed the loose strands of hair off my brow. "Yes. I guess I *was* trying to kill him." Then, defiant, I looked up at the two Kenneth Lawsons sitting in front of me. "You stopped me, though, didn't you? Men. You always stick together."

"You have problems," Scott interrupted. "Problems only a professional can handle. Serious man problems."

"When did you get a psychology degree?" I asked, leaning forward, itching to stand up, jump in anybody's face and yell, *You know jackshit about my problems.*

"Look," Ted said calmly, "you two have to chill. Okay?" Then, coming closer to me he said, "You know most of the guys here didn't want us to let you in the dojo in the first place. So what's up with you? You charge in here huffing and puffing like a bull. You act as if you're ready to do a friendly spar, and then you turn into some black Xena, Warrior Princess."

I slammed the towel onto the desk. "I don't have time for this shit. Put me out. Go ahead. What's that old bullshit saying—'A man's gotta do what a man's gotta do?' Go for it. I don't give a fuck anymore. A woman's gotta do the same damn thing a man's gotta do—protect her ass."

Scott jumped up, papers flying from the desk, his blue eyes flashing uncharacteristically under his blond hair. "Cut the crap. No cursing in the dojo, remember? You never could follow the rules. Master Ted and I fought for you to be in this dojo, but you couldn't cut it, could you? That's your main problem. This is a spiritual dojo. Not some hotshot go-out-and-kick-butt karate school. This is a way of life. But you. You . . . "

"Master Scott, please," Ted said, waving him to sit.

Ted looked me in the eye. "You're trouble here, Patricia. I don't get it. You say it won't matter that you're a woman. We, *we*, both of us," he pointed a finger to Scott and then slapped his chest Tarzan style, "go against the rules for you—and like some Shannon Faulkner you set out to prove *us*, your *defenders*, wrong—and the guys who didn't want you in here, black and white alike, right."

"I'm no Shannon Faulkner," I said weakly. "I kicked butt before I left." I wished, at the very moment I said it, I hadn't. That *this* was all over. And that all the hurt, pain and loss still crushing me were gone. That what happened before I entered the dojo tonight was not real, and that I was not sitting here getting my ass chewed out by the only semblance of family I had left.

"Man," Scott said, blowing out a breath and shaking his head from side to side, "you're pathetic."

Ted grimaced, his emotional pain obvious. "And you know what's ironic? I think you might have been right, Patricia. I mean about letting women in the dojo. The real problem here is you've got the nature of a savage, undisciplined, calloused, angry, out-of-control male.

"We tried to persuade you to do katas, to connect with your chi. But no, you don't want to do that. You also refuse to meditate. We let that pass. We let you continue on in that macho path, knowing where it leads. But this . . . you've gone too far."

I grabbed my gym bag and with one hand untied my brown belt.

They sat in silence, heads bowed.

I let the belt slip from my fingers in a heap onto the desk and turned to walk out.

Neither of them moved a muscle. Stillness filled the distance between us.

I had actually made black belt months ago, but since I refused to incorporate the spiritual requirements, they had refused me the honor. Irony. Me and Bald Jake were the only two in the dojo who had never done the required spiritual stuff and the only two refused black belts in this, the class of thirteen. I had made the thirteenth member of the team. And who says thirteen is not an unlucky number?

At the door, I looked back at them. They were right. I knew it, like a child running in the house knows he's going to break something.

After all this time I still wore all the orphan-abandonment shit like it was a big grin and I was the happiest person on earth. Until recently, my stone-cold heart had been my only protector. I let my guard down, and look what that got me: fragments, shards, broken pieces of shit.

I stared back at them, both holding their heads down, declining to witness my walking out the door in ignominy.

"I'm sorry," I said finally in a mumble. "I know you tried." I bit my lip and felt my stomach lurch—apology never came easy for me. "Maybe I'm a lost cause. No one wants me. No one cares about me. I have nothing. No family. No love. Nothing."

I slammed the door and ignored the question that wavered as Ted yelled after me, "Hey, wait. What happened between you and Kenneth Lawson?"

CHAPTER THREE

Other than Kenneth Lawson, the dojo was my only family. I should not have gone to the dojo after seeing Kenneth and that witch together. I should have walked in that restaurant and ripped them apart. But the thought of fighting over a man turned my stomach. My pride prevented me from doing that, and instead I decided whipping any man's butt would do. It was stupid, yes, but satisfying in an Arnold Schwarzenegger kind of way.

Shihan Ted, my old friend from the foster home, was a counselor by profession, and he'd used all he was worth to get me to open up. But what happened to me was none of his damn business.

Shihan Scott, a TV journalist, had lost his cool for the first time since we'd met. Neither of them had wanted to give up on me. No doubt, all the guys in the dojo would be singing the rap "We told you so" by now. So what.

Ted and Scott founded the martial arts kai five years ago.

Ted had explained to me, "*Dojo* means the school where your training takes place. *Kai* means society, and *shihan* means master instructor in the Japanese styles."

Ted was an eigth-degree black belt shihan of Sanuces Ryu jujitsu, with over twenty-eight years of experience. Scott was a sixth-degree black belt shihan of Bu Kyoku Ryu karate, with twenty-five years of experience.

They'd gathered together four other top martial artists in the schools of Hop-Gar kung fu, Wing-Chun kung fu, Capoeira and Kwasafo, the last two originating in Africa. Each master could choose two students, making a school of twelve.

Ted invited me to visit when I told him I'd been thinking of doing an article about the boom in martial arts schools in Atlanta.

On my first visit I felt right at home. The men were kicking butt and taking names. I talked to Ted until the wee hours of the morning. I wanted to join.

His answer was no. And I garnered another no from his partner, Scott.

I continued to pester them, giving them all the reasons they should take me on as a student. Finally, they decided having a female might be all right. I would be their thirteenth student.

Things didn't go so smoothly with the other men. They wanted no women involved. Period. But the dojo's rules are made by the shihans, not the students. I was in.

Then came the serious training. At first I sailed along like a ship on breezy waters. And then the gale hit. The notion was that this particular dojo put emphasis on building spiritual character. The inner person. Katas. They wanted me to practice the repetitious, prearranged series of movements every day. I am not a creature of repetition. I'm easily bored. Particularly when the idea of spiritual development is mentioned in the same sentence.

I had not counted on that. Spirituality and me were sworn enemies. Few things scared me in life. Fire, because I'd been caught in a foster home that burned down and I'd had to jump out the bedroom window to keep from going up in flames. Closeness, of course. And anything to do with God or spirit. I didn't want in on that part of the martial arts; I wanted only the physical stuff.

Scott and Ted promised they would give me time to adjust. But they assured me daily for the four years I'd been there that adjusting was absolutely necessary for me to remain. I had planned to leave next year, after I felt confident I could wipe the floor with any man's butt. Now the leaving had been done for me.

"Who needs a stupid group of kung fu–wearing pricks?" I shouted, taking a sip of spring water. "And who needs a damn Kenneth Lawson?"

Peppy, my Persian cat, leaped onto my lap. "Okay. You. You're my only family," I said, stroking him. "I'm warning you, don't start that clawing me either. I'm not in the mood today, cat." I held his face up to mine so he could pay attention to my declaration. "I should have scratched that damn Kenneth Lawson's eyes out when I saw him. You know that, Peppy?"

Lord, the things I did to keep that man would make your stomach churn until you threw up butter. Cooking special meals for him, buying expensive wines—French wines I couldn't even pronounce and sure couldn't drink. I let him live here with me, for God's sake.

Professor, my ass. I don't believe he even tried to get a job anywhere. Shit, there are a zillion colleges and universities here and he couldn't find a job? No way.

I did everything short of pulling a Shirley Brown, calling some woman up and, like the song, saying, "Woman to woman, you know that car he's driving you around in? I pay the note on that car." But thank God, that's not me. My thing is, why admit how stupid you are to your competition?

I can't even pull a Bernadine, like in *Waiting to Exhale*, because it's my car. All I know for sure is, there are days I understand why *The Atlanta Guardian*'s editorial page opposes the NRA. Because if I had had a gun, I would have popped his butt right there in that restaurant. But I didn't have a gun, and now all I'm left with are the keys to that very Audi I had once paid the note on.

Until the moment I sat starry-eyed, waiting to be herded into a room with a bunch of strangers to collectively swear "I do," Kenneth Lawson was the only man I'd ever trusted. Then, less than five hours later, I spot his butt sitting in a restaurant with another woman.

Sucker. I believed him when he told me we had a bond together. He claimed to be alone, like me. Wrong. Sure, he was a few years older— okay, maybe ten—but what's that got to do with it? I'd been dumped by men ten years younger than me too. Supposedly he wanted a bright future for the both of us. Now I knew why he smiled when he said it. He was lying.

Staring at the key ring that read, KENNY L IS MINE, a lie I paid to have engraved myself, all I could think about was Why do women do this to themselves? It couldn't be about loving because what I'd been through had nothing to do with love. At first everything is great, then suddenly it deteriorates faster than a slumlord's apartment building.

I had to face it—no matter what our relationship had been, it wasn't *all that* anymore. No, there were only two people I felt sorrier for now: that weave-wearing, miniskirt baring chick he was with, because I knew for sure what she's got, and the next poor brother who came along. Because I was going to cut his balls off, whether I intended to or not.

Bang! Bang! Bang! That must be him, the lowlife dog. Where's his damn key? I wondered, while peeping out the window. Wait until I get my hands on him. But there was a dusty, dark-green, late-model Ford Taurus parked under the street lamp. "Who is it?" I asked.

"Police, ma'am."

Police. My mind raced. *Police?* "Yes!" I whispered, pumping my arm like I was playing a slot machine and all the coins were tumbling to the floor. My prayers had been answered. He and that she-devil had been in a car wreck. When it rains in Georgia, it might as well be ice on the roads. Drivers skid everywhere.

"Oh my God, no," I rehearsed, feigning shock and hurt in my voice while moving farther back from the door to yell, "Just a minute," like I hadn't been checking out the window.

I practiced the scene over in my mind, recalling how Monzorra, one of my foster mothers, had collapsed onto the casket of her brother while it was being lowered into the grave. Now, that's Hollywood. Me, I'm distraught.

Finally I opened the door. "Yes. Can I help you?"

"Are you Miss Patricia Conley, at 522 Rosewood Street?" the policeman asked.

I fought the urge to say, No. I have no idea why 522 Rosewood is on the metal plaque beside my door, idiot. Instead I said, in a why-in-the-world-would-the-police-be-here voice, "Yes, I'm Patricia Conley," flipping my locks back off my face. "Is there a problem?" Knowing full well the problem was that I looked like crap.

"May we come inside?" The WE was a six-foot-eight brother who probably had a bad knee; otherwise I was sure he'd be shooting hoops instead of guns. He also had a nasty keloid scar on his right cheek that went across his lips in a diagonal slant.

The other one was a short, redhaired, freckled woman who could have passed for a mix of Columbo and Raggedy Ann. Her hair looked more like a mop and was unmistakably her own burden growing out of her scalp.

Somebody needs to talk to you about wigs, my dear. The woman had on a maroon blouse and gray slacks, but the guy was dressed to the nines. "If you don't mind, could I see your badges?" I asked them.

Red Columbo glared at me, while her partner whipped out his billfold and held it up. A gold shield with blue writing that read, DETECTIVE DAVID GRIFFIN, CITY OF ATLANTA, glowed at me.

I don't know why I'm like this under pressure, but I said, "Yeah. I bet you can buy those at Kroger. They have everything, you know."

Red Columbo wasn't having it. She grunted, pointing to the badge swinging from a black cord around her neck, "Miss, we don't have time for this. Are you going to let us come in or not?"

I stepped back and made a hand gesture for them to enter.

After spotting my swollen face, the ex-ballplayer asked, "Are you all right, miss?"

"Yes," I lied. "I have an allergy."

"No one called you already, did they?" Red Columbo asked.

"No one like who?"

They both looked at each other.

"Miss Conley, I think you'd better sit down," the ex-ballplayer finally said, pointing to my yellow-flowered overstuffed chair, as though this were his house and he was directing the traffic flow.

"Why? What's the matter?" Don't overreact Conley, I reminded myself.

"Ma'am, do you own a blue-gray ninety-two two-door Audi, license tag JA 2789957?" he asked, reading from a notepad.

"Yes," I said. I didn't want to give anything away until I knew exactly what was going down.

"Is it registered to you?" Ex-Ballplayer asked.

"Yes, why? Has there been an accident?" I said, distracted by Red Columbo's sweeping my house like her eyes were a damn broom.

They both passed glances. It was Red Columbo's turn. "Were you driving your vehicle tonight, Miss?" she asked, leaning forward in her chair.

"Where're you going with this?" I asked. Something wasn't right here. I didn't know what it was, but they weren't here for a routine accident.

"Where are we going?" Red Columbo repeated looking at her partner, her lips turned up smugly.

"Yes, where are you going?" I repeated, glaring at her. "Are you by chance a shrink?"

She acted as though she didn't catch my drift or sarcasm and continued, "No. Why? Did you expect a shrink, Miss?"

"No, it's just that shrinks always repeat your questions back to you. You know, like a parrot." *Damn, Conley, chill out.*

"You know, I'm going to let Detective Griffin here handle this, because to be honest, you're pissing me off." She sat back and rested her hands in her lap in tight, white-knuckled fists.

Ex-Ballplayer knew the signal and had possibly executed this switch-off many times before.

It was something about Red Columbo that could grate on any self-respecting woman's nerves. It was sort of like she forgot she *wasn't* a man.

"Miss Conley," Ex-Ballplayer said in a soft, consoling voice, "we have a problem here and we were hoping you could shed some light on it for us."

I held my tongue but thought, Do I look like a fucking flashlight to you? Red wasn't the only one who could get pissed off. "Look," I said, "believe me, I have no idea what you're talking about."

Red Columbo lifted her hands into the air and flopped them back down in her lap, like she might be doing the Wave at a ball game.

I ignored the gesture and continued directing my body language toward Ex-Ballplayer. "But go ahead, I'll try," I said to him in my sincerest tone.

"A few hours ago someone left a blue-gray Audi, same make and year as yours, and registered to you, by the way, in an alley in downtown Atlanta. Now, we need to know what happened and we'd hoped you'd cooperate. If you're having trouble, we're here to help you."

What in the hell was he talking about? Did Kenneth have an accident or not? Finally I said, "Was my car in an accident? Wrecked? Hey, you've got more answers than I do. You're the ones with my car."

Sighing heavily, Ex-Ballplayer said, "Miss Conley, we can do this easy or you can come downtown."

"Downtown? Come downtown?"

Red Columbo couldn't resist.

And I couldn't blame her.

Obviously, she had caught my drift earlier because she said, "Miss, are you by chance a shrink?"

I smiled. She was good. Damn good, and I respected that. I answered, looking her dead in the eyes, "Touché."

"Could you answer the question?" she said, tipping her head in my direction to acknowledge her point. "Were you driving your vehicle tonight? Or is anybody else authorized to drive it?"

"Ah, no. No, I wasn't." They looked serious. Sounded serious. I was beginning to understand this was not just about the car. And the understanding was making me nervous. The last thing I needed was trouble with cops. I continued, "I got a cab home. Actually, no one's been driving my car but me. As far as I know it's in my garage. And if it's not in the garage now, I suppose someone must have stolen it." Why was I lying? Covering up for that no-good Kenneth after what he'd done to me?

I didn't have to ask myself the whys of this behavior. A tattletale in a foster home is as good as maimed. It's a sick code of ethics, but like police officers who stick together, it's second nature to you after a while.

Here I was lying worse than a schoolgirl covering for her roommate. Besides, I wanted to get to the bottom of this my damn self, on *my* terms.

The two officers stared at me.

The ex-ballplayer spoke first. "Listen, Miss Conley, we know you're a reporter, and to be perfectly honest we expected a little more cooperation here."

"Journalist. I'm a journalist. And I'm sorry," I lied. "You caught me off guard, that's all."

"Or on guard," Red Columbo scoffed under her breath.

"Where exactly is my car?" I asked, pretending she wasn't there.

"Impounded right now for safe keeping until it's converted to property," the ex-ballplayer said.

"Why? If it wasn't in an accident, where did you find it and why impound it for safe keeping? Are you saying I can't just go get it?" Alarm tightened my stomach. Did that damn Kenneth commit a crime in my car?

"That's funny," Red Columbo said. "You haven't asked us whether whoever stole your vehicle was arrested. Why is that, Miss?"

"Probably because I know Atlanta is New Carjack City and more than likely some young punks snatched it from my garage and were joyriding and got caught." Where was Kenneth? Why would he go off and leave my car somewhere—let it get impounded or taken for a joyride? He must have rode off in the sunset with that damn bitch. That mother . . .

"We don't think that's what happened, Miss. But if you don't know who could have been driving your vehicle and it was stolen from your garage, then we have to look elsewhere for answers. By the way, it'll be a few days, maybe longer before you can pick it up. Give the impound a call, let's say in . . . "

She looked at her watch, for a calendar, I presumed, or effect, obviously enjoying this.

After a much-too-long pause she said, " . . . three to four days minimum."

I could see somebody strangling her. "Three or four days? Look elsewhere? Where did you find my car?" I asked her, struggling to control the fear building in my gut.

Ex-Ballplayer answered, "Behind a restaurant downtown in its back alley. It'll be on the report when you pick the vehicle up. The door was left open, no keys in the ignition and blood on the steering wheel and the seat. Fresh blood. We're checking now to see if it was human blood.

But you don't care because you don't know anything about this, right?"

I didn't respond. Couldn't. What the hell were they talking about? Blood on the steering wheel and the seat? Blood? Fresh blood?

It was clear Red Columbo was tired of her partner dick-footing around. She cleared her throat. "Listen, Miss, I'm sure you can tell us what cab company you used to get to and from work. We know you work for the *Guardian*."

Her implication was clear. She thought I was lying.

"I rode with a photographer this morning to an assignment and then he drove me to work. After work, I took a cab to my dojo and then I got one home." All of that was true, except why I took a cab to the dojo and home. Kenneth and I were supposed to come home together to celebrate our marriage. "Both Yellow Cabs," I continued. "But I'm afraid the names and numbers of the cabs escape me. You know, the mind is a terrible thing to waste, isn't it?"

Red Columbo was all business now. I could see the line drawn sternly on her forehead. The party was over and any more smart remarks might have her yanking out those shiny handcuffs dangling from her patent-leather belt.

Chill. It was time to chill. I didn't deal with cops often on my beat, but as a journalist you learn when to stop pushing and instead pull. "Listen, I'm sorry, Miss—what was your name?" I said, smiling slightly.

"Detective Watson. Detective Sarah B. Watson."

"Yeah, well, Detective Watson, I'm not feeling so hot today. You know—the pollen. I don't know, you guys just caught me at a bad time." The queen of understatement had spoken. I didn't know if I'd ever felt so betrayed. "Please accept my apology. I assure you I'll cooperate as best I can from now on."

A tiny slither creased the corner of her mouth. She'd won the battle. "I can dig that," she said. "Okay, we'll start from scratch."

Her partner looked skeptical and maybe even uncomfortable, since he ran his finger inside his collar to loosen it. He'd seen her before in this pose for the kill—make them think you've softened up and then, *bang!* right in the kisser.

This was my kind of woman. Use all the tricks of the trade, both male and female, until you come home with the prize.

"Let me ask you something, Miss Conley."

So she did know my name. "Sure, go for it."

"Do you know anyone who could have been using your vehicle with your permission? Someone with a key, maybe?"

27

"I told you, I'm the only one who drives my car. There's no one else. Nobody with a key." I cleared my throat and followed her eyes to my hands, which were now busy twisting my key ring that read, KENNY L IS MINE.

"Are those the keys to your vehicle, Miss Conley?" she asked, pointing to my hands.

"Yes; yes, they are. And my door key. Why?" They could be lying and my keys were still in the car. If so, they weren't buying that some thief stole my car and had a duplicate key ring made with "Pat" engraved on it, like the one Kenneth used. "Well, actually," I continued, "these are my keys. But I keep a spare set attached underneath my car. I'm absentminded. I'd lock myself out at least once or twice a month if I didn't have those stashed. You know criminals, though. They're hip to all the hiding places." At that moment, I was hoping these two detectives weren't hip to me.

Red Columbo stood up and motioned for Ex-Ballplayer to follow suit. When he towered over me, he said, "Here's my card. We may have more questions for you, so keep your day job." No smile. Nothing. All the consolation gone from his voice.

"Sure. Hey, I'm here. And if I think of anything, I'll give you a call." Now, was that lame or what? I am not thinking, that's for damn sure. They know I'm lying. It's now or never. Be nonchalant. "Oh, by the way," I said, as they touched the doorknob to let themselves out, "you said something about my car being behind a restaurant. What restaurant were the lowlifes eating in when they ditched my car?"

They turned, both offering me a blank look and a shrug, like they couldn't read a thing into me asking the question.

I braced. Couldn't show any emotion on my face. Maybe I'd chuckle when they told me. Anything but scream like I was gonna want to if they didn't say McDonald's.

A locked-eyed look passed between them, followed by a few moments of silence, and then the answer I damn sure didn't want to hear.

A slight smile from Red Columbo.

Did she know what had happened to me earlier?

"Oh, it was the . . . " A brow cramping up. "What's the name of it, Detective?" Red asked, looking to her partner.

"The Le Chef restaurant," Ex-Ballplayer said, not taking his gaze from my face.

Incredibly, I held my breath and composure until they were in their car, fastening seat belts.

What in the name of God had happened in that alley? The least

Kenneth Lawson could have done was bring my car and keys back home. Blood? Maybe he'd cut himself? Maybe that witch was on the rag? Yuck. Maybe what, Patricia Conley? Maybe he freaking just didn't want to marry you.

Granted, I know that men will go to great extremes to avoid marriage, but this, this was a new low. I cursed so loudly, Peppy stopped playing with his sheepskin mouse to stare up at me. Something was seriously wrong and even Peppy knew it.

> "In the Dogon word,
> all things are manifested by thought;
> they are not known by themselves."
> —*The Pale Fox*

CHAPTER FOUR

I leaned against the door, my hands trembling. God, their visit unnerved me. I unconsciously twisted my keys back and forth until one of them popped off the key ring and landed on the carpet. I scooped up the key and walked into the living room, even though I felt so dejected I ached to crawl on my hands and knees. I felt lower than a snail. My sore eyes roamed the room, each corner heaped with memories and pain.

I live in a small, eclectic magnolia-tree-lined community in a gray and white wood-frame house in Decatur, Georgia. It borders Atlanta so closely that even the police don't always know what jurisdiction they're in when they come to arrest somebody. Flowering purple and pink azaleas planted by the previous owners bloom in my front yard. Two white wooden swings bang against the porch windows whenever it storms. Large white columns grace the front porch, as close as I'm allowing to a Southern plantation.

Inside, piles of papers and magazines litter the floor near every chair. A vase, large coffee-table books, a bonsai, all gifts from Kenneth, adorned the square, dusty, glass-topped table. The Chinesoie gold-flowered drapes were drawn shut, just the way Kenneth liked them.

Next to the Victorian rocker he'd bought at an auction, the fringed ivory floor lamp was still on. It was as though he sat there reading, the way he often did, long into the night. Tomes on economics, world conspiracies, World War II and by some author named Swedenborg were neatly stacked beside his chair.

Books tossed close to my chair spoke volumes on our contrasts. Arthur Flowers, E. Lynn Harris, Gloria Naylor, Toni Morrison, John Edgar Wideman and the writer I admired most, Ernest Gaines, struck different chords in me than the books Kenneth consumed daily.

Yet he could talk to me at length about the flowery words of Naylor and Morrison, the jazzy, love-cast style of Flowers and the pride I felt in my own race whenever I read Gaines. He'd read them all and loved them, but I couldn't say the same for his books, at least about the few I'd struggled through.

The only book we both owned was one I received as a gift from a college professor, the *Kybalion*. Some metaphysical-type book I would never pick up and read, but every night Kenneth studied it religiously.

What the hell. I knew nothing about him. Because I had no past worth mentioning, I often assumed the other person didn't either. If I didn't ask them, they wouldn't ask me, was my modus operandi.

I rubbed my forehead. Exhausted, I clutched the keys and dried my eyes with the back of my hand. Damn. Fuck him. I'd get over him. Hadn't I always been alone?

Men are all the same. It's either a) I'm not ready for a commitment speech or b) you're not ready for a commitment speech, but it's never like that Goldilocks story where it's just right. Not ever. And now I can add c) Baby, I'm just no damn good.

I punched the pillow a couple of times, cursing my swollen eyes. I had cried until my defenses rose up to protect me. Enough of this crap. Forget this damn crying.

Abandonment, like a parent, walked with me through the major events of my life. I had been left someplace unknown, probably on a doorstep, before being shipped from foster home to foster home. I truly couldn't remember the early years.

My first memory was of old Cooney in Baltimore, Maryland. A tall black man with a limp. His wife took in foster children of all nationalities as a way to make ends meet. I don't suppose they ever really wanted any of us, black or white. They had two children of their own, a boy and a girl. To their credit they treated us all the same—like shit.

Cooney hated us. The foster kids and his own. I was thirteen years old before I knew what hate was, and I applied it to Cooney—after he raped me.

I remember the cops grabbing him and placing the handcuffs on him. With his hands behind his back, lips snarled like a dog's, looking at me with bloodshot eyes, he yelled, "You little nigger, I'll get you for this."

I cried as a policeman grabbed my shoulder and shoved me out of Cooney's reach. Anger, not fear, gripped my stomach so tightly I shook all over. The police nudged me out the door and dropped me off at a shelter, where a counselor tried to explain that it wasn't my fault.

It took her a while to realize that I hadn't thought it was my fault. By that time in my life, I believed the nature of man to be nothing but evil. No, that wasn't what had worried me. What worried me was the fact that they'd carted me off like a criminal and Mrs. Cooney let them. I had been abandoned once again.

After that I was like a robbery victim: always wondering whether my shit would be gone when I got back home.

The nerve—that Kenneth actually drove my damn car to pick up that witch and then just walks off and leaves it. Goes to show what an asshole he is. And to think I fell in love with the jerk.

I had wanted so much for this to work out for both of us. He's probably run off to marry her right now. Maybe he's already married, Sucker.

Remembering now, I started getting madder, sitting there hugging a pillow. I looked over, saw Kenneth's face and threw the pillow at his chair. I missed. The lamp crashed to the floor, the bulb splattering into tiny fragments much like my heart.

And in our world, "The only thought, then, which can
possibly be cognized is thought in signs.
But thought which cannot be cognized does not exist.
All thought, therefore, must necessarily be in the stars."
—Charles Sanders Peirce

CHAPTER FIVE

Then the phone rang.

I hesitated. My first instinct was to ignore it. Let the machine pick it
up. I'd been tripping so much by now, anybody who knew me would ask
me questions I was in no mood to answer. It rang again. Last chance to
pick it up.

Maybe it's him. I hate that. Here I go. Waiting by the phone for a
ring and an apology, every woman's nemesis. Didn't you promise yourself never again? *Ring.* So, if it's him, so what? Stay strong, my sister.

Click. "Hello, you have reached 555-5212. If you've got a hot news tip,
beep me, 555-8330. Otherwise, leave me a message. Oh, and if you're
trying to sell me something, leave me your home number so I can call
and worry the hell out of you." Pause. *Beep.*

"Hello." A tiny whisper. A woman's voice, speaking breathless and
fast with an accent. French, I think. "Hello, are you there? Pick up. This
is Clau . . . never mind my name."

I picked the receiver up and held it to my ear. A feeling triggered inside. This was no friendly phone call. I could sense it. This was clearly
somebody calling to mess with me. My hands trembled violently, "Who
the hell *is* this?"

"Look, I've got to talk to you. Listen. Kenneth didn't want me to talk
to you. But now it doesn't matter. You could help find—"

"*Bam. Bam. Bam.*" Sounds like bangs on a door emanated over the phone.

The woman's accented voice shrilled, "Oh, *Mon Dieu!*" but it was clear she wasn't talking to me. She'd dropped or thrown the phone down.

I stood still, trying to make out the noises.

Then nothing, until scuffling, like furniture being shoved across a floor. Crashes.

The phone was silent. Then I heard it. Heavy wheezing. Shuffling. In the background, a scream, a whimper, two thuds. Then the wheezing coming closer. Closer. *Click.*

Somebody had hung up the phone.

I needed to call the police. And say what? An obscene phone caller's house got broken into while I was on the phone?

I didn't have a clue who it was or where they were. I hit *66. *Hurry, hurry.* Silence, then a dial tone. Shit. What *is* the number? I'd used the callback because if you don't have the service, it cost money to use it each time. Okay, so it's not much money. But hey, it's money, isn't it?

Dammit. I pitched a scarf and books off the table searching for my phone book for instructions. Okay. Calm down. You know what it is. Remember? The joke, the phone company acknowledging that they're screwing you from both ways.

The number popped into my head at the joke prompt. I dialed *69. A dial tone. A few beeps. Then a message: "This is your automatic call-back service. The number of your last incoming call is a private number and cannot be automatically called. The call was received . . ." I zoned out on the date and swore. Then the voice intruded again: "To activate automatic callback, dial 1." I did. And then I got my third shock of the day: My phone number had been blocked from calling this specific number.

Who was it? I tried to recall whether I knew the voice. A woman with a French accent. Who? *Who?* It had to be the witch Kenneth was with. Why else would my phone number be blocked from calling *that* particular number?

Yes. That's it. She's the whore in the restaurant with Kenneth calling me to fuck with me. But why? Maybe he wasn't with her right now. Coming home to me? He wasn't with my damn car, that's for sure. But what did she mean by "now it doesn't matter"?

I felt the urge to do something. Anything. I picked up the phone and dialed the phone company. They couldn't help me. All their modern technology and the most they could do for me was repeat what I already knew: I cannot get the phone number if the caller has blocked my number. But, the rep chimed, "It means the caller had to actually program your telephone number from their phone in order to block you from calling them back."

Shit, how did Denzel get somebody to trace his calls in *The Pelican Brief*? Some journalist I am.

Blood. It hit me. Maybe Kenneth was hurt? Maybe that's where the blood came from? Maybe she hurt him when he wanted to call it off? Right. He didn't look like he was calling anything off to me.

Then I dialed all the area hospitals. None had treated Kenny or Kenneth Lawson in the past few hours or ever, for that matter.

Stop it. Get some tea, drink it and carry your butt to bed. You're tired and you have to work early tomorrow. Forget Kenneth Lawson.

But I wasn't about to do that. Obsessive compulsive behavior goes a long way for a journalist who's not locked up in a mental ward. Persistence is the key to finding out stuff. And going after information was my lifeblood. I had chosen journalism because it allowed me the freedom to employ my basic nature. Journalism was different from the old notion of reporting. Journalists didn't just report the news, they dug up the news. They pushed and pulled and moved crap around, until the shit began to stink.

A newsroom is the ideal place for a cynic. Every rock you lift hides a snake. Hardly anything is as it seems and evil abounds, confirming all that you believe about the world.

And people wonder why journalists don't do more stories about good things. Because people don't want to read about the good out there; instead, they want to read about shit they've somehow managed to avoid. Spin out a paper with nothing but positive headlines and I promise it won't last a month.

Me, I'm a natural digger for dirt. After all, when you've been buried in a mud slide most of your life, scum is what you're most comfortable digging up.

In this case, I'd never been engaged before and I wasn't going out like that. No way. Kenneth Lawson was going to tell me to my face what the fuck was going on and why he left my damn car in an alley and walked away.

There is an old saying that if you love a man, let him go, and if he loves you, he'll come back to you. I say hunt him down and kill him. One thing was sure, I was going to find his trifling ass in order to know exactly why he had picked today of all days to jerk me off. Hell, I'm not that bad.

I started in the bedroom. Nothing out of place. He hadn't taken his clothes, including the Versace suits, from the closets. His slip-on Laurens lined the floor of the closet. But no leather case beside the dresser.

I checked the dresser drawers; underwear still folded in neat piles. Nothing to indicate he wasn't planning to come back. And that's what let me know that the motherfucker must be crazy, if he thought he could stand me up, abandon my damn car, hold hands with another woman and still wake up in my bed on any morning. *Crazy-ass men.*

Next, I stomped back into the living room. I cut the computer on. He worked on it day and night. It was a Pentium-run trick with some newfangled MMX. It was the only thing other than books and clothes he'd brought into the house.

Being a secret person myself, I'd never touched the machine before. Futile. He'd coded it for privacy. I tried his name and mine. Still nothing, except the blinking request for a password.

Now, if you're close to a man, you can come up with his password after a while by putting yourself in his shoes. A computer guy at work told me that. But hell, Kenneth and I weren't really close, evidently.

When you're orphaned, sometimes you confuse closeness with companionship. Obviously that's what I'd done, since I didn't have a rat's chance surviving a science lab of figuring out Kenneth's password. I shut the machine down and looked around the room for any other clues to his disappearance.

I checked the kitchen drawer he sometimes dropped coins into. The only thing I found were matches from Le Chef. So he'd been there smooching before. I set them all ablaze on impulse.

This was from shit. It didn't make any sense. Hell, he could have told me he'd changed his damn mind. The chicken-shit-eating, suck-egg dog.

"Knowledge lies in knowing man,
but also all that which is not man,
for it has been given to him
to know that which is not himself."
—Falani Initiate

CHAPTER SIX

Every car passing in the street woke me. It seems like I got up a million times during the night. Two times I thought the phone was ringing. My heart sank when it wasn't. Damn, I need help. Even if it was Kenneth, what was I left to do but curse him out? Nothing. I was going to have to act just like a parent with an adult child still living at home. No matter how bad it hurt, for my own sake, I was going to have to throw his ass out. But I wanted to do it in person. See him squirm and sputter out excuses. Witness him as uncomfortable as I had been earlier at the court. I wanted to shout, curse and throw a literal fit so I could count on his last few minutes with me being unforgettable. I didn't want his sorry butt back. No way. I pushed my face into the pillow and cried.

When I did manage to fall asleep, I dreamt about all sorts of monsters and shit. And, of course, they were all after me. Why do dreams have to be so narcissistic?

The next morning I got up early—well, early for me—even though my eyelids couldn't have felt any heavier if the singing group Two Tons of Fun were sitting on them. I turned on my CD and listened to Stevie Wonder's *Fingers* while I dressed. I loved old music and I knew the beginning words to all The Supremes' songs.

I looked at my reflection. It's incredible how puffed and swollen your eyes and nose can become in one night. My angular, dark-skinned face now looked like that of a woman on a drug binge. Thirtysomething was messing with me.

Dressed, I grabbed some toast even though there was no doubt in my mind that I could live comfortably feeding off pure anger. I checked the clock; it was 8 A.M. I called a cab. I walked back into the bedroom to find my purse and something caught my eye. My desk. It was off to the left, in the alcoved area the real estate agent so eloquently referred to as a sun room. Real estate agents, car salesmen and preachers must go to the same school of description. I walked over to it.

I hadn't even looked at the desk last night. Kenneth didn't use it often, except to write notes late at night. There was always a message pad he scribbled on next to the phone. I picked it up. The sheet was blank. "I've seen too many movies," I said as I lightly shaded pencil over the remaining blank sheet. I held the pad up to the light, hoping, like in the movies, some secret would be revealed. It wasn't. The cab driver blared a horn and I left feeling like a broken-down robot.

♊

At work, I phoned the police number for impounded cars and got a recorded message that made it clear I would not get my car back without doing the equivalent of walking through fire with poisonous snakes coiled in my mouth.

I downloaded my voice mail with great dread, amazed I was still able to walk, like my whole world hadn't crashed on top of me last night. Women are some strong mothers.

Beep. "Pat, what uuup? You holdin'? I need to borrow a few bucks, cousin. Marky, you know, your snitch."

Get one or two tips from somebody and damn if they don't think you're obligated for life. He made me glad I had no damn cousins.

Beep. "Patricia Conley, this is April from First Step public relations office. Could you tell us which reporter to invite to cover a program we're having? Please call me back; you have the number."

I stopped. What does she get paid for? Damn.

Beep. "Patricia. Something's come up. I might be late." It was Kenneth's voice.

Yeah, right. Something came *up*, all right. His damn dick. This was getting on my nerves. I hit the 8 for the time the message was left. The mechanical voice droned the date, and time—4:00 P.M.

Yesterday at the same time he should have had his butt at the probate court.

The machine continued on with the next message while I spewed curse words in my head. Kenneth had encouraged me to stop cursing. And I had except at work, where cursing was a part of the culture. And where if you didn't curse in the heat of an argument you'd wobble away crushed like a duck.

Beep. "This is John Biggers's secretary. He asked me to give you a call to tell you, thank you. Please excuse my language but he's instructed me to read this verbatim. 'Thanks for the intro to your friend, little filly. He's a damn good old boy. And from my home state, too.'"

Why would John Biggers call me now? It'd been several months since I interviewed him for a company profile. He got on my nerves calling me damn horses and shit then, and it was no different now.

I could have spit when he told *Greater Loafing*, the local tab, that he'd granted me the interview because he admired my work. Then when my editor informed me that Biggers had granted me an exclusive for his anticipated Washington contract for a new immunization program, I wanted to curl up and die. I didn't have time to worry about him now though. I hoped his contract wasn't a done deal today.

But what did the message mean? I hadn't introduced him to anybody. Probably had me mixed up with another journalist he'd dealt with. Maybe Phyllis Clor?

The funny thing about voice mails in an office is that you can say your department, your name, and even if it sounds in no way like the person the caller wants, damn if they won't still leave a message. People must think the newsroom is the size of a phone booth and we're all sitting on that one funky-shaped stool inside waiting for their call.

I walked over to Evan, the city-desk assignment editor. If anyone got hurt in an alley last night, he'd have the police report even if it didn't make the newspaper. His journalists covered the crime beat.

No shooting, no cutting, no nothing of a black male, he assured me. Not last evening. Not last night. Nothing. A rarity in and of itself.

No shooting and the Olympics weren't in town? Scare me. During the '96 Olympics, the Atlanta area had had over ten homicides in five days and not one lead story about them. Go figure.

I dialed the private number Jeff Samuels, an undercover cop, had given me to contact him during day hours. He worked out of the Nineteenth Precinct.

I'd smiled when he told me he was undercover, because it didn't seem like much cover was going on if he could tell people. He said that he told me because he was cultivating a few journalists to help him if he ever needed to leak information. I suppose I should have been insulted but I wasn't. Journalist—a leak? Never.

He answered on the fourth ring. "Jeff? Look, I've got a problem. I need you to find out about my car that was impounded last night."

"Impounded for what?" he asked.

"I don't know for sure. The detectives weren't that helpful when they dropped by my house."

"Who? Burglary?"

"I don't know. Detectives is all I know."

"Who was it? Their names, I mean."

"A detective Griffin and a woman, Sarah somebody. Could you just check it for me, please?"

"Sarah Watson? Homicide? They're homicide detectives. They came to your house? Did someone get hurt? Die in your vehicle?"

"Look, you know more about this than I do. Could you check it or not?"

We'd not been on good terms since I'd called off our brief fling. He'd been trying hard to continue dating me, and I'd been trying hard to blow him off. We'd met soon after I met Kenneth, and at first I was a little interested; then when Kenneth and I got serious, I backed off but Jeff didn't.

"I'm on deadline, Jeff, so I need a yes or no that you will or won't. Simple." It dawned on me that he sounded different when he'd realized the detectives were from homicide. Like the surprise of it made him more professional, no drawl. He usually had a terrible country drawl that sounded like an announcer's on the country music station.

"Okay. I'll check it, Patricia. Were you driving the vehicle?"

Why can't police say *car* like everybody else? "No. No, I wasn't driving the *car*." I hesitated. "I think someone stole it. Look, can you call me back as soon as you know? I'll do you a favor sometime."

"The movies?"

"Yes, yes. I'll consider you taking me to the movies one day."

Fool, I thought as I hung up, not sure whether I meant me or him.

CHAPTER SEVEN

The copy carrier had brought the first of the morning papers up, but I hadn't bothered to look at them.

Carol Erickson, another journalist and the closest thing I had to a friend, covered local news. We ate dinner, went to movies, plays and stuff together. I don't know if it was out of mutual admiration or something more realistic; we were both single and lived in the city.

She was helping out the A1 section, proofing the national and international news with a red grease pencil. I hated local and had avoided it as much as possible until I came to Atlanta. *The Guardian* wanted everybody to work a beat at least once.

I'd already done my stint and was working on a newly created desk called the South Task Force, sort of a dumping ground until they decided where to stick you next. I'd been doing a few specials on computers for the business desk from a Southern perspective.

I scanned the A1 top fold sitting on a distant desk. A large-point header read, PLANE CRASHES NEAR SWITZERLAND. THREE ATLANTANS ON PASSENGER LIST. I could also see a small photo of a woman topping the story next to it. She was possibly black, light skinned, with long hair, your typical model type, but that was about all I could tell.

"Hey, Carol," I said, walking over to her desk. "Can I buy one of your doughnuts?" I needed some sugar, bad.

"Sure," she said. "How much do you owe me already? You gonna owe me a thousand bucks more if you take my only chocolate."

She was a bit overweight. One of the things I liked about her was that she didn't seem to be bothered by any need to pretend to diet. If you needed a sugar fix, she had it.

If Carol'd been thin, with her fiery-red hair she could have passed for Lucille Ball. She dressed very neatly, with that Irish Spring kind of look. You'd expect a brogue to come out of her mouth; instead what you got was a long, low, Southern drawl.

Carol's desk was always in order and her reporting was detailed and precise. Her house was twice as neat. For her, everything needed to be analyzed and left neatly closed and resolved. Carol was the kind of woman I imagined could piss in a bottle.

I walked over and studied the doughnuts, while she held the paper up with both hands. I glanced at the paper as I scooped the cream-filled doughnut into a tissue. She had turned to the inside, and the jump's slug line drew my attention. FRENCH CITIZEN FOUND. "What's that about?"

"A woman swimming in her bathtub."

"Swimming in her bathtub? She must be awful daggone small. But since when is that newsworthy?"

"She was swimming in blood. She drugged herself, then slit her wrists. Anyway, everybody is freaking because she was a French citizen. She's only been here a short while. Worked for some theatrical supply company named Les Miserable, a business nobody here's ever heard of. But you know how they carry on. If she'd been a prostitute, she probably wouldn't have made the local briefs. They kill me."

I took a bite of doughnut while thinking, there's nothing like a liberal white woman defending the downtrodden.

Carol closed the paper. I could see the woman's photo clearly. A fraction of a second later, my doughnut was splattered on the floor.

She was the same woman who had been clutching hands with Kenneth the night before, downtown in the French restaurant. A French woman with a French accent? Damn. Possibly the same woman who called me last night? If so, she must have been beating her damn self up, before she drugged herself and slit her wrists.

My body trembled. Bile rose in my throat and I knew I was going to be sick. I ran in the bathroom and splashed water on my face. I held the sink, shaking.

Carol followed me into the bathroom and offered me some wet paper towels. She stood by looking concerned. "Are you okay? What happened? You—are you pregnant?"

"No. I think I have a virus," I lied.

"Don't give me that. You look terrible. I know you, remember? Miss Cool-as-a-Cucumber Pat. Tell me. What is it?"

"Look, I think I'm going home. But you could do me two favors. Would you tell Carter I'm not feeling well? I'll check with him later. For the budget, tell him the follow-up story on the computer company is in the queue ready to go to rim for the copy editors to tag a headline and chop up."

"What's the second favor?" Carol asked.

"Oh, would you check out the French . . . never mind. That's okay."

"What is it? I want to help. We're friends, remember?"

"I know, Carol. Forget it, though. Okay?"

"No, it's not okay. Come on, let's go get some coffee. Otherwise, I'm not telling Carter jackshit. You're not getting off this easy. I want to know what the fuck is going on. If you're doing a story on that French woman, I'm in. That's my beat, remember? Plus, your eyes are swollen, your nose all red. Something is happening."

We walked to the elevators, heading for the cafeteria on the third floor of the building. I held my head down and Carol didn't push me to talk until we were sitting in the Deadline Diner, named appropriately for the consequences of eating its food, as well as the news angle.

"Okay. Come on. Tell me. Is it Kenneth?"

Carol was with me the day I met Kenneth at the computer seminar. She thought he was the most gorgeous man she'd ever seen when we later actually saw him. He'd had on a hat and shades in the seminar and you couldn't see that much of his face. After colliding with him and knocking all his papers on the floor, Carol invited him to have lunch with us. Even though I think Carol might have secretly been scoping him out for herself, it was me he'd invited to dinner.

After that she was always pumping me for information on our progress. He was the only man she'd ever pushed me to date.

With the mention of Kenneth's name, tears had reflexively popped in my eyes.

Carol handed me a Kleenex. "Watch it," she warned. "That shit'll cut your face if you're not careful."

I loved her natural wit. Actually, she could be smart-assed and extremely secretive about her private life. That's probably why I liked her. Why she could be counted among my short list of friends. She was a kinder, gentler me.

"I'm going to make this short, okay?" I said, recognizing at the same moment I was pissed that Carol was witnessing my crying. I'd been crying more in the last day than in my lifetime. "Listen and no wisecracks." I took a deep breath. "Kenneth and I were going to get married."

"What? Married? You're shitting me, right? Coldhearted Hannah herself, married? I don't believe it."

"Look, are you going to listen or what?"

"Sure. You're serious, aren't you? So what happened? Don't tell me. You got cold feet."

I grabbed for another napkin. "Can we get out of here?"

"Sure. Come on, let's go to the bathroom on the eighth. It's early; the prima donnas aren't in Features yet."

In the bathroom I splashed cold water on my face again, while Carol leaned against the wall handing me brown paper towels. "You're scaring the shit out of me," she said. "You know that? I've never seen you this rattled. Actually, I've never seen you even jarred. I know you really liked Kenneth and all, but, shit, marriage?"

"Would you stop saying that word, please?" I sat on the tattered orange couch that must have been a holdover from before the floor got remodeled, since the walls were now a harsh blue and burgundy. "Look, you remember the conversation we had when you gave me that eggnog when Peter Bronstein left the paper for Paris and I didn't know it was spiked? And I got so wasted I confessed to you that I really trusted Kenneth?"

"Do I remember? Shit, you bring up the fact that I should have known you didn't drink alcohol only every day. But what's trusting a man got to do with this? Obviously, if you were going to marry him, you trusted him. So why'd you renege?"

She held up her hand and then looked under all the stalls. "Okay. Go on."

I sniffled, fighting the tears. "We, we were getting married yesterday. You know, at the Wednesday all-you-can-marry-at-one-time Moonie gig and . . . " I shrugged. "He stood me up."

"All right. Maybe *he* got cold feet. He'll get over it and come to his senses. You know how men can be. Stupid as shit. There's always another Wednesday." She smiled at me and winked. She'd never been married herself.

"I saw him. I saw him after I left the court."

"And what did he say . . . ?"

"He couldn't say anything since he had his fucking face stuck in the face of that French whore in the A section."

Her hands went to the side of her face and I couldn't help thinking of the movie *Home Alone*. Advertising is a bitch.

"No shit," she continued. "You mean your Kenneth Lawson was with the French woman found with her wrists cut. Are you sure?"

"Please. Of course, I'm sure. I stood watching them holding hands and gazing at each other in the Le Chef restaurant until I couldn't take it anymore. I wanted to walk in there and rip both their hearts out."

"What did you do?" she asked in a whisper. Like maybe she didn't want to know. "You didn't . . . ?"

"Didn't what?"

"Well, you know; blowing up a car like Angela Bassett in *Waiting to Exhale* is one thing, but slitting somebody's wrists, well, that's something else again."

I laughed. Out loud. "Don't be stupid. I didn't slit her damn wrists. Sure, I was mad as hell, so I went to the dojo and tried to rip Jake Fuller's balls off, but that's about it."

"You don't think Kenneth had anything to do with her killing herself, do you?"

"That's just it. It gets deeper. See, later on, these detectives came to my house and said they'd found my car abandoned and . . . well, I'm not going to get into that. But the bottom line is, something is going down. I think maybe Kenneth or somebody got hurt while in my car behind Le Chef. If it's true, then how did she slit her wrists soon after without Kenneth being there?"

Carol shrugged. "Maybe she was married and her old man showed up and didn't have a dojo to visit to kick anybody else's butt except theirs?"

"Yeah. Maybe." I didn't mention the phone call I suspected the French woman had made before slitting her wrists. But, hell, the entire thing was confusing me. "Did the police think it was a suicide?" I asked Carol, while sweat beaded my forehead. "What was her name again?"

"Claudette Duvet, I think. The paper doesn't say what time she died or whether they bought the suicide. Maybe Kenneth told her that he was marrying you and her favorite opera was *Madame Butterfly*. You never know what women will do nowadays."

"Uh-huh. Then, where is he? He damn sure didn't come home with me last night. Listen. I know Kenneth must be involved in something that's not kosher, only I don't know what it is. And I don't know if he hasn't gotten me mixed up in it. God, he was using my car—my house. It better not be no damn drugs."

The thought made me mad as hell. Kenneth Lawson and everybody else knew exactly how I felt about drugs in the black community. If I saw drug shit going down, whoever it was might as well put on handcuffs and carry their own ass to jail. Because, friend or foe, I was turning them in.

"If that motherfucker," I said, "was in my damn house dealing drugs, if he's not dead, I'll kill him. I swear on that."

"Don't jump to conclusions. You have no evidence Kenneth was using or dealing drugs, do you?"

"No," I lied. Actually, I did have some evidence he might have been using. But I couldn't believe it about him even now. Sometimes what you believe is solely based on what you can bear at the moment.

"Okay," I said, slowing my breathing. "All I have to do is find out what is going on and find him so I can tell him off and I'll be all right again." I said this like I believed it was that simple.

"Well, maybe he thinks he had to go away because the police would connect him to the woman's suicide."

"I don't know shit anymore," I said, rubbing my head.

"Well, maybe you don't know shit anymore, but one thing you should know—detectives in Atlanta don't come to your house for abandoned cars."

"Maybe. Look, I've got some checking around to do. You cover for me and I'll call you as soon as I know anything. . . . It's funny. For the first time in my life I actually thought, God, I'm going to have a family. But I guess it's not meant to be."

She put her hand on mine. "Don't say that. You must still care for him, or why go to the trouble of looking for him? Maybe this'll be straightened out and you can get married like you planned. Look how far you've already come. Shit, you're confiding in somebody and you're not even drunk."

I got up. This was getting too weird for me. "I'll call you, okay? Cover for me."

Carol got up and squeezed my hand. "Hey, at least you're still sober."

> "And having sprung into existence,
> the thing becomes conscious of itself,
> 'comprehends itself,' and thus
> the sign of an 'intelligent soul.'"
> —The Dogons

CHAPTER EIGHT

Carol was right; I wasn't drunk but I damn sure wanted to be. If I was drunk none of this crap would mean a keg of beer to me. *Drunk.* The word danced on my tongue and I wet my lips. Being drunk is a dream come true if you're trying to avoid feeling pain. At least for a hot minute.

It's been years since I drank three—to be exact. Being involved in the dojo slowed me down, and then, finally, a kid made me quit. I'd been drinking like a fish swimming in water since I was fifteen years old. It started off fun. You know, a beer stolen out of the fridge here, a bottle of wine there; never whiskey, though. Old Cooney turned me against whiskey.

When I was in college it was cool. Shit, everybody who was anybody drank and I was trying my best to be somebody, so I had to drink. Then it was social; at least that's what I said. After college I kept on socializing until booze got so intimate with me it was reeking from my body every morning like expensive perfume.

I stayed by myself most of the time, never had a lot of friends, so drinking seemed like the answer to my woes. Hell, it didn't talk back, didn't stand me up, was always there, could snuggle in the bed with me, dulled my senses until masturbation seemed silly. Hell of a lover booze can be.

But then I started skipping stories. Good stories. My career was flushing down the toilet with every piss. I kept telling myself I wasn't an alcoholic, and there was no one around to argue the point.

At first, I wasn't an alcoholic because I only drank socially. Then when it dawned on me one night that I was tipsy and alone, I changed my definition: I wasn't an alcoholic because I only drank on weekends. Then because I didn't drink every day. Then I wasn't one because I didn't drink hard liquor. And I couldn't be one because I worked every day. Hey, at least I didn't get drunk. Finally, I wasn't one because, because, damn, I just *wasn't* one.

My colleagues at work didn't complain; hell, half of them are drunk at home or at work, the other half snorting like hogs or smoking like chimneys. And any left have so many emotional problems, merely getting to their therapist is about all they can handle.

The newsroom is the mental ward of print. We are the living version of the *DSM-IV*. We got it right there for you. Half my editors are manic as hell. Feature writers tend toward more exotic-sounding illnesses, and most copy editors are so embalmed they'd all blow up if you lit a match near the copy desk.

Don't get me wrong. Not all journalists fit this bill, but so much of what we do is hazardous duty. Newsrooms are like dumps. Every piece of filth and trash nobody would dream of living with is heaved on us, sometimes even dug up by us, and then we're expected to smile and go on. We don't whine "not in my neighborhood." And just like a toxic waste dump, we never get rid of it all. Somewhere deep down in a journalist's soul we know that the shit simmers like a raging fire and sometimes we need to put the flames out.

Mental health workers experience it too, but the difference is at least they're trained to help somebody. All we're trained to do is record the facts, pry into folks' intimate thoughts and expose their most painful moments. It's a shitty job but somebody's got to do it. And if you're drunk, it's a hell of a lot easier.

So, for seven years, I drank before work or after work, sometimes on breaks, or for breakfast, lunch or dinner—anywhere, anytime and then, finally, everywhere.

Then one fuzzy evening in the West End, one of the few historic black sections of Atlanta, I'm speeding down the street like a goddamn maniac and a wisp of a thing rolls out in front of my car. The crunch is loud. I stagger out and see twisted iron under the wheel. I lean against my car. Shit. I've run over a freaking bike.

I get back in the car and start my engine. I'm pulling the gear down to put the car in reverse when I hear the scream. A woman is running to-ward the car—no, past the car—to the other side. She kneels in the bushes. I look, mesmerized at the confusing sight. My head spins and I'm sick. I lean my head out the door, throwing up the enchiladas I ate earlier. More screams tear from the woman's throat, adding to her inaudible words cruising the air.

Other people run to her. I hear sirens, but they seem far away. I'm in that hazy place where alcoholics live to escape the reality of a world too painful to live in. I'm in a blackout. I bang my head on the wheel and fall asleep.

When I wake up I'm in a hospital ward. My head bandaged. My boss, Phillip Dowry, is sitting at my bed. When I open my eyes he strains out a smile.

I know the look. All is not right with the world. I've fucked up, but how I don't recall.

Later I know. A ten-year-old boy was thrown from a small blue bike. One broken arm, a crushed leg, a few broken teeth, but otherwise okay. I'm not charged.

Why? No one tested me for alcohol because they saw my journalist's ID badge swinging from my neck. *The Atlanta Guardian* is the major news gig in town. This is before the time people wanted to spit on jour-nalists. And, I've got pain medication open in my purse.

The ambulance crew assumes I was out on a story. With the fog, the pain medication, the little boy in dark clothes, and his skin dark to match, it is an unfortunate accident.

The pain medicine, Tylenol 3 with codeine, is loose in my purse on its own. I hadn't used it since I had my tooth pulled three weeks before. Everyone understands and forgives me. Except me, that is. I know better.

CHAPTER NINE

I didn't go home like I probably should have. Instead, I walked up toward Macy's to Le Chef. There was no sign there'd been any disturbance. The white tablecloths were not stained with blood as I had imagined. One red rose was at the center of each table in a crystal vase. I asked the maître d' if I could speak to the owner. My eyes fixated at the back table where only yesterday I'd seen the two of them, Kenneth Lawson and Claudette Duvet, clutching hands.

After a few minutes a tall, thin man with long black hair, a silk sky-blue Armani shirt, tight navy Calvins and navy alligator cowboy boots came from behind the bar. He had a swing in his walk and I thought he might be gay.

"May I help you?" he asked with no accent at all.

"I'm waiting for the owner." I figured he wasn't French so he couldn't be the owner. Wrong.

"I am the owner. Now, may I help you?"

I'd annoyed him by assuming what probably a lot of other people assumed—that he wasn't the owner. "Okay. Sorry. I'm a journalist with *The Atlanta Guardian* and I received a tip that you had some problem here last night. Possibly in your alley?"

He swung his head around, glaring at the waiters bustling back and forth from the kitchen. He whipped it back around. "Who told you that?"

"I said it was a tip, that's all." I could see blood coloring his cheeks. I'd hit some button. Obviously, no one here was supposed to talk about what had happened.

"No. I don't know what you're talking about. Nothing happened. Now, if that's all, I have to see to the bar." He turned to walk away.

I grabbed his shirt.

"Excuse me," he shrilled, flapping his hands at me like a seal. "Why are you touching my clothes?"

"I didn't mean to," I said. "I meant to grab your arm."

Shooing me like a fly, he whispered, teeth clenched, "What is it? I've told you everything I know. Why don't you ask the police?"

"Police? The police were here?"

"I don't want to get involved in this. I've got work to do."

It was time to pull. "Listen," I said, putting on my fake, weaker-than-thou face. "This is off the record. I'm just trying to find out what happened to a friend of mine who left my car here. You're the *only* person who can help me. Please."

"What kind of car?" he asked, less defensive.

I knew it. When a person has been taken for granted, overlooked because he doesn't appear important, all he needs is reassurance that *you* are not like the others, because you know he's important—voilà.

"It was an Audi," I said, lowering my voice, "and it was behind your restaurant in an alley. Did the police talk to you about it?"

He looked around again, a squirrel snatching birdseed. No one was watching us. He motioned me over to a corner booth.

"The Audi was *your* car?" he asked in a conspiratorial whisper.

"Yes," I said, not wanting to give him anymore in case he was one of the bad guys.

"The only thing I can tell you is that the police talked to us and then detectives left a sketch here for me to show the customers of a man who supposedly was involved. But I'm not pulling it out, waving it in front of customers. You know they already think it's unsafe downtown. Why give them a reason not to eat here?"

"May I see the sketch? Please?"

He sighed. "Why not. You work down here. You have to be downtown."

He came back with a manila folder and slid himself onto the seat beside me. I moved over to make room.

"Look quick, okay?" he said, waving one hand in the air. He appeared to be more relaxed.

51

I didn't want to open the folder. But I did. My eyes filled with water. "You say they said this man was involved?" It was a likeness of Kenneth Lawson. My heart fluttered. I looked up at him, allowing myself to show him my pain. "What happened? Was he hurt? Anybody hurt? Did they take him or anyone to the hospital?"

"No. According to the police, they didn't know where the people in the car went. But ask the witnesses. They probably can tell you."

"What witnesses?"

"Well, all I can say is there are three vagrants who live out back, and they're the ones who told the cops the man in the car got shot and was helped away by another man and a woman."

My head jerked up. "What do you mean? *This* man? Shot?"

A waiter walked over and leaned down. "Excuse me, but the chef's back there cursing everybody out. If you don't get in there, I think you're going to have a brawl on your hands."

"Sorry," he said, jumping up and snatching the folder from me. "I've got to see to this. That chef is crazy."

CHAPTER TEN

Before I could speak, he raced through the swinging doors of the kitchen. I considered running after him, but then what? It was still early and if the witnesses were vagrants, there was a possibility they'd not gotten up and left the alley yet. Vagrants in Atlanta kept old-time-banker's hours.

I walked out and headed around the block to reach the back alley. I was confused. The sketch was of Kenneth Lawson. Kenneth was shot? But if he was, who was the other man who helped him away and where did they go? I didn't have a clue what was going on. But I had a good idea who the woman was. Now to find those vagrants.

The alley was narrow and boxes were stacked up on both sides. Even though the sun was shining, it was dark and dreary. I walked carefully, trying to breathe through my mouth so the full brunt of the rotten smell wouldn't knock me down. I saw an old woman rummaging through a brown paper bag. "Excuse me. Could you . . . ?"

She didn't look up. "You sorry son of a bitch," she mumbled. "I'll kill you." Then she broke into song: "'Precious Lord, lead me on . . .'"

I stepped over her underwear, strewn all over the alley's entrance, and walked more warily into the darker recesses of doorways and trash Dumpsters. Directly behind the restaurant I saw a cardboard-erected shelter with a red-and-white gingham curtain hanging across the entrance.

There're a lot of vagrants in Atlanta. Community mental health put all these people on the street. Otherwise, I'm sure most of them, who are either mentally ill or addicted to substances, would be in hospitals being treated long-term.

I pulled the curtain back with a Kleenex from my pocket. Three people were piled inside along with a scrubby, brownish dog with long matted hair.

"Excuse me. Could I talk to one of you gentlemen, please?"

The tattered green army blanket stirred. Then a head popped out. A dark-skinned man with unkempt braids and a full wooly beard sat up and yawned. Then a dingy-haired blond white man with his hair almost locked, it hadn't been combed in so long, flung the blanket aside. The last lump didn't move and I was tempted to ask if their friend was okay.

I wasn't surprised to see the black man and white man together. I'd always found it curious that the most integrated community in Atlanta was among the homeless population.

"Who you be?" the black man said.

"I'm a journalist and I thought maybe you could answer a few questions."

Blondie spoke next, "Hey, we already been in the damn paper 'bout our dog. Shit got him a home better than us for 'bout two weeks, then the stupid sons of bitches brought him back. Like he wanted to be in this hellhole with me."

"Shut up, Ralph. We don't want no publicity, lady," the beard said. "For one thing, it's too damn early for you to even be up."

"You shut up yourself, Bobby Ray," Blondie shouted. "Ain't nobody talking to you. She talking to me."

"I don't mean to interrupt your communication," I said, "but I'm talking to whoever will answer my questions about what you witnessed last night in the alley, in exchange for"—I reached in my purse and pulled out twenty dollars—"this."

"You thinking we can be bought? You insulting us, lady?" Bobby the Beard shouted. "We are law-abiding citizens like you. We do our civic duty. We overstand where you're coming from."

Blondie snatched the money from my hand. "Ask away. I ain't studying Bobby Ray's stupid-shit lecture. Just 'cause he been to law school he thinks he's better 'n us. Don't he, Pat?"

I was stunned. How did he know my name? I stood there staring in disbelief.

Then the lump moved and sat up. It was a white woman with ragged jack-o'-lantern teeth, wearing a thick gold sweatshirt that read, GRANDMA LOVES YOU.

"Both you idiots shut the fuck up. I'm trying to sleep," she said. "You see a piece of ass and you both go crazy." While grinning at me, she stood up, snatched the money out of Blondie's hand and stuck it down inside her bosom. "I'm Grandma Pat, dear. What can I do for you?"

"Wow. For a moment you had me spooked," I said. "My name is Pat, actually Patricia, but often people call me Pat."

They all laughed. "Hey, baby, you've given us an idea," Bobby the Beard said. "We can be the Alley Psychic Network. Now all we need is a phone and a TV to watch ourselves sucker the suckers."

Grandma Pat moved slowly, throwing the blanket off her shoulders. "Give me a minute. My old body ain't what it used to be," she said, and walked out to a metal bedpan filled with greasy water. It was sitting on a makeshift table outside the cardboard house. She splashed some water on her pruned face and dried it with a stained towel.

She was old and I figured it would take her a minute to collect herself. Probably arthritis slowing her in the morning.

She bent over and then dropped down, stretching out on the pavement in front of me like she was kissing the ground.

My heartbeat quickened. Had she fallen? Passed out?

But, damn, if she didn't do the Suriya Namaskar, the yoga Salute to the Sun in perfect form. I was still standing there gawking when she grabbed me by the hand and pulled me off to a corner behind the Dumpster. If I hadn't seen her do the salute with my own eyes, I'm sure I wouldn't have let her pull me back there, but, hey—I was impressed.

"What's your full name, girl?"

"Patricia Conley."

"What you need to know?"

"I came to find out what happened in the alley last night. The man involved was my boyfriend."

"I'm so sorry, I know how it is. I know pain like a hog knows slop," she said, her eyes watering. She patted me on the shoulder. "See, we come back here. We go to bed early now that the weather's changing. Anywho, we done missed the shooting. When we come we see this man helping another one out of the car. There's a woman with 'em, but she got her head held over and her long hair is in the way, so we don't see her."

"How do you know the man was shot and not stabbed or just cut or something?"

"Young'un. I done been shot, cut and beat up bad. I know what your chest look like when it's been opened up with a bullet and I know what it look like when a knife done you in. The man was shot."

"Did you see the man's face? The one who was shot?"

"Naw. The man who shot, we don't really see him neither as he's bent over double and all. We only sees the man helping him. The man who helping look sick hisself, but he ain't shot, though. They get into another car at the other end of the alley and drives away.

"Then the police come asking a bunch of dumb questions. And then detectives come. One of 'em is a woman, nose stuck so high up in the air, pigeon droppings ought to fall in it. Anywho, we tells 'em what we can, and then, honey, it was way past our bedtime and we goin' on to sleep. You know."

"Can you describe the man you *did* see? The one helping the shot man?"

"I can do better than that. Them police done drawed a picture from what we say. Here." She reached inside the same bosom where the money went and pulled out a folded piece of paper.

My hands shook as I took it and unfolded it, hoping it was the same sketch the restaurant owner had shown me. I gasped. "This is the man who was *not* shot, right?"

"Right. That's the man who helped the man who was shot. Shit. He looks like Denzel Washington, don't he?"

I don't know how it happened but my legs gave way. I thought, Kenneth Lawson wasn't shot but sick. *Sick.* How sick? Sick from what? AIDS? Maybe he's given me AIDS?

The alley spun and darkness engulfed me. I felt Grandma Pat grabbing for me, but I couldn't stop falling. I knew the cement was covered with garbage and I didn't want it on me, but still I couldn't stop falling. How far away is the pavement? I wondered as I fell. I remembered the few times I'd smoked marijuana, how something inches from my reach seemed miles away.

I heard her calling, "Bobby, Ralph, get over here. She's done passed out."

Kenneth Lawson. He was not the one shot in the chest. Wherever he was, he was still alive. Thank God, but what did she mean by sickly? was my last conscious thought.

♊

My mind swirled into a cloud of light. I could hear the blood flowing through my veins. I saw an old dark black man dressed in tattered and dirty clothes standing in front of some boulders. He was beckoning to me. I couldn't hear what he was saying but I saw his lips moving. It seemed odd that I could see his lips but not his face. Dreaming. I must be dreaming. I heard a man's voice. Could it be the old man inside my head? Talking?

"He's sick and alone," he mouthed. "Alone just like you now."

That's what the old man was saying to me when the penlight hit my pupils.

Opening your eyes with a flashlight poked in your face and the smelling salts of alley sewage is as jarring as any remedy you can get in a drugstore.

I sat up and removed the damp, Clorox-smelling rag off my forehead, and brushed the limp lettuce off my shoulders.

Grandma Pat was leaning over me. I realized that if she were darker skinned, she would look a lot like Grandma Dixon, one of my foster mothers, and the only person I'd ever opened up to other than Kenneth Lawson. "How long have I been out?"

"A bit. Time don't matter, now do it?" she said, jostling the others away.

"What happened?"

"You fainted. You sick? Pregnant?"

"No, I'm not sick," and then louder, "And I'm not pregnant."

"Hmmm. Sin, ain't it? A body can't be a woman and be sick without some old hag thinking she pregnant."

"It's all right," I said, feeling terrible. "I didn't mean to raise my voice." I'd never raised my voice at Grandma Dixon but once, and it was the last time I saw her.

"I'm not sick, though," I continued. "I've not had much sleep in the last few days and I haven't eaten anything in a while except a piece of toast."

I didn't want to tell her that I'd not slept well in over a week and that I couldn't eat for three days because I was too nervous about getting married. The funny thing is, I wanted to tell her. Odd. I'd never fainted before and I decided it was a warning sign of something bad on its way.

"That car? Was it your'n?"

"Yes. Yes, it was," I said.

"Then I got somethin' for you," she whispered, taking me by the arm and helping me move with her farther away from the others. "I got it from the man who was shot in the car."

"I thought you said you didn't see the man who was shot."

"I don't tell folk all my business till I'm sure 'bout hows I feel 'bout 'em. You all right. Anywho, we never tell the cops everything. Miss Tit Brain made me so mad talking down to us, we wouldn't tell her the time nohow."

"So what *did* happen?"

"When I come, a man was in the car, shot. His head was lapping over on the steering wheel. I thought he was dead. I'm a collector, you know. Got all kinds of stuff over yonder in my grocery basket. Anywho, I start to go through his pockets, 'cause you know if he dead and he got stuff, it ain't gon' really do him no good. His throat is gurgling and I figure I'd take it 'cause, shit, he's gon' die anyway. I swipe the money and whatever he's clutching in his fist."

"What was it?" I held my breath. This didn't make sense. If it wasn't Kenneth, why would some other man be in the driver's seat of my car?

She goes into her storeroom bosom again.

I had a flash. Grandma Dixon kept her money in her bosom too.

"Here," she said, handing me my car keys, the ones whose ring says, PAT. "You can see why I kept 'em, don't ya?"

I looked at her. "Yes. Yes," I said. "I see. The name. Your name." My keys. Why would this man be clutching my keys? "Did he say anything? Anything at all?"

"Naw. He might woulda but the woman and the other man was coming toward the car. The woman was sorta helping the other man along, but when they got here they both lifted the shot one out, and took him to a bluish car down there." She pointed to the other end of the alley.

"I don't get it."

"I done told you the truth. The shot man had some cash on him. When I seen them coming, I hid. You can't have the stash back, though; it's mine."

"Sure. Sure. But the guy you described for the police, the one on the sketch, was my boyfriend. I can't figure why another man would be driving my car. Can you describe him? The man who was shot?"

"That's just it. I don't know 'bout the picture on that paper, 'cause I don't see that man walking with the woman up close like they do. See, Bobby Ray and Ralph told the cops the way that one look on that police drawing. I just shake my head to the cops that I agreed with them for the hell of it."

"So what exactly are you saying?" I said, exasperated.

"I'ma saying, I saw the man in the car that was shot, not the one with the woman. That's what I'm saying. See, I didn't tell the police what the man look like who was shot in the car 'cause don' nobody know I seen him up close.

"Bobby Ray and Ralph, they come in the alley late. They sees the man and woman closer than me, but not the man shot in the car. I didn't tell them two clowns neither that I saw the shot man in the car. Didn't want no fighting from them sorry coons trying to take my money."

"Okay. Don't worry. You can keep the money. I only need to know how the man in the car, the man who was shot, looked. This is important. Please, help me."

"Hey, what you think I *been* doing? The man in the car who was shot looked like that picture too. It was like seeing two Denzel Washingtons. Now, who wouldn't love that? Shoulda been six of 'em." She pointed to the police artist sketch. "That woulda been nice, huh?"

"Are you sure? You mean they looked alike?"

"Two Denzels, I'ma telling you. Two of 'em."

"You're sure? You're sure they both looked like this man? The one on the picture? The Denzel Washington–looking man?" I recalled how I had thought everybody in the dojo looked liked Kenneth Lawson, but I had a reason to be seeing all men that way. But with a white woman, there is only one reason she wouldn't be able to tell them apart. So I said, "Listen, Grandma Pat. I realize that sometimes because white people are not accustomed to describing how—"

"Don't go there, gal. You trying to imply 'cause I'm white I can't tell black men apart? If'n that be so, hell, I'da said they both look like that ugly Bobby Ray, now, wouldn't I?"

After apologizing for my slip in stereotyping, I left. Now I was truly baffled and scared. If the man who Grandma Pat saw in my car was shot and that man was Kenneth Lawson, then who was the other man? Why did she think they looked alike? Twins? No, it couldn't be. No. Kenneth said he had no brother. No sisters. So what went down? Makeup? Yes. Yes. Maybe they were planning to pull off some theft and needed to have any witnesses confused. A botched holdup? Yes. But where was Kenneth Lawson now? And then, against everything in my mind, my heart screamed, *Please, God, don't let Kenneth Lawson be dead.*

CHAPTER ELEVEN

I stumbled dazed from the alley. I looked up at the buildings but they were blurred. I felt wheezy and sick. I wanted to lie down and rest, forget all this. But another part of me wanted answers. I examined my key chain. There were three keys on the ring.

When I'd given it to Kenneth, there'd been two. One for the car door lock and ignition and one for the house. I held the unfamiliar key out and looked at it with a discerning eye. Now, what could it fit? A post office box, maybe? Kenneth never received mail at my house. I'd questioned him about it but he'd shrugged and said there was nobody to write to him.

The main post office was across the street from the Federal Reserve, only a few blocks away. I'd try there first.

On my way, I shunned the unfamiliar derelicts that had taken up corners on Atlanta's streets in the time-honored tradition of prostitutes. At least prostitutes offered you something in return for your money. Which is more than I could say for these vagrants.

One of them, an older man with a gray beard and a dead-fish smell, followed behind me. "Hey, little sister," he said, like we were bosom buddies.

I held my hands out, palms up. "I don't have any money," I said, cutting him off at the pass.

"Hey, all I wanted was fourteen hundred dollars," he said, smiling like I was his fairy bank teller.

I burst into laughter and handed him a buck. Finally, a vagrant offering something in return—a good laugh. That was worth something to me about now.

The post office was busy as usual. The line continued outside the rope. There were five windows but only three were open. I dropped my head in disappointment when I got the man on the end. I hesitated, hoping the guy to my right would get free first, but he was still counting out money into an elderly woman's hands.

The corner man reminded me of the opposite of eight ball in the pocket. If you drew him you lost not only time, since his snail movements were legendary, but any empathy you might have for postal workers.

Attempting a smile, I asked him, "Do you think this is one of your keys?"

"Nope," he answered while fumbling in his drawer. "Haven't lost any keys."

"I don't mean *your* keys. I mean one of the keys to one of your post office boxes?"

"Nope." Still not looking up.

"Would you mind looking at it first before you make a decision?" He was pushing me.

He looked me straight in the eyes. "Nope. Not ours."

"Well, do you have a guess if maybe it's for one of your other post offices?"

A big sigh escaped his puckered, are-you-done-asking-questions lips. "Nope. All our keys are from the same company. Try a locksmith."

Even though I'm sure from his tone of voice that he suggested a locksmith to be a wise mouth, it was a good idea. There was one only six blocks away, not far from the Five Points area. Not so bad, since I had on my walking shoes.

The locksmith also sold beepers, so I had to wait through three customers, all with wads of cash and no credit. While I waited, I wondered if this man was legit. I'm always suspicious of a storefront selling beepers. The place smelled of illegal people to me and I don't mean aliens. The last thing I needed was to be in the center of some freaking laundry raid with not a stitch of dirty clothes in sight.

"Looks like it could fit something like a safe deposit box to me," he said, giving the key a look. "I only cut the keys with this machine, sister. I'm not like a locksmith for real or nothing. Did you try the bank?"

I should have gone there first. I headed for First Federal. If that didn't work, I'd try the bus station, the train station, and then maybe some of the pay-as-you-go workout gyms.

Now what? I went to the customer service desk. I banked with First Federal because it was located only three blocks from the paper. Not close enough for everybody to know my business and not far enough to be inconvenient. I had tried to get Kenneth to open an account here but he refused.

Louise, a young black woman with a warm, friendly smile, was the customer service rep. She and I often dished out wrath on the brothers together. After meeting Kenneth I'd stopped doing it. Louise continued undaunted.

Kenneth offered me tangible reasons why brothers did what they did during our long, heart-to-heart conversations. Now I knew he had a vested interest in dissuading me since he probably knew one day his turn to be dissed would come.

"Louise," I said, sitting in the customer chair and offering her the appearance that this was a typical day in my life, "I have a little puzzle for you. See this key. Do you think this might be a safe deposit key?"

She took it in her hands and felt along the edges while her eyes searched in her forehead for answers. "Wait a minute," she said, disappearing into the back.

A few minutes later she returned, smiling. "I think it might fit our safe deposit boxes upstairs," she said.

"Your safe deposit boxes?" I said it like they might be UFOs. Of course, I knew what they were in theory, and had come here looking for them, but I'd not considered that they'd have safe deposit boxes here, in this bank. It was so small. On the other hand, I'd not given much thought to them before. I'd never actually had anything in a safe deposit box.

"Go through the doors, to the right, to the second set of elevators. Go to the twelfth floor, then to your left until you dead end. There's a door there that says First Federal Deposits. A woman is there who'll help you."

My legs wobbled slightly as I rose to leave. The excitement plus no food was beginning to take its toll on me. This was taking me too fast. I needed time to digest what was happening. To think about the connections, implications, the puzzle of recent events. I was never good at puzzles, chess or checkers because the big picture often eluded me. This was no different.

At the elevator I punched twelve. It was filled with brass, and was more elegant than the other elevators I'd ridden in this building. On the twelfth floor the carpet leading to the dead end was burgundy, plush and thick, confirming my suspicion that if you had a safe deposit box, you ought to have something valuable to put in it.

Inside the deposit door, the attendant, gray-haired and pale-complexioned, as though she'd been dancing with Dracula all night, offered me a seat. "How can I help you?" she asked, a plastic-food smile on her face.

I didn't know how. I'd never had a box, so I handed her the key, like I might have been mute.

"I'll need your name," she said, sounding out the phrase as though she were singing a cappella.

"Uh . . . Patricia Conley," I answered, feeling inadequate about this whole encounter. Not knowing what to expect, I shifted in the chair, a child waiting for the dentist. I knew what happened on television, but it hadn't taken me long to know that television and real life were two very different phenomena.

She checked some file cards. And, like magic, once again, just the mention of my name seemed to ring some bell. She smiled a bit less plasticly and said, "Oh. Of course. The note." She pulled out the card and looked up at me. "Your skin is so wonderful, you know, dark and smooth looking. I've been tanning for years with no luck. You're a lucky woman."

I quelled the impulse to ask: Would you like to trade? Be a black woman for a day? Yeah. I didn't think so.

She continued, "Plus, how could I forget the elaborate train of questions your husband devised so even you would have to be tested to get in? I told my husband about that."

"Sure, of course," I said, puzzlement stretched across my face. And annoyance, because even though I didn't have knowledge of any questions, it occurred to me that she shouldn't be spreading my business around so freely.

She reached in her drawer and took out some papers. "You'll need to fill these forms out in person this time. But I'm supposed to ask the questions before you start—or was he kidding me when he instructed me to ask them of you?'

"No. Of course he wasn't kidding," I said, wishing I knew what he wasn't kidding about. "Okay, ask me the questions." I smiled at her, trying to hide my pensiveness. What did she mean? I'd never signed any forms or written any note.

"What is your favorite ice cream?"

"My favorite ice cream?" I repeated incredulously.

"Yes, please." She didn't seem impressed that that was the answer to her question.

"Uhhh. Ben and Jerry's New York Style Chocolate Chunk." That wasn't exactly the correct name but that's what I always called it.

"And who is it that you feel you were supporting in his career at one point?"

"What?" Then it dawned on me where this was headed other than *Wheel of Fortune*. "Robert Holland, Jr., a former CEO of Ben and Jerry's, who is a black man," I answered.

Kenneth and I joked about this, since when I met Holland, I made a point of telling him that I supported his career by increasing my Ben & Jerry's allotment from two pints a week to four. The sad part was, I was serious.

"And what is it that you believed yourself to be when you were twelve?"

I stared at her. He wouldn't. Then I answered, clearing my throat as the word seeped out, "Alone."

"And now—what is it that you believe yourself to be now?"

"Alone," I answered, meeting her eyes. Understanding the implication of Kenneth Lawson adding that last question. He must have planned to leave me.

"What is the book you and your husband both owned before you met?"

These were the answers only I could give. "The *Kybalion*." Husband? Did this mean he meant to leave me even if we'd gotten married?

"Please fill out the forms, be sure to sign your name exactly as it is presented on your signature card and I'll take you back."

Seeing my signature already on the card shook me up even more. While I filled out the papers, my hands trembling, I thought about what this little scenario could mean. Maybe Kenneth meant for me to find the key? Maybe the answer to where he'd gone was in the safe deposit box? Maybe this was some complex, incredibly complicated scheme to surprise me on some exotic wedding excursion? Yeah, right. And I believed Michael Jackson really loved being black and he and Lisa Presley were going to be married forever.

Dracula's bride rose, pulling a key ring from a drawer. The ring had so many keys on it I was tempted to offer her help to carry it.

She walked around her desk in front of me. She wore a black linen dress with a white lace collar. I thought Drackie must have picked it out.

She said, "Follow me, please."

And once again, thanks to the elements of surprise and shock, I was following some woman.

The vault had an echo. Inside it was as cold as Alaska. At one time I would have thought "cold as hell," but that makes no sense. I watched her fumble through the keys until she came to the one she needed and slid it into the lock. She looked at me and smiled.

I smiled back, while my mind tried to rewind scenes from the movies so I'd know what to do next. . . . *Oh. My key.* With my teeth chattering from the cold and the fear of uncovering what was in the box, I stuck my key in the second keyhole. Every sound reverberated; even the key sliding into the lock echoed.

"Would you like to be alone?" she asked, looking away.

"Yes," I answered, unsure of what that meant or what my options were to not being alone.

That was it! I was destined to be alone. Forever.

She led me to a small cubicle in another area and left. I looked around and suddenly felt claustrophobic. My hands quivered and my fingers fumbled with the top of the box. I lifted the lid. The box was the size of a medium gift box.

There was a disk labeled Simone Ratcliff Songs plus a letter addressed to me with a note underneath my name. My hands were shaking and I couldn't breathe. The message read: *If you're not authorized to open this box but you've somehow gotten into it, beware. I may still be out there and coming for you. There are still a few of us left. Death to those who would destroy us.*

What? I opened the envelope and slid the letter out. I unfolded the pages and began reading them through my blurred eyes.

Dear Pat,

If you're reading this letter I must assume I'm in serious trouble or dead. Because I'm not completely positive this is a secure approach, I must remain cryptic in my words, but not when it comes to my heart. From the moment I set eyes on you I loved you. I spent many hours wishing we'd met earlier, when I had no mission. Nothing to do but live my life. When I didn't know what I know now. Maybe in reality that time never existed but I'd thought it did. As it stands you may eventually come to think I've used you. That I came to live with you because you were a journalist and a good cover. That is not true. I assure you, I agonized over falling in love with someone who was in your line of work. I was not ever convinced you could help or that I wouldn't put you in danger by merely being in your house. I can only say one thing to you. If you're reading this and I'm not there squeezing your fingers in my hand, I want you to know I wanted you to be my wife more than I've ever wanted anything. Remember that no matter what happens.

I apologize for not telling you about the box, but I did make sure you and you alone would be able to access it if something happened to me. I knew the bank would eventually notify you. I didn't want to involve you in any way in whatever was happening to me or around me. But I decided if you came to open it or found the key, as in all things in the Universe, it was meant to be. To that end, I must ask you to be careful. I still don't know the nature of the beast but I do know there is one out there and he or she is hunting for us. My benefactor is in Atlanta. He has been attempting to help me with this problem but has yet to find an antidote. Others, however, have questioned his intentions. I cannot divulge to you his name at this time since I don't want him to become a target either, and I must assume that someone other than you could be reading this letter. Take the necklace and the ring. Tell no one you have them. The ring brings great danger. Try to find a way to get rid of it. Sell it without revealing that you're the person selling it. The disk was given to me by a woman and if it is in the box, it means I've not figured out everything yet and am still working on it. Take it and put it in my computer at home. It will automatically open up the program and ask for a prompt. The name I called you when we made love the first time will open it. Please don't do it until you remember that name. Any incorrect attempt and the program will automatically erase.

Trust no one, my love. Tell no one what you've found in this box. The money is for you to use as you see fit. It is my life's savings.

Don't look under rocks. If information comes to you, though, and you are left with no choice than to pursue it, do it with my blessing. I know how you are. Relentless in your pursuit of information. Expose them. But be careful. Remember the Guerin woman you told me about. Don't fall into that trap. If it gets too spooky, walk away. I pray you do not need to use anything in this box except the

money. Believe me, I am in the dark now and if you're reading this it means I died pretty much in the dark. I can only
assume death overtook me. Whether it was natural, only
you know. If, per chance, I died a violent death and not one
borne of illness, then please drop this and pursue it no further. Your safety is more important to me than any amount
of revenge.

> Love, Your husband always,
> Kenneth Lawson

Sniffling and gasping for air, I lifted the necklace, hung with symbols
I didn't recognize. It and the disk had been placed on top of a thin black
velvet cloth. I lifted the cloth slowly, not knowing what to expect. A
black velvet pouch was on top. I pulled the drawstring open and turned
the pouch upside down. A diamond ring fell into my palm. I stared at it.
It looked like a real diamond. The diamond ring Kenneth Lawson
couldn't afford?

The bottom was lined with money, hundred-dollar bills, to be specific. The fear gripping my heart wouldn't let me touch the money, let
alone count it. I dropped the ring back into the box like it was a hot
sweet potato.

This was more than a sour-milk problem. This was beginning to
stink—not just any foul odor, but the skunk smell that can never be
washed off and will cause you to give your car away once you've run
over one. Skunks are more than roadkill; they are car kill, too.

CHAPTER TWELVE

I slid the disk and necklace into my purse. I closed the lid slowly, afraid any abrupt sound would break open another Pandora's hell. Then a thought surfaced in my head: A diamond, after all, is supposed to be a woman's best friend. I slipped the ring back into the pouch and stuck it into my purse.

The coldness in the room migrated down to my fingertips, and the money felt like velvet. Why did it have to be so cold in here? I counted out two bills with shaking fingers.

I figured if I had an emergency I'd probably need to get to this money more than I needed the disk, necklace or diamond. But I was too scared to take all the money with me. Was he telling the truth? His life savings? That meant he didn't steal it.

Get real, I thought. No one saves this much cash. Not legally. I replaced the cloth, closing the lid over it. I folded the bills into my wallet. A premonition floated forward: Money was not going to be enough to save me.

I walked out of the bank looking over my shoulder, scanning the street and gazing up at tall buildings. Bringing up Veronica Guerin was a bad omen. A warning for sure.

People think journalists have exotic ways to dig up news. What they don't realize is that most news falls into our laps. Journalists don't have snitches in high places. Snitches in high places make decisions to tell, and find us. For the most part anything a journalist can find, so can the average citizen. But then there's that handful of us—the Veronica Guerins of the world—who accidentally start scratching a sore, not understanding that festering right under the skin is a pulsing boil ready to explode in our faces. Veronica Guerin was one of those journalists. In Ireland she had fought organized crime openly and defiantly. The more they threatened the more she dug, until she was almost chiseling the sore out of her community as if her words were a scalpel. Then, *boom*. She was shot to death. The world of news still goes on but you—you're dead.

I'd told Kenneth I wasn't going out like that. As of yet, I'd not run across a news story that volatile. And at this moment I hoped I never would. If I did, I'd act like somebody with some sense and let the authorities handle it. And honest to God, I wanted to leave this whole mess alone. Carry my butt to work and forget Kenneth. So he dumped me. So what? I could live with that. Couldn't I?

No matter how I fight it, at times I still catch myself responding like a lovesick woman. You can show me the strongest, bravest woman on earth, but start her heart pumping love-jones through her veins and she will go to smithereens before it's all over. I told myself it's the principal of the thing. Gotta know if Kenneth Lawson had a pocket full of bubble gum. I headed for the jeweler two blocks away.

The shop owner, Ira Bernstein, is an expert gemologist and a personal friend, as friends go in my world. Actually, he's the closet thing I'd ever had to a father, which is certainly not puffing a lot of smoke considering what I'd had in the father line.

He deals mostly with other jewelry stores and very wealthy clients. After working in South Africa much of his young life, he worked on Jeweler's Row in New York for many years before moving to Georgia for a slower pace. He said he couldn't bear to go to Florida, since that's where everyone expected him to go.

It was funny how I met Ira. *The Perspective* editor Larry Conley, no relation to me, came up with the idea to have a round-table discussion with Jewish people and some of the Muslims in the Atlanta area.

It seemed like a bad idea to me when I was assigned to sit in on the group. I kept having visions of them all fighting each other before it ended. I could see the participants pulling out Uzis and shooting everyone in the room in the name of Allah and in the name of Abraham. Thankfully, I was wrong.

They were civil and exchanged ideas about stereotypes held by many people about each group. I was fascinated by Ira's participation. He, of all the participants, understood the significance of them being together at the newspaper.

After becoming comfortable with the group, he haltingly revealed a long-term friendship with a Suni Muslim albeit African-American brother who had a shop next door to his. Both the Jews and the Muslims around the table seemed shocked, and Ira appeared embarrassed to have admitted it.

I did the follow-up on the group later and became friends with Ira. We bonded after he told me things about black and Jewish people I didn't know. For instance, that black people in the civil rights movement inspired the Jewish people to speak out collectively about the Holocaust. Before that they'd felt it was best not to spend a lot of time talking about it. Some of them had even been ashamed that they'd "let it happen."

He and I talked about the irony of how blacks didn't want to belabor slavery or teach their children about the atrocities done to them either. It was my belief, after long conversations with Ira, that maybe black people were ashamed too. Much like a rape victim feels somehow complicit in what has happened. Like she'd done something to bring the molestation upon herself.

Perhaps much of the anger in our youth stemmed from us refusing to deal with the pain and shutting off our feelings since our enslavement.

"Ancestral memory is real," Ira Bernstein often reminded me. "Your people in this country," he would say, "need to mourn their loss. We, the Jews, are doing that now. We are cleansing ourselves. We are brothers and sisters, you and I. We, the Jews, the black man, the Native American—all know what it is like to be maimed and in ill repair. We are the kings and queens of suffering."

"Hi. May I speak to Mr. Bernstein?" I asked a tall, thin youngster who must have been a new clerk, since I'd never seen him before.

"Just a moment. I'll see if he can come out," he said, watching me from behind a high counter with a window. He rang a buzzer on the door behind him and went inside. Minutes later Ira shuffled out.

"Patricia. How nice to see you," he said. "I hope you're having a fine, fine day. Did you meet my new clerk?"

I shook my head no. He made the introductions, but I wasn't paying attention. After a moment Ira stopped talking and cleared his throat.

I looked up, taking him in.

He wore a smile on his pockmarked face. He was small statured with a wisp of gray hair on each side of his ears and a sweeping whitish beard that he probably wished transplanted to his balding head. He wore a gold chain swinging from his neck with a monocle attached, his loupe—or "jeweler's eye"—on a chain by itself. Red suspenders kept him from being teen vogue, because otherwise I'm sure his oversized pants would have been around his knees. His pastel shirts looked hand starched even though the collars were always frayed badly under his worn, shiny, old-timey suits.

"Got a puzzle, Ira. I've got something I'd like you to look at for me," I said, taking the ring from the pouch and holding it up so he could see it. "To see if this is even worth a plug nickel." One of his sayings.

"Let me take a look at it," he said, taking the ring from my hand. He popped his monocle on his eye and gave it a once-over. Then reached for his loupe. He pulled a lamp over onto the counter where he could see better and examined the ring through the loupe.

"Very, very interesting. Hmmm. Incredible. Do you mind telling me vhere you got this?" he asked me, raising both his gray caterpillar brows as his eyes met my stare.

"It's not exactly mine, so I'm not sure where it came from. Why? Does that matter?" I dropped my head slightly. I didn't want to let him see the fear that had crept into my stomach and was spreading to my face. Was it stolen? Maybe Kenneth was a diamond thief? That would explain the money. There had been a ring of diamond thieves operating in Atlanta for years. Why wonder? "Do you think it's stolen?"

"No. No, my dear. I don't know whether it is stolen or not. I know it is a magnificent stone. *Magnificent* stone. Rare. I'll need to keep it for a vhile if you'd like it appraised."

"What's a while?" I asked him. Ordinarily, leaving a diamond any-where is a risk. But as jewelers go, Ira was reputable and a friend.

"Vell, maybe a few days. You see, I'll have to do some research. This is not an ordinary diamond, you see. Not ordinary." He wet his lips and ran a finger under his collar. "Do you think you could find out vhere it came from in the meantime? Or at least who your friend got it from?"

"I could try," I said, attempting not to arouse suspicion that I didn't have a fly's chance in a frog pond to find out where it came from.

"I vill try to have it for you soon. Do you want me to call you at the paper?"

"No. No," I said. "If you don't mind, I'll give *you* a call. I think I'm going to be working away from the office for a while. But do you think you could sort of guesstimate how much the ring is worth? I know you can't tell me for sure, but a ballpark kind of figure?" I was fishing, I knew, but something about his manner unsettled me. He'd become so edgy since I'd handed him the diamond, like a runner getting ready to break from the starting point before the gun went off. Generally, he was a calm man, easygoing and chatty. Today, this wasn't him.

He continued to inspect the ring as though he were alone.

"Ira. Excuse me, but can you sort of guess its worth? This is not for an official appraisal or anything. I mean, it's not for sale."

"Not for sale? Not for sale? Who wants to sell?" He looked up, wrinkled forehead plastered on his normally serene face.

My voice got testy. Was he going to answer me or not? "No. No, it's not for sale. But could you guess, maybe?"

"No. I'm not sure of its vorth. I can tell you this—it's too rare to be passing it among friends, if vhat you say is so." He added, almost to himself, "I hope your friend keeps it in a safe," while still staring into the diamond as if hypnotized.

"Thanks. I'll tell him that," I said, a little pissed. We'd sat many hours talking politics and philosophy. He'd even given me personal advice before. But what did he mean by, "if what you say is so"? Was he implying I was a liar?

It's funny how indignant you can become even when you know you're lying or telling only half-truths. I wished at that moment that all the answers had been tucked away neatly in the safe deposit box and I could relax again and breathe.

I watched Ira shuffling into his back office while staring so intently at the ring that he almost walked into his door frame.

CHAPTER THIRTEEN

I asked Ira's assistant if I could use his phone. He passed it through the window to me. It was times like these I wished I had a cell phone. I'd had two beeps, one from the newspaper and one from Jeff Samuels.

I dialed Jeff.

"Hey. I didn't get much information, but I do know a few things."

"Why are you talking so soft?" I said. "I can barely hear you. Did you find out about my car, the shooting?"

"Yes, I think I did. But I need to see you face to face to talk to ya 'bout this. Why don't you meet me at The Varsity in about fifteen minutes?"

"Look. I don't really have the time for this now. Could you tell me over the phone?"

"I reckon we ought to talk. Meet me. I'm gittin' up now." He hung up.

Now see, that was the very reason I couldn't date him seriously: *Gittin' up.*

I stopped back by the paper and checked out a car with the security guard at the front desk. No, I wasn't on assignment but I needed a ride. The car was a white Dodge with *The Atlanta Guardian* logo on its sides. I could bring it back in an hour or so and then catch a cab when it was time to go home.

At The Varsity, I found a table in the back. If you're nostalgic for times gone by, The Varsity is a popular drive-in where people still skate up to your car. It's one of the most famous and colorful places in Atlanta. The hot dogs drip grease and so do the fries. Clogged-artery doctors ought to be passing out cards at the door.

When Jeff and I first met, Carol and I were there eating lunch. I was buying a second hot dog with onions and he said the lamest line I'd heard in years: "You won't be able to kiss your man if you eat those onions, ma'am."

"Are you serious?" I asked, looking up at him, a little annoyed after gazing into his face. How could anyone this fine be so dumb?

He wasn't dumb, though.

"Ain't I seen you before?" he asked.

"No, I don't think so." He must be getting these lines from the old TV movies on American Movie Channel, I thought. Plus, if I'd seen him, I'd remember. He was a looker. But country as hell. He had a Southern twang when he talked and he wore polyester even out of a police uniform. His tall, lean physique and dark brooding eyes didn't go with polyester.

"I know," he said, his eyes twinkling with a memory. "I saw you at a computer seminar a couple of weeks ago."

"Well, I was at one but I don't recall seeing you there." I didn't think he was lying.

"I was in the back, working security. I'm a security guard. I work private security often. No one suspects an undercover cop to work as a security guard."

"Oh."

"How about you and me going out sometime?"

The forwardness startled me. I'd pegged him for country and shy.

"No, thanks." Kenneth and I had just begun dating regularly. Not that we went out much; he refused to go out with me in public except the movies and dinner.

Jeff was a head-turner. When you're single as long as I've been, you never burn your bridges with men, especially fine ones, in case your present situation bombs and you need someone to accompany you someplace. So, in a flash of inspiration I said, "Hey, maybe this will work. I've got to go to a dinner that requires an escort tomorrow. You down with that? Escorting, I mean?"

"For you—yes."

When I introduced him to Carol, who'd been observing us from our table, she barely grunted. "You look familiar somehow" was all she said.

Later I told her he'd been at the computer seminar the same day we'd met Kenneth Lawson, but she swore she'd seen Jeff somewhere else. She didn't trust him, and after that whenever she saw him she was barely civil.

For a few months he served as an escort whenever I needed to go someplace that required a man's arm. I made it clear that that's all it was and all it could be.

Kenneth Lawson moved in with me during that time. And he moved into my heart.

Anyway, Jeff's escort service turned out not to be the greatest. Jeff was from Kentucky and he talked about horses, dogs and fishing like most men talk about football and women. He often said corny stuff. I'm not easily embarrassed, but twice I felt the sting of it when we were at parties together and he'd said something so hokey I'd expected some clogging music to be playing in the background. At one party, in front of a couple of bigwigs whom I was trying to get interview time with, he blurted out that he cared about me like hogs love slop. I almost fainted.

But today, when I saw him enter The Varsity, it struck me again how truly handsome he was, his muscles bulging out of his sleeves, his dark, bronzed skin glistening from the heat. I smiled as I realized he probably didn't mind the polyester uniform when he was a beat cop.

"Howdy," he said, smiling broadly.

We'd not seen each other in almost seven months. I stopped using his escort service a few months after my relationship with Kenneth became more serious. I failed to mention Jeff's services to Kenneth, but Jeff knew all about Kenneth. He also knew my relationship with Kenneth was why I fired him.

"Hi," I said, hoping nobody had heard his "Howdy" to me. "I'm sort of in a hurry, so could we make this quick?"

"Yeah, sure. I thought maybe you'd rather talk in person."

"Why?"

"Well, are you mixed up with this? Evidently from what the police can piece together, somebody in that alley got shot, and shot badly. And they were in your car."

I knew that much, but *he* didn't have to know it.

"Do you know who was in my car? Or who was doing the shooting?" I could hear the anxious tone of my voice and I warned myself to calm down.

"This is the dangdest thing," he said.

There is a time in a relationship when a strong point is that you can draw something out to the *nth* degree. However, if you're not in bed with someone, drawing things out is not a strong point. We'd never slept together in the three months we had our arrangement, so for now it was a definite weakness.

"Please," I said, as calmly as I could. "I've got a lot of things to do today."

I started drumming my fingers on the table. He hated that, said impatience was not a virtue in most instances.

"First off, no one saw the shooting. Period."

"No one? That's hard to believe. I thought I heard around the paper there were witnesses." I didn't want to tell him I'd questioned the witnesses myself. "What do the police think happened, then?"

"Yeah. Well, there were no witnesses to the shooting itself. And I'm not the amateur you think I am, you know," he said, sighing like I'd planted a foot on his chest. "First, I know Kenneth Lawson was involved, even if the police haven't ID'd him yet. Second, I know if he got shot you'd be the first to know. I reckon y'all still live together. Am I right so far?"

I shrugged, annoyed at the chastisement. And hoping he didn't know I'd been jilted by the jerk.

"So no," he continued. "I checked everywhere like you asked me to do and according to all reports, they don't know for sure what happened last night. Apparently all they know is that your car had blood inside. And third, I know you only called me because once again you had a use for me."

My stamina was slipping away. Why would anyone shoot Kenneth Lawson or anyone else in my car? "I think you're not telling me everything you know," I said.

He looked directly into my eyes for a split second and said, "I'll ignore your last statement."

I wanted more information and my frustration pushed me to add, "Remember, I never promised you anything more than for you to be my escort. You agreed to that, so could you tell me whatever it is that you think is going on, so I can get on with my day?"

"Okay. Okay," he said, holding his hands up as if he were being held at gunpoint. "I think Kenneth Lawson is involved in some illegal activity. I'm not sure what, exactly. I think if you're hiding something, anything, for him or about him, you ought to let me check it out. Maybe I could take a look at your computer at home. Notes he might have. Anything like that. Let me help you. What do you say?"

I could not speak. *I say bullshit.* Trying to remain calm I said, "You're off base. What makes you think Kenneth was anything other than the victim of a crime? Or that he was doing anything illegal?"

"Just forget I said that. By the way, why didn't you ask Kenneth yourself what happened? Won't he tell you? I'm sure he was driving your car. I've seen the police sketch, you know. Where is he?"

He looked serious. Maybe he told the police about Kenneth Lawson. God. Why didn't I think of that? I shouldn't have called him. The cops were probably looking for Kenneth now.

"No," I said, finally, "there's nothing for him to tell me. He didn't do anything wrong, I'm sure. Someone stole my car. Kenneth is out of town. You're wrong. He wasn't involved." I hoped he didn't continue this line of questioning. I stared into space.

He got up and went to the counter and placed an order. He came back and handed me a black coffee with two packs of sugar and a large glass of ice water.

I looked up, a little taken aback that he remembered. I must drink ice water when I have coffee or something will happen to me—or at least that's how I act if I don't have the two together.

"I think about you all the time," he said, looking down at his hands.

"Let's don't go there, okay?" I said, hating that the conversation was drifting in the direction of "us."

"No problem. I'll let you call the shots. Didn't I always? Nothing's changed." He paid for the coffee. "Look, I'll leave you be." He began rising.

"Wait," I said, clutching his hand. Panic rose inside my gut as his words that Kenneth was doing something illegal repeated in my ears. "What about the woman who cut her wrists? You know, the French woman in the paper today. Do you have any information about what happened to her?"

"Are *you* in trouble?" he said, making the "you" sound like it was coming from a hoot owl. "Do you know something about this woman? If you do, you'd best tell me." It was the most serious expression I'd ever seen on his face. He sat back down.

"No. No, of course not, it's just that I might write something about her. You know, do a follow up." I said it quickly, attempting to make my laughter lighthearted, even though it sounded like a shoe landing solidly to squash a roach.

He looked at me, raising his thick black eyebrows upward. "To make it plain, I would say it sounds like a swell idea. But I'd say you don't poke around with this one."

"Why? Why this one?" The word "swell" swam in my head. Why did he have to say that? Who says that? Not even white people say that anymore.

77

He didn't answer right away. He stared at his hands like he was pondering the answer. It frightened me to see him do that. He was straightforward. Pulled no punches. An "Ask me no questions and I'll tell you no lies" type of man. He blurted out stuff, whether it was right or wrong, appropriate or inappropriate, good or bad. So to see him sitting there, eyes staring at hands, made my heartbeat speed up like an allegro in a symphony.

Finally he looked up at me. "I wasn't going to tell you this. The dead French woman came to Atlanta shortly after Kenneth Lawson moved here. I think she knew him."

He might have been country but he was a good policeman. He saw the terror leap to my face and he took my hand in his and squeezed it.

"What makes you think that? I hadn't even mentioned her to you until a minute ago? What makes you think she knew Kenneth?"

"Listen. If you're in trouble, tell me. I'll do all I can to help you out. You know how I feel about you."

I pulled my hand from his. I gathered my purse, dropping it twice. How did he connect Claudette Duvet to Kenneth? How? I had planned to show him the hundred-dollar bills and ask him if they were counterfeit. I'd heard rumors about counterfeit money surfacing from Iraq for several years. Forget it. I wasn't asking him shit. At least they were old bills and I wouldn't be like the robber in Atlanta who threw his bank cache away because he thought the new hundred-dollar bills were fakes the teller passed off to him. The idiot.

Now I really needed to get away and think. Some kind of monstrous thing was rising up from the muck and I was going to get caught up in the dirt if I didn't wash my hands clean of this quick.

This was not about something in the milk not being clean; this was about something in the white lightning being poison, other than the alcohol itself, as Grandma Dixon used to say. This was the shit that hit the fan and if I didn't watch out it might end up all over me. Damn that Kenneth Lawson.

CHAPTER FOURTEEN

*Exhausted and against my better judgment, I headed back to the newspaper. It was time I did a little re-*search myself. I could call in and ask news research but I wasn't even sure what I would be looking for. Besides, the fewer people who knew about this, the better chance I had of getting to the bottom of it before some-body, namely me, got embarrassed or, worse, hurt. First, I needed to try to figure whether it was Claudette Duvet who called me on the phone last night. Seeing her photo in the paper, knowing she was the same woman with Kenneth, and now having it confirmed that she could be traced to him left me with very ambivalent feelings about her death.

With that thought, I concluded I'd better go home. I knew the answer-ing machine recorded the French woman's call because I'd picked the phone up after she'd started speaking. Finally, technology that was on my side. Maybe somewhere I could find a tape of Claudette Duvet's voice and match the two. If it was her, why was she phoning me? And who killed her?

I contemplated swinging the car around in the middle of the street, knowing full well a U-turn would get me a big fat ticket, one I couldn't afford. The hundred-dollar bills floated in my mind. I said what the hell and made the U-turn. I needed to get that tape. Maybe if I played it I could figure out what she'd meant, and why she called.

When I stuck the key in the door I knew I was in trouble. Peppy would always sit at the door when he heard a key because he'd associate it with food, a Pavlovian kind of thing. I'd have to nudge him gently away from the door. Because for some ungodly reason he'd have it backward and think that whoever was feeding him was on his side of the door with the food and he wasn't letting them out. I've not quite figured the cat logic yet, but as a rule I'd have to inch the door open unless Kenneth was holding him when I came in.

There was no more Kenneth, so I was surprised when the door glided open.

I'm not neat, but this was from shit. The room looked like a damn goat had cleaned it up. Shit was everywhere, ripped and torn. I stepped in over the stuffing from my favorite yellow chair and saw poor sweet Peppy floating limply in the fish tank. An irrational thought sprung into my mind—*the fish killed him*—but quickly dissolved. I walked over to him and the weight of all this crashed down on me. Tears blurred my vision as I went to pick him up but couldn't. I picked up his mouse instead and placed the chewed remains against my cheek.

Peppy had been with me for four months, a gift from Kenneth to me. I looked up. *No, the computer's there.* But as I looked at it, it dawned on me that it wasn't all there. The hard drive was gone. Now everything breathing associated with Kenneth was out of my life. And I was alone. Completely alone. Again.

After I'm sad, I'm usually mad. I stomped into the center of the room and looked around for effect. Somebody had robbed me, dammit, and drowned my fucking cat. An idea rushed to my mind—they might still be here. A chill rippled through my body and I shuddered. What the fuck. "Come on out," I shouted, stomping my feet up and down in a frenzied war dance to let the intruder know I wasn't playing or taking this bullshit. I flailed the mouse around my head by the remnants of its tail as I whooped worse than an old Arsenio audience.

But then I saw the television and the CD player intact. Robbers in this neighborhood weren't about to leave a TV and a CD. Shit, they don't know enough about a computer to only take the hard drive. I reached for the answering machine tape. It was gone too.

As I dialed the police I let my eyes settle on each pile in the room. Someone had been searching for something and my hope was they'd found it. Otherwise, like Arnold Schwarzenegger, they might be back. And now that my adrenaline was down and my breathing coming slower, I wasn't so sure about this come-on-out invitation I'd posed. Sparring in a dojo was not the same as kicking a lowlife criminal's butt.

I disconnected and dialed another number. Why I didn't stick with

911, I couldn't say. "Jeff," I whimpered into the phone while the room became a hazy stream of colors for me. "Please, can you come over?"

I stumbled into my bedroom. It was in shambles. Shit everywhere.

I sat down on a pile of clothes and started to fold them for some asinine reason. Time whirled around me and I folded and refolded.

⠃⠇

Jeff cleared his throat. He stood in the doorway, poised to knock on the bedroom door. I guess I'd left the front door standing open for the crooks to return, so he had walked in and followed the trail of destruction to the bedroom.

The minute he saw the room he walked over, taking me in his arms. "Listen, Patricia. You're all right. That's what matters. Tell me what happened."

I pulled away. Kenneth had said trust no one. For all I knew, Jeff could have done this. Maybe he found out about the money. Could police get records of safe deposit boxes?

He reached for me again. This time, depleted and exhausted, I let him. Jeff was a good man. A nice man, almost too nice. That was the problem. I felt like he was no challenge. I had actually said that to him when we stopped seeing each other.

The hurt branded itself on his face that night even though he hadn't argued. He'd kissed me on the cheek and said, "I'm sorry you feel that way. Maybe another time," and left. He called for several weeks after, offering tickets for all kinds of events, including freaking square dancing, plus the damn rodeo.

That's when I'd had my limit and told him no thanks in the way that only nice guys can understand. "Bug off, please. I'm sorry, but Kenneth and I have so much more in common."

Now he comforted me like I'd never breathed a cross word to him. Like I'd not shunned him for another. And I still wasn't sure I wouldn't sell his soul for one glimpse of Kenneth Lawson.

Kenneth Lawson and I had been standing on the bridges of Madison County. We sparked electricity within each other, making the power company seem dull. He was dashing, handsome, suave and sophisticated. He'd read Chaucer, Nietzsche and knew who Frederick Douglass and Sojourner were. We could talk all night long on any given subject and still have more to say in the morning. Any news item I talked about, he knew something about it.

Kenneth was soft-spoken and gentle, yet he exuded a strength and power that was unquestionable. He called the shots and I followed. A rarity. As always, everything was wonderful until, as Chinua Achebe said, "Things fall apart."

Actually, if I'd been married and he'd gone away pining for me because I couldn't leave my family, then we'd have had the greatest love story ever told: *The Black Bridges of Fulton County*. But this is from shit.

While I thought of Kenneth, Jeff massaged my shoulders and alternately stroked my hair. When I spoke I felt torn and confused but I said it anyway: "Please. Don't report this. Things are happening too fast and I have to figure this out. I don't want to get anyone in trouble."

The truth was, I had begun to suspect that Kenneth was involved in something illegal *before* his disappearance. Drugs, guns, murder—I wasn't sure, but I knew deep inside that lately he had been hiding something and that our relationship was strained. He had always been discreet out in public, but he'd not even wanted to be seen at the movies.

What cut most is that one day I'd found matches from Le Chef in the car and asked him if maybe we couldn't go there together sometime. He outright lied and said he'd never been there. He claimed to have picked up the matches while at the public library.

I didn't know his mother's name, for God's sake. He never talked about family or friends. I'd never known him to call anyone from our house or, should I say, *my* house. He didn't want his name on anything, and at first, I must admit, I thought it romantic.

The last guy I'd hooked up with had wanted half of everything we'd bought together, including the futon when we broke up, even though I had caught him snuggled up on it in my house with another chick. But with Kenneth it was like he was saying to me, Okay, I'm not bringing material things here and I won't take any away from you.

But the last couple of weeks I had begun suspecting some really funky stuff was going on. He left the house late every night. Twice I could have sworn he had needle marks on his arm. He was sick some days like he might have been experiencing drug withdrawal. Some nights I could hear him throwing up in the bathroom. On those occasions he'd swear he had a bad stomach. He always had some excuse.

Then when I spotted him holding hands in the restaurant, it all came together. He had another woman. The thought of the other woman, the French woman, in that same restaurant was a stab in my heart, or ego. I refused to cry again. Damn him. Maybe she was pregnant. Wasn't it true that sometimes men felt the symptoms, too? That bitch.

Maybe it wasn't like that, though. Maybe Kenneth was in trouble and didn't know how to ask for help because he didn't truly trust anyone, the same as me. Maybe he needed help. He needed me. My help. I was the closest thing he had to family, or so he said. I could not abandon him. He obviously didn't want to leave me, otherwise why leave me the diamond? The necklace? The letter? And the money?

I wanted to believe that after all I'd shared with him about my past, he wouldn't abandon me unless he was in serious trouble. It's funny to me that no matter how down black women are on the brothers, if they're in love they can always manage the benefit of a doubt. . . .

"Are you okay?" Jeff murmured, bringing me back to reality.

"No. I'm cool. I'm shook up a little, that's all," I said, straightening out my clothes. "Listen, I don't think I'm going to stay here tonight. I've got to go to work now, though. Really. What if I give you a call later?"

"Are you sure? Are you sure you don't want to report this?"

"Positive. Really."

He didn't look convinced and I became afraid he would report it anyway. So I kissed him on the mouth, long and deep. He sunk into me and for a split second I felt his member rising on my leg. Then he straightened and whispered, "I'm sorry."

"I kissed *you*, remember. I'll call you tonight. Now I need to be alone, so could you please go?"

"Let me take you where you're going."

"No. Please. I have to take the paper's car back anyway. Just go."

He let himself out the door. I sighed when I heard his car come to life and move on.

I needed to get out of my house in case whoever trashed it returned and caught me here, but most of all I needed to think. I searched my desk looking for a tape to put in my answering machine. I didn't want to admit it, even to myself, but I wanted Kenneth to call. To tell me what was going on. I didn't want him to be shot or sick. I wanted him to come back. I pushed the new tape into the machine and rewound it. I quickly put a simple one-line message on it and grabbed a few of my things. As I got ready to leave, I thought of Jeff.

Jeff's kiss had not been what I'd anticipated, and to be honest, all my thoughts had shut down the moment his tongue had glided gently into my mouth, like a probing hot ripple through my body. Warmth. A tingling. Not what I'd expected at all.

I thought of Kenneth, and the song "I've Got Two Lovers" played in my mind. Evidently there were two Kenneths out there, or Alley Pat was as looney as she looked.

I drove to the paper, quickly checked the car back in and called a cab. I went to the four-star Peachtree Plaza Hotel, in the heart of the downtown area. Top security specialists roam the halls, so they claim. It's generally ignored that at least two women have been attacked in the hotel. But it was the only place in town the newspaper kept a running account, and I checked in under its name. That way no one could poke around and find me. I left instructions that I was there for the paper and no one was to know about it. I took the plastic key card and went up to my room on the ninth floor.

The room was large with a mahogany desk. Three phones. I could make a call from the bathroom if I so desired. I couldn't imagine grunting on the toilet while I made small talk, but who knows, there must be people who think they don't even have the time to take a shit. Sad.

I laid back on the bedspread fully clothed. I needed to call work and talk to my editor. Get some time off, maybe two or three weeks. I had plenty of vacation and comp time. What could he say? I'd tell him my aunt who lived in Michigan and had raised me was ill and I had to go home for a while. Of course, I had no aunt anywhere, but he didn't know that. I kept my personal business out of the newsroom, a feat in and of itself. The newsroom was like a carbon copy of its mission—to keep informed and to inform. Someone was always digging into someone else's business. If you want to know where a journalist really spends time asking questions, look no farther than newsroom gossip.

I'd caused trouble for the one journalist who'd attempted to get in my business seven years before, when I first came to the paper. I'd come from a weekly in Baltimore. I found out this busybody female journalist had inquired at the paper about me. When I finished dressing her down, there was no doubt in my mind that no one else would be trying that again. And as I'd figured, I got more respect after that. For some reason, an I-don't-give-a-shit attitude and a sailor's gruff will take you a long way at a newspaper. That, and cursing like one.

I figured either I'd resolve this quickly or I'd be dead. Isn't that the way of all mysteries? I dialed the paper. It was already getting late, but Thursday is a late work day. My editor understood. No problem, he said.

I knew it would be at least a month before he'd chew me out for running a tab at the Plaza on his dime. But I might not even be around in a month. When you're a journalist the worst that can happen is what you think will happen. In the news business, all news is bad news.

I asked my editor to transfer me to Carol, since she'd beeped me hours before. A part of me wanted to talk to her; the secretive part of me didn't.

When she heard my voice, she leapt right in. "You know the deal on the French woman? Fishy. Real fishy. Kathy Scroggins gave me something but, hey, I know you told me not to bother. But I said, what the hell, maybe I'd check it out. Anyway, Kathy says there is a rumble that the French woman didn't kill herself. What they hadn't put in the paper was that she had a nasty gash on her head. They're looking for a connection to her death and the Le Chef shooting. Check this out. Their lead started with some books they found checked out from a library. Revenge for an overdue fine, maybe, huh?"

I didn't breathe. Carol meant it to be funny. She had no idea how close they were to being right. Carol didn't know about the French woman calling me. Or about my suspicions that I was on the phone with her when she was probably hit in the head. This was feeling scary, not funny. "Thanks, Carol. Do me a favor. Don't mention this to anyone else. And please don't tell anyone you talked to me or know anything about this. Tell Kathy I said thanks. And, hey. Don't beep me. I'll call you. Beeper calls can easily be monitored."

"What's going on? What do you care if beepers can be monitored? Are you all right? You haven't made one wisecrack since we've been talking."

"Nope," I answered, "I don't know a thing about what's happening," and hung up, hoping that was wise enough for her.

I thought about Kenneth and a pain surged through my chest. I bit my lip with determination. There was no doubt in my mind he was in trouble. My gut screamed it. Illegal, probably, but trouble just the same. And as long as it wasn't drugs I would probably help him. Loyalty *was* one of my virtues.

Women are a funny breed. I can understand why men don't know what to do when it comes to us. I, for one, seldom know what is good for me, and even when I suspect something is, then it's something else I want. How could I explain why I was willing to do battle over someone whom I knew nothing about, and yet wasn't interested in going to the rodeo with someone who'd slit his wrists for me? How was it that I'd risk my job, my reputation and possibly my life for a man whom I couldn't swear I even knew his real name? And on top of that, stood no chance of seeing again? I might as well have been a guest on the Jenny Jones show.

Go figure. And we wonder why the brothers are confused. Shit. I was confused. And with that revelation, sleep dived on top of me, and I was down for the count.

CHAPTER FIFTEEN

An old man, dark as soot, was talking to me. Actually beckoning me to follow him into a mountain cave. I went inside and looked deep into a crevice. I thought I was falling into it but he caught me by the hand and pulled me back up. When I saw him again we were sitting down around a fire, in a circle of rocks. Though he was talking to me and I couldn't hear him or see his mouth move, I knew what he was saying. He held his hand out for the diamond. The band had fallen away. I reached out to give it to him and it dropped into the fire. He told me to reach in and get it. I wouldn't get burned. I shook my head in terror. No. No, I can't. I won't. I'm afraid. Without coming any closer, he whispered in my ear that I wouldn't get hurt. It was my duty to get the ring and give it to him. I must place it in the palm of his hand so he could take it home. The legacy was mine now. I was the regent. I began to cry hysterically. He spoke in a calming voice and said he would come to get it when I was ready. I looked into the fire, and the flame and the diamond were one. I cried tears on the flame and it went out. The diamond shimmered, a red glow, there waiting for me to grab it. I was too scared. Suppose the fire burns me? I reasoned. A strong force pulled my hand into the fire and snatched the ring out.

I was examining my hand when I woke myself up. The beauty of the ring made me cry. My pillow was soaking wet. What time was it? I had no watch. I'd kept planning to buy one, but then I'd decided that until I could afford the Movado I wanted, without feeling guilty that I could have taken the same money and fed some kids, I'd do without. So I pulled the clock radio around and jumped up in alarm. It was nine o'-clock at night.

Jeff. I'd promised to call Jeff. But for what? To get his hopes up? No, I'd wait.

I'd wanted to try the disk when I'd got home. But no hard drive. I had packed my laptop, so I pulled it out and opened it on the desk. I removed the disk Kenneth Lawson had left for me from my purse and laid it on the desk. I stuck it in the laptop's slot. Nothing happened. I couldn't get it to open.

Now I wish I'd paid more attention to the newspaper's computer orientation classes. If I'd tried it on another computer, would it have opened? Darn it. I didn't use the laptop for anything but sending in my stories and checking Documaster. Technology was kicking me to the curb.

Then it occurred to me that the direct connection to the newspaper's Documaster archives might be worth checking out. I could browse our files for the stories on the French woman's death. Her name was Claudette Duvet. The woman who called me had begun by saying "Clau . . . " something before saying "never mind."

It was her, all right. No coincidence was that big. Claudette Duvet came to the U.S. one year earlier on a work visa. The French embassy considered her a valuable asset and that was about it. The rest of the article I'd found was about danger in the U.S. for foreigners, *yada, yada, yada.* It didn't even state her age. It was an Associated Press story and it occurred to me that the managing editor probably shit bricks that a local angle was not pursued. Sometimes the paper could really slip up. But why now, when I needed more?

I absentmindedly clicked to the next article. The headline read, HACKER'S BURN TEST SITES. Hacker?

The hacker, Bobby Stevenson—that was the ticket. I had interviewed Bobby, a young student, recently for a story on an upsurge in computer espionage. He'd gotten into some pretty testy places, like the SAT databank in New Jersey. He'd given me his private line. We sort of clicked, as misfits often do. Can you believe it? Rich kid with a private line doing all kinds of dirt on-line and getting news coverage, positive at that. Only in America.

I fished his card out of my bag. Dialed. Waited. He finally answered, sounding like he was asleep. The minute I said who I was, he woke up.

"Sorry 'bout that. Thought you were my folks checking up on me. I'm a Dungeons and Dragons game to them. What's up?"

"Could you check on a visa for me?"

"Don't know. Haven't scooped that yet. MasterCards, yes."

"I don't mean that kind of visa. I'm talking about foreigners working here."

"Oh. Gotcha. I'll check it out and get back to you. What countrinos?"

I'd known him long enough to know he meant countries. "France, maybe. Is there a way to do sort of a browse on a name?"

"I'll go after that. I'm not too down on it yet, but I will be by the time I call your sack."

"I'll call you. Is there a fee?"

"No gravy. Your article made me the most likely man to succeed. Getting that stuff."

"You mean with girls?" I asked, feeling a little annoyed with his tone.

"No. With hackers, babe. Since your article I've hooked up with some powerful dudes."

"Oh. I see," I said, thinking, Damn, I'm talking to Rod Serling. "Listen. The visa is in the name Claudette Duvet." I spelled it for him. "One more thing. Check out an anthropology professor named Kenneth Lawson for me." I gave him the little information I had about Kenneth, praying he wouldn't turn up on a most-wanted list somewhere. I almost felt like a traitor. But I wasn't the traitor here, Kenneth was. "When should I call you back?"

"You caught me at a wammo time warp. I went over the moon—you know, government spy dope, and I've got no down time. Give me a few days."

"I thought you told me when I did the article, you weren't going to be doing it to the government anymore."

"Hey, you've got me going wrong. I'm doing it for the government now. Check it ouuuuuut."

We hung up. The world is scarier and scarier.

I stretched out on the bed, tired. I jumped back up and went over to my purse. I pulled the necklace out. It was a locket and looked like it opened, but it didn't. I lay on the bed fingering its symbols. I concentrated on the one in the center, the most familiar: II.

What did it mean? Two? Or maybe it wasn't a Roman numeral. But what? Underneath the sign was an oblong shape with open rings on each end of it. Inside the shape was a figure that looked like a primitive animal with a long tail. To the right, toward the front, something that resembled a five-year-old's drawing of a tree. To the right, toward the back, some dots. In the middle, to the left, a stick man figure and then on the right edge, three notches.

I flipped the locket over and back a couple of times. Then I checked the clasp to see if it had "sterling silver" or anything written on it. No, nothing, not even the usual carat designation. I got out my magnifying glass that I used for map reading. Nothing.

Why didn't Kenneth just tell me in the letter what was going on? And who was the other man who looked like Kenneth? Why did the old woman Pat, who I'd actually begun to think of as my namesake, think the man who was shot looked like Kenneth Lawson? Maybe all three of those alley cats were drinking. They might have not recognized even each other if they were drunk. I didn't ask her if they'd been drinking. Maybe that's why she was seeing double? How many times had I seen more than one person dancing in front of me while I was drunk? Damn. I fell asleep not counting sheep but possibilities.

♊

I woke up Friday morning feeling a little bit more refreshed than I had the day before. I showered, dressed in jeans and a T-shirt with a saying by Thomas Jefferson: THE ONLY SECURITY OF US ALL IS A FREE PRESS. I pulled on my socks and sneaks, pondering why I wore the T-shirt anymore. Journalism was changing rapidly in the face of instant information. I couldn't be sure a paper would go to the mat to take a business or government entity down. For a long time TV had been exempt from the advertisers' death knell, but now even ABC had felt the pinch. Print media was more and more vulnerable these days. The big boys could pull their advertising if somebody stepped on their toes. And newspapers, swallowed whole by the bottom-line theory of economics, didn't want toeless feet. It was clear to me that the newspaper had gone from being the voice of the people to the whim of the richest or loudest people.

I picked up the telephone. It was 8:30 A.M. I needed to check my messages at work and home. Maybe Kenneth Lawson had phoned me.

At home, a frantic, unfamiliar voice whispered the third message. "Kenneth Lawson. This call is for Mr. Kenneth Lawson. I'm sorry to phone you here but I have no choice." Her hurried cadence continued, "A woman friend of yours told me about you. She said if something happened to call you. You are one of them, according to her. I've been calling her and I haven't been able to make contact with her. Anyway, I can't say more on this phone. But please call me as soon as possible at this number. Greetings. Oh. Please ask for me, Dr. Kia———."

I replayed the message three times. Kenneth had never gotten a message on my machine before that I knew of. I scribbled the number down on a hotel notepad. The woman had spoken so softly her name was garbled. She had a singsong cadence or lilt, as though she were from Jamaica or Trinidad. I knew some Trinidadians here who owned a bookstore and spoke with similar inflections.

Her phone rang six times. I was hanging up when I heard a woman's voice with a Southern accent chime, "Centers for Disease Control. How may I direct your call?"

I slammed the receiver down. Sweat popped out on my face.

CDC? *CDC?* All right. Let's suppose the woman who called Kenneth works at the CDC. I had not been prepared to phone the CDC. I redialed the number. "May I speak with a Dr. Busota or a person with a name that may sound like that?"

"We don't have anyone by that name," the receptionist said.

"Yes, but what about a name close to it? I'm not sure. But I do have this number for them left on my message machine. It was a bit garbled."

"Hmmm. Maybe it's . . . No. How about . . . No. Oh, do you mean Dr. Mutota? Dr. Kia Mutota?" she asked.

"Yes. Yes. Dr. Mutota." What did I have to lose?

"I'm sorry, she's not in yet. Would you like to leave a message?"

"No. I'll call her back. Oh, I'm a journalist with *The Atlanta Guardian*. Would you mind telling me what Dr. Mutota does there?"

"She's a geneticist."

"Oh. Thanks. Thanks. I'll call her back. What time do you expect her?"

"Any minute."

"Thanks," I said, hanging up the phone. I pulled out a journalist's notebook and made a list, something journalists love to do. Okay, I had one or two shot and/or dropped-out-of-sight-like-most-men-bordering-commitment boyfriends. One rare diamond ring that was probably stolen. One suicide/murdered French other woman (who I should have killed). One safe deposit box full of big cash. One weird charm with drawings on it. Oh, and let's not forget, one house junkier than usual (which is hard to accomplish). One dead cat. One geneticist other woman. Oops, and one big case of the love-jones that was going to get me killed. Uhmmm. A true conundrum.

I looked at the number again. Why would someone from the CDC call Kenneth? It didn't make sense. My mind raced. AIDS? Pat had told me that one of the men who looked like Kenneth was sick. She had no doubt about that. What illnesses could render you so visibly ill: cancer,

AIDS or possibly kidney disease. Or maybe some other disease? Now I had it. Maybe that's what this was all about.

I'd recently seen the movie *Outbreak*. Maybe it was something more complicated. Or maybe Kenneth Lawson and Claudette Duvet were having a baby. The unborn baby had a disease and they had contacted this doctor to help them. That would explain why the son of a bitch hadn't told me about either one of these people, that's for sure. But what did she mean he's one of *them*? Kenneth had mentioned an *us* in his letter. His benefactor was working on an antidote. I pulled the letter out and reread it. It made no more sense now than when I'd read it earlier.

I dialed again, madder now. "May I speak with Dr. Motota?"

"Dr. Kia *Mu*tota," the new voice chided. "May I ask who is calling?"

"Yes, Claudette Duvet," I said into the phone, with the kind of French accent Andy Griffith might use.

"Greetings. [A whisper.] What's happened? Why haven't you called before now? What of the others? I must tell you things here are going badly."

I couldn't even fake an answer I was so perplexed by the questions. She obviously didn't believe what she'd read in the paper. A lot of people from other countries didn't trust newspapers to tell the truth. Actually, a lot of people in this country didn't either anymore.

"Who is this?" she whispered into the phone. "I'm hanging up."

"No. No. Please listen. This is Patricia Conley and I'm the girlfriend or was the girlfriend of Kenneth Lawson. I think you knew him or knew his other friend, Claudette Duvet." To describe Claudette Duvet this way hurt, and I caught my breath involuntarily.

Silence. A cleared throat. A whisper. "Don't talk;" then, much louder, "We must get together for old times' sake. Why not for lunch? Today?" Then whispered, "In front of the Five Points Marta station at twelve-thirty." Loud again, "I would love seeing you again, my love. *Au revoir.*"

She was gone. What the . . . ? I was losing my grip here and I needed to get out of this hotel room. Maybe walk for a while so I could collect my thoughts.

Outside the sun continued shining as though everything in the world were still normal. Pink and white dogwood blossoms bloomed on the trees, and flowers of varying species popped up in pots along the sidewalks. A typical Atlanta spring. I walked to a coffee shop and sat in the corner. I ordered coffee, a large glass of water and two Danish. If somebody didn't kill me, all this sugar would.

The string-bean waitress asked, "Do you want them on separate plates? You expecting company?"

"No," I snapped, rolling my eyes at her, since it was obvious she was trying to get in my health business.

I rehearsed in my mind what I would say when I caught up with Kenneth. The level of impatience you can experience to tell someone off is unfathomable. Okay, I'd confront him about these two women, not that he'd admit to anything. What man did?

How is it that the same person who holds you close and whispers in your ear can then turn around and cut it off? How many times will men walk away without so much as an explanation? Damn, give us some credit.

Then I thought of the excuses I'd heard and almost laughed out loud. "Uh, hey, baby. You see, I'm falling in love with you and that's not cool. I'm scared to get too close." Or, "Honey, you're too much woman for me." Or, "I'll be back once I get myself together," and, my all-time personal favorite, "You are my soulmate, but I don't think I'm evolved enough for you, baby, and I don't want to hold you back." Some brothers should write greeting cards.

But then, if I was fair, I'd have to admit I knew women, including myself, that had used similar, if not the same, lame-duck-out-of-this-shit excuses. Maybe, when it all boiled down to it, we weren't that different. All a bunch of sorry pissants trying to avoid commitment. One thing is clear to me as I grow older: When you get what you want, most times you want something else.

A different waitress came over and asked me if I'd like a coffee refill. I didn't understand her words at first and it took several repetitions before I got it. I couldn't understand her English and she wasn't a foreigner either. She was speaking what Californians were now calling Ebonics. Well, they hadn't heard Ebonics until they came to Georgia. I had to give credit to Grandma Dixon. She had told me over and over that if you learn how to speak good English and have a solid education, you've won half the battle. The other half was applying it. If you were demanding your rights but the very person you wanted to hear you couldn't understand what the hell you were saying, how was that going to help?

I thought about why I'd come to this job in the first place, to this town. I'd heard it was the black Mecca. But what someone failed to tell me was that if enough people migrate to a city looking for opportunity, pretty soon there isn't any. No wonder I didn't major in economics.

A man with a wide straw hat read a paper by the window. I think I noticed him because he looked familiar, or maybe it was that hot-ass jacket. I tried to recall where I'd seen him before. In the newspaper business that happens a lot. Then I thought I'd seen him recently, maybe even this week. But thinking you recognize someone you haven't seen happens a lot too.

I drank the coffee, slowly, savoring the Danish. Finally, I rose to leave.

I noticed him put his paper down and his right leg involuntarily move out into the aisle like he was getting up. But he didn't.

I strolled out and glanced back over my shoulder. He was there, walking behind me, with his paper rolled up like he was prepared to paper train a dog.

The drugstore was three blocks away. I picked up my pace. He picked up his slightly. I entered the drugstore and looked up at the security mirrors. Sure enough, a few seconds later he entered, his eyes sweeping the aisle. I had no doubt now. I stopped at the card display and browsed. He finally spotted me and walked in my direction.

How foolish of me; maybe he's coming over to the cards. I walked a few steps over to where the reading glasses were to see if he was coming to talk to me or look at cards. He passed the card display and stopped very close to me. He'd had garlic for breakfast.

"Wonderful day," he said with a smile and no accent at all. I prided myself on knowing accents and the sound of a language even though English was the only one I could speak.

He looked into my eyes. His nose was huge, bulbous. His eyes pinpoints in his head. I responded, "Yes," even though his closeness was making me nervous. That and the fact he wore a wool jacket. Something you didn't do in Hotlanta, not in spring.

I stepped closer to the glasses rack and examined a pair of navy blue ones.

He stepped in closer to me. He lifted a pair of green glasses up from but not off the rack. "Nice, huh?"

I nodded.

He pushed something into my side, either a hollow iron pipe or my favorite guess, the barrel of a gun.

"Let's go," he ordered.

I couldn't tell if he was American, but he was about five seven, with no muscles, and under his huge bulbous nose, he had a thin line for lips. I noticed what looked like cat scratches on his hands. He was lanky and I probably could have wiped the floor with his puny little butt; however, right now he had the advantage.

I started walking toward the front but not before slipping, like a common thief, the glasses I held in my hand into my pocket.

I worked my fingers on the glasses and walked as slowly as possible to the front entrance.

"Don't try anything and you won't get hurt. Only want to have a little chat. It seems you're a bit too nosey and messing around in something you might find dangerous," he said.

"Chat my ass, Garlic Breath. And speaking of noses . . . " I said to him, my teeth clenched, still working my fingers.

At the door I slid my hand along the side of his jacket pocket, enough to drop what I held in my hand inside. I scooted through the metal swing gate quickly.

He tried to follow. It didn't work so easily for him. "Bong, bong, bong!" sounded the alarm.

Two security guards raced forward, straddling his legs on both sides. He relaxed his aiming arm while looking at me as though I might suddenly be Alice in Wonderland and had slipped down the rabbit hole.

It happened so fast he wasn't prepared to play innocent. Anger and hostility shrouded his face as the guards patted him down, looking for the stolen merchandise. They did not come up with the stolen property, but in the process, what do you know, they found a gun. An unregistered gun, no doubt. I watched from the corner as the guards barked into walkie-talkies and then three police officers entered the drugstore, their own guns pulled. A concealed gun was a no-no in Atlanta.

I sighed with relief. Since the Oklahoma bombing the police were on the ball. I'd mail the glasses back. I hadn't wanted to take them, but I needed one of those white security tags. Once I'd pried it off the glasses, I'd placed the white tag inside his pocket. How long had I waited to use that trick? Actually, when I'd thought it up I never guessed I'd get to use it.

I had a few more hours to kill if I didn't get killed first, so I decided the safe thing to do was to call Jeff and lay low. Then I needed to sort out where Bulbous Nose came from. I walked to a phone booth and dialed Jeff's private line at the precinct.

"Jeff. I need to talk to you. Something's happened. Someone was following me and I—"

"Where are you? I'll be right there."

"I'm at the corner of Peachtree and Cambridge Way. Near the public library."

"Stay there, I'm on my way." He hung up.

How could he come so easily, I wondered? Most police officers don't have such flexible schedules. In fact, any time I'd ever called him, he'd been able to drop everything and come. How was that? I put in another quarter and phoned the Nineteenth Precinct. "Hi, this is Patricia Conley. I'm a journalist at *The Guardian*. Is there any way I can check on one of your undercover cops? I need to make sure that this guy who is asking me stuff is legit. I can verify I know him by giving you his private number and his name."

"I'm sorry, ma'am," the man said, sounding as if he would rather be wrestling bears than speaking to a crazy woman asking a stupid question on the phone. "See, that's the point. You know, *undercover*." He disconnected.

Calm down. You can't go around suspecting everyone, kiddo. You're going to have to trust someone. Why not him? But didn't Kenneth say to trust no one? Hell, I couldn't trust Kenneth.

Jeff was there in a few minutes. The precinct wasn't exactly around the corner.

"Get in."

"What's the matter?" I asked him.

His face was drawn, and I saw frown lines in his forehead. He offered me no smile as he leaned over and swung the door open. "I've been suspended," he answered with a slow cadence.

"Suspended. For what?" I couldn't believe it. "What for? What did you do?"

"It's a long story and I can't really get into it. This will all blow over. I've got some information for you."

"Information on Claudette Duvet?" I asked, hoping.

"The police think she was doing something illegal. And that may be the something that got her killed."

"Killed? I thought the police reported it as a suicide." I didn't want him to know that I knew anything. This was beginning to scare the hell out of me.

"I know, but one of my friends says she was probably murdered. Do you know anything about this?"

"Of course not. Why are you asking me?"

"I know that she knew Kenneth Lawson, that's all. And you certainly knew him."

"I didn't know her and I don't believe she knew Kenneth. And why would someone kill her?" Even as I said it, the idea didn't really seem so outrageous. I'd heard the knocks on the door, the fear in her voice, and I knew that she didn't hang the phone up herself. Should I tell Jeff? No. I need to know more about what's going on first. As stupid as it may have seemed, I didn't want to implicate Kenneth in her murder. And I wondered what made Jeff think Kenneth knew her. He had to know more than he was telling me about this whole situation. Damn.

"Hey, don't look so grim. I don't know what is happening, but it looks like I'm going to have plenty of free time to figure it out."

"Wait. You didn't tell me what makes you think Kenneth knew this woman—what's her name? Duvet?"

"Take my word, he knew her. And I'm sure he was in your car and that he's the one who got shot. It's just a matter of time before he surfaces."

"Look, this is getting out of control. Maybe you shouldn't get involved. After all, it's my problem and I've not exactly been a friend to you."

"You have. A body can't be held responsible 'cause they don't love you. Don't fret none, okay? I want to help you. Besides, now I have nothing better to do.

"You know what? Why don't you take a vacation? You know, git away? Git away in case he does come around, because it may be that Kenneth Lawson was not on the up-and-up. Maybe he wasn't the guy you thought he was."

"What is that supposed to mean?" My defenses were rising in my throat, almost choking me.

"Well, for instance, where is he now? Today?"

I didn't answer but looked out the side of Jeff's window.

"Okay. You don't want to tell me where he is? Then maybe you can at least tell me what he told you he did for a living. I don't believe you've ever told me. Where was he from originally? And did you ever meet this woman Claudette Duvet?"

He stared at me and I felt queasy. Maybe he was only trying to protect me. That alone was making me squirm.

If the truth be known, I'd thrown all the good guys back in the water for as long as I could remember and set my bait out for the sharks. When I'd had to make the choice between a handsome, country, blue-collar type guy and a handsome, suave, out-of-work type guy, I'd settle for the shark. Now that I'd been thrown into this cesspool, I knew I'd probably made a mistake. This guy was attempting to protect me.

"Look, I told you. I only asked you about Claudette Duvet because the paper wants me to do a follow-up. You know, foreign tourists have been murdered here in the past.

"As for Kenneth, he doesn't know her, I'm sure. He doesn't know anyone here. We are both orphans. As for his line of work, he is an anthropologist. He was doing some contract work. What time is it?" I asked him, tired of thinking about all the things I didn't know about Kenneth and wishing at that moment I could have made better choices in my life.

"Ten-thirty."

"Where did the time go? Look, I've got to meet somebody. I called you because a man followed me and pulled a gun on me."

"A gun? He didn't hurt you did he? Where is he now?"

"It's a long story but everything's under control. I'll tell you later. Now I need to get my stuff from the hotel and find a new hideout. Obviously, I wasn't hidden."

"You can bunk with me. No strings attached. You'll be safer. Honest."

"I don't think so. For all you know, whoever trashed my house could be on to you."

"I'm a country boy, remember? I've got a hiding place outside of town. We can go there for a while."

"I'll think about it. Right now I need to get my stuff and haul ass out of that hotel."

He headed in the direction of my hotel. I hadn't told him where it was. My heart speeded up as we approached the entrance. He continued past it.

"So where is it you're staying?" he asked, looking over at me. Then, "What's the matter?"

"Nothing. Nothing. You drove past it. I'm back at the Plaza."

He made a left and headed back around. He went with me to help pack.

"Goddammit," I screamed when I opened the door. "Somebody has been in my fucking room."

He moved around me, his gun drawn, sweeping the room quickly. He went into the bathroom and then reappeared. "You've got one foul mouth."

"Sorry," I said, remembering how he didn't curse. "I told you it's a habit from trying to survive in a newsroom that's an old-boys' club." I didn't want to curse in front of him, but this shit was getting old. And I could see they'd taken my laptop, so I wasn't at all sure it was an innocent robbery, whatever the hell that would mean. I was glad I'd put the disk back in my purse this morning.

We called for house security and by the time they'd asked questions that wouldn't help them find Waldo, I excused myself and left Jeff to finish packing my stuff. He would pick me up in an hour in front of the Peachtree Five Points station, where I was to meet Dr. Kia Mutota.

I jogged to the station so I wouldn't be late, wondering on the way how it was that if Jeff had been suspended, he still had his gun. But maybe it was an extra gun; police always have a stash.

It occurred to me as I approached the Marta station that Dr. Mutota wouldn't know what I looked like and I didn't know what she looked like. Fine clandestine meeting this was going to be. How much more secret could you get?

At the station I could hear the street preachers yelling out warnings of hellfire, damnation and doom. It was hot enough to make me believe them. "Doomsday is here," one shouted in my ear.

I spotted a tall black woman with a white lab coat under a navy blue raincoat that looked about two sizes too big come up from the west substation. She carried a black briefcase and I could see she wore a badge clipped onto her coat's lapel. I walked in her direction. It had to be her.

She looked around, discreetly scanning the crowd, then walked in my direction. She smiled at me as if she recognized who I was. She held her arms out like we were old friends.

I walked over and hugged her. Did she recognize me or was I duping myself? As I pulled back I read her name tag: DR. KIA MUTOTA, CDC GENETICS ENGINEERING LAB. "Hello, Doctor. I'm Patricia Conley." We stood on the right side of the sculpture closest to the steps that led back inside the station.

"Yes. Yes, I know who you are. Duvet showed me your photo before."

She might have been Ethiopian, Jamaican, I couldn't tell, but she was not an African-American with that accent.

"What do you mean, Duvet showed you my photo? What photo? Why?"

"We shouldn't be seen together," she said, ignoring my questions. She continued very quickly, "Time is running out. They came looking for me last night at my apartment. I know it was them."

"Them who?" I asked her.

"Them. Didn't Kenneth Lawson tell you?"

She didn't give me time to answer.

"I'm going to have to go underground. Tell Kenneth that I'm still working on the antidote but I'm not sure if there's time. I've analyzed the samples but I need more time."

She stopped talking and stepped back. She looked at my stomach. "You aren't pregnant, are you?"

"No. Of course not. Why would you ask me that?"

"Thank God," she said, wiping her face with her coat sleeve. "I'm glad Kenneth sent you to get this." She motioned to the briefcase. "I think that Dr. Delecarte is on to me. I don't think he really is trying to help them like he says he is. I think he is the one who set them up. Tell Kenneth and Claudette to be careful."

I noticed she was still concealing something under her coat. And the thought of a gun surfaced in my mind. How much should I tell her? Why doesn't she know Claudette Duvet is dead? Maybe she didn't watch the news. There are people who don't. I'll let her finish and then I'll tell her.

"It's all here," she continued, her chest heaving in and out. "Of course it's cryptic, but you must find someone who can decipher for you. Claudette said Kenneth might know who . . . Oh my God . . . "

Dr. Mutota shoved the briefcase in my hand and took off running back into the subway tunnel before I could tell her that Duvet was actually dead. And, at the moment, I had no freaking clue where Kenneth Lawson was.

Two men ran on the other side of the sculpture, one black and one white, racing after Dr. Mutota. They ran down the steps so quickly, I couldn't see their faces. I decided to follow. Because of the sculpture, they must not have seen who she was talking to, or that she'd given me the briefcase; otherwise they probably would have stopped with me.

I couldn't let her run without any help. I glanced around, surveying the street people. I saw the preacher with the wig who carries a walking cane and actually pokes it in your face to make her points. I walked over and put the briefcase into her hands. A big risk, but at the moment my choices weren't so great. I could take it with me like most dumb women in movies would, only to have the villains snatch it and run, or I could leave it with God's chosen.

I raced down the steps in the direction I saw the doctor run. I jumped the turnstile and heard the buzzer go off to signal I hadn't paid.

The platform was crowded with people and at first I didn't see her. The station rumbled, vibrating loudly in my ear. All heads were watching the train's approach, trying to figure out which door they could get into without being knocked around. All except me. I was scanning the platform in the opposite direction of the approaching train.

When I spotted Dr. Mutota again, she'd rounded a post, the two men dead on her heels. I didn't pause but ran in their direction. The two men wrestled with the doctor as another train squealed in the background. A third train on a different track rumbled forward near where they struggled. Dr. Mutota flung a briefcase, identical to the one she'd handed me, across the tracks. It must have been what had been concealed under her coat, not a gun as I'd surmised.

One of her pursuers jumped down and raced to the briefcase while the other continued the struggle. I saw the man throw her on the track of the moving train.

I reached her too late. There would be no heroic rescue. She lay in a pool of blood on the tracks. Neither the briefcase nor the two men were in sight.

People, or should I say vultures, moved to gape at her body. I jumped down on the tracks, looked both ways, prayed I wasn't near the third rail, and knelt down beside her, shaking like a bad motor in a car. This was way out of hand.

I heard someone calling the police on his cellular phone. "There's been an accident. A woman has thrown herself down on the tracks in front of the moving train." Evidently they'd all been focused on the doors of the other train as it approached. Witnesses.

Other Samaritans had dropped down onto the track with me. One young black woman was kneeling down beside the doctor's mangled body, leaning her head near her chest. Maybe she was a doctor or a nurse. Either way, I figured it was time for me to get up and get the hell out of here. The last thing I needed was an interrogation. Accident, my ass.

I walked away like I'd not been there. No one noticed. Everyone, young kids included, gawked openly at the doctor's body like she was a Cirque de Soleil act. Our society is desensitized to violence, I don't care what anyone says.

I found the street preacher clutching the briefcase quietly. The picture of her mouth shut stunned me for a second. It was like she knew doom was in that briefcase and there was nothing more to be said. Salvation was too late.

I pried the briefcase from her arthritic fingers and walked toward the corner where Jeff would pick me up. But I couldn't help but wonder what was up with her as she sat mesmerized in the same spot. Her fist was closed around the air as though she still held the briefcase, her cane leaned on her dark blue dress, and her gaze was fixed someplace in front where maybe she could see what I dared not even think about.

Fear crept over me as I watched her stillness from the corner. Something larger than I wanted to handle was swimming around in this milk, like an old, dead fly. I hoped that fly wouldn't end up being me. Behind her stood an old man clad in tattered, dirty clothes that barely held to his body. It was hot here but not that hot. He stood so close to the old woman I wondered if they were together.

I turned my head to scan the street for Jeff and then turned back. The old man was gone. I looked past the old woman for him but he'd disappeared. I thought to myself, He'd better find some clothes before his behind gets arrested. Cops in downtown Atlanta don't tolerate much from vagrants anymore. Hell, people don't tolerate much anymore.

"The life force benefits from all the contributions
due to these different sacrifices,
offerings and consummations."
—The Dogon

CHAPTER SIXTEEN

In the car with Jeff I was quiet. He didn't disturb my thoughts nor ask me about the briefcase or what had gone down with my meeting. He drove out into the country toward the mountains. When he pulled off the main highway I didn't open my eyes. My thoughts spun like a top, tilting to one side.

Death, that's what. Death always shook me up and dragged me back to the moment I knew Grandma Dixon was gone and not coming back. I could see her now, Miss Minnie Dixon.

Grandma Dixon was a fully rounded woman who cared for foster children. She was the last foster mother I had and in many ways the only one I had.

All the children fought for room on her lap, except me. I was the oldest and too big to sit on her lap. But I longed to, from the day I'd broken her great-aunt's vase.

I'd been with her only a few months. Every morning when she woke up Grandma Dixon dusted the antique vase that her great-aunt had left her. She said it was the most expensive thing she'd ever owned. It was beautiful glass that caught the light in rainbow prisms.

Sometimes when Grandma Dixon wasn't home, I'd sneak in and finger the vase even though we weren't supposed to even stare at it hard. I wouldn't dare pick it up. But then came the blowup. My temper was always like a firecracker. Once the fuse was lit, I'd burn, burn, burn until

I'd explode. That day Grandma Dixon had walked to the corner store. I walked past her bedroom and saw Stevie, another foster kid, rummaging in her stuff.

"Get out of her room!" I shouted. I wasn't going to tell on him, I just wanted him to get out. He started shouting and then in a rage shoved me into the mantel. I hit him squarely on the jaw. And that was it.

We pummeled each other until he burst my lip. The blood shot out like a whip. When I saw it spill down onto my hands, I turned to grab something, anything to knock him out. Nobody was ever hitting me and walking away. Fury swelled as I groped for something on that mantel. I clasped my hand around the nearest weapon and crashed it into his head. It was not until the sparkling rainbow colors shimmered on his wooly black hair that I realized it was Grandma Dixon's vase. And dog-gone if his thick Afro hadn't protected him and he wasn't even bleeding. I stood there in shock, my lip and hand spouting blood.

I heard Grandma Dixon shriek as she ran into the room. I thought, Oh, shit. She's going to kill me. I was going to have to fight her, too. I threw my hand up. She grabbed it and said, "Oh my Lord, child. You're bleeding. Come on now, baby. Come on. Let Grandma look at you."

I heard her but I couldn't comprehend what she meant. I tried to push her away. She grabbed her prized chenille spread off the bed and attempted to wrap it over my hand. I struggled against her while she yelled to the other children to get her some ice, water, towels and a piece of steak from the freezer. "I don't want this girl's mouth to swell up. Quick now."

It hit me all at once. She wasn't concerned about her vase or her bedspread getting messed up. She was concerned about me being hurt. *Me.* From that moment on I loved her even though I never told her. At least not while she could hear me. But me, Patricia Conley, really, really loved somebody.

One frosty night Grandma Dixon called me into her room. She sat in her rocker, the electric heater in front of her, with a blanket across her legs so the heat wouldn't burn her.

"Come here, Patty Watty," she whispered. She gave all the children nicknames. She said it was a black tradition since slavery, to keep from calling you by the name the slave masters gave you.

"Yes, ma'am," I answered. It was about time for her arthritis medicine so I had brought a glass of water with me.

"There's something I must tell you."

My eyes bugged out. Was she sending me away to another home or worse, juvenile? "What did I do?" I asked fearfully, pain rising up into my throat.

"You ain't done a thing, chile. Now, do what you been dying to do since you come here."

"And what is that?" I asked, anger putting a spark in my voice. She must be sending me away.

"Come on. Give me a hug."

She looked at me, her eyes glassy. I got up awkwardly. I'd never really hugged anyone before. The closest I'd come was digging my fingernails deep into old Cooney's face when he got on top of me.

Finally, I surrendered and began crying, allowing all the anger and fear of seventeen years of uncertainty to flow out of me. I sobbed into her neck and a warmth embraced me that I'd never felt before.

She whispered in my ear, "Forgive me, young'un. I know you like it here. And that's why I'm so very sorry. I love you like you're my own."

After a while I became consciously aware that saliva and snot were getting all over her skin and dress. And that's when I realized she was no longer hugging me. Her chest lay still. Her head lulled over on my shoulder. She was dead.

I remember thinking when the funeral home men came to take her away how shitty life was. In my child mind, she too had abandoned me. It would be a long time before I hugged anyone else.

Death is such a final thing. Maybe I would know death myself soon. What had Kenneth Lawson gotten me mixed up in? I could see images of Dr. Kia Mutota's body, bloody and oozing. I could hear the rumble of the train. I could smell the blood, and see it curdling like buttermilk. Three times I asked Jeff to pull over for me to throw up on the side of the road. Death was the one thing I didn't stomach well.

The increase in bumps let me know our destiny was probably someplace where the smooth sailing was over.

Jeff touched my hand lightly, then squeezed it as we eased on down the road. Oz might as well have been waiting at the end, because I felt a foreboding that I would never be able to go back home again as the same old me.

The trees' rustle, the birdsong, the engine of the motor all suddenly sounded different to my ear. And in my mind I could hear Sam Cook singing "A Change Gonna Come" as dusk settled on the Georgia mountains ahead and I wrestled with the question, Am I really ready to die?

I thought of the irony of death. You tire of the struggles of life but somewhere in the back of your mind you're not quite ready to die. To die is to give up.

I recalled a funny story Grandma Dixon used to tell. The preacher asked, "How many of you want to go to heaven?" All the hands went up except that of a slow-witted man named Jim Pulliam. The preacher said to him, "Jim, you don't have your hand up. Don't you want to go to heaven?"

Jim was not slow-witted that day. In an innocent and enthusiastic voice he boisterously proclaimed, "No. I wanna go to Greensboro."

How I would love to be in Greensboro now.

CHAPTER SEVENTEEN

The cabin was Jeff—clean, neat and warm. A dark wintergreen upholstered couch with pillows and a throw were featured in the center of the living room. A fireplace, now cold and sooty, faced the couch. The house smelled of cedar and pine with a whiff of sandalwood, as though incense might have been burning in an eternal flame. The floor was oak with two large Navajo rugs covering most of the center.

The walls held prints by Romare Bearden, Elizabeth Catlett and a few other artists I recognized. I walked over to the Catlett and realized it might actually be an original.

I looked around the comfortably furnished room. CD player, VCR, large floor model TV, leatherbound-book collections in glassed-in bookcases, not easy to come by without big bucks.

A small den area held a huge desk with the most computer equipment I'd ever seen outside a computer store.

"What's with all the computer stuff?" I asked him. What would a police officer need with all this?

"A hobby. Just a little hobby. Actually, I don't even know what some of it is myself. I'm keeping most of it for a friend."

Hooked up? I followed the cords with my eyes and saw that they were all connected. A friend—uh-huh. A bar separated the kitchen area from the dining area, which was done in royal blue and white with hand-painted Italian ceramic tile behind the sink.

This was not the shabby bachelor cabin of a country boy. The architectural lines of the winding stairway, the balcony, the cathedral ceiling, and the overlook bedroom upstairs did not fit the country ease of this man I'd come to know.

I knew exactly what policemen made in Atlanta after one year on the force, and it sure as hell wouldn't buy this. In fact, I didn't know too many people, black or white, who could have bought it unless they were playing some kind of sport or exercising their lungs for money.

"Is this real?" I pointed to the Catlett.

"No," he said and cast his eyes to the floor.

Lying. But I didn't say anything.

"What about this place? It's gorgeous," I said. "It looks like it would have set you back, let's see, maybe two thousand years of your salary?"

"My family built it for me."

"Your family? Come on, this is me you're talking to. I thought your family was in Kentucky. I guess next you'll tell me they own the Kentucky Derby."

He didn't rise to the bait. Silence. Head hung.

I sat down on the couch and picked up a well-worn copy of *The Black Man's Guide to Good Health*, by two physicians and Charlene Shucker, an ex-colleague of mine at *The Guardian*. I'd read it, and felt it was under-read by black men. I'd teased Charlene about the title, telling her, "You should have named it *The Black Man's Guide to Poor Health* and recommended only the worst stuff for them to do. Then they would have bought it and done everything in there the opposite. Haven't you read the statistics? Put a warning on anything and a large number of black folk increase their usage."

Charlene hadn't thought it a joking matter. Jeff obviously didn't either. I could see that he cared about his health and grooming.

Then it occurred to me: Maybe he's got a well-read rich wife who bought the book and this house for him. A wife I conveniently didn't know about, or maybe, yes, maybe he's a kept man. Just because you're country doesn't mean you can't be slick. I hadn't thought of that before.

"I know it seems like a lot of unanswered questions. All I can say is, it is," he said to me, like we'd been talking nonstop.

"It is what?"

"A lot of unanswered questions. You hungry? I've got the best trout you've ever put in your mouth."

"Yes, I forgot about eating the last few days. Doesn't feel like I dropped a pound, though." He wasn't getting off this easy. "How often are you able to come up here?"

"Not too often." He busied himself in the kitchen. "I remember your rule: You don't cook for men; that way you won't feel used when you break up."

"Right. Hey, let me ask you something?"

"Shoot."

"Please, could you not say that?" I said to him, a slight smile forcing itself on my face despite what was going on inside me. "Anyway, are you married, a kept man or anything like that? This cabin thing is tripping me out here."

He put the frying pan down and walked over to the couch, where I had settled down and pulled a pillow in front of my heart for protection.

"I'm not married, not kept, not anything, and most of all I'm not a liar. You're asking me questions I can't answer right now, that's all."

His twang was gone. I'd noticed it with that lightbulb flash you get. I didn't even know when it left, but his drawl had disappeared too.

"You know something else? Your accent is gone."

"Really. I hadn't noticed."

Lying again. Not only was his accent gone, his speech bordered on the formal, stilted, even. I'd noticed it several times before over the months I'd known him. Certain words didn't quite go with his Southern persona. The changes were difficult to pinpoint, though, since he never talked a lot. This was probably the most I'd heard him say before in one short span of time.

Maybe coming out here with him was a bad move. Hopping from a frying pan to an iron cauldron sort of thing.

He went back to the kitchen. I watched him take out cornmeal and oil. He turned on the stove and took a plastic container from the freezer that looked like precooked vegetables. The kind of thing a woman might leave for her man while she's away somewhere. He began humming an opera tune. Last I heard he was a Charlie Pride–humming man.

I toyed with different scenarios in my mind about him, the fact that I'd never actually seen him at the police station, or met another police officer who knew him. I became so preoccupied I almost forgot about the briefcase—or maybe that was deliberate amnesia. I dreaded opening the briefcase every time I recalled the street preacher's face.

I got up and opened it on the couch. It contained a bundle of papers bound by black clips. I thumbed through the pages of the thick document. Greek to me. Not one recognizable thing on its pages, unless you count the repetition of the Roman numeral II at intervals.

"Do you know anyone who might read gibberish?" I asked Jeff merely to break the heavy silence that had fallen between us, knowing full well he barely knew people who spoke good English. At least that had been my impression until now.

He didn't respond.

"Okay," I said, "how about a phone? I need to check in with some people. You do have a phone, don't you?"

He didn't answer right away; instead, he sighed deeply. Finally he said, "No, I don't have a phone out here. Sorry." He proceeded to place two Lenox china plates on the table. When he walked back to the counter, I sneaked the plate up and checked the bottom as though the plate were a Hallmark card. The inscription said, "18kt gold trim."

He walked back over, placing on the table what I guessed to be real sterling silverware and hand-painted linen napkins that matched the tiles on the walls. He then lit the white candles gracing the table in what looked like genuine gold candleholders. He did all this with the skill of someone who dines in this type of elegance every day.

In the most cultured tone he asked, "Would you care for some juice?"

"No, whiskey would be better," I answered. "I need to calm my nerves."

"I thought you couldn't drink alcohol."

"And I thought you didn't lie. You have all this computer shit but no phone," I snapped quicker than a crab. I'd seen the phone jack and the wire connecting the computer to the wall. Did he think I was that ignorant?

"Okay. I'm sorry but I don't keep alcohol here. Will juice do?"

"Hell no, but I'll take some anyway."

"Look, I have a modem in the computer hooked up to the phone line. But no physical phone, okay? Could we call a truce?" he asked me.

"The same kind of truce the white man gave to the Native Americans, you who speak with forked tongue? You want me to believe that you're a police officer stuck out here in the middle of nowhere without a way for them to contact you?"

He took a small black gadget from his shirt pocket.

"And what is that?"

"A beeper."

"You think I'm stupid, don't you?" I'd never seen a beeper that small, but I knew if they made them that small they'd cost more than a police department would foot the bill for, that's for sure.

108

"Okay. No truce," he said, sitting down at the table, sighing heavier this time. "You are going to eat, aren't you?"

He served salad with the fish. The trout was smothered with onions, scallops, parsley, assorted herbs, butter, carrots and potatoes. It smelled delicious. And I was starved. I'd not eaten much of anything in two days and now it measured out as a week in my stomach. My mouth watered. If I'd have been a dog, Pavlov would be up from the grave checking me out. I needed to eat.

At the table I bowed my head. He didn't. I said grace silently, a rote action you pick up living in foster homes. Maybe he was an atheist. I wasn't, even though I lived like one.

"I think I know someone who can decipher your stuff for you."

"How convenient," I said sarcastically. This setup didn't work for me. I hadn't trusted him much since this started, but after coming out here, my trust level had zoomed below zero.

How would he know people who could decipher this? And how could he afford this place?

We ate our food in silence. The atmosphere between us was thick as smog in California. I felt betrayed once again.

But there was no doubt in my mind at this point about my mental status: I needed a shrink—and bad. Because the entire time I sat there watching him eat, his left arm in his lap, I wanted him to reach over and take my hand. All of a sudden he was no longer the country bumpkin, and to my discredit I felt more attracted than ever. Shallow? Maybe. Insane? For sure. But true just the same.

After dinner we sat on the porch. I sat on a swing, he in an Adirondack chair nearby. It was cooler here than in Atlanta. Butterflies flitted close by the porch's rhododendrons. Neither one of us talked.

Finally I broke the silence. "You know, people often speak differently with their friends, Jeff, more relaxed, I mean, than they do at work or at social gatherings. But your change in speech is miraculous. How do you explain that?"

"If you don't mind, I'd prefer not to talk about that. What do you think is going on with you and Kenneth? What do you know about his past? His friends? Tell me why you've been covering up the fact that he was the driver of your vehicle. Did he, by chance, tell you anything or leave anything with you? It's obvious somebody thinks he did."

"Hey, if you can't tell me anything, I certainly can't tell you." Now that was childish, but whoever said I wasn't a child?

"Okay," he said. "Let's talk about something else. What about your

109

future goals? How's that coming?"

"Do you really care?"

"Of course. When did I act as though I didn't care about your future? Tell me."

"Never," I said, suddenly feeling embarrassed about the negative thoughts I'd had about him.

"So tell me. You told me once you had plans for a school. But you didn't tell me what kind or why."

"Okay. I've been saving money to do this school. Like the Jewish one that houses kids who are at risk of not graduating high school, plus accepts top-notch students who fight for admission. I want to start a similar school for kids here. And to keep it from becoming a negative stigma or a dumping ground, I'd make it so exclusive that families with money, or the illusion of it, would die to have little Courtneyroy attend."

"You mean like the Mae Boyer School in Jerusalem?" he asked, looking out into the wooded area immediately off the property as though he could see it there in the distance.

"How do you know the name of it?" I asked him, impressed and confused. Few non-Jewish people even knew this school existed.

"I just do. You would do well to start one. Do you have venture capital or investors?"

"No. Right now I don't even know of anyone who's interested. At least past lip service. I don't have much saved so far, but I figure in a couple of years I can do it. I've already written a working plan."

"You're serious, aren't you? Why? Why do you want to do it? You could go to work for a private school if you want to teach or work in administration, couldn't you?"

"I want to save our kids. I see what's happening to them. Images are created that are tough to fight with Band-Aid programs. Of course, there aren't going to be many programs left soon. Our kids think negative of themselves. You can say what you want, but if every time your name or your family's name or your racial group's name is mentioned, crime and drugs follow like it might be your surname, you're going to be in trouble.

"I believe in Carter G. Woodson's *Miseducation of the Negro*. I want to give our youth education, not to go to work for anyone else but to work hard for themselves and their community. I want my school to be like a mini Harvard Business School, focused on the entrepreneurial spirit. Without it we're all lost."

He clapped his palms together and said, "*Ita est.*"

I couldn't have felt any more surprised if *Star Trek*'s Scotty had beamed me up. "*Ita est*" was an idiomatic confirmation, like "Okay." Who the hell was he? He was not the Jeff I knew. Why would someone fake being country, backward, illiterate and use poor diction who could also quote Latin?

He got up and went in. I followed close behind him.

Inside I picked up my purse and plopped down in the leather high-back office chair. Thomasville. Expensive, I thought as I sunk down into it. Well, if he's telling me nothing, then I'm telling him shit. I tried turning on the computer.

"What are you doing?" he asked.

"What does it look like? I need to check something out. Can you turn this on?"

"Sure. If you insist. What are you checking out?"

"None of your business. Can you turn it on and then go find something to do, maybe?"

"This is my house."

"Like I don't know it. Damn, give me a break."

He turned the computer on and the screen hummed to life. He didn't punch in anything but sat directly in front of the screen. A camera mounted on the monitor flashed a red beam into his eye and the screen saver popped to life with Oriental prints. They were gorgeous and designed to alter every minute when you didn't touch the keyboard. Windows 95. I had not upgraded so I was going to need help after all.

"What's the camera-looking box? What's it do?"

"It identifies the person using it."

"How?"

"It's an iris scanner. It scans the iris to make sure the person using the computer is the right person."

"You mean you don't have to even touch it? You sit in front of it and that's that?"

"Well, the crosshairs must come together," he said, pointing to two lines overlapping each other. "But otherwise, that's that."

It didn't seem the kind of thing a cop would have in his home. The Atlanta police weren't that sophisticated when it came to technology. Besides, if it wasn't his, why would it be able to identify him?

"Excuse me," I said, as he walked into the kitchen. "On second thought, I could use your help."

"Sure. No problem." He walked over and pulled a chair close to me. Too close. His energy was like a blade, cutting through my space, disruptive.

I watched his fingers move rhythmically across the keyboards as he logged himself on the system. He moved so fast I was not able to detect the password, which was a series of clicks and passes, not the average six letters. I sighed. No using this alone, that was for sure.

"So what do you want to do?"

"I want to see this disk." I pulled it out of my purse. "Alone," I added. "I think I can handle it from here."

He didn't argue. He inserted the disk, hit a few keys and got up.

I followed the prompts. The password Kenneth was talking about was Patty Watty. It is what he called me the first time we made love. I entered the name and waited. I glanced around to make sure Jeff wasn't spying over my shoulder. He'd moved away. I stared at the screen. But nothing happened. There was no response. "Shit."

"What's wrong?" Jeff asked.

"Nothing. It's just that I was supposed to read this on my own computer," I lied, "and now it won't do it on yours."

"No problem. I can override the codes."

"No," I screamed, much too loudly as he hit a key, remembering the warning Kenneth had given for using the wrong password. Maybe it could be read only on Kenneth's machine.

Jeff's fingers stopped in midstroke.

"I don't think you can do that. The disk was formatted to erase if the wrong password was used. And also it was supposed to open automatically only on my machine."

"No problem. I can handle that with this." He made a few keystrokes.

I watched the screen fill with something that looked Greek to me, as he walked away. "What the hell is this?" I said aloud. It didn't matter if he saw it. Hell, no one could read the shit.

He walked back over and leaned over my shoulder. "It's encrypted. Probably in case the wrong person got it but had the correct password. This wouldn't have happened on the originating system, but the program knows it's on a different system so it's a bit more complicated, that's all."

"Meaning?"

"Meaning it's like secret coding."

"Well, fuck," I said, jumping up.

"Patricia, please."

"Please what?" I asked, knowing full well he meant the cursing. "This is not going to do me a damn bit of good."

"Want me to try?"

"Try what?"

"Figuring it out."

I laughed. "Yeah. Try."

He sat down and began working the keys. I pulled my chair close to him. Too close. I watched, mesmerized by whatever the hell he was doing. A new screen popped up and flashed off. I thought I saw something about the U.S. government, but I'm not exactly a speed reader. Then scrolls started going on the screen:

```
M'''Z''''5PT''''''''''''''''''''''''''''''<\#212>H''''''''N'@''''''
>M'''''P'$''$''O''N'@''''''*X''''''''''''''''''''''''''''''''''*X
>M''''''''K@H''''''!7#O''''''''/H'''''''''<\#212>H'''''''!P'@'''''
>M''X''''''''''''''''''''''''''''''*X''''''''''''''''''''O''''''''
>M'''''''O''''''B:'8%VKL!O'''''B:'8%VKL!'P''''$''''#''''_'''
>M'',''''=!O'''P''''''''#OSQ'@H;$:XO'''''''''''''''''''''^'','
>M_O\)''8'''''''''''''''''$''''+''''_O\''O'@''''''''''''''''''
>M''''O''''+5S=6"LL^:XP'''L''''@''''!''''2''''''\'
>M''!O''''!''''%P''''%'''9'''''8''!L''''P'''O'''O''''?'''
>M''P''''$''''@'''.O$'''>''''@'''''''$,#'''''#X''','''''+''''
>M'P''''('''+'''''''''''L'''''''''#!''''('''>''''$O'''$-R:7-T
>M:6YA($MEWL97('P''''''''''''#OSQ'@H;$:XO'''''''''''''''''''
>M'''^''','_O\)''/_____
>M_____
```

"What the hell is that?"

He grimaced. I knew he wanted me to stop cursing. But why should I stop? The hell with what a man wants.

"Binary," he continued. "Checking binary first. Then it will check other possibilities of encryption. It might take a while but eventually you'll know what it says."

"Uh-huh. You believe that?"

"Sure do. Look, no need waiting here. Nothing's going to happen for a while, I can assure you of that. Let's get a drink. Nonalcoholic."

"Why'd you say that?" It seemed odd he'd say that. It was like he knew I had a problem with alcohol. Earlier he'd commented that "I couldn't" have any, not that I didn't *want* any.

Whenever we'd been out together, I'd told him I wasn't drinking because I was working, and the two didn't mix.

"Say what?" he asked, looking innocent.

"Never mind," I said. Maybe he'd guessed I had a drinking problem. I moved over to the couch. I didn't believe for one minute that that ma-

chine was going to do a thing but spew out more jabber in exchange for the jabber going in.

"So do you think your machine can decipher this?" I handed him the papers from the briefcase, confident no one could read them.

"Nope. Written in scientific logarithm and another type of encryption language. Nope. We'll have to see someone else for this."

"How do you know?"

"Take my word, I know."

"You sure know a lot for a cop."

"What's that mean? You think all cops are ignorant?"

"No. No. Let's change the subject." I hated stereotyping. I felt black people should stay away from stereotyping folk and being discriminatory since we know exactly how devastating and debilitating both could be. I'm always dismayed when black people have a problem with homosexuals. Like what is wrong with this picture?

"Want to hear some music?"

"Sure. But I'm not into country."

"I have other stuff. How about 'Deep Forest'?"

I shook my head yes, but I didn't know what "Deep Forest" was. When the music came on it was soothing. Drumming and such, but soothing. I leaned my head back and drifted.

Jeff sat down close to me, our knees touching. It felt like the heat from his body was actually massaging me. I opened my eyes to make sure it wasn't his hands. It wasn't, but it felt like it.

He smiled and I wanted to dissolve right then and there. I looked at his hands. Strong, sturdy with large fingers.

"You can sleep upstairs," he said. "I'll bunk on the couch." He picked up my bags and headed up the stairs.

My eyes fastened on his firm butt.

When he came back down my eyes stopped at his crotch and I said a silent prayer: *Get a grip, girlfriend. You don't trust him, remember?* I did remember. But I also remembered his gentle touch in my apartment earlier. And I remembered the sting of Kenneth Lawson skipping out on me for whatever the reason. I could see Kenneth leaning over that white-clothed table holding hands with Claudette Duvet. Imagine him whispering to her in his low-metered voice. I hated them both. The bottom line was, Kenneth wasn't here and even if I found him, there was no guarantee he'd ever be mine again.

Then I recalled something Grandma Dixon told me: "All dogs have teeth but they don't all bite."

But why would I wait until now to have these feelings for Jeff was a better question. Vulnerable. That's the kiss of death to women when they lose someone. They are all vulnerable. And then I heard Grandma Dixon's voice saying, "Men are vulnerable, too."

Lying in the bed upstairs was torture. A ceiling fan blew cool air onto my body—a body that felt like it was burning up with fever, but I knew it was desire. I had on a black silk teddy (unconscious choice) and I'd pulled my hair back into a ponytail. I lay there listening to the crickets outside the window and wondering if—no, hoping—Jeff walked in his sleep. That's when I heard the creaking. I stopped my breathing.

Creak. Creak. Was he coming up here? I arched my head to hear the sound better. *Creak.* It was not inside the house, but on the porch.

♊

I jumped from the bed and squinted out the window. Nothing. I walked over to the railing and looked down into the living room. I couldn't see the couch. Panic flooded my mind. I tiptoed to the edge of the stairs and whispered, "Jeff. Jeff?" No answer. I looked around the room for a weapon. I didn't see anything. My shihans had drummed into my head, "Your body is the only weapon you need." Yeah. Tell that to the man who shoved the gun in my side.

Okay. Okay, I told myself. Why pay all that money for lessons if you're never going to use them? I placed my bare foot on the first step and listened. Nothing.

I moved down the stairs, holding the railing. I tried to pace my step with my outward exhalation, something the shihans had told us to do.

Creak.

Whoever was making the sounds was outside on the porch. The stairs ended only a few feet from the door. There wasn't much moon so I couldn't see very well in the room. I called to Jeff as softly as I could. No answer. It was going to have to be me. Maybe Jeff was asleep. Maybe he'd been knocked out. Or maybe it was Jeff planning to come in the upstairs window and kill me.

I yanked the screen door open, extended my right leg, foot arched, prepared to make contact with whatever fool lurked on the other side of the door. Thank God it was air, as I stumbled forward.

Jeff sat on the step, twisting his body around, looking up at me. "What's the matter? You attacking some unknown assailant, or did you think it was me?" he asked.

"You scared the shit out of me."

"You don't look scared to me," he answered. "I'm awful glad I wasn't standing at the door. My guts would probably be chopped liver by now."

"Sorry. I thought you were a prowler or a hit man come to get me."

"Then, you thought I was dead? I'd have to be dead, you know, for anyone to get to you."

"My brain stopped functioning a while back, to be honest," I said, trying to erase what he'd said from my mind. "I couldn't think rationally. For all I know, someone could have come in the door, stabbed you, gone back out and was out here throwing gas on the house to set it on fire."

"My. What a vivid imagination. Maybe you should try fiction."

"You're a witty ass."

"Look, you've got to stop that cursing. I hate that."

"Why, because I'm a woman and you think it's okay for men but not women?"

He stared at me. Then asked, "Have you ever heard me curse?"

I didn't speak but shook my head no.

"Have you ever heard me make any reference to what women couldn't or shouldn't do?"

"No," I said weakly.

"Then I think you should give that lecture to someone who deserves it. That wouldn't be me."

"Oh, because you hate it, I have to stop." I'd lost the punch out of this argument and I knew it. And even though we were sparring verbally, I could feel the fire rising between us. I sat down on the step next to him. My thighs showed. "Look, I think I'm ready for that truce. But you owe me some answers."

"Thanks. I'd like that," he said, smiling. "I could use a truce. I'm tired."

The moon reflected in his dark eyes. I literally thought I would pass out.

"You're right," he continued. "I do owe you some answers. But I can't give them to you. Not now. I'm sorry." He wrapped his hand around mine.

I jerked my hand away.

He gently took it in his and kissed my fingers slowly.

I attempted to snatch my hand away again.

He held firm.

I stopped pulling.

He kissed my wrist, then up my arm, to my neck, my cheek, my lips, and then his tongue was inside my mouth and I went limp. His arms wrapped around me and I moved into him.

116

"If you don't want to be with me, I mean *really* be with me, I'll stop now," he whispered in my ear.

My mind blanked. No rational thoughts left.

How could I? I loved Kenneth. Remember? But Kenneth had dumped me. Left me. Abandoned me. So, he left a letter. How did I know Kenneth wasn't giving me a line? How did I know he didn't steal that money, the diamond and leave me holding the bag? He wouldn't be the first man that had offered a creative reason for leaving. If Kenneth really cared for me, wouldn't he be here now?

I looked into Jeff's eyes. There was a spark in them I'd never witnessed in a man's eyes before. I wanted someone to love me. Maybe—maybe *he* did. I felt something for Jeff whether I could admit it or not. So I kissed him. Pushed my body into his. Let him know it was all right to touch me. This was not about lust, sex or love. This need was about loneliness, but I didn't tell him that, I just kissed him.

He nudged me upward and we stumbled our way inside the house.

I whispered something that might have been "stop," but even I couldn't hear it. I felt my leg touch the couch and I let my body go as his arms caught me behind the shoulders and gently lowered me down.

I held his body, his chest to my breast, only for a second before his tongue slid from my mouth to my throat to my breasts. He took each breast into his mouth one at a time. He kissed them lightly and licked them as he might have eaten an ice cream cone as a child. Then I felt his fingers unbutton the remaining buttons that had not popped open on their own volition.

He slid down between my legs and licked my inner thighs, then kissed his way to the mound of flesh that houses the future of the world in a woman's body. His tongue probed and caressed the folds of me until my body moved to a rhythm played out in a world of instinct and lust. I felt my thoughts collapsing in upon each other so that the only sensation I had was one of movement and vertigo.

The trembling started in my lower back at the base of my spinal column, moved like a wave into my core, and rushed up like a spring, gushing forth the liquors of life. I could not have stopped the ecstasy if my life had depended on it.

When I slowed, shuddering convulsively, he entered me, and the crescendo began again, slow and jazzy until I could no longer breathe. I held my breath, my eyes rolled up to the top of my head, and I believed at the instant his shuddering began we were both in flight, soaring to unknown space frontiers. Heavy sighs escaped our mouths at the same time and he held me close and kissed my cheek, my eyes, my mouth, my neck, until, like a newborn baby, I drifted off to sleep in the cradle of his arms.

A feeling stirred in my heart for the first time, and I refused to name it—even though considering the state of things, I preferred it to be lust.

The next two days, Saturday and Sunday, I slept late and spent my time walking and thinking about my life. What I'd done and what I planned to do in the future. How things had gotten so messed up for me that I didn't feel safe at home. What was I going to do about Kenneth? My mind said forget him. But something, my loyalty to him, said keep trying to find out what had happened. What made him leave me without a trace? That weekend Jeff and I slept together upstairs in his bed but he didn't approach me for sex and I didn't offer. I fell asleep cuddled in his arms.

♊

Monday morning, waking up slow and groggy, a picture swam up in my mind from twilight sleep. I could still feel the gun in my side and smell that garlic breath close to my face. I saw a blur passing me with that same garlicky smell on the sidewalk. And I knew where I'd seen Bulbous Nose before, in front of Le Chef the day I'd seen Kenneth Lawson and Claudette Duvet. The vagrant who'd bumped into me.

The sound of Bulbous Nose's voice was metallic, like it had become an extension of his weapon, now being shoved in my side hard, signaling me to walk. Then the sound was more muffled, like faraway rumblings of thunder, and I opened my eyes, realizing someone was talking out past the porch.

I threw off the cover Jeff must have placed over me and tiptoed to the window. The morning air was cool and damp. Fine bumps quickly covered my arms. No one in sight.

I walked downstairs and over to the computer. Miraculously a list of names was there in place of the gibberish. I didn't recognize any of them except Claudette Duvet. I copied this information onto a new disk and slipped both disks into my pocketbook, praying Jeff had not seen the list.

I looked out the living room window. Now I could see Jeff pacing a few feet away from the porch, his hand held up to the side of his face. I could barely hear him, but I could hear enough. Words tumbled from his mouth, not English, maybe French sprinkled here and there with another language that I couldn't recognize.

It didn't compute: a bilingual hillbilly from Kentucky. He spoke into a cellular phone, the conversation heated. Into the phone he didn't have here.

I stepped quietly onto the porch, down the steps and in front of him.

He was a possum caught in headlights.

I placed my hands on my hips and spread my legs. A gunslinger couldn't have looked more threatening.

He hung up.

"What in the hell was that all about? I thought you had no phone? And you, you who could barely speak English, have not only lost your Southern drawl but have acquired other languages? How extraordinary. Now, do you want to tell me what the fuck is going on? Are you a part of this shit or what?" Tears from my anger made him shimmer like a mirage in front of me. I *wasn't* going to cry.

He walked closer and I stepped back, moving my feet forty-five degrees apart, in case I was going to have to use them.

He held his hands up in surrender. "I assure you, I would tell you if I could but right now I can't. When you must know I'll tell you what I can. The one thing I want you to believe, though, is that no matter what, I'm going to take care of you. Just trust me." He took my shoulders firmly in his palms.

I jerked away. "Trust you? Trust you? Do you have your fucking head in the sand or something? Black women don't trust black men to take care of them. Hell, I doubt even white women trust white men anymore. You don't get it, do you? Black woman see the things black men can take care of. They can take care of their own feelings, they can fuck up and land in prison big-time and, oh, don't let me forget, they can lay more women than chickens can lay eggs. And you want me to trust you? Sorry, buddy.

"And furthermore, I'm not a cop, I'm not an agent for the government and I'm not your fool, and I'm tired of being fed information on this need-to-know bullshit basis. Do you get my drift?"

"Yes. And I don't blame you for being disturbed. But I can't—"

"Disturbed? *Disturbed?* Shit, I'm mad as hell, I'm not disturbed. I'm—"

The phone rang. He flipped the end out and answered. "Yes. *Qui, qui.*" Then more French words. Then he hung up. His face was drawn as though someone had told him his mother was dead. He looked up at me and said, "We have to go someplace now."

I stood staring at him. Who the hell was this man? I'd known him for several months, fighting every step of the way the fact that he was way

119

too country for me and we had little in common. When I wanted to go to the symphony or a jazz concert, he wanted to go to a tractor pull. When I wanted to go to see an arthouse film or a lecture, he wanted to watch a cartoon festival. And I never saw him read even a cereal box.

Sure, he always did what I wanted in the end. No arguments, no back talk, as Grandma Dixon used to say. A perfect flunky. I'd been misled, but why? Now he stood here giving me orders like he thought I'd follow them. "Go where? Where do we have to go? I don't think I'm going any fucking where with you."

"I think you will," he said, his face still grim. "They've found Kenneth Lawson's body."

CHAPTER EIGHTEEN

Jeff Samuels was wrong. I made him drop me off. I'd called Carol from his nonexistent phone and asked her if she'd take me to the Dekalb County medical examiner's office, where I'd have to go to ID Kenneth Lawson's body.

Carol didn't answer at first. "Are you still there?" I asked into the quiet line.

"Yes. I'll come get you. Are you at home?"

"No. I'll meet you at the International House of Pancakes on North Avenue. We can go from there. It's going to take me about an hour and a half to get there, but wait for me in the parking lot."

"Where are you?"

"I'll tell you when I see you, okay?"

"Sure. Okay. And Patricia, I'm sorry."

"Don't be sorry yet. It may not be him."

I didn't want it to be him. If there were two Kenneth Lawsons, I wanted the dead one to be the one I had not slept with, the one I had not agreed to marry, the one I had not fallen in love with.

Guilt swam up out of my gut and grabbed me in the chest. What was wrong with me? I might have been screwing my head off while the man I professed to love was dying. Obviously men are not the only dogs out here.

Jeff must have recognized the expression. "Look. I'm sorry about what happened. Honest. It's my fault. I knew you were vulnerable.

121

Please forgive me. I shouldn't have touched you. But you know how I feel."

I didn't respond. I turned and walked back into the house and began putting my things together. I couldn't think about what I'd done. Right now Kenneth Lawson should be the focus of my thoughts. I couldn't hide from the fact that I would have obviously made a lousy wife, sleeping with someone before his body was cold. *Damn, girl. You screwed up.*

Jeff walked over to me. "Here," he said.

"What?" I refused to turn around and face him.

He laid a disk on my purse.

"What's that? That's not the disk I put in your computer. Where is it? I thought you said the disk had been compressed and it was going to be five disks in all."

"That's true," he said, sighing, "But this is the only one that is complete. I'll see to it that you get the others. Promise."

I didn't have the energy to argue. I'd ask for my original back, but then what? I couldn't read it and I didn't know anyone who had the equipment to decipher it. I closed my bag and walked outside.

Tears stung my eyes, but I felt too guilty to cry. In the car on the way there I gazed out the window but didn't see anything. A hole in the ground was too good for me.

When I spotted Carol's car at the I Hop, I grabbed my purse, the briefcase and my bag. I opened the door before the car came to a full stop.

"Wait a minute," Jeff said, putting his hand on my shoulder.

I wanted to pull away, but I didn't. It wasn't his fault, but mine.

"I want you to know something," he said, trying to nudge me to turn around and face him.

I couldn't.

"I love you. I'm going to protect you, no matter what happens. Remember that, okay?"

I turned and stared at him. What the hell did he mean? Protect me? I still didn't speak. I didn't want to punish him; I was the one who deserved punishment. I had enjoyed the last three nights. *Loved* would be more accurate. It had been a space and time filled with warmth that I'd not experienced before, not even with Kenneth. The longing, the hole inside me closed itself around his body and we were one, soaring off into the outer reaches of space.

But here, now, I would deprive myself of the pleasure of his lips on mine, a penance for my transgression. I stepped from the car and without looking back closed the door on him, shutting him out.

He didn't come after me, but watched me get into the car with Carol.

"What are you doing with him?" she sneered. "You haven't been fooling around with him, have you?"

"Carol," I said, warning in my tone, "if you're going there, I'm getting out. I can catch a cab."

"No. No. I'm taking you. Okay. No questions. No third degree. Come on."

Under ordinary circumstances, the ride to Dekalb is pleasant. I'd never been to the Dekalb medical examiner's office.

If you watch movies and television, you get the impression that every journalist works the cop beat. In real life, many journalists do the majority of their business by phone, fax and watching the news. When you begin working you might spend a few months doing the cop thing, but if you're lucky you move on. Pursue other interests. There are some journalists cut out for daily doses of mayhem and murder. I was not one of them.

When Carol pulled into the medical complex I said, "This is a medical park. The medical examiner's office isn't here, is it?"

"You know Atlanta, unpredictable. Wait until you get inside."

We might have been waiting in any doctor's office furnished with rentals: floral-print stuffed love seat, four wingback chairs, French-provincial tables, inexpensive accessories placed around the room. Discount-store framed paintings hung on the wall. A large tabloid magazine, *The American Medical News from the American Medical Association*, was on the table. Newt Gingrich grinned on the cover.

A notice beside the door frame that led into the back offices read, BY INVITATION ONLY.

I fidgeted the same way I do in a doctor's office. The only difference was my eyes were filled with water. "Carol. I'm not prepared for this," I whispered. "I'm nervous." It was a strong admission escaping my mouth. Me *nervous?*

"Hey, don't worry. Once Chief Brown comes out, he'll put you at ease. You're lucky. The medical examiner and his chief investigator are the best men around, not only in their jobs, but in their spirit, too. I'm sure it'll be okay."

A young, very attractive black woman in a white lab coat and pants and black rubber-soled lace-up shoes walked out from the back. She came over to Carol and me. "Hello, I'm the senior forensic technician. Chief Brown asked me to take you over. Which one of you is Ms. Conley?"

I attempted a smile and said, "I am," sounding as shrill as a member of the United States women's gymnastic team.

She extended her hand. "I'm with her," Carol said, pointing to me and sticking out her hand to shake Ms. Lorie Bradshaw's hand.

Carol and I followed Ms. Bradshaw's car to a building about two blocks away. The Dekalb Police Department was upstairs but we went to the back. It looked like we were headed into the back garage of a hospital.

I could hear my shoes click on the concrete as we went up the three steps that led to the entrance, a half steel door with a Plexiglas window. It reminded me of the last time I'd been aware of the clicking on cement on the day I'd been stood up. The hallway was snug and the three of us standing together in it made a crowd.

Ms. Bradshaw stepped into a room not much bigger than a walk-in closet and handed us some white disposable slippers that fit over our shoes. I noticed the silkiness of the paper material. For an instant, I felt the urge to run to the bathroom and slam the door shut, sit on the floor and scream. But I didn't. I stood waiting for her to take us to the next step.

She was calling my name. I looked up, not knowing how long she'd been repeating it to get my attention.

"Are you going to be all right?" she asked. "You can take all the time you need before you go in. Let me go inside first. I need to do a few things and then I'll open the door." She pointed to a door almost in front of us. "Then you and your friend come in whenever you're ready. Okay? Oh, and you two can call me Lorie."

She appeared to be kind, considerate and warm. Her professional air had appropriately dissolved the minute we stepped through the door of this building. Maybe in this job she knew the pain of death more intimately than most people.

I stared at her. Then finally I nodded my heavy head up and down.

She smiled and disappeared into the room. A room that held death on a regular basis.

Seconds passed, maybe minutes before she opened the door.

Fear gripped my throat. I was hardly ever scared. Mad, angry, pissed, hostile, uncomfortable, arrogant—those were the emotions that permeated my life.

I was not a praying person. Grace over food was not prayer, it was a practiced litany, like standing to say Bible verses. *Jesus wept*, I said in my mind, the one I recalled most often in Grandma Dixon's house.

In the past, I'd not considered who I'd even pray to if I were to pray.

I was your average shut-downist. I'd shut my thoughts, feelings and de-
sires off along with any spiritual life when I was young and understood
the misery of living. God didn't seem to be partial to me and he sure
wasn't into giving me what I needed, let alone what I wanted or asked
for. But now, at this moment, I would have given anything for an ounce
of faith that when I walked through the door Kenneth Lawson would
not be the face that stared back at me.

Please God, I thought, not to any image in particular, *don't let it be
Kenneth*. Because for me, if it was Kenneth, then it would mean I would
have no way to say to him, "I'm sorry for being unfaithful."

And with a stab I realized I couldn't say I was sorry for being with
Jeff—just for being unfaithful. I knew if it ended this way, the heavy burden of guilt would be mine to claim forever.

Carol had me by the arm. "Are you ready?" she asked me.

I looked at her. Ready? It registered. On television the stoic family
members walk in and say, yes, this is her or him, before tiny whimpers
escape their mouths. They don't stand forever in hallways, afraid to walk
through the door.

But this was not television. This was real. Once I was through that
door I couldn't change the channel if it was not what I wished to see. I
would be stuck with the picture for life.

"Patricia. We don't have to go in until you're ready."

"I'm ready," I lied. Because it had come clearly to my mind that given
my state of terror, I would never be ready to step through that door.

♊

The room was clean, sanitized, brightly lit. Glass-front cabinets lined
the top wall; steel cabinets with drawers sat under the spotless steel
counter. I spotted a batch of sparkling vials for collecting blood, waiting,
as well as several sizes of plastic cups with screw-on tops. A Tupper-
wareish nightmare to linger with me.

Blue latex gloves sticking out of the top of a box like the ones Lorie
was wearing struck me as too kitcheny. On a hook some smaller, cottony-
looking white thick gloves. Ones I knew they used underneath the latex
gloves when cutting, further protection in case they sliced through. I saw
a tiny worn spot on the thumb of one of the white gloves and I wondered
why they hadn't thrown it away. If blood got through, it would certainly
be on their hands. The phrase *blood on their hands* rang in my brain.

I looked past the metal stretcher sitting in the center of the room and foolishly imagined it rolling closer to me. An intruder on my empty mind. I spotted a steel door leading to another room with the kind of handle you find on freezers. To the right of the stretcher was something that resembled an oversized toilet bowl with no seat and a beige plastic hose running out of it. Behind the table on the wall was a shelf under a phone. On the shelf lay a metal drill with a circular attachment. I identified this as a skull saw.

But to identify objects was not why I was standing in here, I reminded myself as my eyes settled on Lorie's kind face. Neither she nor Carol had rushed me. I felt Carol's hand resting lightly under my elbow.

My journalist's mind asked how a woman like Lorie came to a job like this one—slow-dragging with death daily. And then that same journalist's mind told me to get on with this.

I looked down at the end of the metal stretcher. A blank tag dangled from the end of a toe silhouetted under a stark white sheet. The tag, rectangular except near the top, where a brown round circle kept the silver wire attached to the toe, was beige paper. The same tag you might find in a butcher's shop, a dry cleaner's, a store.

I shivered and followed the line of the toe up to where I surmised the ankles, legs, and knees would be. My eyes stalled where the midsection began. Moved up slowly to the chest. I stared, wondering if there was a gunshot hole now cleaned under the sheet. I coughed. A slight odor had filled the air since I'd come into the room, musky and rank. Not the smell of Drakkar I remember whiffing from Kenneth's chest.

This neck was covered, white sheeted. I thought of the Klan. Georgia. Sheets. Georgia. Injustice. Sheets. Georgia, and then my eyes were there. At the face. Uncovered. Open. Unmasked. I stared at the face. Death danced on it like a samba. Tears dripped faucetlike down my face.

I reached my hand toward the face. I could not identify this body. I could truthfully say this was definitely not the man I loved. I could confirm for the Dekalb medical examiner's office that I had not ever been held and caressed by this lifeless carcass lying here looking as though he had chosen to take a nap.

Lorie moved close to me and took my hand in hers. "Can you identify him as Kenneth Lawson?"

To my right I could feel Carol's head moving up and down, offering her opinion.

"Yes. Yes, yes, yes, yes," I whispered over and over like a doll with a malfunctioning string. "It is the body of Kenneth Lawson."

And for the first time I knew what "spirit" meant. Ted and Scott had attempted to drum this idea into me at the dojo, but I could never get it. Not here, in my heart, until now. Finally, I understood that we are more than our bodies. That we are truly more than we can even fathom. This body might have borne Kenneth Lawson's name on the tag swinging from its foot, but the spirit of Kenneth Lawson was still missing.

I touched the face.

Lorie did not stop me.

The mustache. The beard. All there. Him, yet not him. Lover, yet no love was left in this body. He was hard, his skin like the skin of an elephant in a museum. I slumped down. There was no seat in this room.

Carol and Lorie caught me under my arms, led me to the hallway and helped me sit in a chair. My hands hid my face. It was not true. It could not be him. It was not true. I looked up, tears flowing.

Lorie was a blur standing beside Carol. Both silent.

Carol's own tears slinked down her face.

"I must see his penis," I whispered.

Carol gasped, "What?"

"I must see his penis. He has a birthmark." I continued talking, hearing myself but not able to stop this request. "If I see it, I'll know it's him. Please," I pleaded to Lorie.

Kenneth Lawson and I had teased about the possibility of this very scenario when Michael Jackson's little fiasco had occurred and he'd had to show his penis to prove it was not *his* that had violated a child. It had been a great joke for us to share—then.

Lorie understood. Had probably had even more bizarre requests in the past. "Sure. It'll take a minute. I have to prepare him. I'll come get you when I'm ready."

She was gone. Carol stooped down in front of me. "Are you sure you want to do this?"

I could not speak, so I nodded, yes.

"He's ready," Lorie said, standing in the doorway.

I thought of the body as *it* now. Kenneth Lawson was not in that body. I followed Lorie back into the room. My white faux-silk slippers made a snakelike noise on the cement floor. Carol stayed beside me, supporting me. A friend. A good friend.

Lorie had rearranged the body. Now the face was covered. But two sheets were folded neatly across the middle of the body, and only his penis was out for viewing. His chest, legs and feet were still covered with a sheet.

The penis was not shriveled but looked more like an uncooked sausage. I lifted it and rotated it gently in my trembling fingers. The birthmark was there.

I didn't know whether to be relieved that I finally knew where Kenneth Lawson was, or die now myself.

The face and body looked like those of Kenneth Lawson. But who was the other man? It was not possible, but here was a man who looked exactly, not merely resembled, but looked *exactly like* Kenneth Lawson. I refused to believe it was my Kenneth Lawson. There must be some mistake.

♊

We drove back to Carol's place. My mind was going over every detail in that room like an army of ants marching back and forth on a work detail. I told Carol about the vagrants, the diamond and the money. I told her Kenneth had also left me a letter but I didn't tell her what it said. "Don't you see? It can't be him. He's somewhere hurt. That's why he hasn't called me. I know it."

"I think you're wrong. I think that *is* Kenneth Lawson," Carol said. "I know it's difficult for you to face, but you have to accept his death. Lorie said they're checking out his organs because he looked as though he was suffering from some illness. But, on the other hand, I can understand. Denial is normal."

"I'm not in denial. It's just not him."

"Then explain it to me, Patricia. Lorie told you they found him in a rented car in the back of your house. She said it looked like he was getting out of the car to come inside when he had a brain aneurysm. They say his brain exploded inside his head. *And* you identified him."

"Yeah, well, what about the gunshot? He didn't have a gunshot to his chest."

"That's right. He didn't. Just like the Kenneth Lawson those men described for the police who helped the shot man out of the car. Remember? You told me that. They said the man appeared ill, not shot. Remember?"

"I know I did, but then, who was shot? Somebody who *looked* like Kenneth was shot, I'm telling you; that's what the old woman told me."

"That old woman was probably drunk. Seeing double everything. What makes you believe her story over what the men said? You said Kenneth didn't have brothers, remember. Maybe they are all lying. You don't know those people.

"Patricia. Face it. You've been under tremendous strain since this all started. And you might eventually see pink rhinos if you don't get some rest."

"Can you let me use your car for a couple of hours?"

"For what? I thought you were coming home with me to rest. Get yourself together to make funeral arrangements for Kenneth."

"You said you'd help me with the arrangements, right? Then, you start them and I'll come back later. Besides, Lorie promised me she'd talk to her boss about running the fingerprints. It may not be Kenneth Lawson. Look, if you won't let me use your car, drop me off at a rental."

"Damn it. You can be so hardheaded."

"Please," I pleaded, my voice softer. She'd stuck by me thus far and didn't deserve my hostility. "Really, I need to check on something."

"Okay. Look, I just don't want anything to happen to you."

"I know, and I appreciate it. I'll be back."

We'd pulled up in her driveway. She got out and wrestled her house key off the key ring. Whenever I'd used her spare, I'd forgotten to put it back.

I walked around and took the key ring. She reached out to hug me.

I stepped back and held up both my hands. I didn't want to be hugged. Didn't deserve it. Right now I wanted it all to end—the pain, the hurt, the confusion. If she hugged me I might break down. Who knew? Fuck it. I knew where I was going.

I started the engine. Felt her staring after me. I didn't look back. I headed for a small restaurant where I knew I could experience—God.

CHAPTER NINETEEN

At the tiny American restaurant, red-and-white-checked cloths covered the tables. Glass vases sprouted fresh-cut flowers. The sun spilled through the window, glistening off the chrome cafe chairs. It was too early for any customers but I knew they'd let me come in. At one time I'd been a regular visionary in this holy place.

Jess Garner, the owner, had been a freelancer who wrote the wine column for *The Guardian*. She'd finally gotten tired of the writing life for more reasons than one, and opened her own restaurant.

"What are you doing here?" she asked, walking over with a white chef's apron on that read, THE WINERY.

"Hey, I can slum with the best of them," I said.

She gave me a look. The kind of look that says, Yeah, well, why do you look like a rat's catch?

My eyes were puffy with pent-up tears, but I smiled and grimaced my way to a seat in a back booth.

She came over and handed me a menu. "You know you're early. We don't serve breakfast, but if you want I'll stir up an omelet for you."

"I need to think and be alone."

"No problem. You've got it," she said, sweeping her hand in the air at the empty tables. She headed toward the kitchen.

"I came here because I wanted to see God's face." I spoke in a voice I remembered from long ago.

She turned slowly. "What?"

"Don't make me repeat it," I said, dropping my eyes from hers.

"I thought you quit drinking."

"You thought wrong. Now, could I get that drink?"

"Do you want to talk about it?"

She knew this scene like people knew the scenes of *Casablanca*. Her own husband was an alcoholic. And he had a lot to do with why she gave up her wine column. It seemed he could give better descriptions of her samples because he'd done more than just sip them.

"Listen," she said, walking back over to the table. "Maybe you need to call somebody. An AA person or something."

"Didn't use AA, girlfriend. Couldn't handle all those freaking strangers gawking at me while I told my life's story. Plus, I don't need anybody to keep me from drinking. Now, back to *my* business. Either you sell me the drink or I'll go to Harry's Market and buy as many bottles as he's got. Either way, I'm getting drunk."

She stopped in her tracks. Having been married to an alcoholic probably gives you a sixth sense of when arguing is useless. She turned and walked to the kitchen.

I sat there hating myself, my life, my history. At that moment the only thing I loved was the glass of wine she was walking toward me with and the bottle in her other hand.

Jess had coined the phrase that described this American wine, now sparkling toward me, in one of her columns: "Silver Oak, a full-bodied cabernet sauvignon, costing only about $35 a bottle but tasting like the face of God in a bottle. It is divine."

She had not lied. The winemaker, Justin Meyer from Napa Valley, became my hero. I provided income for him and his partner, Raymond Duncan, for at least one fifth of the year until three years ago. In my drinking heyday, Silver Oak was my constant companion. My crème de la crème. My boyfriend, my girlfriend, my family. Right now I needed a family that wouldn't let me down or abandon me. I needed God—even if it was God in a bottle.

In the movies, about now, something happens and you don't take that drink. In real life sometimes you do. I drank until I couldn't hold my head up. My tolerance had changed drastically. In the old days it would have taken two or three bottles to get me this drunk.

Someone told me once if you're an alcoholic and you have stopped drinking, when you start back it's like the culmination of all the years you've stopped in that first drink. In other words, you are in deep shit.

CHAPTER TWENTY

When I woke from the blackout the next morning, I knew "deep shit" was an understatement. I sat up, startled to be in my own bed. Banging. I heard banging. The banging on the bedroom window woke me from the pissy place my mind was stuck in. I stumbled toward the window. Got ready to raise it but the thought of what had been happening surfaced in my mind like a dolphin soaring out of the water. I swung back out of the direct line of fire and shoved myself beside the window, flat to the wall.

I squeezed my thighs. I had to go to the bathroom.

Then I heard Carol calling my name. Carol, not an assassin. I opened the window. "What is it?" I asked angrily, my head splitting.

"Let me in," she shouted, moving away from the window, a look of disgust on her face. I passed my mirror. Shit looked better. At least the ax that felt like it was splitting my head wasn't visible. I opened the front door. I was fully dressed. I even had my shoes on. I ran back to the bathroom and threw up.

"I've been looking everywhere for you! Are you crazy?" Carol yelled into the bathroom.

"Yes," I said, wondering why she'd asked the question.

"You got my damn car towed. Did you know that? What's happening in there? Are you all right?"

"No," I answered, wishing she'd stop yelling so loudly. My eyes were refusing to focus.

She banged on the door. "Let me in if you're not all right. What are you doing?" she yelled. "Are you hurt?"

"Stop yelling. I meant no to whether or not I'd gotten your car towed. I'm fine if your yelling doesn't burst my skull open." I stumbled to the door, opening it.

"You shouldn't even be here," she said, sounding and looking relieved. "Jess Garner told me she sent you home in a cab drunk last night. She called me this morning, right after the police pound called to tell me I owed them seventy-five bucks for keeping my car from being in a tow-away space. The thoughtful bastards.

"Jess didn't even know you drove my car there. Says she got worried, called the paper and they told her you were on vacation, but that I might know where you were. You could have been killed sleeping here."

"I'm sorry about the car. I'll pay the money."

"Goddamnit. I'm not mad about the car or the fucking money. You'd better get with it. I don't think you can afford to be drunk right now. Do you get my drift?" She threw a newspaper at me.

I was sitting down now, rubbing my head. "What's this?"

"Look at it."

I picked up the paper. Six men stood, huddled together on a golf course green, on the top fold of A1. They looked blurred. A bad run. The tagline read, THE BIGGERS'S GOLF TOURNAMENT KICKS OFF TO A GREAT START. I checked the date. A week ago. "What am I supposed to be looking at?"

"Look at the men's faces."

I squinted. I knew the man in the middle. John Biggers. I'd done the article on his newly formed company. He was the fool who thought all women were part of the animal kingdom. He was on a crusade to legislate the privatization of the immunization of children. Of course, his own company would be the designated company. First in Georgia, then the Southeast and later the U.S., with its ultimate altruistic goal to use all the marginal profit for immunizing Third World countries for free.

I found it odd that he was in the medical business at all. He was a good-old-boy, politically connected high roller from Texas. An engineer by trade. Born and bred hillbilly, called himself a redneck, but liked "the coloreds," he'd assured me during the interview. I'd not thought of him since I'd gotten that message from his secretary, thanking me for introducing him to one of my friends from Texas. Which, of course, I'm sure I didn't do. That animal-labeling idiot.

Next to him was Ralph Spears, one of former President Carter's press secretaries. And next to him, Jeff Samuels. "What's he doing here?" I asked, the shock registering on my face.

"You tell *me*. I called the photographer on the story. He tells me he got a group of men for the shot who happened to be sitting with Biggers on a couple of carts. Didn't even get their ID's on the photo. Strictly a promo publicity shot to advertise the benefit."

I could see two or three other men in the background, standing off to the side. I opened the paper.

"Don't bother. There is no related story except an advertisement in sports, full page, about the benefit golf tournament and how much money they expect to give to orphanages. I say it's all bullshit."

"Maybe Jeff was working? You know, an off-duty gig? He told me he works security as part of his cover. A lot of cops do, you know."

"And Biggers let him be in the shot? I doubt that. This is the fucking South. Hierarchies mean something here. That would be like Biggers pulling the caddy into the shot. You see where he's standing, don't you?"

The caddy's shoe and half his body made the photo background. These six men, on the other hand, were huddled together in the good old boy's closed-rank position. A position of power, money and influence. What in the hell was Jeff Samuels doing in the photo? Goddammit if I wasn't going to ask him.

"I told you there is something about him that doesn't ring true. And I'm going to find out what it is. I've seen him before but for the life of me I can't remember where." She grabbed my purse off the floor. "Let's get the hell out of here. When you said you were junky, you weren't kidding."

"Go to hell," I replied, mustering a smile. "Did you get a call from the coroner's office yet?"

"No. Nothing. However, I made arrangements for the funeral home to pick up the body as soon as it's released. Carl's Funeral Home will take care of the body. No ceremony, right, since you said there was no one to invite? They'll let us know. You still want cremation?"

"Yes," I said, coming to the ultimate conclusion once again that even drinking can't keep you drunk forever, though God knows I wished it could. "I need to clean up, get a shower, brush this awful dragon breath away and get myself together."

"I'm taking you to my house. You can do it there, put on one of my dresses I've saved for the day I go back to a size twelve. Ha. Like I believe that. Hey, I picked up your mail. It was scattered all over your throw rug inside the door. Some of it was still stuck in your mail slot."

"Thanks, but I don't have the strength to care. I know it's time for my bills, but who gives a shit? I'm tired, my head hurts—"

"Well, okay, let's do this quick. I'll take these with me and I'll do them for you. How about that? Let's see, your electric, phone, credit card . . . what's this? Emory?"

"Emory?"

"Well, it says Circulation Department, Emory University. Never mind."

"Wait. Let me see that."

I'd forgotten the card. I'd gotten a research card for Kenneth to use in my name. It cost me $100 and I wouldn't have done it if he hadn't paid the money. I'd never seen him bring any books here, so I assumed he hadn't used it. I opened the envelope.

It was a letter informing me I owed money and if it wasn't paid my borrowing privileges would be suspended. There was a number for questions to the circulation department. I stuffed the letter in my bag. Maybe this would help me. But right now I had to get the hell out of here, since I was sober and thinking again.

In the car, I didn't speak. I laid my pounding head back on the headrest and prayed that I'd not go back to drinking. Knowing full well I wouldn't if I just kept away from the alcohol. That shit still felt bad in the mornings.

I glanced back at my house. It looked like the same man, who had been standing near the street preacher, was now sitting on my curb. "Carol," I said, "stop the car."

"What is it?" she asked, slowing to a stop near the side of the street.

"Look. Damn it, do you think that old man is casing my house?"

"What old man?" she asked, turning around.

I looked back. He was gone. Maybe he'd gone in the back. Daggone bums. "I don't care. What can he do that's not already done?" With that I laid my head back and closed my eyes. "I wish this shit was over."

At Carol's I dressed and ate a Danish. "I'm going to talk to Ira. I think I'll put that darn diamond in the urn with Kenneth."

"You can't be serious?"

"No. I'm not. I don't know what I'll do with it."

"If it's real, fucking wear it. He wanted you to have it, didn't he?"

"Yes. Yes, he did, I guess. But he didn't want me to wear it. He told

135

me to sell it. Wait. Maybe they're looking for the ring. Maybe the ring is the key to this."

"If it's real I could see that." Carol put on her jacket. "Drop me off at work. Keep the car."

"You trust me with it again? I'm going to call about my car tomorrow."

"Sure. Why not? If you feel anywhere as beat up as you look, I don't think I have to worry about you drinking anytime soon."

"You're a perceptive woman," I said, realizing that she was the kind of person I would have liked to be my family.

"Thanks. Now let's move or I'll be late for my appointment."

Before she stepped out of the car I said, "I know you think I'm losing it but—"

"No. I don't think that. I think you've lost it. And it's going to be worse if you don't get some help with this."

"What do you think I'm doing?" I asked, letting her off at the curb in front of the newspaper.

After dropping her off, I parked a block from Ira's shop. I passed by a pay phone. I had the urge to call Jeff Samuels, but I wasn't ready to talk to him. I wanted to confront him about the photo, but then what? Being in a photo with a zillionaire wasn't exactly a criminal indictment. First things first, I said to myself, and hurried to Ira's shop.

Ira Bernstein had a bomb for me.

CHAPTER TWENTY-ONE

When I walked into the small office the clerk buzzed a switch and disappeared inside the main door that led to the back. I rang the bell on the counter, thinking that maybe by some miracle I was invisible and that's why he hadn't seen me enter.

Ira came out of the back with his clerk, locking the door behind them. He held his key in his hand as he approached me, offering me a slightly drawn mouth. He and I were better friends than that.

"Hello, Patricia. Hope you're having a fine, fine day."

"Hi, Ira," I replied, smiling at his familiar greeting. "To be perfectly honest I'm having a holocaust kind of day."

He smiled only briefly. "Since you mention that, I must speak to you privately. Vould you mind stepping into the back?"

I had not been in the back of the store before. Most of the time if we talked, we'd walk up the street to the Dunkin' Donuts and have some coffee together. This was not a convenient time for personal chitchat at either place for me.

"I think I'll take a rain check today," I said, attempting to hide my anxiety and head pain. "Did you find out a price for the ring?"

"I must speak to you privately about the matter, if you don't mind," he said, peeping at the clerk.

Mata Hari had nothing on me now. Everything in my life was a secret. The problem is, I was the one the secret was being kept from.

"Sure. No problem." What now? "I'll step back to your office. But is this about the ring or something else?"

He was already holding open the metal gate to let me through. I took a fleeting look at the counter where his clerk worked. Splintery-looking diamonds were lying on the white pad called a diamond pad. I'd asked Ira before, why white? And he said it was so the tint of the diamond would show up. Why paper? Because jewelers scribble notations about the diamond on the paper. Made sense.

I followed close behind him into the narrow hallway. Musk and the odor of decaying bananas filled the air. I felt a slight vertigo. Ira stepped back behind me to double lock the door and reset an alarm. It seemed like a lot of trouble but I suppose the idea was that thieves wouldn't think too much of the procedure either. He shuffled past me into a room in the back hallway off to the left.

A dark scarred mahogany desk with two tattered bronze wingback chairs furnished the room. He motioned for me to sit in one of the wingbacks. He took the other.

"Vould you like a drink of water?" he asked, pointing to a cooler behind the desk. "Vater is good for you, soul and body. I drink plenty of vater. Crystals, that's my life," he said, giving a little chuckle.

"I'm sorry. I'm not following you."

"No mind. No mind. A jeweler's attempt at humor."

"I don't mean to be impolite or ungrateful, but I have had a rough few days and I'm sort of in a hurry."

"Of course. Of course, my dear. You don't mind me saying 'my dear'? I think of you like a daughter; you know that. Of course. Of course. I think you're a very good young voman. Very smart too. Real smart."

Ira gave this same speech every time. I waited while he shuffled through some papers on his desk.

Obviously the word "hurry" must not mean the same in Yiddish.

He looked over the papers like he'd forgotten I was there. Finally he said, "To the point. To the point," slapping his wrinkled hands on his knees.

I watched specks of dust fly up from the fabric. I smiled. Grandma Dixon used to say, "Rich folks don't spend all their money on new clothes; new clothes is for poor folk. Spend their last dime on a fancy name-brand frock while the rich man sitting back ragged, laughing all the way to the bank."

"The diamond," he said, leaning forward in the chair, his bushy eyebrows close together. "Were you able to check with your friend as to

138

where the diamond came from yet?"

"To be honest, no," I replied, wishing he'd stop asking me about where it came from. I couldn't recall him questioning me like this before. "I'd like to know a general estimate of what it's worth," I said, sighing heavily, hoping the sigh might help him get the hint.

"The diamond, it is vorthless," he told me, his eyes flickering.

I dropped my head. Tears sprang to my eyes. I couldn't acknowledge to him that his words hurt me or left me feeling so let down, but they did. With all his class, I expected more from Kenneth. I, at least, thought the scum cared for me enough not to take me for a zirconian fool. It was the thought that counted, but in this case his thought must have been "sucker."

I put my purse strap on my shoulder and stood up. "Thank you, Ira, for taking a look at it for me." I held my head down to keep him from seeing my tears. "How much do I owe you?" I looked up.

"No. No, my dear," he said.

"Look, I know you don't want to take my money, but for this one I want to pay."

"No. I'm sorry. You misunderstand. More of my humor. Not that kind of vorthless. Sorry I confused you. Another attempt at jeweler's humor," he said. "I meant that the diamond is beyond the normal market. Priceless. It is a rare diamond, museum quality, if you know what I mean; it is priceless."

I flopped back down in the chair. Shocked. Then fearful. Then mad as hell. Kenneth a thief after all; a diamond thief. How could he? No wonder he wanted me to sell it on the black market. Not even caring if I got caught holding the bag. Damn. Damn. Damn. I wanted to swear aloud, but I never cursed in front of children or old people.

"Did you report this to the police yet?" I asked.

He looked puzzled.

"Ira, believe me, I didn't have anything to do with it being stolen and I sure wouldn't risk involving you in anything like that. Whatever goes down, I gave it to you, so it's my problem. If it is stolen, they should have it back immediately." I felt nauseous.

"I'm not sure vhat this is about," he said, looking at me, smiling. "No. I don't think it is stolen. Not stolen. Definitely not from any museum or company that I know of. Actually, I've never seen this particular diamond facet and I've only heard of it once in my life.

"An old diamond cutter from Germany vorking in Antwerp. Supposedly later he cut some of Hitler's treasures. Once he understood vhat

Hitler was doing to his own people, he killed himself to keep from cutting any more.

"The story is that he stole the ones he'd cut and hid them. Hitler cried . . . cried like a baby when he found out they vere missing. Then, he vas so angry, he had the old man's body mutilated and burned."

"What are you saying?" This was too much for me to take. Way over my head. Journalists should be prepared for all kinds of news. That is our business. But I was not prepared for the kinds of news I'd been getting the last few days. "Are you saying this is one of those diamonds?"

"No, my child," he continued. "I don't believe that tale; that's a myth. No, but I am saying that I believed the diamond you gave me, after examining its color, clarity, and cut, vas so rare I sent it to some old professor friends of mine at Georgia Tech to examine it. They could not believe vhat they were seeing. And neither could I. It is a red diamond. The rarest in the vorld."

"You're sure this isn't some mistake?"

"No mistake. Diamonds come in eleven colors. The poorest quality is either yellow or brown, but the rarest in the world, red. Red." His face looked like he was experiencing an orgasm when he repeated *red*. "And it has no flaws. Not one. I've never seen such a thing. Never. Ever."

I sucked in a breath and shuddered before breaking down.

Ira moved around behind the desk and pulled a cup down and filled it with water. "Tears of joy. Vonderful." He walked back and handed it to me.

I was sniffing into the leather of my purse. He handed me his handkerchief. I cried more now since I had something to catch my tears.

"No, Ira. I need to be rid of this ring and everything that goes along with it." He must have thought I meant sell it.

"Oh. I thought it not for sale. Your friend wishes to sell it, hey? Vise, maybe. Maybe unvise," he said, shaking his head up and down, flecks of dandruff shedding from his beard. "Vise. You two can live like king and queen. Vonderful. Unvise, it may have other meanings."

"What? What other meanings?"

"Come with me to their lab. They vould like to meet you. Ask you questions."

"I don't know any more than I've told you, Ira."

"I think it is best they explain to you, then. Come. We take the bus. I do not own a car."

"I have a car. I'll drive. But Ira, remember, I don't know for sure where it came from. Nothing about it. It could be stolen from a museum, a jeweler, anybody."

"It may have been stolen, ya, but if so, it vasn't from any place I know. I am certain of that."

We hurried to Carol's car and I drove to Georgia Tech.

CHAPTER TWENTY-TWO

*Ira knew where the lab was and we walked in without anyone noticing us. Two men in lab coats stood be-*side the usual lab equipment.

When they saw us they stopped fiddling with a microscope and walked over, hugging Ira. "Hello. Is this the woman with the diamond?" one asked.

Ira introduced me. Excitement danced across all three men's faces.

"Have a seat," one said, pulling up two chairs for us. The other one said to me, "You have no idea, do you? I can see it on your face."

"No. Thank God. I have no idea what you're talking about and no answers, and I'm grateful you can see that. It'll save a lot of time."

"Ira, did you tell her about the Bucky ball?" the taller man asked.

Ira shook his head no.

"The Bucky ball? What is that?"

"We think it's inside," the older, shorter and more perceptive one said.

I named him Yoda.

Yoda continued, "Or at least something like it is in the center of your diamond. How it got there I couldn't guess in a zillion years, and it probably could have taken that long to form inside it. Whatever it is, we think it is in the class with Bucky balls."

"Stop vith the tormenting her. Can't you see she doesn't know vhat a

142

Bucky ball is? Tell her, speak English," Ira said, looking exasperated. "You explain this to me and I know carbon."

"Carbon?" I said, frowning. "I know that diamonds are carbon, if that's what you mean. And the other form of carbon is graphite."

"Ah-ha!" Yoda said, smiling. "She knows as much as you do, Ira." Then he winked at me. "Now let's get to the nitty-gritty."

The two scientists laughed.

It must have been an inside joke because I sure as heck didn't get it.

Yoda continued, "Have you heard of Buckminsterfullerene?"

"You mean like the American architect who did the geodesic domes? Buckminster Fuller?"

"I was wrong. She knows *more* than you do, Ira. Yes, well, a few years back a third form of carbon was discovered. Well, we scientists acted that way at first, but since it was here on earth all along, it was a new discovery only to us.

"Anyway, it's a hollow cluster of sixty carbon atoms shaped like a soccer ball. So since the geodesic dome had a similar structure—the roundest, most symmetrical large molecule known—it was named after Buckminster Fuller, thus Buckminsterfullerene. Now it's coined Bucky ball."

"Excuse me," I said, "I truly enjoy science but I don't think I can do a lesson right now."

Ira said, "Listen. Patricia is vorried someone stole the diamond."

"*Ira*," I snapped, glaring at him.

"Don't vorry. These are old friends. We have been through lots together."

I knew he meant the concentration camps or some other indignities during their time so I didn't pursue my anger. "Yes, I do think that, but I didn't have anything to do with it."

"Of course not, my dear," Yoda said. "I doubt seriously if it's stolen. And if so, I couldn't imagine from whom. However, you're right. Now is not the time for a lecture. To make a long story short, we don't know what is in the diamond. *We* think it's a Bucky ball. But we don't know."

"So," the tall one, now the Green Giant to me, said, "since we didn't know we tried to find someone to tell us or you what it was. We found an old friend who'll be back in town soon and he will know. We'll give you his name and number. Tell him we sent you. He'll take care of you from there. He's a material scientist who works for NASA."

Yoda smiled. "Here's your diamond back. You will tell us what he says about it, won't you?"

"Yes, sure," I lied. I sat there staring at the diamond. I held it up to the light. "I don't see anything in it."

The Green Giant looked amused. "Of course you don't. It's so tiny it can't be seen by the human eye. But it's there. Believe me."

I sat thinking with my head down. Maybe Kenneth knew I'd show it to Ira and then Ira would lead me here. Hmmm.

"Patricia?"

"Oh. I'm sorry. I'm thinking. Give me a second?"

"Sure," Ira answered, motioning them to walk over to the microscope.

What I needed to do was hide it. But where? Not with Ira. If someone knew about me, they might know about him. Plus, I didn't want to put him in any danger. What about leaving it here? No. That wouldn't do. I didn't want anyone else to be in danger. I could mail it. Heck, no. Then it would be another zillion years before it got delivered, if at all. What choices did I have?

It came to me. I'd hide it where I'd hidden stuff as a young teen. When you're in foster homes, you must protect your stuff from snoopers. Every kid knew that. I had a perfect hiding place.

I walked over to the huddled group. "I'm going now. Thank you all for your help. I *will* let you know what I find out about the diamond."

"I hope you're going to keep it someplace safe," Ira said. "No matter what is in it, it's very valuable. And in my experience that means dangerous."

"I'll keep it safe. Don't worry."

"And you," he added. "You need to keep safe."

"And me," I added, slipping the ring into a Kleenex in my change purse.

"I hope that's not what you call keeping it safe," the Green Giant said.

"No. No." I smiled at him. "I have a place for it."

Ira followed behind me. "The shop. I must get back. Not to vorry, I can take bus."

"No. I'll drop you off. I wasn't thinking."

We walked in silence to the car. I drove him back to the shop. Before he got out he said, "Patricia. You are like my daughter. The daughter I never had. Please. I can keep it safe for you."

"No. You're right. A ring like this might be dangerous. I wouldn't want to put you at risk." I didn't tell him, but there was no doubt in my mind this diamond was dangerous.

"I'm an old man," he said, smiling. "Risk *is* my life."

"The answer is no. I'll be in touch. Don't worry. I have it covered.

Honest. Now you better go back to work. It looks like you've got company."

I could see two men inside chatting with the new clerk.

"Call me. Please. Take care," he said, and then added something in Yiddish, which I figured must be some kind of prayer. I sure as hell needed a prayer from somebody closer to God than me. And a God that wasn't in a bottle.

I stopped at a convenience store and bought what I needed to hide the ring. I sat in Carol's car debating what to do next. I felt heavy. Like I weighed a ton. Too many things had happened. I couldn't focus. Couldn't get my bearings straight.

The diamond was an added burden. Kenneth Lawson left it for me for a reason. But what the hell for? It couldn't have been an engagement ring because he didn't want me to wear it.

I stepped back out of the car, locked the doors and walked a few steps to a pay phone. I finally got up the nerve to phone my voice mail. It's funny how much avoidance behavior we can employ.

Beep. "It's Mark. Hey, girl. How could you go on vacation without leaving me the money? Damn."

His was the only message. I transferred to the city desk. "May I speak to Herb?"

"Hey, kid," he said into the phone. He was an editor who called everybody, young or old, kid. "Thought you were on vacation?"

"I am. Listen. Can you get me the address for the French woman who died—you know, the one who slit her wrists in the bathtub? I'm thinking about doing a follow-up story but I want to talk to some of her neighbors first."

"You're doing this on your vacation? Eager, aren't you? Can't it wait? Guess not if you're calling. Hold on." I knew he'd ask the clerk to see if they had a home address from the police report. Routine. Much of our information came from the faxed police report copy or the phone. The days of print journalists scouting behind police footprints are long gone.

It took forever. I glanced around the parking lot for any signs of Bulbous Nose or anyone else suspicious. There weren't many people out. I thought about the ring. Why did Kenneth have the ring? Why leave the ring to me? And what was in the center of the ring? I couldn't think clearly. My mind had truly taken a vacation.

I waited. I hoped Carol was out or away from her desk. It dawned on me too late that she didn't sit that far away from Herb. Conversations were never private in the newsroom. I should have thought about that. I hadn't called Carol for the address because I knew she'd be saying I had no business going to the dead woman's place. She was right, of course, but I didn't want to hear it. Carol would be pissed. But what the hell.

"Hey, kid. I got it. It's 622 Filmore Lane. You know where that is? I think it's near the Red Cross building."

"Yeah. I think so. Thanks, Herb. And Herb, do me a favor?"

"Sure, kid."

"Don't mention this to anyone. It may be a dud and I don't want some editor putting it on the budget before I'm prepared to do the story."

"My mouth's shut, kid."

I hung up and hopped in the car. I jotted down the address on one of the covers of the many journalist's notebooks Carol had lying on the floor of her car. There was a time when I didn't have to write everything down, but as I get older, so does my memory. At times I can't recall my own office phone number, so I've taken to writing it down on slips of paper.

I drove to the house. It was up a slight hill on a dead end street. I could see the back of the Red Cross building across a small creek. Stuck in the city, the brick house was nestled in a neat suburban neighborhood with manicured lawns.

The yellow police tape sagging in front of the door was the only thing out of place. That and the black soot along the white door and its frame. They'd taken fingerprints. They sure hadn't cleaned up after themselves.

As I let myself in through a side window, hoping no neighbors saw me, I wondered who the police intended to keep out with that plastic yellow tape.

The house was a split-level with a dark, wood high-beamed living room. There was hardly any furniture. A freestanding stone fireplace separated the living room from the dining area. The kitchen was to my right. I went down the steps to the bedroom.

It smelled terrible. Rotten. All the furniture was in place but some of it had fingerprint powder added to the accumulating dust. I opened some of the drawers.

Claudette Duvet's house had probably been neat before the police waltzed through. I looked in the small French desk. Nothing of interest. I noticed no photos around anywhere. I picked up the phone book from the desk and thumbed through the pages. I often marked numbers that I thought I might call again. Maybe Claudette Duvet did the same. Maybe I could find out something about her.

When I got to the C's, I noticed a slightly turned down corner. I scanned the page. The CDC was not on it. I'd hoped I could find the link to the CDC here. Okay. She didn't mark anything but this time she'd turned down the page. I scanned the businesses. Did any seem like a place she'd call? I went down the page slowly. I fished out a piece of paper and a pen. I didn't want to touch anything that belonged to her unless I absolutely had to. She'd been violated enough. I wrote down numbers I thought might be possibilities.

I opened her desk drawer. Stationery still sealed in a box, what looked to be an expensive ink pen, some blank sheets of paper were all that lay there. I looked around the room.

Beside her bed was a white leatherbound Bible. I picked it up and shook it. A rosary bookmark fell out. I put it back and began thumbing through the pages absentmindedly as my eyes scanned the room. I looked at the front of it. No entry in the blanks. I flipped through a few more pages. I stopped. My heart raced. Heat burned my nose. I bit my lip and pushed my tears back.

It was a Polaroid of Kenneth Lawson and another man hugging each other. The photo was stuck to the page with glue so that if you picked it up and shook it, the photo would not fall out. This Bible must have belonged to Kenneth. That dog *should* be dead, I thought angrily as I envisioned the two of them, he and Claudette Duvet, holding hands. Lying here on this very bed together entwined.

"I hate men," I whispered.

I didn't expect to find anything belonging to Kenneth here, in her place. Sure, I thought the two were lovers, but a Bible? Here? It meant something if a man gave you a Bible. Especially a religious man. Why did I think that thought? Was Kenneth religious? I didn't know. I knew shit.

The Bible looked new. I examined the photo. I guessed it might have been recent, since I recognized the clothes Kenneth wore.

He was embracing an old and frail-looking silver-haired white man, who had on some kind of robe. Black and white. Was he in a choir? A church? I couldn't recall ever seeing a robe like it. But, face it, I hadn't seen a lot of robes. I knew little about churches and Bibles. I only knew the rosary thing because Carol was Catholic and had one.

Kenneth and the man were standing outside a greenhouse-type building. Nothing in the photo looked familiar except Kenneth Lawson himself.

I ripped the photo, tearing some of the page off with it. I stuffed the rosary bookmark in my purse. Neither Claudette Duvet nor Kenneth would need the beads anymore. Now what? I looked around. The bathroom, in a far corner, was off limits.

I started to go out the door when it hit me: the mattress. I was sure the police had looked at the mattress but Grandma Dixon had told me once that if you wanted to hide something in there, remove the manufacturer's tag and then sew it back on. Was Claudette Duvet that smart?

I examined her mattress. Removed the tag with a nail file. Nothing. I was about to leave the room when I spotted a small blue gilded box. I opened it. It was full of business cards. And there it was.

A business card with Kenneth's name embossed on it. DR. KENNETH LAWSON. In the right corner it read, COMPUTER CONSULTANT, DIRECTOR OF TECHNOLOGY, DELECARTE LABORATORY. The lab was in Seattle, Washington. The edges of the card were frayed and dingy. A computer consultant? Director of Technology? What happened to the anthropology professor? Was that a lie too?

And here was that name again, Delecarte. Dr. Mutota had mentioned that same name. What had she said? That Delecarte was onto her? He wasn't trying to help? Onto her for what? That meant they all must have known each other: Kenneth, Claudette Duvet, Dr. Mutota and this Delecarte. Kenneth evidently had either worked for this man before he came to Atlanta or he had been working for him here. No wonder he couldn't get a job teaching at a university. Shit. He'd told me he'd been a professor of anthropology all his life. And before coming here he'd been in a town outside of Detroit teaching in a small college's anthropology program. I didn't even remember the name, but it didn't matter since he'd probably made the crap up. Why? God, he could have gotten a job here in computers. That explains why he was at the seminar where we met. But why wouldn't he want to work in his own field here? Maybe he and Claudette Duvet were stealing from this Delecarte. Maybe they had stolen the diamond from him.

I decided my next step would be to figure out who the other man in the photo was. Maybe *he* was Delecarte. That would be like killing two snakes with one ax. But how to find him?

I drove around thinking what to do next and wondering what in the hell was happening to my life—a life that was never too great in the freaking beginning but now had gone straight to hell. How could Kenneth Lawson have done this to me? Why live with me?

I spotted the Catholic church unconsciously. The priest was stepping out of his car. I swerved into a parking space on the street and raced toward him. He looked up in terror, attempting to get back inside his car, fumbling with his keys.

I realized what it might have seemed like to him, some wild woman running toward him at breakneck speed. This could be a scary neighborhood. I slowed and called to him, "Father. I'm a journalist and I need to talk to you a second."

The terror left his face and he stopped the struggle to make the wrong key fit in the car door.

"Whew," I said, catching my breath. "I'm sorry if I startled you." I couldn't be mad. I know that a lot of black men feel insulted that people assume they're going to bother them, that they snap down their door locks when a black man walks past their cars, but I'm a realist. I snap down my locks for men and women no matter their color. It's a shame, but in this day and age everyone is suspect.

"No. No apology necessary," he said, his chest heaving like he'd been the one running. "I'm a little jumpy. Some punk-head white boy stole my car a few weeks ago and I finally got it back. Now, how can I help you?"

I sighed relief at the mention of a white boy. All minorities know that whenever anyone in their ethnic group commits a crime, by some unnamed law it reflects on them. It doesn't seem to work the same way for white folk. Nobody fears that every white man will eat them, say, like Jeffrey Dahmer. If old Jeffrey had been black, black folk wouldn't be able to lick their lips in peace again.

"Maybe you can help me. I hope so," I said, finally continuing after catching my breath and my thoughts. "I have this photograph I found with a rosary. I thought maybe you could tell me if this is someone Catholic in the picture. The man's wearing a robe."

I heard myself and wondered how stupid that sounded. Like only Catholics wore robes? I was losing it for sure.

"I meant—" I started to explain.

He interrupted. "Let me take a look."

He studied the photo. I saw the moment recognition came into his face.

"Ahh. I'd say from what he's wearing he's a Trappist monk. And if he is, I'd say, if the picture was taken around here . . . was it?"

"I'm sorry. I don't know. I think it's recent so it's possible it was taken around here."

"Then if it was I'd say it was out in Conyers at the Cloister."

"Excuse my ignorance, but the what?"

"The Cloister. It's a monastery out in Conyers, Georgia. I haven't been there myself but I know that's the robe of a Trappist monk and I heard they have a greenhouse out there where they specialize in the bonsai."

"Oh. I don't think I've heard of it, but thank you. I'll check it out.

Thanks, and I'm sorry for scaring you." I was remembering the bonsai Kenneth had brought me a few months before as a gift. He'd actually taken care of it himself when I'd forgotten about the plant. When it came to plants I was root kill.

A Trappist monk? Conyers? I didn't want to go that far now. Time marched on and Carol would shit bricks if I was late picking her up. I was getting hungry anyway. So I decided I'd get something to eat and ponder what was going down.

I drove to Little Five Points. I thought about going to Suzy's but I was afraid she'd ask me why my face was puffed up like a frog's.

I went to the Bridgetown Grill. It's a funky place where half the waiters are white guys with locks and Rastafarian crocheted crowns on their heads. It was one of those guys who told me it's insulting to call Rastas' hair "dreads." He claimed it was coined by others, who dreaded seeing the locked hair on the brothers and sisters.

The Grill has a place all the way in the back where you're not so conspicuous to passersby. I always feel like I'm sitting in the belly of a peacock in the Grill, it's so bright and colorfully decorated with pink flamingos and other tropical items. The specialties are burgers and jerk chicken.

I ate slowly, not thinking about my problems as I'd planned, but instead missing Jeff's touch. I hated to admit it, but I longed for him. I went over in my mind what a terrible person I must be. I wanted to call Jeff and I was thankful I was too cheap to get a cell phone or I'd be dialing up his number.

I examined the map I'd brought in from the car and found Conyers. When I got a chance I'd call the Cloister and get directions and go out there.

I still needed to hide the diamond. So I finished eating, paid and left, glad that no one said anything to me. I headed for the Grant Park area, to the cemetery.

Often as a young child I'd lived within walking distance of a cemetery. I loved cemeteries. It was not the dead who frightened me. It was ordinary people—living foster families and shit. In the cemetery I had found a foolproof place to hide my personal writing. Writing was the only thing that kept me sane in those days, but, since I mostly wrote wicked things about my foster parents, I needed to make sure they couldn't find my journals.

Finding good cemeteries was part of my moving-to-a-city ritual.

The Grant Park Cemetery, established in 1850, takes up about eighty acres of green space. It is where you can locate a real Southerner, born and bred in Atlanta, Georgia. Most people who work at the newspaper aren't from the South. Hardly anyone is from Atlanta proper. If you walk the streets, a large percentage of the people you meet will not be Southerners and even fewer will hail from Atlanta.

The cemetery's arches shadow around six thousand mourners and visitors each year. The centuries-old sculptures in the garden act as sentries, guarding the forty thousand or so dead, from all ethnic groups, buried there. Magnificent Victorian-style stained-glass mausoleums cover the vast lawns. There are even signed urns from the infamous Gorham foundry.

The park itself holds the remains of Confederate and Union soldiers, a Jewish section, former Atlanta mayors, the golf great Bobby Jones, the founder of Morris Brown College and many other notable personages. Margaret Mitchell, author of *Gone With the Wind*, holds a spot. The cemetery may be one of the few integrated resting places in the Southeast, and maybe the U.S., and other than the homeless population, it is also probably the most integrated neighborhood in Atlanta proper. Never mind all the residents are dead.

I'm familiar with the park because of a story I wrote on Carrie Steel Logan, the founder of Georgia's first black orphanage. I've done a lot of stories on orphanages, since it haunts me that maybe I would have been better off in one, instead of shifted from foster family to foster family. And then I remember Grandma Dixon and think better of the notion.

The mausoleum I wanted stood on the northern end of the grounds. There weren't many people there. With each step my shoes sunk into the ground. The cemetery's soil always reminded me of quicksand. It was like the very earth itself was making an attempt to pull you under since you, while still breathing, had the guts to walk on its hallowed ground.

I sat down outside the mausoleum. It was a place I came to regularly. All the descendants of this family were dead and gone. Maybe they made ghostly night visits, but no one came in the flesh. I sat hugging my knees like I had no place to go and nothing to do. My body and mind needed rest, so I just sat there.

Finally, I opened my purse, pulled out a small brown bag and laid the ring on my lap, the rare red diamond with the unknown center I couldn't see. I took out the condom I had bought and slipped the ring inside it. I opened the mayonnaise pack and squeezed some out onto the condom. I dug a hole and stuck it inside.

Dogs didn't dig up condoms, and even if they surfaced, people didn't touch them. Condoms are the untouchables of this society.

> "The means of protecting oneself against
> 'bad words' of the dead is to give them water."
> —*Words and the Dogon World*

CHAPTER TWENTY-THREE

I dropped off Carol's car and left a message at the paper that I'd left the car in the garage. I'd call her later.

When I got a cab, I asked the driver, an older black man, if he knew where the Cloister was, expecting him to say no.

"Sure. I know where the place is. Don't know if you can still get in but I'll take you out there. Don't know their operation anymore. Used to, though. I'm born and bred in Georgia and I remember when they come here. Let me see, that would have been 1940 or thereabouts. I been out there many a time since then, taking folk to visit."

It had been a long time since I'd ridden in a cab with a person who'd been in Atlanta longer than I had without an accent or the poorest diction you've ever heard. I noted from his ID tag that his name was William Shepard.

You could tell this black man was from the old school. The school where black people knew that it was important to communicate to whites in their language, so they couldn't pretend they didn't understand your demands.

I held the photo over the seat, more assured now that he might recognize this robe or at least save me the trip. "Do you know if this is the kind of robe they wear out there?"

He glanced at the photo and slowed down the cab, like a good driver should. "Yep. That's what they wear, all right."

His voice turned reflective. "I'm a religious man, deacon in my church. But I ain't so dumb that I think I'm the only one knows how to get to heaven. So I got one of the books about the men out there once. It said that the blacks didn't like the whites so they split. But when I asked one of 'em about it, he said they weren't talking 'bout skin color but the color of the robes they wore. That's how I know they wear black and white.

"Funny, huh?" he continued. "Black folk in this country so messed up, when you say black and white they can only think of one thing, skin color. It's a shame what white folk done to us. A shame."

After that he didn't talk. I closed my eyes and tried to force all my thoughts from my mind. It didn't work.

The Cloister. Why would Kenneth Lawson have a photo with a man from this place? *Cloister* means "secluded" in plain English. I wondered what it meant to Catholics as we left the city limits of Atlanta.

It was getting to be dusk now, but I could see we were moving out into a rural area. The only thing I knew about Conyers was that since last year, some white woman had been claiming to have visions of the Virgin Mary on her land. Supposedly the sign that the vision would appear was the smell of roses. Carol and I had joked that we bet they had little sprinkler nozzles in the ground that went off intermittently spraying rose perfume. My mind drifted and I dozed off to much-needed sleep. . . .

"Hey," Mr. Shepard called. "We're here. You're going to have a problem getting a cab from out here late, you know. Cabs are funny 'bout coming out now since so many of us been shot, so on and so forth."

I stretched and tried to rub the sleep from my eyes. We were at a gated entrance. The sign said, OPEN 6 A.M. CLOSED 9 P.M. We were fine; it was barely 7 P.M. We rode through the gate. Through the dusk I could see magnolia trees blossoming on each side of the paved road. After about a quarter of a mile the buildings came into view.

To my right was a one-story building with a stained-glass window in the top and a sign indicating a gift shop. Ahead to the left was a white plaster building with an archway that led into a Spanish fort–like enclosure. I got out of the cab and paid Mr. Shepard.

He grasped my hand gently. "God bless you, sister. Take care. Whatever you're looking for, I have a feeling you might find it here."

I felt awkward. Very seldom did people touch me, and certainly not strange men. But I didn't feel like jerking my hand away. I avoided his eyes, not wanting him to recognize the unnatural vulnerability I felt. It sounded like an afterthought when I finally said, "Thanks."

"Hey, do you want me to wait for you?" he asked, tipping his hat.

"No. Thanks, though. I'll be okay. What's your cab number? Maybe I'll call you when I'm ready to go."

"I'm off at seven P.M."

"I'm sorry," I said, realizing that he'd brought me out here when he hadn't had to make the trip.

"No problem. Hey, think about coming to church sometime. I'm at Sixth Street Baptist. You're welcome anytime."

I didn't lift my head. "Sure. I'll think about it."

I hadn't been to church a lot in my adult life. When I had, I'd been uncomfortable. An uneasiness would settle over me and I'd think irrationally, They all are feeling sorry for me. They know I'm an orphan and that I have no one. I'd gaze around the church looking at people sitting with their families and those alone whispering to the person next to them and feel anger. God ripped me off. Left me in this world unwanted and abandoned. Alone.

After being with Kenneth, though, I had begun thinking of going to church. I don't even know what brought the thought on. One day I was sitting next to him on the couch and the next moment I imagined the two of us sitting together, shoulder touching shoulder, in our own special church.

I looked up. Inside the second archway, now facing me, was a plaster angel or maybe it was the Virgin Mary. I wasn't sure which. I've always found it odd that the Virgin Mary holds such a highly esteemed position in religion. Standing there now staring up at her, at the entrance to an all-male establishment, I considered how churches seemed to feel about women, according to many male ministers I'd talked to over the years.

A man with the now-familiar robe on walked toward me on the brick path, beyond the gate where a sign read, THANK YOU FOR NOT VISITING BEYOND THIS POINT, in both English and Spanish.

"Excuse me," I called, noticing that the robe he wore was actually white with a black apronlike open-sided cloth on top. He had a leather belt around his midsection, which I couldn't call a waist.

"Yes, may I help you?" he answered, a friendly tone in his voice.

"I hope so. I'm looking for someone. It's the man in this photo."

I held the photo up to him and pointed out the man dressed exactly the way he was dressed.

"That's Father Fred. Where did you get this?" he asked me.

"From the man next to him. Is he here? Father Fred?"

"Yes, he's here. But he doesn't see anyone from the outside. I don't know how anyone would get a photo of him. I tell you, go in the bookstore and see Brother Joseph. He might be of more assistance."

He pointed me back through the archway toward the building that said, GIFT SHOP, in English and Spanish. I wanted to explain to him that I doubted anybody working in the gift shop could help me, but before I could complain he walked to my right toward a greenhouse.

Inside the gift shop I spotted another man in a black-and-white robe behind the counter. There was a blond woman also helping behind the counter. Three people stood in line. On a dusty shelf, I spotted a Bible like the one I'd seen at Claudette Duvet's house. I picked it up and carried it to the counter.

The man was busy waiting on the three people in line so I walked over to the woman.

"I'd like to get this, please." My reasoning was if I bought something, they'd be more apt to give me information.

"I'm sorry, only the brothers run the cash register," she said, smiling. "I'd be happy to help you in any other way."

I must have looked dismayed because she continued, apologetically, "I can't see the cash register very well anyway because of a detached retina."

"That's okay," I replied, and moved over to the line. When I got up to the counter I placed the Bible in the man's hand. He looked up and smiled. "Good evening." He punched in the cost. "That will be $39.95, please."

"Sure," I said, counting out $40.

He put the money in the drawer and offered me my change.

I glanced around behind me. There was no one waiting. I sighed, inwardly relieved, and handed him the photo. "Do you know the man in the photo wearing the robe like yours?"

"Yes," he said. "Where did you get this?"

What was this, the Inquisition? "Do you know him?"

"Yes, I know him. It's Father Fred. But he doesn't see anyone. He's very old and he remains cloistered inside the community. Is this a recent picture?"

"I think it is. Actually, I didn't take it. I think it belonged to the other man in the photo. Do you know *him*, the black man?"

"No. I don't believe I do." He stared at the photo.

"I think he, that man," I continued, pointing to Kenneth Lawson, "came out here recently and met with your Father Fred. I know he had one of these Bibles. And a rosary like that." I pointed to a black-beaded rosary with a rose-colored cross hanging from it.

"I'm afraid I can't help you. You might try Father Ignatius. He's at

155

the retreat center. If this man did see Father Fred, then I'm sure he would have been the one to get the father's permission."

"What do you mean, get his permission?" I asked, not following this very well. Not that I'd followed any of it so far.

"You see, this is a cloistered community. We live the monastic life. We do not go outside the community except for hospital visits. Some of us go twice a year to see family. But there are those of us who never even come outside the cloister walls unless there are no visitors about. That means out here or anywhere on the grounds.

"In other words, Father Fred has not seen an outsider in many years to my knowledge. Of course," he looked at the photo again, "it looks as though he saw this gentleman. As I said, try Father Ignatius."

I followed the brick path toward the retreat house. The blond woman called to me from behind.

"Miss?"

"Yes," I answered, turning back and waiting for her to catch up with me. As she approached, I wondered if she'd been sent to ask me who I was and why I was asking questions. It had struck me that not one of them had been curious as to why I wanted to know about either man.

"I overheard you back there. Father Ignatius will be happy to help you. They are all lovely men."

"Thank you," I said, wondering what the hell she was talking about and where this was leading.

She shifted her weight. I could tell she wanted to say something else to me but was hesitant. I stood staring at her, wondering how long she'd stand looking down at the grass.

Finally she spoke again. "I think you should go in the church while you're here. When I came here I was very alone and troubled. My father died recently. I was an only child and my mother died fifteen years before. My father was all I had, and after he died I felt alone. I came here and went in that church and it changed my life. The Holy Spirit filled me and I've not wanted since."

I didn't know how to respond. Obviously she wasn't sent to ask me anything. Maybe she was nuts. I stood staring at her. "I'm sorry, but why are you telling me this?"

"I don't mean to intrude. You seem so spiritual, that's all. I didn't want you to miss going in the church. And," she lowered her eyes, "I recognize aloneness now."

"Well, thanks. But it's okay. I don't know anyone who'd mistake me for spiritual. And I'm not alone. Sorry." I smiled at her.

She knew better. But she smiled back and said, "Good luck on finding what you're after."

I wanted to scream, "Am I wearing my vulnerability on my face for makeup so the entire world can mess with me?" I wanted this to end. All these people feeling sorry for me. All these people in my freaking business.

I stopped. Cursing here was out of place. I looked up at the white-bricked church she'd pointed out. The steeple reached to the sky. The windowpanes were stained glass. I walked swiftly past the church, afraid something would reach out and pull me in, as I headed to the retreat center. It was getting dark and lights were popping on around the place.

Inside there was an open window. The carpet was cheap but clean. I was in the small lobby, which reminded me of being in a university dorm. No one was inside the small office behind the lobby. I peeped around the corner, noting a long, empty hallway. In front of me was a larger room with chairs. I didn't see a bell or anything. I leaned against the door frame wondering what to do next. Then suddenly someone tapped me on the shoulder. I turned and was face to face with a tall graying man with a crew cut.

He was solidly built and I noticed liver spots on his hands. He wore sandals with white socks and he had on the robe. On closer inspection I could see that the white was yellowing, and that the black and white were two separate pieces. The black slipped over the white as if they were two connected panels, and there was a pointed hood attached in the back from the neckline.

"Please, may I help you?" he asked gently.

"I hope so," I replied, wondering how many more times this phrase would be repeated to me before I'd meet this Father Fred.

"I'm here to see this man." I pointed to Father Fred. "Because of this man." I pointed to Kenneth Lawson.

"I'm Father Ignatius." He motioned toward the photo. "May I?"

"Sure," I said, handing it to him and biting my lower lip.

He looked at the photo and then back at me. "I'll need to get permission for you first. He doesn't see people but I do recall this man coming to see him. When I told him who was here, he was so excited."

"You mean you remember Kenneth Lawson coming here? Do you know when?"

"I'm afraid time escapes me. And I don't remember the man's name. Only that Father Fred recognized who he was right away. They spent time together and then he left. Let me go tell him you wish to see him. Will he know your name?"

"No. No, he won't. Tell him that I was going to marry Kenneth Lawson."

The monk disappeared through the door. I sat down in one of the wood and leather chairs and glanced around. On the table next to me was a thin book, *Open to the Spirit, A History of The Cloister*. I thumbed through it.

Mr. Shepard had been right: The monastery was founded in 1944 by twenty Cistercian monks. The monks followed their patron, Saint Benedict of Nursia, who abandoned the excesses of life in late-fifth-century Rome, withdrawing to the desert to seek God.

I let the book relax in my lap, trying to imagine why people would live a monastic life. Then I read on. An abbot was their leader here. These monks were known throughout the community for their bread, bonsai trees and stained glass, which they made for churches, both non-Catholic and Catholic.

I had read the entire pamphlet before Father Ignatius returned. It was dark outside and I realized it was approaching 9 P.M. Were they going to lock me out?

"Miss. I'm sorry to say it is past the visiting hour. The father does not know the name of your friend; however, he said he will speak with you tomorrow."

"Oh," I said, disappointed. "Could you call me a cab? I realize I've stayed late." I checked my watch. It was after 9 P.M. now.

He wrote on a piece of paper: *We are in the period of the Great Silence, the only time of strict silence in our community. Please feel free to stay the night. Father Fred insists. I will show you to a room if you wish to stay.*

I was tired and spent. I nodded, too exhausted by the past events, emotionally and physically, to argue or wait outside the gate in the pitch dark for a cab that might not ever come and too frustrated to talk to anyone anyway.

Father Ignatius went into the small office and returned with a key numbered 225. He handed it to me and directed me up the stairs.

I expected a stark, colorless room with one hard bed with a sheet, no chair, one candle and a cross on the wall. For some reason I always associated this kind of life with prison. But the room was not too drab, sort of a cross between a college dorm room and a cheap but clean hotel room. The Fairfield Inn of solitude.

I threw my purse on the bed and walked over to the sink. I washed my face and dried off with one of the white towels waiting for me on the bed. When I lifted my face to the mirror, I didn't recognize myself.

Lines that I'd never seen before graced the corners of my eyes. I'd aged somehow in this process.

I flopped down on the bed and wished I could cry. No tears came. I was a tad hungry but it was clear there was no place to get food. I searched in my purse for my stand-by candy bar. I bit into it and lay back on the bed, wondering why this Father Fred didn't recognize Kenneth Lawson's name.

I drifted off to sleep.

CHAPTER TWENTY-FOUR

In the middle of the night I thought I heard Kenneth Lawson calling to me and I woke up disoriented and unnerved. I looked around the room, but nothing seemed disturbed. The chocolate had melted from my half-eaten candy bar onto the bedspread. I got up to wipe it off.

I had fallen asleep fully dressed again. Grandma Dixon used to whip me for that. She could never understand that before I had come to her house, I slept ready to run out into the night, prepared for my foster mother's husband or boyfriend to come to visit my room or for whatever else might disrupt my sleep.

I looked out the window and I could see the church's steeple and the stained glass sparkling in the moonlight. The church beckoned me. I could almost feel fingers pulling me forward. I picked up the three-fold pamphlet on the wooden desk and read it. Visitors, it said, could go in the church anytime day or night.

I closed my purse and stuck it under the pillow. Then I wrapped the blanket at the foot of the bed around my shoulders, and slipped out of the building to take a stroll. I was not going in that darn church.

I walked into the church on my second stroll past its doors. The silence hit me and on some level, I knew what the deaf world must be like. The interior of the church took my breath away. Four rows of pews separated the other rows by a sign that asked people not to go farther unless they were staying at the monastery. That qualified me.

The room pulled me forward. The ceiling demonstrated a version of Gothic design, but the intricate Gothic detail work I'd witnessed in other churches was replaced by clean lines. There were no images. I'd read earlier that the monks designed stained-glass windows without images, because the Cistercian imageless, geometric designs would free the mind from obstacles to contemplation. Each window in this church had its own character, since an individual monk was allowed to arrange the set number of pieces to fit his own personality.

I walked slowly toward the altar. Shades of blue and rose reflected off the dimly lit walls. The stained-glass window over the altar was the only exception to the rich geometric designs that surrounded me. An image of Our Lady holding the enthroned Christ Child was overshadowed by symbols of God the Father and God the Holy Spirit.

According to the booklet I'd read, the color scheme of the church was related to this window: *As the worshipper's eyes are drawn toward it, so too do the colors in the church progress toward it.*

When I'd read this line, the words had held no meaning for me. Me, the shut-offist. But here in the night light, I understood as something inside me stirred. As I contemplated the altar's image of Mary holding her child, for the first time I fully acknowledged the pain the separation from my mother had continued to cause me. In that moment some notion nudged my mind.

I had been living the monastic life among the living. Alone. In contemplating my pain, my bitterness and my abandonment, I'd cut myself off from everything. But the one thing I'd failed to do was contemplate my inner soul. Or God.

My shihans, Ted Maverick and Scott Brooks, were right. The only real battle one must fight is with one's own spirit.

Here in this place I felt the pain of all those years, all the bitterness rushing forward, engulfing me. Tears burned the corners of my eyes. A wave of heat moved through my body and I let the blanket slip to the floor. My heart was full.

Tears streamed down my face. Of all the things that had touched my life, I had avoided God. Now God wrenched my heart, and in this woman's face I saw the essence of my life. She was not merely holding her child, but the world—mankind. I knew at that moment the female spirit. The influence it served in the world. Nurturing love even in the desolation of man's creation. Neither power, nor money, nor another human could take the place of the love offered by God.

The thoughts startled me. Frightened me. Were they my thoughts? The chapel's silence must have affected my judgment.

I sank down on my knees. And then I uttered my first real prayer. "Oh Lord, help me."

My mind raced on with alien thoughts that I had no words to describe. I let my head lull forward in the abyss of an ecstasy I'd never known, and drifted to unknown and unspeakable peace.

CHAPTER TWENTY-FIVE

*Someone tapped me gently on the shoulder. Startled, I looked up. A skeletal hand lacking its pointer fin-*ger rested on my shoulder. I wiped my eyes.

The same old black man I'd seen with the street preacher and again sitting on my curb was beside me. He motioned me to come with him outside. He still wore dirty, battered clothing, and he smelled to high heaven. He continued to beckon me to follow.

I wanted to stop. Where was he going? But it felt like he had me attached to him, pulling me along. It occurred to me that maybe he wasn't talking because of the vow of silence.

He looked too frail and weak to be harmful. Senile, crazy, but not harmful. He walked in front of me, carrying an oak cane. The cane was forked at the top.

I followed him to a clearing not quite in the woods on the edge of the property. What I saw I could describe only as a small room masquerading as a house. It looked like what we used to call a lean-to, meaning if you leaned too hard on it, the crap would fall down.

This place must be another rendering of their monastic life, I thought, recalling the Indians in India who flagellate themselves, and the first monks with whom the Buddha had studied, who vowed total poverty.

The floor inside the structure was earth. In the center of the room the oldest man, black or white, I'd ever seen with my own eyes sat down, crossing his legs in front of him. His bones stuck out all over his body and I expected him to cough up phlegm any moment, since I reasoned only illness could emaciate a body as his had been.

He motioned for me to take off my shoes.

I did as he asked, wondering if this setup was some type of tourist attraction. I buried my toes in the black earth and wondered what had happened to the red clay that is most of the earth of Georgia. Did he bring this earth with him?

He smiled and planted a gentle kiss on my cheek, like a whisper, but he never moved his mouth near me.

I started to cry. And the memory of Cripple Cooney raping me vanished quickly, like a shooting star passing out of sight.

The old man wore a cap, and a leather pouch around his neck and entwined copper, bronze and iron bangles on his right arm. There were scars on his wrist joints that appeared to be some type of ritual marking. He wore a leather belt swelling with ornaments of old and decrepit-looking leather weaved together with cowrie shells. In front of him was a stone hearth, on which rested a spotted clay pot the color of bricks. A blond wooden board also sat in front of him, along with a cast-iron bell. He lifted the bell and shook it back and forth until it knelled. It sounded like a cowbell. The kindling in the hearth lit and fire danced in front of us.

My hand flew up to my mouth in shock as the fire sprang up without him touching it. I'd never seen such a thing. Was this some kind of magic show?

He shook his head no.

I thought, God, don't let him be responding to my thoughts.

He nodded yes.

Finally, he spoke. "I will speak to you in the primordial language so you may understand my words."

I could hear him but his mouth did not move. He was the man in my dreams. I thought, I'm dreaming again. I never even got up and walked into that church. That's what this is. A dream.

"No dream. All things are dreams. I have consulted the oracle. Where there is order, there must be disorder. All things must possess the duality in our physical reality as in our spiritual reality. The rock holds the primordial seed. The beginning. The she and he of the world. The he and she are still in its time. We, my people, were wrong, misled by the reality of the physical world. We misinterpreted the signs. We should have understood what the absence of the eighth articulation meant. But we failed to see it. Now in the valley of the dead I see it. And finally before the time of the Sigui, we can prepare for her coming back.

"You must make sure the primordial seed is embraced by Akwette, the one you call Kenneth Lawson, one last time before I can return it to the earth. You will know the time and the hour. There are things of value we must do everything to retrieve. The legacy is yours now.

"You must fulfill the prophecy as the other half of the whole. You are now Akwette's part. It must be finished one year before the Sigui ceremony, or we will miss the sign of the eighth articulation again and thus the coming."

When he finished speaking he patted my hand and stood up. He looked as tall as a giant and as strong as metal forged by fire. His bones looked like the foundation of the world, and for the first time in my life I knew what it meant to be blessed by a holy man.

He helped me up and I felt the strength of his touch surge through my body like a lightning bolt. I could have fought Goliath and won.

He pulled me close and kissed me on both cheeks, and the smell of him was sweet and pungent. I stood mesmerized.

The old man sat back down, as though I were already gone, and stuffed something in the mouth of a land turtle.

CHAPTER TWENTY-SIX

When I realized that other people were shuffling into the church, I looked up in embarrassment and fear. How was this? I was in the lean-to. Or was I merely dreaming? Oh God. What was happening? This was not me. Me, Patricia Conley, kneeling before an altar. I checked my watch. It was 3:40 A.M. I'd read that the monks all rose at three-thirty, so I hurriedly picked up the blanket and slipped out the side door.

Outside the cool Georgia breeze swarmed around me. Goose bumps spread rapidly on my arms. I pulled the blanket around my shoulders and ran to the room.

I lay on the bed, refusing to consider what had happened inside the church. I preferred to think of it as an aberration, a hallucination, a dry-drunk experience. Certainly I couldn't be "spiritual" as the woman had said. This did not happen. I knew it. It did not happen. Not to me. Me. Patricia Conley.

But I no longer felt alone. Something deep in the core of me had altered. I could not put a name to it and I didn't try as I let sleep take me in its arms.

CHAPTER TWENTY-SEVEN

When the sun burst through the window I got up and found the shower. I dressed, dried my locks and went searching for food.

At breakfast no one spoke. It felt like having an itch that you couldn't scratch. I wanted to talk. And badly. A couple of times while eating the wholesome hot oatmeal, I wanted to say to the monk sitting next to me, "This is good," but I didn't.

After eating, I couldn't find any of the monks, so I walked down to the lake. Geese quacked and squawked to one another not far from my bench. I looked out across the water.

This may very well be the most peaceful I've felt in my life, I thought. I feel safe, comfortable, at ease and at home.

The monastic life here was not what I had imagined—a cesspool of sexually deprived, grouchy men. It struck me that of the men I'd met, the energy I'd noticed most was soft and compassionate.

I heard a light tapping coming toward me. That would be him. The old black man. I twisted around and spotted a pale white man with a white cane tapping his way down the mulched pathway toward the lake. He had on shades and I decided he must be blind. I turned back to enjoy the lake.

The tapping stopped beside me and the monk said, "Good morning, Ms. Conley."

I stood up. "Good morning, Brother . . . "

"Allow me. I'm Father Fred. I believe you and I have a mutual friend. May I ask who sent you here?" His tone was friendly but no-nonsense.

He looked fit but his hands trembled along with his head in tiny little twitches. And I thought of Katharine Hepburn in the movie *On Golden Pond.*

"No one sent me," I answered. "Kenneth Lawson and I were going to be married."

"Kenneth Lawson?" He looked puzzled. "I'm afraid I don't know the gentleman. Were you under the impression I did? I told Brother Ignatius I'd see you but I didn't recognize that name."

"Yes. Since you and he were in the photo together, I thought you must have known him."

"The photo?"

"Yes, I have it right here." I held it out. Then I withdrew it, realizing he couldn't see.

"Come with me," he said and began moving toward the retreat office.

I followed, wondering if I should help him. But his step was sure and he walked fast for someone who looked so old. I was the one who was breathless when we entered the small office. We sat opposite each other on folding chairs. He pulled out a scrapbook and handed it to me. There was a rock labeled VOLCANIC connected to it with a gold string.

"Take a look inside. If you find the person you're talking about, I can then help you."

The photos had Braille labels beneath them.

"I have not received many visitors since I came here more than thirty years ago," he continued. "So if you have a photo of me with someone, it may not be too difficult to determine who it is." He folded his hands in his lap and bowed his head.

I didn't know if he was praying, tired or had merely fallen asleep.

I opened the scrapbook. The first few pages displayed newspaper articles, yellowing and torn. Midway the photos began. Some were clearly taken among indigenous people in different countries. I flipped through quickly and got to the ones in the back of the book.

I guessed he probably had the photos in chronological order. I was correct. The last page held only one photo. A Polaroid of Father Fred and Kenneth Lawson standing together in front of the church door. There was no label beneath it, and my body tensed. Suppose he couldn't recall?

"Here he is," I said, dreading what he might say. I handed him the book and rested his hand on the photo. "I'm sorry, but there is no Braille underneath."

He didn't say anything for a while. Then he said to me, "What is your name again?"

"Patricia Conley."

"Wait here," he said, getting up with great effort and leaving the room.

All kinds of possibilities raced through my mind. Suppose he's not coming back? Maybe he's senile and can't remember. Maybe he will bring the old black man back with him.

Twenty minutes later, he returned. "I'm sorry to keep you waiting so long. I needed to make sure you were giving me the correct name. You know, when you're aging your memory is not as swift."

He seemed more relaxed yet more feeble to me now, and I wanted to help him back into the chair. His head appeared to be shaking more than it had been, and I thought about going to get someone. Then I realized how foolish I was. Because he was old I'd attributed this mannerism to aging. He was shaking his head as a result of remembering.

"Is this who you are inquiring about?" He handed me a rectangular-shaped picture frame out of a white paper bag.

I stared at a black boy about two or three years old, being hugged by a young white man. I looked up and examined Father Fred. Yes, the young white man was him. But was this Kenneth? It could be him, I supposed. But I wasn't sure.

Finally I replied, "I don't know. I guess it could be. Do you not remember Kenneth Lawson?"

"The last photo in my book is one of this boy," he pointed to the frame, "who is now a man. But I know him as Saul Bernard. When he was a child, I christened him, after Saint Bernard. He was like a son to me."

I heard him but I didn't hear him. Saul Bernard. I was engaged to marry Saul Bernard?

"He told me about you. He told me that he'd fallen in love right in the midst of his troubles. Did he tell you of his troubles?"

"No," I replied, choking back tears. "I don't know about his troubles. Was he mixed up in drugs? On drugs? Is that what you mean?" I'd been lied to from the beginning. There was no Kenneth Lawson. I'd been tricked. But why?

"Oh, no. He never used drugs. Didn't believe in it. No, that I assure you was not his trouble."

"Did you know Claudette Duvet or a doctor named Kia Mutota?" I asked.

"No. I've never heard of them. You see, Saul came to see me not too long ago. He was sick. He didn't tell me a lot about what was happening. He wanted some information. I gave him what I could and he left. My suggestion to you is to ask him about all this. He is an honest man. He will tell you if he can."

"Tell me . . . " I looked up, startled. Of course, he didn't know. I wouldn't tell him. I wouldn't tell him about the stolen diamond, either, and all the crap his Saul had put me through. Let him think Saul was an honest man if he wanted to. After all, not a lot of white men feel black men are honest these days. Let him live with the delusion I wished for now.

He cleared his throat. "He is dead, then, I take it?"

He could have slapped me across the mouth. "Why do you say that?"

"When you are blind you use other senses to see. Curious, I don't know that I'd thought of that before my blindness a few years back. But what about Paul?"

"Paul?"

"You don't know, do you? I'm sorry. I may be speaking out of school."

"Please. Who is Paul? I must know!" I could hear my voice rising. I was getting out of control. No need to badger this old man because I'd been so freaking stupid.

CHAPTER TWENTY-EIGHT

"I see no harm if Saul is dead. Paul is probably dead too. They were both suffering from the same thing. I'm not sure what that was exactly. Saul said it was complicated. He knew he would be dead soon."

"Dead? Dead from what?" I was getting hysterical.

"I don't rightly know. He thought it had to do with a study he was in as a young child."

"Who is Paul? What do you mean?"

"Paul was his brother." He reached inside his bag and pulled out another photo, this one in an oval frame.

This photo was of Saul, or the person I knew to be Kenneth Lawson, and a boy who looked exactly like Kenneth.

"They're twins?" I asked, realizing now why both men in the alley had looked alike. I hadn't seriously considered that possibility since Kenneth had said he had no family. God, just another lie.

"Yes, monozygotic twins."

"You mean identical? They were identical twins?"

"Yes."

"How did you know them?"

"They both were very bright boys. They became very successful businessmen. Their mother would have been proud. Computers, you know."

"But how did you know them? You said you knew them when they were children. How? Where's their mother?"

"Their mother, Kai, died. She was an African woman who came to America to work. I knew her father in Africa years before when I was a missionary. I was probably the only person she knew in the United States other than her employers. After her death, I visited the boys when they were still youngsters, at her request. That was before I came here to live."

"What happened to their mother? What was her name again?"

"Her name was Kai, pronounced with a silent 'a.' She died in a terrible accident."

"So what do you mean you visited them at her request *after* her death?"

"I mean she asked me to see to them long before she died."

"You act as though she knew she would die."

"Yes, she thought she would die early."

"Whatever happened to her? How did she know?"

"She had a premonition of her death."

"Yeah, right. If there is something wrong with Kenneth or Saul or Paul, I'd like to find them. I think one of them is alive. Do you have any idea where he would be now?"

"I thought you implied that they were dead."

"Well, I don't know. As I said, one of them is dead, but I don't know which one. I can't believe it's Kenneth, though. I just can't believe it."

"Maybe, then, he is with William Delecarte. William was like a father to the two boys after their mother died."

"Delecarte?" I could see the card from Claudette Duvet's house with DELECARTE LABORATORY embossed on it in black ink. "Who is William Delecarte?"

"He is the man Saul's mother worked for. She was their housekeeper. After she died the Delecartes sort of helped the boys until a couple they knew, a black couple, adopted them."

"Where is this couple now?"

"I think they died not too long ago. An accident."

"Do you know their names?"

"I think they lived in Seattle. Their names were Lawson . . . hold on. I have it written someplace."

He rummaged around in his paper bag and finally pulled out a wrinkled slip of paper with jagged, cut edges, obviously how he told one slip of paper from another.

The paper held the names Kenneth and Mabel Lawson, along with a Seattle address. I sighed relief. Kenneth, at least, had not lied about his name. He must have been a "Junior." I don't know why this news soothed me but it did. At least I had known his real name.

"Why did Kenneth—Saul—come to see you recently?"

"I'm afraid if he didn't tell you, I'm not at liberty to."

"That's just great," I said, gritting my teeth to keep from swearing. "Here I am stuck with some daggone diamond, got people chasing me, and I don't know why, and you are not at liberty to tell me." I had not thought about telling him about the diamond; it had just popped out.

"Excuse me. Please repeat what you said about the diamond. You have the diamond?"

"Yes, I have it. Saul, or Kenneth Lawson, left it for me to sell."

"To sell? Are you sure it wasn't Paul? Saul would never sell his heirloom. Never. I don't believe it."

"I don't care if you don't believe it. I have it and he said if I wanted to I could get rid of it. And believe me, at this stage of the game I'd give the thing away."

"You mustn't," the old man whispered, grasping my hand. "Their mother swore me to secrecy before she died." He squeezed my hand. "She came to me and for a minute I was afraid of her. She was so intense. I can see it now. We had walked into the woods. Over there."

He pointed to a wooded area that I could see outside the window.

"You know, in the Church we believe in the possibility of miracles. But not sacrifice. When she came she carried a large gunnysack that she dragged it into the woods with us. She pulled four wooden double cups from a backpack. I'd seen the cups before in Mali. They are the special earthenware reserved for twins. I watched mesmerized even though I should have stopped her. Her long dark fingers pulled a chicken from her sack, a knife from her backpack and slit the chicken's throat. The blood squirted onto her face and hands. The squawking filled the air and I couldn't breathe. I wished to scream but I didn't. I wanted to run away but I could not move."

He grasped my hand tighter. He was horrifying me but I couldn't move either. *Sacrifice.* Even the word scared me.

"The blood hit my face and I touched it. I touched it with my fingers. And I must tell you," he said, leaning into me, whispering, "I felt the hand of God embrace me. Honest. It is the holiest experience I have ever had. I heard her incantations, and even though they were in the Dogon's sacred language, *Sigi so*, I thought I understood it. I was close to God. I was there with God. For the first time in my life I knew God intimately. No intercessor. Just God and myself."

I could see tears streaming down his face. I didn't know if he was hurting, and I wanted to tell him he didn't have to go on if he didn't want to tell me this. But I knew he needed to say it. And I needed to hear it.

"I wanted to stay with Kai in those woods forever. In seconds she had performed a ritual with eight chickens all together. She laid two trapezium-shaped pieces of leather on the ground. Eight cowries were sewn on each one. Out of her bosom she pulled a handkerchief and removed the diamond. She dripped the blood onto the diamond and each leather strap, her incantations getting louder. She raised the knife into the air. I foolishly thought she was going to stab herself. And still I could not move to help her.

"But instead she drove the knife into the ground. And I swear to you upon what is holy, the diamond was there, glowing red in between the two straps. No longer clear like it was when she'd removed it from the handkerchief, but red inside. Glowing there on the ground like a fire. And in that moment I collapsed.

"She helped me up and then in her own gentle way gave me the instructions for keeping the diamond. And then she swore me to secrecy. And until the moment I placed the diamond in Saul and Paul's hands, I never spoke of it. When I gave it to them it was white again.

"The diamond and a necklace is the only thing of their mother's the boys ever had. Saul knew the significance but he told me Paul tried to sell the diamond through some broker without telling him. Saul found out and took the diamond from his brother before the sale. And that's when their trouble began."

"What was it? What trouble? You mean his getting sick?"

"No. The trouble had to do with someone trying to destroy the diamond."

"Destroy it? That doesn't make any sense. Who would destroy a diamond? No one in their right mind."

"I know it doesn't make sense but that's what Saul saw in a vision. And he believed it."

"A vision." Give me a break, I thought. He was probably dreaming like I was last night. I'd heard of vivid dreams before, so real you think you're there, experiencing it. Of course, there is *psychosis*. "Is that what was wrong with him?" I asked. "Was Saul losing his mind? Is that the illness?" I tried to remember if a brain aneurysm had anything to do with mental status. I didn't think so.

"No," he said. Again he reached into the bag, this time pulling out a yellowed black-and-white photo without a frame.

"Their grandfather, Laye, was a holy man in his tribe. His name Laye means consumed by, or surrounded by, light or fire. The Dogon. Oh, what a fascinating people. When I was in Mali, even before the twins were conceived, the grandfather asked me to keep an eye out for the boys when they came to America. Twins are sacred among this tribe, and he knew they would need all the knowledge they could get to take care of their legacy."

The word *legacy* lingered in my head like a splinter.

"So was this wishful thinking on the grandfather's part or are you saying that he knew before they were born they'd be twins and end up in America?"

"The Dogon were a very spiritual people but refused to conform to the Catholic Church, or Islam, for that matter. Yet I had great respect for Laye, even though I was a Catholic priest. I understood holiness in all forms. Laye could predict many things. He told me that their seed would one day help the world understand the two stories of Genesis."

"I don't know what you're talking about. You mean Genesis from the Bible?"

Father Fred nodded.

"I'm afraid I don't know the Bible. And I don't mean to sound flippant or ungrateful, but I don't have time for a lesson right now. I'm trying to understand what is going on and find Kenneth, or Saul, before something happens to him. That is, if Kenneth is alive. I can find him help, I'm sure of it."

"This symbol," he said, showing me a necklace around his neck, "this is a gift Saul and Paul sent to me. And this is their grandfather." He pointed to the photo.

I examined it. The picture was faded but the outfit was the same. He was exactly as I'd seen him, even to the land turtle. It was the old black man in the lean-to, except he had the diamond on his pointer finger. Maybe the missing pointer was on the other hand. "You have no idea how relieved I am," I said. "That explains it. Can I talk to the old man again?"

"Again? He is dead. Someone killed him in Africa years ago."

"Killed him?" My fingers trembled. My body spasmed all over. My stomach involuntarily contracted and I felt all the air leave me in a whoosh. I grabbed for my throat.

"Yes, brutally. Both he and his wife. Tortured. Then murdered. Tragic. He only had one child, Saul and Paul's mother, Kai. She was pregnant at the time. After his death, the Delecartes, who were there working with an anthropologist team, offered her a job in America. I was surprised when I learned she took it. It was not the kind of thing I would have expected her to do. But she was young."

"He can't be dead; the old man can't be dead," I muttered, only half hearing what the monk said. "Impossible. I saw him. I talked to him. Their grandfather. I talked to him."

"My dear, calm down. I'm not sure who you saw or spoke to but it was not the boys' grandfather. Where do you think you saw him?"

"Here. In this place. Last night. Out there." I was losing control. I pointed out the window. "By the woods. This is not funny. Please. This is not entertaining or funny. What kind of trick is this?"

"I assure you, this man, the man in this photo, the twins' grandfather, Laye, has been dead many years. You couldn't have possibly seen him. Or anyone like him, for that matter, not here. He had no brothers or sisters. Unusual for the Dogons. His only heir was his daughter, the twins' mother."

"Who killed them?" I asked. "Maybe people only thought they were dead."

"No. They were dead, all right. As for who killed them, no one knows. Some in their village said it was outsiders and that it was about the diamond."

"The diamond?"

"Yes. When they found the twins' grandparents, the diamond was missing. The grandfather's finger had been cut off."

"Oh my God. No. No. Which finger?"

"As I said, he was a holy man. It would have had to be sacred for him to have a ring on. Let's see, he would have worn it"—he felt his hand, then held up his pointer finger—"here."

I let out a tiny scream. "I can't hear any more," I said loudly. "No. No. *No.*" I think I was screaming. I was lost. Tired. Scared. And now hallucinating. This whole thing had driven me mad.

I could feel Father Fred placing a cup of water in my hand and helping me sip it. The water flowed down my throat, odorless, tasteless and nonexistent, much like the old man.

"Please tell me," I whispered, still shaking. "You don't suppose the diamond that I have is the same one?"

Now I thought he was fainting. His hands went to his face and he turned beet red before whispering, "Do you know about the Ark of the Fox?"

"The Ark of the Fox?" I said, much too loudly. He was scaring me. I recalled the old man's words, drifting slowly upward into my consciousness.

"The boys always knew what the significance of the emblem was. At least Saul did. See the rock attached to my photo album? This symbol was engraved on that rock but it wore off. The boys had the rock with them until they were adults. Then they gave it to me when they received the diamond. The diamond came from the center of a similar rock buried in the earth somewhere in Mali. This photo is from Mali.

"In the forties, their grandfather told me that the rock would become very valuable sometime just before the millennium. People would want to buy it for a lot of money but it wouldn't be for sale then or ever. Others, however, would want to destroy it.

"Laye said that the twins were here to deal with the Ark of the Fox. But the Fox was in the West. The grandfather knew the nature of these boys before they were born. Don't mistake me. Both boys were good children and fine young men, but Paul was always the weakest of the two. He did not embrace his African heritage. As a young child he wrote me once that he thought that they were primitive. On the other hand, Saul always loved his Africanness. He was always the spiritual one, whereas Paul was the practical one. Together they made a great business team. But all of this the grandfather had told me before they were born.

"Later, I asked the twins did they know what the Ark of the Fox meant. And they said, yes, it meant the Fox chased its tail. In the symbolism of the Dogon the Fox is the polar opposite of good. The Fox is the essence of greed."

"Do you know what that means? The Ark of the Fox?" I asked, hoping he'd offer a clearer explanation.

"Other than what I've told you, no. But wait," he said, leaving the room.

Again he left me sitting, only this time I was trembling. Something scary and unnatural was going on and I didn't like it. I couldn't even complete Stephen King's *The Stand* because it seemed too plausible. This was scarier and it didn't seem plausible at all.

I scrambled in my purse. The necklace. I picked up the photo again and looked at the paintings scrawled on the large stone boulders behind Laye. They were of stick men and geometric figures. The writing on the bottom of the photo said, "The *tonu* of the *po pilu*—great vault at Sanga." That meant this place still existed somewhere in Africa. I compared each drawing with the necklace Kenneth had left in the safe deposit box. And then I saw it. The same design.

My hands shook. I felt nauseous. I got up and went into the bathroom across the hall. I splashed water on my face. I looked in the mirror. The puffiness was gone from my face but it was now replaced with fright.

I heard Father Fred tapping his way back into the office.

"Ms. Conley," he called softly.

I slid against the wall. It would be irrational not to answer. But I didn't want to answer. Somehow I felt if I answered this call, I would end up answering a bigger call.

Saul Bernard or Kenneth Lawson, which I still preferred to call him, was dead or his brother was dead or maybe both, and it was something left undone that Kenneth expected me to do. Otherwise, why leave me the diamond?

"Please, come back. It's all right. Everything will be all right." He was pleading, obviously sensing my fear.

I walked out and sat back down. My knees were shaking.

"Here," he said, handing me an envelope. "Take this." He handed me a key. "Their mother, Kai, left both of them letters. They were to have them whenever they were in danger. Maybe they need them now. The key is for a box at the Spring Street post office," he said. "I pay it every month. The box number is on this sheet of paper." He laid the paper on top of the books. "Also, here are some books for you to read. Maybe you can understand the meanings."

I didn't extend my hand. Whatever it was, I didn't want it. "I want to find Saul, not Paul. If I do find Paul, I'll tell him to come and get this from you. . . . I'll be okay. Honest." This is over. If Kenneth, or Saul, is dead, then it's over for me, too. I continued, "I can bring the ring back out here to you and you can give it to Paul if he shows up. How about that?" I asked him, almost begging him to just say yes. "I could do it tomorrow."

He didn't speak.

I hesitated. Should I tell him that there may be people after the ring? Yes, if I bring it and leave it with him, his life may be in danger, too. He has to know.

"Listen . . . " I said, wishing I could take his hand before breaking this news to someone so frail.

He took my hand. "Don't worry. If you decide to bring the diamond out here, it will be fine. I know there may be people searching for it. But I doubt they even know what they're looking for. Let them come. And remember, things are hardly ever as they seem."

I was speechless. At last, I broke the silence and let my emotions take root in voice. "This is scaring me. I'm afraid."

He handed me the books with the key on top.

"Fear is good. It will keep you safe."

I reluctantly looked at the slip of paper. I read "To Akwette," and "To Akuette," and underneath "Kai box 1403." I asked him, "Do you know what Kai means? Or the other names?"

"Yes. It means 'remember.' I don't know what the boys' names mean, I'm afraid. She would never tell me. Now I must go. I must go to prayer," he said, disappearing out the door.

"One more thing," I asked, running after him, grasping the sleeve of his robe.

"Yes?"

"Do you know what the term 'primordial seed' would mean to the old man? That is, if there was an old man."

"You are serious, aren't you? You did see something or someone."

I shook my head, unable to trust my voice to spring from my mouth without screaming.

"It means the beginning. The original. To the Dogon, the primordial seed is the beginning of life on earth. It is the essence of all beings, all things, created by their God, Amma."

I wanted to run after him. To cry and beg him to take this burden from me. I didn't want to know about any of this. I didn't want to remember any of it. I wanted to forget it all—even Kenneth Lawson. I didn't have time for this shit. The diamond wasn't my legacy. I didn't marry Kenneth Lawson. I didn't have any obligation to anyone except maybe to give this man the diamond back. Darn, he was about to get on my nerves.

What was I thinking? Probably nothing he says is true. He's probably senile or worse. Maybe being stuck way out here can make you a little crazy. Hell, a whole lot crazy.

I called the cab company and asked if Mr. Shepard was on duty. They said they'd send him right away.

I sat out at the lake, waiting. Waiting and not thinking. My fingers clutched the key and the slip of paper. I balled the paper up and threw it in the trash can and then walked back to the parking lot. I would mail Father Fred his key later. I was finished with this. If Kenneth Lawson was still alive, I didn't want to know now. It was over. Done with. I'd mail the diamond back out here and that would be the end of it.

I flipped through the three books and a booklet Father Fred had given me, balancing them in my arms.

179

I saw the Yellow Cab pull up.

"Good morning. Ms. Conley, isn't it? I'm glad you stayed. I forgot to tell you people could stay overnight." He paused. "Are you all right? You look different."

"No. No, I'm not all right," I whispered and climbed into the backseat, wishing I'd not asked for him. Why did I? Normally I hated getting a cab driver who was familiar.

As he drove onto the paved drive I looked back to see if Father Fred was watching. I didn't see anyone.

Speaking of gone mad, I'd been out here only a few hours and dag-gone if I hadn't gone crazy.

"Stop!" I yelled so loudly, Mr. Shepard jumped.

"I left something," I heard myself say. I felt like it wasn't me saying it but some far-off, distant Patricia Conley. I jumped from the cab and ran back toward the lake and the trash can. I fished the paper out and stuck it in my purse. I looked up, expecting to see Father Fred smiling at me. No one was there.

I walked back to the cab and got in. I gave Mr. Shepard Carol's address and squeezed my eyes shut to block out my madness. I sniffed the air. And for the second time in forty-eight hours I prayed—this time, that Mr. Shepard had sprayed rose perfume into the air.

"The things which one draws,
one draws the drawings in order to know
the things which will come in the future."
—The Dogon

CHAPTER TWENTY-NINE

I removed the key from what Carol calls her clever hiding place. The key is attached to the outside of the mailbox by a rubber band. Carol says that when someone broke into her house, before they'd kicked the door off its hinges, it had smashed into her curio cabinet, breaking her collection of decorated eggs. Since then she wanted the thief to use the damn key.

I fished the disk Jeff had made out of my purse. I'd said I was done with this. Yeah, right. I had to at least find out what was on it. I'd thought about reading it before, but in foster homes you learn not to pry in other people's stuff. But that wasn't really why I didn't look. I was too scared. Now, instead, I phoned Carol at the office and left her a message that I was at her house.

Time was racing by me faster than a meteorite, but I was really too overwhelmed to read the disk. I decided the books Father Fred had given me would be the safest bet. I was wrong. Nothing was safe.

The Sirius Mystery by Robert K. Temple appeared the most reader-friendly so I began with the section called "The Knowledge of the Dogon." The introduction talked about astronomers, star systems and the like. According to Temple, the brightest star in our sky, Sirius, is so bright because it's close, large, bigger than the sun and other nearby stars. He began by saying that there is no reason for an astronomer to believe that Sirius, unlike other stars with circling planets, such as Tau Ceti or Epsilon Eridani, would have intelligent life. I was in no mood for an astronomy lesson. But on page 18, he finally moved to the Dogon. Just as Father Fred had told me, the Dogons are from the area now known as Mali. This tribe and three other similar tribes all hold as a part of their religious tradition a belief system centered around the star Sirius, which includes information that supposedly is impossible for them to know.

I continued reading, my mouth open.

I stopped reading and made a cup of coffee. I was tired and spent but I was trying to relate what all this had to do with what had been happening. I decided in some way the diamond was the key—but how? I sat back down on the couch and picked up reading on the subject of the Nommo. The Nommo, according to the Dogons, is the name for the founder who came here from the Sirius system to set up a society on the earth. Wait. *What?* Does this mean they believe we somehow originated in outer space? Come on. Give me a break. The last people I suspect of being UFO watchers are Africans. I mean, face it, how many black people have you seen talking about being abducted?

But the Dogons also believe this Nommo will come back at some point, when a certain star appears again. And when this signal appears balance will be restored to mankind in this universe.

I couldn't imagine the sophistication it would take to even make up a story like this. Okay, if this were really what the Dogons believed—and Kenneth, his brother and the grandfather were all Dogons—I still wasn't sure how this connected to what had been going down. Maybe if I could find out what "the Sigui" meant. The old man had told me the diamond had to be returned exactly one year before the ceremony of the Sigui.

I picked up another book, *The Pale Fox*, and checked the table of contents, then read one passage. According to the authors, Marcel Griaule and Germaine Dieterlen, every sixty years the Dogons hold a ceremony called the Sigui. This ceremony would somehow renovate the world. Supposedly a fault in a rock in the center of a village lights up with a red glow in the year preceding the ceremony. But even before this red glow appears, elongated gourds, which no one has planted, are discovered in a spot outside the village. When these signs are manifested, that's when the calculation for the time of the ceremony is performed. At the ceremony, after two thirty-year intervals, a sign of the Kanaga mask is drawn. But the grandfather, Laye, or whoever it was I'd seen, had told me the ceremony of the Sigui needed to be complete one year before the eighth articulation. According to this book, until an incident with the eighth chief, all the ceremonies had taken place on the seventh articulation. This was confusing me. But one idea stuck in my mind: Suppose the diamond, the rare red diamond I now possessed, was what really gave off the glow? What would happen if it wasn't there?

I picked up another book, *Conversations with Ogotemmeli* by Marcel Griaule, and flipped the pages. On page 127 I saw the Dogon cap, the exact one the grandfather had had on his head. I also read that a turtle is a sacred animal to the Dogon. That might explain the turtle the old man was feeding.

Then I read on the next page about the dual soul and circumcision. It seems the Dogon believe that each person is born with two souls, one a male, the other a female. His or her body is one, but the spiritual part is two. The Dogon believe children have their own life, their own path and their own possessions. I was mystified when I read the next paragraph. "The infant arrives in the world endowed with two principles of different sexes, and in theory belongs as much to one as to the other; his person sex is undifferentiated. In practice, society recognizes him by anticipating the sex which he has in appearance. Symbolically, however, his spiritual androgyny is still present. 'Nothing in them is rigid,' says Ogotemmeli." The Dogon believe we are both male and female.

The Dogons perform circumcision because of their belief that one soul must be dominant in order to keep the child from growing up confused. Both the men and women are circumcised to sacrifice blood back to the earth, since according to them, each soul is connected to the earth. Fascinating. Wouldn't this explain why we have people who are attracted to the same sex in this country? But I couldn't accept any explanation for the practice of circumcision. This excuse didn't make me feel any better about it. Actually, what was so wrong with being both male and female spiritually? Was that *me* thinking this? Oh God. What was happening to me?

I picked up the one remaining book, Genevieve Calame Griaule's *Words and the Dogon World*. Some of Marcel Griaule's work, including the work of his daughter, Genevieve, had been written in French and translated to English.

I decided to look up the Ark of the Fox and came away with the understanding that this was comparable to a greedy person who would cut off his own nose to spite his face. Hmm. And then as I read the next quote, my heart stopped. "The eighth articulation will be in the sex, the reproductive organ that will permit the adult to give birth to a new being." I read it again. A new being? What could that mean? My head hurt like hell. I couldn't read any more of this.

I turned on Carol's computer and thanked her for not using passwords. I put the disk into the computer and read. I read until my neck ached. It was four o'clock before I got up. I fixed another cup of coffee and sat at the table eating powdered doughnuts.

Carol came in the door with a bag of groceries. "Boy, am I glad to see you."

"Hey, how are you?" I said, powder all over my mouth, hoping my face did not give away my inner fears and confusion. Too many people had seen me vulnerable lately. It had to stop.

"I'm okay, but how are you?" She put the groceries down on the counter and walked over and sat down at the table. She picked up a doughnut. "So what's up with you?"

I wiped my mouth with a napkin. I could tell she didn't know whether to ask me questions or leave me alone. Against my own nature and probably my better judgment, I wanted to talk. I was as full as a tick but I needed a push.

"You okay?" she asked, smiling. "Hey, I'm not going to press you." She took a bite of doughnut. "Your business is your business."

The lines were drawn. Often to a secretive person, a line drawn is all she needs to know that you're not going to step over her boundary or *on* her.

"Today I read the most incredibly unbelievable shit I've ever read. Of course, I spent my morning hearing the most incredibly unbelievable shit, so now all that is left is for me to speak the most incredibly unbelievable shit to you and I will have come full circle."

"Go for it," she said. "But can we sit in there?" she asked, pointing to the living room. "This chair is kicking my butt."

"Now that you mention it. You sure don't plan to have people dilly-dallying after they've eaten your food, do you?" I chuckled. It had been a while since I'd laughed and it felt good.

She laughed too and grabbed the doughnut plate. "Let's don't leave this."

We settled on the sofa and I said to her, "What I'm about to tell you will self-destruct when I'm done, meaning this is some weird, scary, secretive shit."

"Get on with it. I love weird, remember?"

She was right. Even though she had figured out the psychic hot lines were phony, she still believed in a heck of a lot of mumbo jumbo. I found it disconcerting that a sharp, organized feminist could believe in some of the shit she believed in, but hey, that's life, nothing but contradictions.

"Okay, I don't know whether this was a science fiction novel synopsis or if Kia Mutota or whoever compiled it was for real. Let me start with first things first."

I told Carol about my meeting with Kia Mutota, the diamond and the disk.

"By all means," she said. "Now, can you get on with this? I don't need all this foreplay. I still believe in the tooth fairy."

"Okay. Okay. Kenneth Lawson is not Kenneth's real name. His christened name is Saul Bernard. Named after Saint Bernard. I'm sure you can relate to that. Anyway, that's not the half of it. He's a twin. A monozygotic twin."

"What the fuck is that?"

"Identical. He was an identical twin. His brother's name is Paul and one of them is in that morgue and now I'm not sure which one. They were both originally from Africa."

"You mean they're African."

"You're a genius."

"What about their father?"

"What about him?" I hadn't thought about the father. I'd assumed automatically that the father was African. "Maybe you *are* a genius. Who was their father? I never thought of that and I didn't ask the monk about it."

"The monk?"

"Yes, that's another story. I'll tell you later. First, let me tell you about what is on the disk. That's where I should pick this up." I couldn't begin with what I'd read in the books. It was overwhelming me in a different way. I just couldn't explain what the words I'd read actually meant in real time. So I said to Carol, leaning over in a gesture of intimacy, "Kia Mutota was friends with Claudette Duvet before she came to work in Atlanta. The two of them were immigrants from Trinidad by way of France and a few northern cities in the U.S.

"For the last couple of years, Claudette Duvet and her twin sister were sick."

"What twin sister? You mean this woman Kenneth was messing with had a twin too? Come on. Next you'll tell me these women were identical twins."

I nodded. "Yes. You're on target now. But you haven't heard the half of it. Last year Marvette Duvet, Claudette's sister, got sicker. It turned out she was pregnant by a Ghanaian. But during her birthing she had a brain aneurysm and died."

"What about her baby? Did it live?"

"Stillborn."

"Oh my God."

"That's not all. The certified midwife practitioner, a Trinidadian, was a friend of theirs. So she removed samples of the baby's blood and tissue along with Marvette's tissue for Claudette."

"Why on earth would she do that? You've got me in suspense here."

"The baby had not developed properly."

"What do you mean? Was it deformed?"

"Some would say yes, others no."

"What the fuck does that mean?"

I grimaced. It was then I noticed that each time I uttered a curse word or heard Carol say one, I felt a tiny ripple up above my stomach. Butterflies, sort of. Weird. "What was your question?" I asked to see if it would happen again.

"I said, 'What the fuck does that mean?' Don't make me into a parrot, okay?"

There it was again. "Carol, I keep telling you, you should do stand-up. To make a long story short, the baby was white."

"Oh, I got it. You mean it was an albino?"

"No. The baby was white—you know, Indo-European."

"So? You mean biracial?"

"Nope. Not biracial. Are you listening? The baby's father was African, pure African. The Duvets were Trinidadian and could trace their ancestry straight back to Africa. But according to Kia, after an evaluation of the baby's DNA and other factors, genetically this baby was classified Caucasian. See?"

"Not really. Unless you're trying to tell me she'd been artificially inseminated, and like with the woman in the Netherlands a few years back who had white and black twins, somebody had fucked up?"

"No. No artificial insemination. I mean what I'm saying. White."

"Don't buy it. Somebody is pulling your leg. That can't be right, and you know it," Carol said.

"It's what's in this report. I don't know. Maybe Dr. Mutota was unstable. All I know is what I've read. I don't believe it either but I do know she must have believed it enough to get her butt killed."

"Listen to what you're saying here. I don't think you're getting this. What you're saying is that two black people had a *white* baby." Her face became drawn as the implication settled in her mind. "That's impossible. Somebody is lying. Maybe it's a lie to get some research money or something. Just because somebody writes something doesn't mean it's true. We should know that. That report's pure shit."

"If it's shit, I didn't write it. That's the deal on the disk. Dr. Mutota studied the samples from this baby and the brain cells of Claudette Duvet's sister. In examining the aneurysm, she detected a new genetic formation in Marvette's pineal and pituitary glands.

"Dr. Mutota asked around about it and found that there had been some early research on genetic pigmentation but that it had been abandoned. One of the doctors who had conducted the research was working at the CDC with Dr. Mutota.

"An experiment, code name Gemini, had been conducted in the early fifties. They named it Gemini because all the kids were twins. You know, the astrologcal sign. Whatever the experiments were, they'd originated because of some information gleaned from an African tribe called the Dogons. Among this tribe the date of births for kids was important—you know, some kind of astrology mumbo."

"I'm lost. And so are you if you believe this shit. But go on, tell me more," Carol said, signing to me to hurry up by flapping her hands in that "gimme, gimme" gesture.

"Guess how Dr. Mutota made the connection that this particular Gemini study had something to do with Claudette and her sister?"

"Duh. How can I guess that?"

"The astrological sign for Gemini. Claudette Duvet had told Dr. Mutota that she and Marvette had taken part in an experiment when they were children. During their early years in the program, all the kids had rings given to them. Supposedly Gemini rings."

"Twins. I suppose I could see that" Carol admitted. "If I knew somebody had been in an experiment as a child and that they were a twin, I'd first search for experiments that dealt with the subject matter and then narrow it down to studies that had twins. Then if I'd known that the children had Gemini rings and found a study called Gemini, I might put that together. But I'd be damned if I'd believe anything like this bullshit," she said.

I felt it. The ripple. But then my brain had a ripple of its own. I jumped up and ran to the guest bedroom. I grabbed the briefcase and brought it to the couch. I pulled out the thick document.

"Oh, so you're going to stop telling the story right in the middle to read, huh?"

"No. Let me show you something," I said, handing Carol the document with the second page folded back. "I'm not too swift when it comes to astrological signs, but isn't this one of them? Here. This?" I pointed to the sign I'd seen repeated in the document.

"That's the Gemini sign, all right. Where'd you get this?"

"It's what Dr. Mutota gave me before she died."

"So this doctor somehow found this document on the Gemini experiments, and then gave it to you, a total stranger?"

"I don't know that part."

Carol interrupted my thoughts. "And—"

"Well, that's all I can tell you now because that's all I know. Other than the list of names and the few pages I described to you, the decoding didn't go any further. Yes. There's more, but I don't have it." I didn't want to admit Jeff still had the original disk.

"Don't you see? This is a hoax," Carol said. "It wouldn't be the first time. Remember the time scientists claimed they'd unraveled the mystery of cold fusion? This is fucking crazy."

"Yes, I know. But explain it. Why would a respected doctor who works at the CDC go to this kind of risk for some nonsense? Dr. Mutota wouldn't get anything out of this and neither would the twins. And what about this Dogon stuff? I've read some of the books. There's been a lot written about this tribe having some knowledge that nobody can explain where it came from or why they have it. Okay. I'm not saying this having a white baby stuff is true. But let's say even a trace of it is true. How about maybe the twins were getting together to sue the shit out of whoever did the experiments?"

"So what's the upshot of all this, then? What is the conclusion? And what the fuck are you getting involved for?"

"I don't know the upshot. That's it. This is basically all that I know. I'm not sure of how it is all connected. I'm not even sure how Kenneth fits in it. Maybe the Duvets turned to Kenneth because they were both twins. Shit, maybe they met by accident and fell in love after Kenneth met me. I didn't get any more off the disk. What can I say? Shoot me."

"Don't worry, if what you say is true, someone probably will if you're not careful. This is scary, powerful shit you've fallen into, if it is remotely true. I say drop it. Now. Walk away. I still don't see what this has to do with you and Kenneth Lawson."

"Do you recognize this symbol?" I said, showing her the Gemini sign on the page again.

"I told you it's the Gemini sign. The twins." A bell went off in her head. I saw it zinging her memory.

"You got it. Kenneth Lawson's ring. Remember? He wore it all the time. That damn Gemini ring. Do you know what this means? I don't remember the ring at the morgue. It wasn't in the things she gave me in the envelope either. It means maybe that wasn't Kenneth in the morgue but his brother."

"Or it means Kenneth Lawson and his twin both had rings. See, even that dog won't hunt. And anyway, if it's the other way around, and Kenneth's not dead, then where is he? I know this hurts you but you're going to have to face this. And if Kenneth's still out there, then wouldn't he have contacted you? Even if it wasn't Kenneth, it seems the other twin would have found you by now."

"Well, whoever is in the morgue was coming to see me because Lorie told me they found him in the back of my house, in a blue car."

"Not *whoever*. You mean Kenneth. Kenneth was coming to see you."

"No, I don't know that it was Kenneth."

Carol frowned at me.

I continued, undaunted. "Either way, one of them could still be alive. I figure if Kenneth got shot he's probably too hurt to tell whatever hospital he's in to call me. Maybe he's in a coma. What I'm going to do is first thing tomorrow, I'll contact the other twins who were in the study. I have to know more about that study."

"No, you don't. You don't have to know jackshit. You can *walk* from this crap, I'm telling you. This is real fucking shit. You get it? This is not a fucking news story. The *Atlanta Guardian* doesn't pay you enough to get killed for a story. This isn't fucking Watergate status."

"Hey, I'm *not* walking. *I must* know if Kenneth is still alive. Now I know there is a chance he did love me. I realize he knew things that he couldn't tell me. But I also know some part of him wanted me to do something about this."

"How? How do you know that?"

"I just know." I got up and went to the bathroom. I couldn't tell her what I suspected about the diamond being more than what it seemed. I imagine Kenneth didn't underestimate my loyalty to him. He probably thought I'd sniff this out at a later date. He practically said that in his letter.

First I needed to talk to some of the other twins, and see if any of them were sick. I also needed to know who exactly conducted the experiments. "Darn," I said, as the horrors of the Tuskegee syphilis studies swam into my mind. What the heck had they given these twins?

It was time to call Bobby Stevenson, the young hacker. He must know something by now.

When I came back into the room, Carol was in the kitchen cleaning up her melted ice cream. She'd left the grocery bag on the counter and forgotten it.

I dialed Bobby the Hacker from her guest room.

He answered on the third ring. "Yes, Mother."

"I'm flattered but I'm not your mother."

"Thank the Hive Master," he said. "She keeps calling me every few minutes asking me what I'm doing."

"Sorry. Listen, I hate to be rushing you but I'm sort of on a dead-line," I said, offering him a journalist's excuse for impatience.

"Yeah. Well, I checked out those pawns for you with some of the most high dudes. Heavy hacking shit. These pawns cloaked-and-daggered back."

"I'm sorry. You can tell me about whatever it is you said another time. Right now I need the information, Bobby." *You nut.*

"It's true that the Claudette woman crashed on a work visa a year ago."

"Meaning?" My mind jumbled up worse than a Scrabble game.

"It means she was working on a French visa, but check this out. You know the other man you told me about—what was his name?"

I could hear papers rustling. This was the clearest he'd ever talked to me, so I figured in his world this might be sticky. After all, he was a child.

"Yeah. The dude, Kenneth Lawson. I couldn't find any jones on his being a teach but he was a heavy dude. Working man. He owned part of a computer company with his parents and brother until a year ago. He lost everything, man. Go figure."

"What are you talking about? Lost everything?"

"Check it. It all went kaboom."

I couldn't take any more. I couldn't ask him what he meant. I couldn't take another second of this talk. I'd find out myself later. Now I wanted to rest. "Thanks. Thanks, Bobby," I almost whispered. At least now I knew for sure who the real Kenneth Lawson was.

"Hey, one more thing," he said.

"Yes?" I said, not sure I could digest one more thing.

The jolt hit me in the gut. Evidently, I couldn't compute it in my brain's computer, because I said, "Please. I didn't hear you. What did you say?"

"I said I think the feds might have been watching Kenneth Lawson. There's a flag on the file."

I was speechless. My head spun around. *Exorcist* had nothing on me. "Watching him for what?"

"I'm not sure. The tag only has '*D heist.*'"

What the heck was going on? "D heist"? That could mean only one thing. Did the feds think Kenneth stole the diamond? Maybe that's what Father Fred meant by Kenneth's troubles. Maybe after his brother tried to sell the diamond, the feds or somebody wanted to know where a black man got a diamond like that. That could be it. But then, the feds wouldn't try to kill anybody without a trial. Would they? There seemed to be no connections that made any sense, and yet they somehow fit together. How, I couldn't figure.

"You there? You okay, reporter dude?" He made few distinctions between gender titles.

"Yes. Yes. I guess," I said, still dazed. "Can you run the same check on this name?" Then with a churning stomach, I added Jeff Samuels's name. Could I pick them or what?

"Bomb, but I'm morphing. My mom is freak right now. So I'll hook you up on Thursday at the Red Light Cafe around 3 P.M. You know the landing?"

"I guess you're saying your parents are after you about hacking and you'll meet me there instead. Okay, if you say so." *Nut.*

CHAPTER THIRTY

Carol yelled from the kitchen, "Want to eat?"

Until she asked the question I had forgotten I was starving. After dinner, I stretched out on the bed, mulling over what I'd do next. Jeff Samuels's smile danced in my mind and I shut it off by creating a pencil and erasing it.

The phone rang.

I stopped breathing, as if that might help me hear Carol answering in the other room. A few seconds later she stood at the door.

"It's for you."

I didn't have to ask who it was. The smirk on her face told me. I considered supplying her great joy and saying I wasn't there. But another part of me tugged inside and I lifted the receiver.

"Shit," she said, glaring at me like I was a teenager who'd violated a phone curfew.

"Hello," I said into the phone. I looked up. Carol rested against the door frame. She wasn't going anywhere.

"Carol. Please," I said, pointing to the receiver. "Is this for you?"

"No, and I'm glad it's not. He's trouble, I tell you."

"*Carol*," I said with more emphasis.

She stood her ground long enough to reiterate her displeasure. Then she stomped away.

"What was that about?" Jeff Samuels asked.

"Nothing. How are you?"

"I was calling to ask you the same thing."

"I'm okay. Tired. Could I call you tomorrow?" Why was I being nice to him?

"I had something else in mind."

"Like what?"

"Well, if you let me pick you up, I'll give you a lesson that I'm sure you want to have."

"If you think I want to sleep with you again, you're out of your mind."

"You have a dirty mind, Patricia. I was thinking you might want to finish the encryption on your disk. In case you need more of the information."

"And who's going to show me how to do that? Not you, who knows nothing about computers." The minute I said it, I wondered how he knew my encryption hadn't been completed. I didn't even know it when I left his house. Maybe this was my opportunity to snoop in his shit. Find out about him.

"I can show you how to run the encryption software to completion and you can let the machine do the work. Honest. I only want to help you."

"I heard a fable like that once. If I'm not mistaken it's what the crocodile said when he offered to take the monkey across the river."

"Okay. I see our truce is over. No problem. Call me tomorrow."

I felt like I had a bit part in the movie *The Year of Living Dangerously,* because I said, "Give me thirty minutes and you can come get me."

"I'll be right there. I'm not far away. I happened to eat near Carol's neighborhood."

"Right. And I'm Snow White." He obviously anticipated I'd say yes.

I needed the thirty minutes to tell Carol I was leaving and keep her from wrestling me to the floor. She could be so protective once she decided she was your friend. She was loyal and that's one of the things I appreciated about her.

She was also loyal to black literature. The latest argument we'd had was over a black romance, *The Way Home* by Angela Benson. Carol believed it was my civic duty to buy a copy since there were only a handful of black women writing romance and this Angela was local. I believed that was bullshit. But Carol bugged me, so I finally bought the book. And after reading it I respected the task Benson had had before her: to create romance in a community that believed itself devoid of good men. Tough job.

Now, upon reflection, I should have hugged Carol for reminding me there was still hope. Sometimes an outsider can see what you cannot. Kenneth Lawson may very well have been a good man.

It's weird. The night I completed the book, Carol and I got together at my house and talked late into the night. I told her some war stories of things I'd endured with black men. And she told me her own war stories with white men. It became clear we'd fought the same battles. But as we began to talk about our male friends, it occurred to me that, much too often, the nice guys could have sat chatting with us about all the women who'd dumped *them*. For me, males and females were not that different. I didn't trust either gender. That was the crux of the problem. I'd confirmed that money was not the root of all evil, but rather the pursuit of power, whether by a man or a woman. That's what made people ruthless. If power was involved, they could all be a bitch.

Now I was going to have to watch her trip out on me when I told her Jeff Samuels was picking me up.

"Hey, you're grown. I've been there, done that."

"What have you done?" I asked, my hands on my hips, foot tapping.

"Waited to exhale."

"It is not like that. I'm not waiting to exhale. I've been exhaling all my life, with or without a man. It's the one thing I have always known. Something you fail to understand is that the answers for me don't lie in the dicks of men. Somewhere inside me the answer is buried so deep I can't get to it. But whatever it is, it's between me and me. Kenneth knew that, and if Jeff gets confused, I'll make sure he knows it too."

She didn't speak for a moment. Then she said, "You know, you've really got your shit more together than most of us, even if you are messed up."

"Is that a compliment?" I asked, laughing.

"Some of us have to die trying to figure out what you said."

"Well, now that I've told you, it won't have to be you."

We both laughed, and a horn blew. "I'm not even ready." I stuck my head out the door and waved so Jeff wouldn't think about coming in. That might be too much for Carol to take. I picked up a few of the things she'd left for me to wear and pushed them into her overnight bag. My toilet stuff was already packed.

On my way out I stopped. "See you tomorrow. Okay?"

"Sure. Don't do anything I wouldn't do."

"If I followed that adage I wouldn't be going, huh?"

"You damn straight."

Jeff sat on the step waiting for me. "She doesn't like me. Why?"

"I don't know. What does it matter?"

"No problem. Let's go." He reached for my bag and I let him have it. Then he took the briefcase handle. I pulled back. "That's okay. I've got it."

We didn't talk. I rode and listened to "Deep Forest." This was different from the first music I had heard at Jeff's house. It was some combination of Eastern music. Less beat but still soothing.

He rested his hand on mine. He might as well have placed a hot iron on my thigh. I could feel his heat through my hand. Every bump in the road sent tiny shivers wrenching throughout my body. I involuntarily leaned toward him like he might be a magnet and me a giant piece of steel.

I don't know that I ever wanted anyone to hold me so badly in my life. This time it was different, though. The hollowness that usually lurked in the pit of my stomach like a steely-fingered Freddy Krueger was missing. The longing to belong, gone.

At the cabin Jeff set up the computer as promised. And I put the disk in and sat on the couch.

"Do you want to talk?" he asked, coming over to the couch.

"No. I'm tired." I closed my eyes and leaned my forehead over on a pillow.

"Me too. But I thought maybe we could take a walk before bed."

"I'm not sleeping with you."

"Didn't expect you to. I'm a man, Patricia, not a cowboy counting notches on a belt. I have no kids and if I did, I'd be with their mother. I don't sleep around. I've never slept with a woman that I didn't love. Can you say the same?"

I hung my head. I wasn't loose, but I sure couldn't say I'd loved the few men I'd slept with. He got me on that one. I could be without a man. Didn't feel one was essential to my life. Owned a darn good vibrator for many years. But occasionally after a long dry spell I'd dated a guy that I wouldn't have taken home to Mama even if I'd had one. I shook my head.

"Then don't put me in the little boy category. I didn't invite you out here to trick you into bed."

"Okay. I got your point."

"By the way, I went by Ira's yesterday looking for you. His clerk told me you and he had stepped out. What was that about?"

His question caught me off guard. I sat up and my body tensed. "Why were you looking for me there?"

"I know you and he are friends. You told me, remember?"

"No, I don't remember. Why would I have told you that?"

"Once when we went on one of your escort-type dates together, you told me that he inspected all your jewelry."

"When? When did I say that? I can't imagine why I'd tell you that." My mind reviewed our conversations as I spoke.

"Hey, don't be so uptight. You had on a necklace. I said the necklace was Japanese pearls. You said, no, you knew for a fact they were Hawaiian because your friend Ira checked out all the jewelry you bought."

I didn't recall the conversation but I couldn't swear it didn't happen; my pearls *were* Hawaiian. I gave him the benefit of the doubt, but . . . "So, I still don't get why you'd go there to find me."

"I saw you go in there earlier when I rode past. Then I came back around and you had left, that's all. I beeped you twice."

I got my beeper from my purse. His number was there, indicating two phone calls. I still didn't believe him. Something wasn't right. Maybe he knew about the diamond. He could kill me out here and no one would find me for a long time.

But Carol knew I was with him. He'd have to kill her too, to keep her from accusing him, considering how she felt about him. It's not like he didn't know it.

"Don't be paranoid. Be careful," I heard Grandma Dixon saying to me. She said that whenever I was accusing someone of being racist or not treating me fairly because I was black or an orphan. For me the two states of being were almost synonymous. "You stay in control. What they feeling don't matter, it's what they do you gonna have to deal with. Feelings are worth diddly-squat in life," she'd say.

"Why did you invite me? Really?" I asked him.

"I needed to sleep. But more than sleep, I needed to know you were safe. So I decided the one way to ensure that you were safe and to get some sleep was to have you here with me." He came over to the sofa and leaned close enough that his lips were a hair's breadth from touching mine. "I love you and I couldn't bear to see anything happen to you. It's that simple." And with that he pulled away.

Thank God. I'd fought my body every millisecond he was there. He was getting close to me in more ways than one. My heart was pounding.

"I've got to get up early in the morning, so I think I'm going to bed," he said, staring at me, his eyebrows raised.

I tilted my head. "So why are you standing there?"

"I'm on the couch, remember? You're upstairs."

"Oh," I said, feeling a little embarrassed. I'd wanted him to sit next to me. I stood up and picked up my things.

"You know what?"

"What?"

"If you don't mind, I'll come up with you and tuck you in."

I shrugged my shoulders. It was the game. The game women play that probably gets men confused when they're with the wrong woman at the wrong time and she abruptly stops playing. You know the game. You're saying no, acting yes. There are men who never learn when it's time to quit playing.

I didn't usually play the game, except tonight I realized I was playing it for all it was worth. I needed to quit.

"Look," I said. "I don't want to play a game. I want to be with you, but I'm not ready mentally or emotionally, for that matter. I suppose I wanted you to offer to hold me." There, I'd said it. Now I was out of the game. There would be no winner take all.

"No problem. I can do that," he said, walking over closer to me. "To be honest, it's what I would enjoy most of all. To stroke you until you fall asleep, knowing you were safe, here with me."

I walked up the stairs and quickly got ready for bed. I snuggled under the covers and waited for him to come up.

When he appeared he had on a navy-blue terry-cloth robe and if he'd been liquid I would have drunk him up. He slid in bed beside me and I smelled the odor of a cologne I didn't recognize. "What is that smell?"

"Arrid Extra Dry for women," he said.

"Don't mess with me. That's not what I'm talking about and you know it. Your cologne?"

"Pheromone. Now go to sleep."

"I have a question to ask, and I'd like an honest answer."

"What?"

"What were you doing at the Biggers's golf tournament with John Biggers himself? I saw your photo in the newspaper and I know you couldn't have been merely working security. It doesn't work that way in the good-old-boys club; neither the caddy nor the security guards get photo ops."

I could feel his body tensing, his breathing growing heavy. He leaned on his elbow, his face almost touching mine. He smiled. "You really don't trust me, do you? You know what I can't understand? If you don't trust me, why are you with me now?"

It was a good question and I didn't have an answer. Women. I shrugged. I couldn't answer him. I was torn between wanting him and distrusting him. I also felt guilt, but like a fly landing on flypaper, here I was.

He smiled. "It's an earth-shattering story. The Atlanta police sponsored me to play for the charity. I'm a good golfer and it was for a great cause. That's the truth. Take it or leave it."

"Okay. Don't get hostile," I said, knowing full well he hadn't said it in a hostile manner, but instead an apologetic one. Still, I didn't believe him. Atlanta police didn't do that kind of sponsoring to my knowledge. No. I didn't believe him one bit. But he was right. If I didn't trust him, what was I doing lying in bed with him?

I'd asked myself the question and the only answer I had was that even though everything didn't seem right about him, when I was with him it felt right.

Grandma Dixon always told me, "Trust your gut." Of course, on the other hand, that's how I'd ended up chasing Kenneth Lawson, so really, I should be more leery about her advice.

I decided to play along with his game, whether I trusted him or not. Which of course I didn't.

The old saying is that if you don't trust a man, you don't love him. I didn't believe that anymore. Shit. I didn't trust *myself*.

I snuggled my head in Jeff's arm and waited for him to make his move. Soon I heard his breathing change to light snoring, and I knew then that he was not playing the game either.

When I thought he was sound asleep I slipped down to the computer. It was on. I inspected Jeff's briefcase and found what I suspected. He'd already made a copy of my disk and labeled it disk one of five, only he forgot to tell me. Yeah, right. I sneaked back upstairs and slid in bed. At least now I knew. He was full of shit.

In the morning, I woke up in bed alone. I smelled bacon and coffee strong in the air. I dressed and walked downstairs. He'd set the table for one. "I thought you might like some breakfast before we leave."

"Thanks. Where are we going?"

"I don't know where you're going, but I'll be happy to take you. I happen to have a meeting around ten, and then I'm free. I could pick you up for lunch if you want, around noon."

"That sounds okay. Did the disk get decoded?" I held my breath as I hoped he'd answer me honestly.

"I don't know. I don't think it's complete. It's only on disk two. It takes time. They were changing the encryptions as they went along. You can check. You didn't want me to see it, remember?"

"Then how did you know it wasn't complete?"

"How'd I know? You think I looked, don't you? Well, I didn't. When the program is done, it tells me how much of the encryption has been completed. In your case it said twenty-five percent of disk two, and it still has three more after that. I think you owe me a tad bit more trust by now. Don't you?"

"Yeah, right. I do owe you," I said. He wasn't going to tell me about the copy he'd made.

He continued. "But even if I did look, curiosity alone never killed a person, only a cat."

"*Only* a cat?"

"I'm sorry. I forgot about your cat. Eat up. I've got to finish dressing and then we're off. Tallyho."

Tallyho . . . Who are you? I mouthed to myself. The breakfast was delicious. I knew who he was. He was a chef. And a big liar.

I had better things to ponder. I was still debating what I was going to do next. I opened my purse and checked the envelope I'd placed the key in with the slip of paper. It was sealed, with no sign of resealing.

I needed to do two things: Investigate the other twins in the study and find out what happened to Kenneth Lawson and his adopted family. I also needed to find out about this doctor at the CDC. Maybe he could decipher the document for me. It was early—7 A.M.

I asked Jeff to drop me off at Carol's. I could dig up past newspaper articles in Seattle about Kenneth or his family and try the Internet for the twins.

When we arrived at Carol's he smiled, got out and came around to open my door. I stepped out. He came close to me. Too close, because I wanted to kiss him.

"Be careful," he whispered in my ear.

"Be careful. What do you think I'm doing, for God's sake?"

"Patricia, there are people after you. Remember that. Stick with your news stories. Don't keep looking for Kenneth Lawson. He's dead, remember?"

"I remember," I said, teeth clenched to avoid slapping him. My urge to kiss him vanished.

"Oh, by the way," he said. "Thanks."

"Thanks for what?"

"Not cursing." He got in the car and pulled off before I could respond.

He was right. I hadn't cursed since he'd picked me up last night. "Damn," I said. Now, that was better. I was not giving up cursing for a man, again. No way.

CHAPTER THIRTY-ONE

I turned on Carol's computer. I figured I'd follow the only lead I had to what might have been on Kenneth Lawson's mind the months before he disappeared.

I hadn't used my research card before so this was new to me. I called the circulation desk and asked for help.

Emory University has nine libraries. The main one is the Candler Library. All of them, thank God, can be found on the Internet.

I couldn't believe my luck. I was able to check on the books Kenneth had checked out by using their on-line system, EUCLID, an acronym for Emory University Computing and Library Information Delivery System. I could see why they'd use an acronym.

I signed on and the screen gave me several options, including user information. It asked me for my Social Security number. Thank God this was my card. I could check on items on loan, bills and items requested. Kenneth still had books checked out, plus books requested. I wondered where the books were since I knew he never brought them home.

The list was not surprising, actually, just foreign to me. The books he had out were all in French. The only words I could make out were "Dogon" and "Griaule," the name on two of the books the monk had given me. Then there were the books he'd requested. The 1938 edition of *The Mind of Primitive Man* by Franz Boas. A primer on the Galton Society, whatever that was. And a collection of essays by leading Galtonist and other eugenics folk from the 1940s until 1970. I decided maybe all these references would be somewhere on the Internet.

Finally, a bit of luck. I found references to the books in several places on the Net. One of the books was on the history of eugenics. It listed different funds for the study of eugenics as far back as the forties and as current as 1970. I didn't recognize any of the essayists' names: Carelton Coon, Sir Cyril Burt, a few others.

I wondered why Kenneth Lawson would read these particular books. Something was missing. What?

Since I had nowhere else to go on that angle, it was time to check out his parents. How? Seattle? I did know a journalist who'd left the *Guardian* to go to the *Seattle Intelligencer* in order to be closer to her ill father. I phoned Portia Hill and gave her Kenneth's name and his family's name. She promised to call me back as soon as she could.

I sat at Carol's table, surfing the Net, and wondering how all this fit together when the phone rang. Portia had had no problem finding what I needed. The mother and father had burned to death in a fire at the Lawsons' computer business. It appeared to be arson but neither Kenneth nor his brother, Keith, were suspects. The perpetrator or perpetrators were never found. Shortly after that, Keith Lawson attempted suicide by overdosing on pills. He disappeared afterward and could not be located for questioning.

After his parent's deaths, Kenneth Lawson went to work for a family friend named William Delecarte at Delecarte Laboratory as a computer expert. But about six months later, Kenneth Lawson also left the Seattle area. It was speculated that the Lawson brothers both left due to their painful memories.

It was clear that Kenneth had come to Atlanta at this point. Why didn't he tell me? And why not tell me about his brother? But he'd said in his letter he didn't want me to be involved. Now I *was* involved—but in what?

I asked Portia to check out William Delecarte for me, and told her I'd get back to her soon. After I hung up, I began reviewing the different newspaper research departments for any mentions of the names of the other twins in the study in their respective cities. There were twenty of them in all. I figured this would take all day. Most people didn't get in the newspaper and so I'd have to go to other sources. It was going to cost me money for search services, but hey, I had plenty of money now.

When I was done I stared at the screen. My task had been made too easy by one simple fact: Every one of the twins were listed in the newspaper's obituaries in their respective cities, all dying of either accidental deaths or aneurysms in the last year.

"The signs of things of the past teach the children
the signs of things of the past, that is the road one follows;
it is so that the children will take again (remake)
the signs of the old customs that one draws."
—The Dogons

CHAPTER THIRTY-TWO

Jeff Samuels was supposed to pick me up later for lunch.

After drinking some orange juice I settled down on the couch with the books again. Not that I was up to reading them. But I needed a better understanding of the Dogon. I figured if I tried, possibly I'd absorb the information similar to Edgar Cayce. Yeah, right.

According to one of the books, the Dogon are considered scientists and hierophants at the same time and thus concerned with both the physical and the metaphysical realities of the universe. Man, in the framework of Dogon belief, is the microcosm. According to *The Pale Fox*, using only the naked eye, the Dogon were able to discern the existence of the two companions of the star Sirius long before scientists, using highly specialized instruments, were able to detect them.

I sat thinking and hugging my orange juice glass. Here was a tribe in West Africa, near Mali, considered primitive by modern standards, who had this incredible knowledge base. I found it amazing that I'd not heard of these people. Sure, I'd heard of the Dogon mask before; in fact, I actually visited an exhibit in Chicago once, but I guess I'd never considered the mask anything other than art. Now I was reading that an African tribe held extensive knowledge of the anatomy of plants, animals and even humans. I don't mean the basics like where babies come from, but knowing about the circulation of blood. We didn't know it until

William Harvey discovered it. The Dogon apparently knew how important the placenta was to the survival of babies long before modern medicine did.

I was most fascinated by the Sirius star information. How could a tribe in Africa without telescopes know that Sirius, the brightest star in our skies, was a star and not a planet? How could they see and calculate the distance of other stars in its orbit? They already knew that the orbital period is fifty years. They knew Sirius A is not at the center of its orbit, but one of the foci of Sirius B's elliptical orbit. They also, miraculously, knew that Sirius B is composed of a special kind of material not found on earth. And that this material is strong but heavier than all the iron on earth. The Dogons referred to Sirius B as Digitaria. They believed this star is so heavy because it contains the germs of all creation. Plus they knew that Earth turns on its own axis before scientists discovered it. God. How could they know the orbital period, the density and the shape of Sirius A and B's paths before they were even confirmed by scientists? I couldn't comprehend it. I recalled from a news story that only in 1996 were 47 Ursae Majoris and a second planet circling the star 70 Virginis discovered by scientists and recognized to be temperate enough to allow water to exist in liquid form. I'd made a mental note of it mainly because I found it laughable that they'd given the planets such weird names. The Dogon elders already had maps placing these stars exactly where the scientists had found them located, and they knew about the water.

Incredibly, the Dogons also knew that the Milky Way contained the earth before this was common knowledge. And they believed an infinite number of stars, and seven spiraling worlds, existed. Twin worlds. Fourteen in all. Always the concept of twins emerging in every aspect of their belief system.

The Dogons also predicted that soon scientists would discover another planet, and it was rumored that NASA had sent a team to Africa to investigate the Dogons' knowledge of a tenth planet. And in the spring of 1997 scientists confirmed a tenth planet's existence. The Dogons believed that by the millennium, not only would we know more about the tenth planet, but the primordial seed, what they call the *po pilu*, would manifest itself on Earth, according to their cosmogony.

I stopped reading and stretched, then picked up an article tucked inside one of the books. It wasn't about the Dogons but it certainly fit what I'd been reading. This article was titled "Primordial Soup." According to a Dr. Stanley Miller, in 1953 he'd demonstrated that amino acids could be formed by passing an electric current through a flask of methane. This suggested that life could have arisen from material and conditions present in early Earth history. I found it curious that a tribe in Africa basically believed a similar origin story for mankind. The Dogons even had a symbol that recalled "the genesis of the primordial seed."

In the Dogon cosmogony, Amma is the creator and there are 266 primordial signs. Amma created the first genesis but was not completely satisfied and then proceeded with a second genesis. In the second genesis Amma created twin beings who are equal male and female.

Some aspect of this sounded familiar to me. It sounded, in an odd way, like Christianity. I remembered that Father Fred had mentioned Genesis.

I got the Bible Kenneth had left at Claudette Duvet's and noticed he'd underlined some verses in the beginning of Genesis, chapters 1 and 2. In chapter 1, verse 26, I read, *And God said, Let us make man in our image, after our likeness: and let them have dominion over the fish of the sea, and over the fowl of the air, and over the cattle, and over all the earth, and over every creeping thing that creepeth upon the earth. So God created man in his own image, in the image of God created he him, male and female created he them.* Then, I read further to chapter 2, verse 6: *But there went up a mist from the earth, and watered the whole face of the ground. And the Lord God formed man of the dust of the ground and breathed into his nostrils the breath of life; and man became a living soul.* As the verses continued God placed Adam in the Garden of Eden and made trees and animals, but not until verse 21 did it say: *And the Lord God caused a deep sleep to fall upon Adam, and he slept: and he took one of his ribs, and closed up the flesh instead thereof; And the rib, which the Lord God had taken from man, made he a woman, and brought her unto the man.*

I'd read Genesis three or four times in my life. Now I read the passages seven times. And noticed something I'd never noticed before.

The way the story was written was almost seamless. As if the writer didn't want the reader to take note of it. I wondered why it was together like that. I knew that some parts of the Bible contradicted other parts and were written by different scholars. But if I was right, there was clearly a demarcation. If I didn't know better, I'd say this was a deliberate coverup.

Right in the middle the story began over again, saying the same thing basically, with one exception. In the first version God created male and female and made them both equal. And in the second version he created male first and then made the woman from the man for the man. The only thought that surfaced in my mind was that a mortal man with some agenda wrote the second version.

I found it curious that the Dogons also had two genesis stories. That God made the world and then started over again but with a different end. Interesting. However, in the Dogons' second genesis, things still get out of sorts.

I read more of *The Sirius Mystery*. There were apparently people who reasoned that the Dogons learned their knowledge from some other groups. These people were having difficulty believing that the Dogons knew this information without getting it elsewhere. On the other hand, Robert K.G. Temple seemed to imply that the Dogons had gotten it from the Egyptians, who'd in turn gotten it from a race of intelligent beings from another planetary system. Well, from what I'd read, there was no way the Dogons could have made up their knowledge or memorized it from some other group. Hell, there was no other group with them. And if this was true, and they were the descendants of the Egyptians, as Temple believed, well, he was one of the few who at least acknowledged the Egyptians were black. I wondered briefly, Would the Dogons' knowledge have been dismissed or ignored if they'd not been African? But all of this information unnerved me and I realized I was shaking. I tried to put the Dogon thing out of my mind. Do something more visceral.

I dialed my office number. When I heard the first message my heart leaped into my mouth. *Beep.* "Miss Conley. This is Detective David Griffin. Remember me? We'd like to ask you a few more questions. I'm told you're on vacation and I've left messages at your home. If you could please phone me at 555-6277 as soon as possible. Thank you."

Questions about what? If I thought I was shaking before, I was wrong. Now my hand shook like I was in withdrawal and I wondered if I should call Jeff and see if he knew anything about this or at least could talk to Griffin and find out what he wanted. Damn.

I switched on the television with the remote. I turned it to Channel 5's repeat news station and lowered the sound.

Then I dialed my voice mail back since I'd hung up without hearing the other messages. I listened to Detective Griffin's message again, trying to determine what the tone of his voice might signify. Then I listened to a few others, including that bum, Mark, still begging me for money.

Ted Maverick, my old friend and former shihan, until all this shit started, called. He wanted to see how I was doing. He, Scott Brooks and the guys were finally going on the long-awaited survival training the dojo had been planning. He was sorry I would miss going. He'd call me as soon as they got back. He loved me. And no matter what he'd said, Scott loved me too.

Yeah, right.

I phoned Carol. "It's me. Any news for me?"

"Okay. Sure, Mom. People have been asking about your pie recipe. You know, where you got it and all. Anyway, I tell you what. Why not meet me for lunch today. Noon at Delectables?"

I knew why she was talking like this. She didn't want anyone to know who she was talking to. The newsroom is one big open eavesdrop hole. Journalists sit almost elbow to elbow. Piles of papers and junk separate your desk, but you have very little privacy if others are of a mind to listen.

"Can you be there?" she continued loudly. And I could almost see Jane Sims, who sits in front of her, leaning forward on her keyboard so she could listen to Carol's every word. Nosey witch that she is.

Carol loved espionage books. Everything was a cover-up to her. She was the ultimate liberal, and often talked fondly about her involvement in the civil rights movement. She could not understand why I wasn't more militant when it came to black folk's rights. She argued constantly about the lack of blacks in news management.

It was difficult for her to understand that some of us were catching so much hell merely breathing we didn't have the luxury of fighting battles we were accustomed to losing. We spent most of our time trying to stay above water, gasping for air. Some people had been dealt such bad hands they didn't have the time to worry about the quality of their lives; they just wanted to stay alive long enough to live them. And I'd come to understand that this predicament included both blacks and whites.

"Sure," I said. "I can meet you there. I guess this means you can't talk, huh? I hope you're not tripping again on some conspiracy kick. But let me warn you. Jeff Samuels is bringing me. It'll be a little after noon. I've already promised him lunch."

"Really. Fine. If he can take the heat, tell him to come on."

I wasn't about to step into that by asking her what she meant. Lately she'd been caught up in the news about the snatched bodies after World War II, where the government was using the organs of the dead to check radiation levels without anyone's knowledge. Carol was positive it went deeper than that. Who knows; maybe she was right.

⠿

At noon, Jeff picked me up. I didn't mention my reading material about the Dogons. I tried to put what I'd read out of my mind. It made me feel disoriented when I thought about it for long.

Jeff only gave me two of the disks and it pissed me off. He claimed they were the only two that were completed. He didn't mention the copy he had made. Either he didn't know about the copy I made or he didn't want to open a can of worms. "Are you telling the truth?" I asked him. Damn. I shouldn't have left it. Asking him if he was telling the truth had as much meaning as a wife asking her spouse if he'd been cutting out on her.

He wasn't so happy we were meeting Carol, but a big disgusted sigh was all the indication he gave. We headed for Delectables. And none too soon. I was starving. I saw Carol waving us down, her reddish curled hair and freckled face standing out among a sea of black people on the curb with her. The only time in downtown Atlanta you wouldn't have seen a lot of black people was during the Olympics. It was like Atlanta put up a barricade to keep us out.

Jeff slowed the car as Carol motioned for us to pull over.

"What are you doing? I thought we were eating here?" I asked, as I watched her jump in the backseat.

"We can't. Let me catch my breath and I'll tell you why. But could you please keep driving and speed up?"

Carol took a couple of deep breaths while I shrugged in Jeff's direction.

"Somebody is following me. At first I thought he was flirting with me. Hey, I wasn't interested, but you know, when you get this age, you take what you can get. Then when I started looking back at him I saw that it made him more than a little nervous and uncomfortable. So I tested it out. I went in three stores and the library and still he was there. So, having read many an espionage novel, I lost him in the stacks. You owe me one, dear. Now, what have you been up to?"

"The man following you. Tall, lanky, no-lipped white man with a bulbous nose? Kind of garlicky-looking guy?"

"No. But I know I'm right. And you said I needed to leave the espionage books alone. Active imagination, isn't that what you said?"

"And nothing's changed. You still need to leave them alone. Hey, I'm sorry if you've been drawn into this, Carol. But he could be the detective looking for me."

"What detective?" they both said at the same time.

"The same detective that I told you about before, David Griffin, left a message on my voice mail that he needed to talk to me."

"About what?" Carol asked, looking behind us.

"I don't know. I was hoping Jeff could find out."

"Yes. Jeff, I'd like to see you find out," Carol said sarcastically.

We both ignored her. "Do you know this brother, Jeff? Could you call him and see what he wants?" I asked, hoping he didn't hear my stomach rumbling Apache helicopter style.

"I'd bet all the lottery money in Georgia he doesn't know him," Carol said. "Do you, Jeffy?"

"You darn tootin'. I'll git on it right off," he said, still ignoring Carol.

It occurred to me that his Kentucky accent was back since Carol had gotten in the car. Actors, lovers, flies and men, all the same to me.

Carol frowned. "You darn tootin', are you, huh, Jeffro."

She was beginning to piss me off. It was uncalled for. I gave her a look that said "lay off."

We circled around the city, attempting to lose any tail we might have picked up. None of us spoke. I continued to glance back at Carol, trying to figure out what the heck was bothering her.

"I've got something to tell you that is very important," she began. "Should I say this in front of this, this . . . ?" She pointed at Jeff as though he weren't there, raising her eyebrows as a signal, like she was a doctor and he a patient. Only doctors do that well.

"Sure. Say it. You couldn't get any ruder," I replied, wishing she'd just say whatever it was sticking up her butt.

"You're wrong; I could," she said, shrugging. "Let me think how to break this to you so that Jeffiepooh here keeps the car on the road."

"Carol, please," I said, glancing back at her.

Her face pouted up. I knew her well enough to know she was deciding something. I hoped it was where we could eat.

Finally I said, "I'm starving and unless I get some food, I'm going to die and no one will have to kill me." Not true. Someone had decided dead people didn't need to eat.

Carol made the decision at the same moment the men in the car pulling up beside us must have made theirs. She said, "You know, Jeff. I've got friends in the police department. I did some checking and guess what?"

A second passed. No answer.

Carol continued, accusation on her face more than in her voice, "There was no—"

The first bullet entered the Volvo at the right rear fender. It sent the insides of the backseat spewing gunk all over Carol. Screaming was her calling. She attempted to climb over the seat and her leg smashed into my head.

The mind is a strange thing. *I Love Lucy* popped into my head as Jeff shoved me down and at the same time banked to the left. He gunned the engine and I could hear the bullets crashing through the back of the car as we zigzagged down the street.

"Both of you git down," Jeff yelled in his Kentucky twang.

Boy, was he good.

I heard a siren in the distance. Gunfire didn't sit well with Atlanta's reputation, at least not in the exclusive Buckhead area. We sped on. I guessed the car dropped back upon hearing the sirens closing in on us, since Jeff said, quietly, "Y'all can git up now," glancing over his shoulder to the backseat.

I didn't lift my head. My hands covered my head and if I'd been drunk I couldn't have gotten the shakes any worse. My teeth were chattering. Real gunfire is some scary shit.

Jeff put his hand on my shoulder. "When we get to the hospital, you'll have to handle this. I'm going to have to keep moving. Take the phone with you. I'll call you."

"What hospital? What are you talking about? We're okay. Aren't we? Didn't we lose them?"

"Yes, but your friend, she's shot."

The screaming had stopped. I figured Carol had fainted. I lifted my head and looked back in terror.

Her right shoulder spurted blood. Flesh clung to her clothes and I began to cry.

Carol, silent, slumped over in the seat among the debris, unconscious.

"There's no time for crying, honey. You've got to climb back there and stop her bleeding before she goes into shock. I'm about five blocks from Grady Hospital. That gives you some time. I'm slipping my phone inside your purse. Please, you need to get back there now."

I cried into my hands. I couldn't. I just couldn't. I fainted when my own nose bled. I thought of getting a hysterectomy once so I wouldn't have to deal with menstruation. How could I climb back there and touch her? How?

"I know you're in shock. I know you think you can't get back there. But pull all your energy up in your breath. Climb over the seat and the rest will come naturally. You don't want your friend to die. I know this. You can cry later. I promise."

Cry? That did it. Damn him, expecting I needed to cry. I climbed over the seat. I tore the bottom of Carol's skirt off. Luckily it had an embroidered hem attached so the bottom was easy to separate. I didn't know what I was doing but I thanked God for television. At least I had a general idea of what I needed to do. I folded the material thickly and held it over the wound. I put pressure on it by pushing the full weight of my body onto her chest. The cloth quickly colored pink, then red; then I looked away.

When we stopped in front of the emergency room I felt like screaming, but it wouldn't help me and it sure as hell wouldn't help Carol.

Jeff jumped from the car and rang the bell, shouting into a speaker. Two attendants rushed out through the double glass doors. One of them, after taking a quick assessment, whisked Carol out of the car in his arms and raced back into the building, saying something loudly to the other, who followed on his heels. Whatever he said was not loud enough for a shell-shocked person like me to hear.

Jeff pulled me to him and kissed my forehead. "You did good, honey. I knew that crying reference would get you hopping." He smiled. "Now go inside with her. Grady is the best place to be if you're shot. I'll call you soon. When I call, be ready to move. Okay?"

I didn't move or answer. The anger had worn off from the crying remark and all I felt were fear and pain.

"Listen. I love you. Please. Go inside. I've got to go. Please," he whispered in my ear.

"Where're you going? Were you lying to me about everything? You're abandoning me now like Kenneth? Like all the others?"

He had no idea, I was sure, what others I meant. He and I had only had superficial conversations. Only Kenneth knew my real fears. Only Kenneth knew how I longed to have someone with me, close forever. Only Kenneth knew what I wanted most in the world—a family.

"Of course I'm not abandoning you. I will be back to pick you up. You've got my phone." He placed my purse strap up on my shoulder. "Go in and see about your friend."

"But where're you going?" I whimpered, still shaking and completely out of control. And at the same instant hating myself for this behavior. What in the hell was happening to me?

"I have to find who did this."

"No!" I screamed, hysteria taking over completely.

The security guard looked out of the doors at us.

"Please, baby. I'm not like the others. I'll be back for you. Trust me."

Not again. Another man, leaving me. I felt him pulling away and I tried to hold on to his arm. He pulled away, gently but firmly, and jumped in his car. And then, in a flash, he was gone.

I stood watching the tail end of the car disappear.

"Miss, we need some information in here," the attendant yelled in my ear.

I jumped, startled. He took me by the arm and led me inside. My next rational thought was how lucky we were to be near Grady. If you've got a bullet in you, there's no hospital in Atlanta more practiced in taking it out.

The nurse began to ask me questions.

I knew nothing. No important answers. Not her blood type. Not whether she was or had been pregnant. Not her mother and father's name, even though they lived in the city. Not her birthdate. Nothing short of her address and where she worked.

Friends are not what they should be. Friends should be able to answer some of these questions. The only question I could answer was that her favorite books were as contradictory as her life seemed at times—espionage and romance.

Now I could see what I couldn't see then. We were living too fast and too shallow in this world. I should have known more about my friend.

I squeezed the cup of coffee a nurse put in my hands. Carol had not gone into shock but she was sleeping due to a shot they'd given her. She was in no danger. The bullet had grazed her shoulder. It was mostly a flesh wound. She wouldn't be playing tennis anytime soon, the doctor said. Was that supposed to be a joke? "By the way," he continued, "I've called the police."

I could not stick around for the police. At the rate this was going down, the police might have been the very ones shooting at us. And I wanted to know what this Detective Griffin wanted before I talked to any police.

Carol would be safe. Her parents were on their way. (She had the good sense to have an information card in her wallet. I copied down their phone number and called them.) The police would come and hopefully they'd guard her. I told the doctor whoever did this might come after her since they knew she'd seen their faces. I really didn't know if she'd seen their faces or not. I didn't even think they'd come after her.

But the police were the last people I wanted to talk to about anything.

People were swarming all over the place. Hospital patients with paper slippers on walked leisurely by, pushing their IV's like strollers. An ambulance pulled up, its sirens blasting. Nurses rushed to meet medics pushing someone on a stretcher. I used the cover of chaos to slip out the side door and walked up the alley onto the street. It was still midday and I needed to get out of sight. But where could I go?

There was an ATM a few blocks away. I walked there, racking my brain to make sense of what was going on. When I got to the ATM I was grateful no one else was around. I pulled the cell phone out and made sure it was turned on. If Jeff called I didn't want to miss him.

I put my plastic card in the slot. I heard the whirring sound and it brought Kenneth's face into view. I hit "Cancel" and waited for the machine to spit my card back out. Thank God for the movie *The Pelican Brief*. She got caught because she was stupid. Using traceable plastic. Not to mention falling for meeting that hit guy. There's nothing I hate worse than a woman in a movie doing dumb shit. Even though I'd been doing an awful lot myself.

I caught a cab and headed to the bank. Why not use the money? The couple of hundred-dollar bills I'd taken wouldn't last long if I found myself on the run. Besides, even if the money wasn't legal, I couldn't be in much more trouble than this. Could I? Yes. Yes, I could, but what the hell? If you're already sinking in quicksand, being still is not going to save your butt.

CHAPTER THIRTY-THREE

In the cab I thought about Carol. She didn't deserve this. Whoever did this needed to answer for running around shooting innocent people. Hell. They were pissing me off now. I wished I could get a grip on who "they" were.

I took the money out of the bank without incident.

I decided to go to Jeff's house and wait for him. I had to see him. To make sure he was all right. After all, it was because of me he was mixed up in this crap. I'd been to his house in town only once. It was in a high-rise downtown over a restaurant.

I could walk there but I was afraid someone would see me. I had no idea who was after me. I was only a few blocks from Ira's now. I slipped into his store.

Ira showed me to the back. "Vhat is it?" he said, concern on his face. "You look like scared vabbit."

"I am," I said, leaning on his shoulder. I told him some of the things that had happened to me, but not about the hallucination of the old man.

"I have answer," Ira finally said, leaving the room.

"How would you like to be a Muslim woman for a while? Vait here," he said. "I go next door."

When he returned he was carrying a bundle of dark clothing.

"A Muslim woman?"

"Shhh. Not so loudly," he said, holding his finger up to his mouth. "Can you keep a secret?".

"Of course," I said, wondering what his secret could possibly be.

"I am friends with the Muslim man next door. We sit for hours playing chess in the back."

I smiled. He'd obviously forgotten I knew his secret.

He held up a Muslim outfit with a scarf. "This way no one will recognize you. You will be a Muslim woman dressed in traditional clothes. People will think you are coming from his shop. You can go out the back way and valk around the corner. You'll come out near the Marta station. I'll call a cab and they vill pick you up. There. Now."

"You are amazing," I said to him.

"And you are amazing too, yah. Now get dressed. I'm so sorry about your friend. She will be fine, I'm sure. I will personally check on her for you. Now go in the other room and dress. Sneak out the back. I'll go up front so my clerk won't come back here."

He gave me a hug and went out the front way. I hurried into the Muslim garment, struggling to put the scarf on my head as well as I could, considering I'd never paid that much attention to how Muslim women wore one.

I slipped out the back, rushed through the shadowed alley and came out exactly where he said I would.

It was a few minutes before a Yellow Cab came up and I hopped inside. Immediately the driver, an Ethiopian, began chattering to me in what I assumed was Arabic or Amharic.

I shrugged. "I'm sorry, I don't speak Arabic. I'm dressed this way for a . . . for a school presentation."

"Oh," he said, immediately detaching himself from the conversation. "Where to?"

"I don't know the address but I can show you."

As we rode, I pondered how much I missed my car. I went over the logic in my decision not to even try getting my car. If they knew my house, they knew my car.

As we approached the building where Jeff lived, I asked the driver to slow down. I could see Jeff's Volvo parked in front of his apartment. He stood on the sidewalk, talking to a man. The driver hadn't slowed and we were almost upon Jeff.

I could see the side of the man's face. Sweat suddenly lined my lip, poured from my armpits and trickled down my legs. As we pulled directly alongside them, I said to the driver, "Don't stop, and I'll give you twenty dollars extra."

The driver sped past. Jeff looked up at the moment we zoomed by, and I saw his perplexed look transform to one of recognition. Some disguise this was.

"Please take me to Jonesboro to Clayton State College," I said to the driver. This could not be happening to me. It couldn't be true.

But it was true. There was no disputing who stood on that sidewalk taking an envelope out of Jeff Samuels's hand. An envelope full of money, no doubt.

How much more could I take? How much more? It was like the struggle to survive my childhood, teens and early adulthood was nothing. Child's play. Now the shit was heaved on me. And for what? What had I done to deserve this? Tell me that? *Please God, tell me.*

A tear escaped and I realized how handy the scarf was as the driver pulled into the state college parking lot. The only thing I didn't ask was, why me? I'd stopped asking that years ago when Cripple Cooney raped me. Since then, I'd been raped in a thousand ways. This was just another time and place.

"I'll get out here," I said, gathering up my skirt. I handed him the money with the extra twenty plus a five-dollar tip and stepped from the cab.

Jonesboro is a small town south of Atlanta, famous for Tara from *Gone With the Wind.* Never mind that Tara never really existed. It's like people looking for the bridges of Madison County. But since moving to Atlanta I had come to this school many times for sanctuary.

Secluded, off one of the campus's beaten paths was a pond. I sat beside it, thinking and crying—yes, crying—over what I'd witnessed. Jeff Samuels handing Bulbous Nose an envelope. The same man who'd followed me into the drugstore and stuck a gun in my side. Bulbous Nose not only knew Jeff Samuels but obviously worked for him.

My only consolation was that I was close to the airport and I had cash. I could either get a hotel or get the hell out of Dodge.

No matter how you're feeling, water calms your spirit. That's what Grandma Dixon used to say to me. "The water, the trees, the grass and the very dirt under your feet are the signs that we need to contemplate God," she'd say, while gardening or feeding the goldfish in her small backyard pond.

I knew as well as most people what she said was true. But it took fear, exhaustion and impending death to force me to think about it.

I'd been abandoned—by Kenneth and now by Jeff. It should have come as no surprise. But Jeff's total betrayal *was* a surprise. It was one thing to think he was sneaking around trying to know what I knew, but to have someone force me at gunpoint? Then it occurred to me that betrayal in its nature must be a surprise.

Seeing Jeff standing on that sidewalk reminded me that he would have been at least the second man I would have killed if I'd had a gun.

Abandonment had been a part of my life from the moment I drew my first breath. And it looked like it was going to hang around until I took my last one. Leaning over the water, I stared into a face, supposedly mine. For a second I had a flashback that nothing had happened.

I glanced over now, my daydream gone, at a man casting his fishing line into the water. His companion, a woman with a baby in her lap, blew air into the baby's belly button, and the baby responded with a squeal. The scene made me ache and my insides feel empty.

I sat there grasping my knees, my legs in a fetal position, thinking no thoughts that I could put my finger on. I was too tired to think. Or too afraid.

I could still see the faces: first, Claudette Duvet, Dr. Kia Mutota, Kenneth or his brother, and now Carol. And with each face the acceptance that pain and death were stalking me.

The worst of it, I thought, is that I will possibly die not knowing why I'm dying. Maybe my own mother is alive somewhere? Maybe she is locked up, crazy. Possibly that is the core of what I'm experiencing now. After all, I don't really know my name. Patricia Conley is the name one of the foster family workers gave me. Now I won't ever know. I am a lost soul.

⚹

The phone's ringing startled me. My hand immediately shook as I flipped it open. I expected to hear Jeff's voice on the other end.

A string of foreign gibberish.

I said, "Uh-huh," as inaudibly as possible, hoping the person, if they thought they were calling Jeff, would speak in English.

Silence. They knew it wasn't Jeff. *Click.*

Now I was scared. It had occurred to me more than once that cellular phones can be traced easier than home phones, if I remembered correctly. I had to get out of here.

The phone rang again. I dropped it on the grass. Wits together again, I picked it up and opened it.

It was Jeff. "I'm on my way," he said. "Where are you?"

"I'm not telling you. Now that you've paid your henchman off, you'll probably kill me yourself. Fuck you," I said, and hung up. I thought about throwing the phone into the pond. It rang again.

I didn't answer and it stopped. I knew he was getting the message that the cellular phone customer was not answering at this time. Fuck him. Yeah. Cursing, that's the ticket. It is the only relief I have from this nightmare.

The phone rang again. I flipped it open. "What? What do you want?" I screamed, not caring if others heard me. "Come and get me, damn it. I'm tired of running. I'm fucking tired of being scared. You've been behind this all along. Goddamn it, you probably had Kenneth killed. Carol shot. Come on, get me. But I promise you, I will not be easy. Hell, no. If you think you can fuck me in bed *and* out, I'll show you." I hung up.

The people in the park were either too caught up in their world to look at me or too scared they would get caught up in mine.

The phone rang once more. "Yes."

"Listen. Just listen for one second," Jeff pleaded into the phone. "I'll tell you, okay? Listen. Can you listen? After I explain, if you don't believe me, throw the phone away and get on a plane, train or bus somewhere, but for God's sake get away from here. If I'm not with you I'd rather you disappear where they can't find you. Do you hear me?"

"Talk," I said. What could he do? He couldn't come through the phone. "Make it quick, in case you're trying to trace the call."

"First, I did hire the guy to follow you. The one you call Bulbous Nose."

"Goddamn you. He put a fucking gun in my side."

"The gun wasn't real. It was a starter gun."

"Fuck you, Jeff."

"Wait. You promised to hear me out."

"I promised you shit."

"Listen, when I realized you were going to look for Kenneth Lawson, I knew it might get dangerous. I wanted to scare you off. God knows I didn't mean to hurt you. See, I had him trash your house and hotel. Don't hang up. I thought if you were scared, you'd stop looking around and they wouldn't find out about you."

"What about my fucking cat? What happened to Peppy?"

"He says the cat attacked him. Swore he didn't mean to kill him. I'm sorry. How did I know he hated cats?"

"Go fuck yourself," I said, hurting and cheering Peppy at the same moment. The cat had heart. I was glad to know he at least went out fighting. He'd scratched me plenty, and I knew if he was mad and fighting for his life, he'd have been a worthy adversary.

"For your own sake you'd better hear me out," Jeff said, raising his voice. "I don't think they knew about you until today, from what I can tell. How they found out is what I'm working on. Honest to God, this is the truth. I swear to you."

"Please, let me talk to you and then you can leave. Never see me again. I need to see you to make sure you're all right. God—please, let me see you."

"Don't beg. I hate begging. How do I know you're not lying again? Who is 'they'? Tell me who the fuck is 'they' because I need to know."

"If you let me come to where you are to talk to you in person, then, and only then, will I tell you who I think 'they' might be."

"What? *Think?* Fuck you. I don't need thoughts. I've got my own damn thoughts. And right now, they're telling me you're fucking with my head."

"Look, you name the place and time. Somewhere there's a lot of people. The police station, even. And I'll meet you there."

"Answer me one thing and I'll consider it."

"Name it."

"Are you a police undercover agent?"

"No. No, I'm not."

"Damn." I didn't want to hear that. I wanted him to say, Yes. Yes, I am.

In *The Pelican Brief* Julia Roberts's character meets her contact, but he's really the crook, and he tries to shoot her. They're in a crowded place. A fucking amusement park. She's stupider than I am.

Or maybe not. "Okay. I'm at Clayton State College. And someone called you and if they're tracking me they probably already know where I am and are on their way. I'm . . . I'm . . . Never mind," I said. Wishing I could have been brave enough to say I was scared.

"I'll be there in fifteen minutes. Come to the first circle parking lot and stand beside the little red maintenance shop."

My mind raced. How did he know so much about the layout? It's not exactly a popular place if you're not in school here. What if it was a trap? Why was he only fifteen minutes away? Unless you're a *Gone With the Wind* fan, Jonesboro isn't exactly a swinging place. One riddle only led to another, and I wasn't finding the answers to any of them. But I couldn't keep running. Shit. I was tired.

♊

I planned an escape route. I gathered a few wine bottles and even one liquor bottle out of the trash receptacles, left by people who're not supposed to be drinking alcohol out here. But they do it all the time—bring their picnic food and drinks.

I saw a girl with an orange and purple hairdo sitting on the grass alone, eating a sandwich.

"Excuse me," I said. "Do you happen to have any hair spray?" Only lots of gunk could have kept her shit standing up. Yet her appearance was what I loved about youth and funkiness. They don't have a lot of rules or questions.

She dug in a suitcase-sized purse and pulled out three different kinds of hair spray, foam and color gel. The spray was what I wanted.

"Can I buy it?" I asked, realizing the request must have seemed odd coming from a Muslim.

"You can have it," she said.

And generous. I must not forget that—they are generous. Thank God.

"I need it for a project. What about matches?" I asked, smiling while my hands trembled.

She opened her bag and pulled out a pack of matches that had skulls and bones on them and offered them to me.

"Here," I said, still attempting to smile, "let me give you something for it." I pulled out a twenty and gave it to her.

She looked at it and grinned. "Cool" was her thank you.

I walked around to the bathroom, but someone was inside. I scanned for a secluded spot. I saw one on the far side of the pond near the trees. No one was there. I walked over, lifting my skirt carefully so I wouldn't fall.

At the edge of the woods I knelt down and broke the bottles with a rock, all except one. Then I put the shard glass into a tissue from my purse. I stuffed some dry straw from the ground inside the bottle along with the glass and then more straw. I sprayed half of the contents of the hair spray onto my open bottle's contents. Then I wrapped the only handkerchief I had, which was a little soiled, around the bottle top and tied a knot. Then I placed my two weapons inside a dirty paper bag and I was ready to walk back to the parking lot.

Jeff arrived and got out of his car slowly.

I held my free hand up to signal him not to come closer to me.

"What's that you wearing?"

"You a fashion critic?"

"No. I'm sorry. Can we walk down by the water?" he asked.

"I can swim if you're thinking of pushing me in," I said. Acknowledging to myself it was probably not good enough to keep me from drowning. But he didn't know that.

We walked back down to the pond, along the water's edge.

I kept my distance, still holding my paper bag. I'd sat my purse down on the ground.

"What's in the bag?" he asked me.

"Lifesavers," I said. "Now talk. I don't have all day."

"Can I come closer? From over here I'll have to shout."

"So," I said, backing up farther. If he attacked me I needed time to get my stuff out and light it.

"For God's sake. I'm not going to hurt you."

Gazing out toward the middle of the pond he said, "Things will be happening that will make you question me, my intent and my motivation. But I hope you would keep one thing clear in your mind. No matter how this started, I came to love you. And I still love you now. But there is only so much I can tell you."

"You know what? That makes sense to me. I mean being in the dark is like . . . goddamn cool. Isn't that the way it's supposed to be? Women, what do we need to know? What could we do? Shit. We can't take care of ourselves, let alone unravel a mystery."

I wanted to cry right then and there, but shit, crying was getting old. I was stronger than that. I'd cry when I was alone again.

"I'm not going into that right now. If that's what you think about women, so be it," he said, still watching the pond.

"It's not what *I* think," I said, hearing my voice rising shrill. Then, I thought to myself, Fuck him. "Look, I don't need you. Whatever is going down, I can handle alone."

"No. I'm telling you, you can't. You're dealing with some really dangerous people," he said, ignoring my words.

"You're damn right. You. You're dangerous."

He continued, disregarding my accusation. "We've got a few more days and this will all be over."

"What's the difference?" I asked.

"There is plenty of difference. Let's hope you don't have to find out. Let's hope none of us ever finds out the difference between things being over—"

His phone rang. I tossed it to him. I was more pissed at his seeming dismissal now than frightened.

He spoke in yet another foreign-sounding language and then hung up.

"How many languages can you speak?" I asked, not expecting a straight answer.

"Six," he replied softly, almost apologetically.

"A Kentucky-pretend-policeman that speaks six languages. Uh-huh. And I'm supposed to believe that?"

Two men approached us from the south. One held his head down, so I couldn't see his face. The other's face I didn't recognize. My heartbeat increased. "Isn't it true that cellular phones are easy to bug or whatever?"

"Yes. But not this one. I knew where you were all the time. It can't be traced but I have a tracking device in it."

"Fuck you," I said, realizing I didn't have time for this. "See those men coming? Maybe they're coming for me."

"They're not."

"How do you know that? Oh, do they work for you?"

"Believe me, they're not coming for you."

I stooped down and opened my paper bag.

I could see the men stopping and embracing. They were lovers on a stroll. They sat down on the grass, one leaning on the other for support. Neither of them looked in our direction.

Jeff walked a few feet from me, his back to me.

I figured he must be getting out of the way because he knew they were faking. I ducked behind the tree and lit a match. Evidently the pretend-to-be-lovers had a job to do, but Jeff didn't want to witness them take me out. It didn't matter. I wasn't going out without a fight. I would throw my makeshift bomb at them even if it didn't work.

Before I could bring the match to the paper bag, Jeff grabbed my hand and twisted the match from me. I spun around out of his reach and started lighting another match.

"Ouch!" he yelled as he grabbed the matches. Then he jerked the bottle I'd taken out of the paper bag from my hand.

"What are you doing? Are you crazy?" he asked, putting out the flame.

"If you think I'm going to let them . . . " I looked toward the two men. They were lying down side by side, talking. Neither of them paying me a damn bit of attention. They were busy; in love with each other.

"You could hurt innocent people with this *MacGyver* stuff. What's wrong with you? Don't you get it? The people who are after you want something. They're not going to kill you . . . yet. Now all I have to do is find them, figure out what they want and make sure they don't get it—or you."

I could see it. I never thought I'd actually be able to identify it. But it was there. *Written all over his face*, as the song goes. He did care for me. Angela Benson was right. I couldn't give it up, though. So I merely said, "Okay, so I'm wrong."

This was turning into a fucking Rubik's Cube. Who needs six languages? Why would he have a phone that couldn't be traced but have a tracker in it? As they used to ask of the only white man who understood the value of multiculturalism in the old Westerns, *Who was that masked man?*

He turned. "Whether you trust me or not, you can't stay here."

"And where is it you think I should go, Kemo sabe?"

He looked at me quizzically. "To my place" is all he said.

I actually thought about saying yes. But I'd been talking about the Julia Roberts character like a big dog, ever since I saw that movie. So I couldn't go with him even though some ignorant-ass part of me wanted to. "Look, I've got to go my own way. You understand," I said. "Could I borrow your phone?"

"Of course," he said.

"Toss it to me."

He tossed it near my feet.

"Thanks. Now, if you want us to remain friends, you'll leave."

"All right. All right," he said, holding up his hands. "You're making a big mistake, Patricia."

"It won't be the first time," I said, smiling. "I slept with you."

I followed behind him until he got to his car, still keeping my distance. "Are you sure you want me to leave you? I'll drop you off wherever you want to go."

"No, thanks."

"Will you take my gun?"

"Don't believe in them." Otherwise, your ass would be dead.

"Then I've got something I want you to have. You can get it out of the car. There, on the backseat."

"What is it?"

"Please, get it and keep it with you. The instructions are inside."

"Uh huh. You do think I'm stupid. You want me to take a case with a tracer in it now?"

I picked up the black case and moved back from the car.

"I promise—no tracer." He got in, waved and drove off.

"Humph," I grunted. I walked back down by the pond's edge. I was ready to drop the phone in it when a thought occurred to me. Shit.

I walked over to a Dumpster and tossed the cell phone in it. The campus trash is picked up at night and transported to the dump. I learned that from a news article. Let him carry his ass out there and check the seagulls out. They were about as confused about their place in the world as I was.

I opened the black case. I checked the inside for anything that looked like a sensor or a receiver in case he'd planned to use it to keep track of me. Nothing was there that wasn't in the owner's manual pictures. The manual said it was an air taser and a stun gun. It looked more like an odd-shaped flashlight or an interesting gun. It was lightweight and could fit in my purse. I opened to a demo picture that said you should always hold it level out in front of you: *The target should be no farther than 15 feet away and no closer than 3 feet. The red line-of-sight indicator should be on top. Aim at the center of the attacker. Two prongs will zip out and attach to the attacker's clothes. T-waves will immobilize the attacker for 30 seconds and then repeat. If the attacker is too close, use it as a stun gun to the chest, just below the chin.*

I would take this with me. It might come in handy. And if Jeff followed me, I'd use it on him. That was one way to find out if it worked. I stuck it in my purse.

I looked around for Spike Hair. She was sitting crossed-legged in the lotus position, her eyes closed.

"Excuse me."

She opened her eyes.

"Would you mind giving me a lift someplace? I'll pay you."

"No problemo," she said, and I thought about Bobby Stevenson, the Hacker.

I tried to remember if I'd called Bobby at any time from that cell phone. Jeff Samuels could probably trace calls I'd made on it. But I hadn't called Bobby from it that I could remember, so I felt safe. At least about that.

"Let's move," she said, picking up her things. "I saw you and the dude. I hate domestic violence. If he touched you I was going to spray his ass." She pulled out a big damn gun and I shuddered.

In her van I decided Jeff Samuels did commit domestic violence. So I convinced Spike Hair that I needed another disguise. Maybe even if Jeff saw me this time I'd be less obvious. We stopped at a service station. And when I emerged from the bathroom, people stopped to admire my green, orange and yellow punked-back hair. Or maybe it was the outfit that only Elly Mae of *The Beverly Hillbillies* could be proud of. Or maybe they were losing their lunch because of both looks.

CHAPTER THIRTY-FOUR

Bobby Stevenson had told me he would meet me at the Red Light Cafe.

Spike Hair knew exactly where the cafe was and dropped me off there. When I walked through those doors I knew my new look was right at home.

The army-green chipped cement floor did nothing for the one beige and one red wall. Funky artwork hung on the walls. Assorted tables matched the eclectic combinations of sofas and coffee tables sprinkled around the room.

They called this place the "living room." A punk rock group set up guitars and fiddles on the stage to the right of the entrance. A battered piano graced the corner of the stage. The furniture was all well worn and antique looking. Different twisted iron sculptures hung from the ceilings along with red, black and yellow flags. The huge space seemed dark and covert.

I walked back to the bar and checked out the overhead menu. The only thing I knew about the cafe was that it was famous for its food, especially a black bean soup, and it catered to the arts community. It even had a poetry night.

The chefs, two brothers from California, made each dish individually, on the spot. I ordered pasta. The chef said it would take a while since he made it from scratch. I said no problem, I was waiting for someone.

He perked up. "You here to meet Bobby Stevenson?"

Damn, did everyone know my freaking business in this town? "Yes. Why? Is he here?" I asked, looking around, realizing maybe he'd gone to the john or something.

"No. He's not coming."

"Damn," I swore.

"However," he continued, "he asked me to let you know that someone else is going to help you. He wants you to give him a call. You can use that phone."

He pointed to a phone sitting behind the bar on the other side of the counter. It was an antique black phone. The kind you can use to slam somebody up-side their head and rest assured they won't be getting up until the morning.

I phoned Bobby. "What is going on? I needed your expertise," I whispered into the phone. "This is important."

"Hey, dude. My folks busted me. I'm on my way to a prison."

"Prison?"

"You know, a rehab. Anyhow, I hooked you up with the most high dude. Check it. Did you copy? One of the emperor hackers of the planetary system is aligned down in Decatur, Georgia. He will space you, reporter dude."

"What in the hell are you talking about?" I didn't have the time or the patience for interpreting this shit.

"Okay. Don't freak. I'm saying that I've hooked you up with the grandpa of hackers. This phone is whacked. Ask the chef, he'll tell you the deal, then you decide. The chief will swoop down in about an hour. Outta here, dude, here goes the time warp again. Rocky Horror to you."

He hung up.

I didn't have a clue what the heck he was talking about. The chef. The chef was taking another order. I waited to catch him before he went in the back.

"Excuse me. Bobby said you would explain why I'm waiting, before you begin your work."

"Sure. My brother can take care of this order. Give me a second and I'll be right back."

By the time he was back I'd found a seat on a beige, slightly tattered French provincial sofa. They were right. It felt like I was sitting in the center of an artist's living room. An artist with superfluous, eclectic taste.

He sat down beside me and began telling me what all journalists in Georgia should already know, but I sure as hell didn't remember. Most people think journalists know the news, but what we really know is one story at a time. And it better be the damn story we're currently working on. Some journalists don't even read their own bylines.

"In the beginning there was the Legend of Doom, better known as LD—the powerful computer hackers known as Rightist, Orville and Prof, short for Professor. These were hackers who could monitor the police, the Secret Service, commit international espionage or, better yet, shut down the phone system, including 911, if they wanted to. But they weren't into that. They weren't trying to crash nothing, didn't do it for money. The LD were elite."

"Yeah, so is this who I'm meeting? Some legion?"

"Hold your horses. I'm giving you the history. The LD would still be stomping if this sixteen-year-old kid hadn't messed it up. See, this guy, who was ignorant enough to give his teen buddies raises at McDonald's and order up tons of french fries, thus the name Fry Boy, pretended to be dealing with them. His shit hit the fan on June 13, 1989, when all the Palm Beach County probation departments in Delray Beach, Florida, found themselves yakking with a phone-sex goddess named Trina, from New York State. Any call to or from this office ended up with sweet Trina. Not funny enough for Fry Boy, he moved on to credit card abuse. After mastering that—wire fraud. Then he later involved one of his teen buddies in Indiana.

"Before it was over, Fry Boy and his cohort, using LD techniques, stole six thousand bucks from Western Union between December 1988 and July 1989.

"The sixteen-year-old foolishly phoned the local representatives of Indiana Bell security, bragging that his powerful friends in the Legend of Doom could crash the national telephone network. After the Secret Service figured out who he was, they installed DNR's—dialed number recorders—on his home phone lines and later on the lines of the Atlanta Three.

"Fry Boy was arrested on July 22, 1989. And even though he never knew nor worked with LD, he fingered them as his cohorts."

"Excuse me, but what has this got to do with why I'm waiting?" This shit was frustrating me. Why did every freaking body want to give me history lessons these days?

"Sorry. But this will help you understand what it is you're asking for and how it gets done. If your contact doesn't believe you cared enough about him to know his history, Bobby says he won't work for you. And that means no amount of money can persuade him—only your ability to convince him you understand he didn't do anything wrong. So do you want me to tell you or not?"

"Tell me." Shit, what else did I have to do?

"Anyway, to make a long story short, possibly the three greatest hackers of all time actually lived right here in Atlanta. Orville, who at the time of his arrest was a Georgia Tech student in microchemistry, was smart but about as connected to reality as Bobby Stevenson.

"Then there was Rightist, a young kid still living in his parents' house and working with computers as a day job. And last but not least, the Prof, who took this thing the most personal and the hardest. He, personally, had written the handy Legend of Doom file 'UNIX Use and Security from the Ground Up.'

"The Prof had already been convicted at age eighteen in 1986 for breaking into Southern Bell's data network. But his mistake was the E911 document."

"What's that?" I asked, recognizing that from a journalist's vantage, this was a damn good story.

"Well, in 1988, Prof broke into BellSouth's centralized automation system, AIMSX, or Advanced Information Management System. No public dial up, so they were invincible, or so they thought. Prof broke in and copied a document known as 'Bell South Standard Practice 660-225-104SV Control Office Administration of Enhanced 911 Services for Special Services and Major Accounts.' That wouldn't be so bad but he made a copy on another hacker's account and left it. He would have gotten away scot free. But he couldn't bring himself to get rid of his copy. So the feds nabbed him with the evidence. He was sentenced to federal prison in November 1990."

"And the connection to all this is—"

"You're waiting for the Prof. In fact, that's him now," he said, pointing to a blond thirtyish-looking guy. He damn sure didn't look like any grand-pooh-papa to me.

After the Prof and I were introduced he walked me over to the computer. The Red Light Cafe was the first cafe in Atlanta that boasted the use of a computer for rent while you ate your dinner. Now cyber cafes were gradually popping up more frequently in the yuppie areas.

The Prof flexed his fingers as he spoke. "Now, I know that what you know of hackers comes from TV and movies and that's sad. Every time I see a show I wonder, what in the hell are they doing? What can I do for you? Bobby says take care of you and I will."

"I'm not sure. It's a long story but I'm trying to find out about some people who were connected to a guy. These people left me in a lot of trouble, holding the bag, so to speak. I'm sure you can relate to that." A push and pull.

He nodded in the affirmative and his features looked more drawn. I imagined his mind going back to the time of his own betrayal.

I took out my photo of Kenneth Lawson and Father Fred and pointed to Kenneth.

The Prof held the photo in his hands and studied it. Then I saw a smile on his face. "And this is the guy we're after. Do you know anything about him?"

"Just that Kenneth Lawson was his name. He once owned a company in Seattle with his brother. I know his adopted parents' name. And I know he worked a while for a man named William Delecarte at a computer company also in Seattle. It's all on this paper. His Christian name given at birth was Saul Bernard and he was adopted in Seattle."

"Then I can trace him."

"You're shitting me? You can trace people with only information from a computer?"

He nodded and replied, "Affirmative. Now what's this name—Paul?"

"Oh, Paul's his twin. He's the brother who owned the business with him. A computer business."

"My kind of men. Where do you think they are now?"

The question brought me back to the world.

"I don't know." I refused to say either one was dead. "See, I have these people," I continued, "that I'm trying to connect to him." I hoped he was as good as the chef thought he was. "Also," I said, "I was given a disk possibly compiled by a doctor at the CDC named Kia Mutota. On the disk she refers to another doctor at the CDC but she never uses his name, only the initials W.G. This was from her records at the CDC. If you could get into her personal notes, maybe she named the other doctor. He was involved in a study of twins Kenneth Lawson and his brother might have participated in a long time ago. Dr. Mutota, Kia Mutota, had an accidental death before she could tell me," I lied. "And then I have this list. It's other people that I think were in this same twin study. It was probably around the fifties. Can you help me with any of this?"

"Let's see your names. Hmmm. Gotcha. Eat and come back over when you're done."

"Oh, the information from Mutota was encrypted. So I suspect any notes she's got at the CDC are encrypted also."

"No big deal. I got it."

I let the chef know I was ready for the meal. It was the best pasta I'd ever had in my life. And considering how things were going, it might be the best pasta *ever*. I asked for more sauce and was told he'd have to make it. Turns out he makes only one serving per person. Okay, I said, figuring I had plenty of time. And I was right. Three hours later the Prof called me over.

"The CDC was a piece of cake. Your doctor friend kept some meticulous notes. All right. This is the deal. A doctor there at the CDC was a part of a study funded by the Pioneer Fund in 1952.

"His name is Dr. Wallace Gramm. The study was called the Gemini study because it was twins, you know. The subjects were all born between May 25 and June 15 of varying years. All Geminis. Evidently, according to the study, it was like an astrology thing. Go figure."

"What kind of study was it?"

"Something to do with theories of eugenics and pigmentation. I ain't really into that kind of science. Computers. You give me computer language, I can break it up."

"What about the other names? Were all the people on that list in the same study?"

"Yep. All of them. Not at the same time, though. Eventually the study lost its funding source. It doesn't give an explanation—you know, why they didn't get any more money. Probably the shit they were studying got unpopular."

After the Prof gave me the doctor's name I felt more confident about what I'd be after. I went to the phone and dialed the CDC and asked for Dr. Gramm. "This is his cousin," I lied.

"Oh. I'm sorry. Dr. Gramm resigned and didn't leave any forwarding information. Sorry."

Not as sorry as I was. "Excuse me," I said, "are you sure you don't know how to get in touch with him? When did this happen?"

"I'm sure I don't know how to get in touch with him. As for the time, well, I can't really give out that information."

"I was supposed to come stay with him tonight. Oh gosh. He probably forgot. You know, the absentminded professor. Are you sure you don't know how I can contact him?"

"Sorry. No. . . . Actually, there is someone here who might be able to help you. They worked together. Hold on, I'll ring her office."

The phone rang and a woman answered the phone. She had a heavy German accent. "Dr. Louise Gerstner speaking."

"Dr. Gerstner, this is a relative of Dr. Gramm. I was supposed to spend a few days with him and they tell me he isn't there. Could you maybe tell me how to contact him?" I didn't want her to know I knew he'd resigned.

"Who is this?" she asked, angry or scared. I couldn't tell which.

"I told you, I'm his cousin."

She hung up.

I looked at the phone. What was that about? I tried redialing. Her line was busy. Damn.

I didn't have much time. I told the Prof what happened. "What am I going to do? He was my only contact."

"Go see her. She can't hang up then. Tell her you're a close friend and you're in trouble. I don't think the cousin thing'll work too good in person. You know what I mean?"

"Yeah. Seeing me might make it a leap for her. But do you have any personal information about her that might make it easier to talk to her? Maybe where she went to school? Then I could pretend he told me all about her or something."

"No prob." In a second he'd pulled up her bio, information about her specialty at the CDC and a photo of a stern-looking gray-haired German woman. "Jackpot."

I felt like the clock was ticking louder for me to get to the bottom of this. Jeff Samuels had my disk so that meant he might know as much as I did or more by now if the other disks were complete. But he didn't know about the Dogons or the diamond. At least, I didn't think he did. Now I'd have to get my information the good, old journalistic way. Go to the source.

I got up to go. The Prof shook my hand. "Luck to you, Patricia Conley."

"Thanks," I replied, gathering up my pocketbook. In the distance I heard my name again. I looked around, but I didn't see anyone gazing my way. The chef was nowhere in sight. Shit. Now I was having auditory hallucinations. I started for the door. There it was again—"Patricia Conley." I spun around and looked up to where the sound spilled out. The Prof was looking up too.

A news anchor on the Channel 5 repeat news was ending her two-minute report with, "As stated earlier, Patricia Conley is not a confirmed suspect, she's only wanted for questioning in the murders of a man named Saul Bernard, alias Kenneth Lawson, and a woman named Claudette Duvet. Ironically, this connection was initially made from some overdue library books found in one of the victims' homes. It just goes to show how vital libraries are in the nineties. If anyone knows the whereabouts of Miss Conley, please call this number." A number flashed on the screen.

What the fuck? Goddamn it. How was this possible? Library books. Oh shit. Kenneth's books must have been at Claudette Duvet's house, and they had traced them back to me. I was getting married, minding my own damn business, and now I was wanted for questioning. Shit. Shit. *Shit.*

The Prof took two strides to get near me. "You are in a heap of dung, friend. Come on back. Let's see what this is all about. I'm itching here. I've not been in the police's business since they sent me to prison for nothing. I'd love to scratch them now."

"Look. I don't want to get you in any trouble. One of us in trouble is more than enough."

"You let me handle my business and you handle yours. Believe me, I can get in and out without them knowing. No sweat."

He didn't lie. A half-hour later, in a low monotone, the Prof explained to me that the police had found my fingerprints on the razor that slit Claudette Duvet's wrist. Awful damn surprising since I'd never touched a razor in my life. With the exception of Kenneth Lawson's razor. I froze. Could it have been his razor? The one he used to trim his neck? But how would the police get that razor? Unless Kenneth Lawson actually . . . I couldn't think that thought. It was not possible. *Oh my God. I'm in deep shit.*

Not deep enough, the Prof informed me. It seemed that Kenneth Lawson did die of a brain aneurysm. But there was also an unidentifiable foreign substance swimming around in his blood that they suspected I might have given him, since he had a fresh needle mark on his arm. Their labs were evaluating the substance now.

The only chance I had left was to get to the CDC before they got off work and watched the six o'clock news. Otherwise Dr. Louise Gerstner or somebody there'd be calling the freaking cops on me. Shit.

I hurried out with Prof, who insisted on taking me to the CDC. His greatest pleasure, he confessed, was helping an underdog. His new job since he'd gotten out of prison was finding people. He described himself as a private detective without a license or a gun. In other words, an illegal computer spy.

CHAPTER THIRTY-FIVE

The CDC's previous director was Dr. Richard Owen, a handsome black man with mixed gray hair and an excellent academic pedigree. I had considered interviewing him before he left, but I'd not done it because I was torn.

It was a tightrope that as a journalist I often walked. Wanting to feel proud of the accomplishments of black people without making it seem like it was a fucking miracle. Hell, any person, black or white, given the same opportunity and drive probably does what they set out to do. I remembered how it was for me. As an *A* student my white teachers would sometimes call me out and say things like "Patricia Conley is one of the smartest black students here."

I loved being black. It was a given, and I would not have chosen to be any other person, but the implication in that statement was you're not the best, but only the best *black* student. The white students were still better. I longed for the day they'd say, "Patricia Conley is one of the smartest students here." But it never happened.

The CDC is a number of old buildings mixed in with new ones. None of them look much like the CDC of the movies. The Prof and I scrunched down in his 1976 yellow Volkswagen convertible. I wasn't sure about going in now that I was sitting out front and wanted for questioning. Suppose someone inside recognized me from the television? Who knew, they might have televisions everywhere, like at the newspaper.

"Here," the Prof said, after rummaging around in the backseat. "Use these." He handed me some high-powered binoculars.

"What do you do with these?"

"I'm a bird-watcher."

And despite the shit I was in, I heard the song "I'm a Birdwatcher" go off in my head. Damn music is pervasive.

I trained the lenses on the building. "There she is!" I screamed. "Over there in the blue sweater, walking faster than a fireman on call." I checked my watch. No one else was walking out of the building.

"She's getting in a car," I said, "over there." My instincts spoke up. "I need to follow her."

"Then let's go."

"No. I have to do this alone. No more people can get involved in this. Really, I appreciate your concern but this is on me."

"Then take my car. I can get back to the Red Light. I'll wait for you there. Okay?"

"Okay. Thanks. You don't have to—"

"She's taking off," he interrupted. "Go on." He jumped out and motioned me to follow her car. "One more thing," he said, sticking his head inside. He handed me a small black plastic thimble shape. "Attach this microphone to the binoculars if you need to. Hit the red button and it will be on. You can see and hear from a long ways."

Dr. Gerstner was pulling out of the parking lot, sliding her card through the parrot-blue box for employees.

"Why do you have this? Never mind," I said, realizing it wasn't any of my damn business. I suppose as an unlicensed PI he was a bird listener too.

CHAPTER THIRTY-SIX

I followed Dr. Gerstner, staying a few car lengths behind. Twice I had to stop and pull over to the side, since she continually turned her body to look behind her.

The Prof had a car phone. I reasoned he wouldn't care if I used it. I phoned my shihans, Scott and Ted, while I drove. This could get nasty. I'd like to have some backup in case somebody else was following the both of us. Something must have made her all jumpy. Maybe it was my phone call to her at the CDC earlier?

No answer at their homes or offices. I left a message for them saying where I'd be and that I might need their help. There was no telling where they were. Tonight was not the night for the class and both of them worked long hours, most outside the office.

And then I did it. I impulsively phoned Jeff Samuels. Thank God he didn't answer. But me and my dumb self, I left a message saying where I was.

We were behind an old abandoned warehouse in an industrial complex south on Marietta Street. The doctor parked her car and rushed up the steps to the warehouse, still furtively scanning the landscape. I parked near her car, in case I had to drag her ass out at some point, and ran after her. I waited until she slipped into a side door. Then I followed behind her as quietly as I could into the warehouse. I hoped I could hide behind the crates and barrels stacked all around.

She turned and looked back as though she heard something.

I slid behind a barrel and held my breath. Where was she going? Maybe this was a trap. I felt inside my purse for the taser gun. For some reason it made me feel more secure. If things got rough, I would use it. My heartbeat speeded up.

I moved further into the warehouse. I held the binoculars up and attached the hearing device. I hit the red button. I could hear the doctor's footfalls sounding like thuds on a heavy punching bag.

A gray-haired man stepped out from the shadows. They embraced like lovers kept apart by spiteful parents.

"You've got to leave town," I heard Dr. Gerstner say. "Someone broke into the CDC and ransacked your old office."

"Did you bring my passport?" the man asked.

Dr. Gramm?

"Yes," she choked out, and even though I couldn't see Dr. Gerstner's face, I knew that choking sound. She was crying.

"You can come join me in Germany when things are safe," he said to her.

They were lovers. That's why the girl had transferred my call to her. She knew they were lovers.

He continued, "It looks to me like they've killed all the twins. Now there is only me left as a witness. I didn't think Oscar would kill his brother, but he did."

"Are you sure he killed him?"

"No, I'm sure he had him killed. He's got those goons working for him now. William told me that much. I swear I wish I'd not gotten involved in this nightmare."

"How were you to know how sick Oscar was?" Dr. Gerstner continued. "God, Wallace, neither you nor William could have predicted Oscar would do the things he's done while he's been living in Atlanta."

"Yes, but William warned me years ago that the Dogon elder had predicted this. That's why the Dogon did not tell them all there was to know about the mythology or the potion. Who knew his heart but the Dogon? His own twin didn't know it."

Shit. The Delecartes—they were twins too? The monk had used the plural when we talked, but it hadn't registered. I had Portia Hill in Seattle checking out William Delecarte for me. Not a brother. This meant Oscar Delecarte was right here in Atlanta. Probably that's why Kenneth had come here.

"Yes. You're probably right," Dr. Gerstner said in an anxious voice, the implications of how dangerous this might be obviously just dawning on her. "But," she continued, almost pleading, "now you've got to get away or I'm sure he'll kill you like he's done the others."

"Did you find out who Dr. Mutota had contacted?" Dr. Gramm asked, maintaining a calming tone.

"No. However, the police suspect a woman had something to do with Kenneth Lawson's death and Claudette Duvet's as well. I saw it on the television, just before a woman phoned me pretending to be your cousin. She could have been calling for Oscar, trying to find you. The suspect's name was . . . let me see. Patricia Conley."

It was my cue. "That's a damn lie," I said, stepping out from the shadows and startling the crap out of both of them. "I'm not the damn suspect."

I had fished the taser gun out of my purse and held it like it was a regular gun, even though the instructions clearly stated not to do that. Shit, these two hadn't read the instructions.

"Hold it right there," I said, switching the taser on so the red beam was directed toward Dr. Gerstner's heart. "You are going to come clean or I'll blast the shit out of both of you." I pointed the taser. "Her first."

"What is that thing?" Dr. Gramm asked. "Is it a gun?"

"It's a lethal weapon," I lied, "new technology. If I shoot either one of you, your ticker will stop. Now, on with our business. I don't have time for idle chitchat. This is not a fucking movie. Tell me what the hell is going on."

"Who are you?" Dr. Gramm asked.

"Please, you can take our money, our watches. Here," Dr. Gerstner said, ripping her watch and earrings off and tossing them at my feet. Then she reached inside her purse.

"Hold it!" I shouted. Hell, old people can have guns too. "Don't reach in there. Throw your purse over to me. Now."

She slid the purse over near my foot. I walked to it, reached down and picked it up, still keeping the taser directed at her. Even though there was no telling where that red beam was at this point. I opened her purse with one hand. A gun. A real pearl-handled gun.

"So you were going to shoot me?" I asked, looking at her with a mixture of anger and awe. I couldn't help it. I loved old women who could take care of themselves.

"You," I said, aiming the taser at Dr. Gramm. "You are going to tell me now what this is about or get your ass lasered."

"What exactly do you want to know, young lady?"

"Don't fuck with me, old man. I've had a bad few days and it's because of you. I'm the one Kia Mutota brought your papers to. And I'm the same one that is asking you what the hell is so important in those papers that nuts are going around killing people for them. People I had planned to marry, I might add."

"You were marrying one of the twins?"

"Yes. Now out with it."

"Are you pregnant?"

"What is this? A right-to-life seminar? Goddamn it. Don't stall."

"All right. All right," he said, shrugging to Dr. Gerstner. "What is the use. I'm an old man. In the late fifties two of my colleagues, twin brothers, heard about this fascinating tribe in Africa called the Dogons. Supposedly they not only knew a lot of astronomy but magic as well.

"It seems my colleagues had gotten this information from one of the people on a research expedition with Marcel Griaule, a famed anthropologist. Evidently there was a whispered legend of two primordial seeds hidden among these people. Supposedly the origin of man and woman.

"The twins, Dr. William and Oscar Delecarte, went there and met with a few of the tribesmen. One of the Dogon elders who had what they called 'deep knowledge' supposedly also had great medicine—a potion that came from God knows where, but when smoked was more powerful than peyote. The old man said that if injected in the pineal gland, it could make the shades of man.

"At that time no one had thought the pineal gland did much of anything. Of course, we would later know differently. After gathering up the information, the Delecartes came back to America to see if any of this information could be useful.

"The Dogons put us way ahead of everybody else in genetics and melanin theory. It was not until 1953 that the double-helix structure was proposed. And 1956 before the twenty-three pairs of chromosomes were identified in human body cells. The Dogons' number was twenty-two and it *was* a double helix.

"We understood back then after studying their cosmogony the fundamental aspects of genetic inheritance—meiotic segregation. The Delecartes and I were thinking of writing it up when we discovered something even more astonishing. The knowledge the Dogons had about amino acids, RNA and DNA could take us to a higher strata all together. Of course, they didn't use those terms but they had the information just the same. Remember, this is before 1977, when the first techniques to sequence the chemical message of DNA molecules had taken place."

"Yeah. Well, I'm afraid I don't remember. Could you get on with this and tell me what it is you were up to?"

"You see, dark pigment created the coloring of mankind. But we discovered, coupled with information the Dogons gave us, we could understand the formation of melanocyte cell hybrids, which contain negative regulatory genes that suppress either the production of melanin or the production of basic fibroblast growth. Using the Dogons' elaborate counting system to determine the possible evolution of humans, we uncovered a way to master the switching system of the chromosomes."

"What the fuck are you saying?" I asked. Hoping this wasn't going where it sounded like it was going. I knew a little about the pineal gland myself.

"Right now scientists are excited that they've made breakthroughs about the human P gene. The latest news is that a common deletion allele of the human P gene is found in Africans and African-Americans with albinism. For us that would have been old news. We knew how to make the pigmentation vanish without any form of isalbinism." He cleared his throat.

"What is isalbinism?" I asked.

"The common term is albinism," Dr. Gramm continued. "To make a long story short, because if you've been followed here, we are all in danger for knowing any of this, we knew how to change the melanin production in the body.

"The Delecartes injected the Dogon potion into the bloodstreams and pineal and pituitary glands of twins in a study, for about thirteen years in varying doses. I was only included because they needed another geneticist to assist them."

"They were using children?"

"Yes. William never wanted us to use children; he fought to use rats instead. William, like many scientists, was always idealistic. Too idealistic for his own good. But Oscar wouldn't compromise. He felt waiting to use humans would take too long, and rats are not humans. Eventually Oscar and I overruled William and we began the studies."

"What happened?"

"Nothing happened. The children seemed to show no changes and eventually the funding for the project was stopped. The project abandoned. We each went our separate ways. I came to the CDC. The Delecartes never resolved their bitter disagreements about the potion and they parted company permanently. William stayed in Seattle. Oscar eventually moved here."

"What happened after the experiments?"

"I don't know. I lost touch with both of them. I expected great things from Oscar. He was a go-getter and at the time I knew him I thought he wanted scientific notoriety among our peers."

"You thought?"

"It turned out Oscar was power- and money-hungry. Recently William found indications that led him to conclude Oscar had began new experiments, plus had a new funding source.

"William confronted his brother. Shortly after that William met with an unexplained but vicious death. Supposedly someone robbed him and bludgeoned him to death. That someone, of course, has never been found.

"Before his death William sent me what he thought to be the only original copy of the notes he'd taken with the Dogon elder."

"I'm not following you. If nothing happened with the experiments, then why the big deal?"

"About a year ago, a set of twins who'd been involved in the study named Claudette and Marvette Duvet had a problem."

"My God," Dr. Gerstner screamed, "don't tell her any more. She's being accused of killing one of them, Wallace. Forget it. Don't tell her. Let her shoot if she wants to."

"Shut up, would you?" I said to Dr. Gerstner. "Or I'll just shoot him. How would you like those test tubes, baby?"

Her eyes widened and I knew she was no different than all the millions of women in love. Scientist or not, she didn't want her lover harmed.

Dr. Gramm continued. I began to suspect he was Catholic and just needed to confess this ungodly shit to somebody.

"One of the Duvet twins, Marvette, got pregnant and experienced the onset of an undetermined illness at the same time. Unfortunately she died giving birth to a stillborn fetus.

"It turned out that Dr. Mutota, who was a personal friend of the Duvets, examined the tissue. After doing some research and connecting me to the original twin studies on the Duvets when they were children, Dr. Mutota came to me. I contacted Oscar Delecarte on her behalf, to see if the illness had anything to do with the injections he'd given the Duvets. That's where I made my fatal mistake."

"How so?"

"I explained to Oscar what had happened to the Duvet twin. I also told him the other twin was ill as well. Her symptoms were that she was more sensitive to light, having problems with her vision; a pink film had circled her retina. Plus, she suffered severe headaches that did not appear to be typical migraines, memory problems and was becoming more and more susceptible to infection."

"And then what happened? Wait a minute. You said more susceptible to infection. Did they have some strain of AIDS?"

He smiled. "You need to read more. No. No AIDS. From what I gathered, she and her twin had experienced subtle but definite shifts in their neuromuscular functioning, their vision, including sensitivity to sunlight; their inner ear; an increase in the activity of their temporal limbic system and deterioration of the central nervous system since puberty. And, I later discovered, for the males in the research there was a problem with low sperm count. They also suffered from alternating bouts of depression and aggression. They'd been seeking treatment on and off to no avail."

"So what happened then?"

"I shared with Oscar Dr. Mutota's conclusions after she'd examined the baby's and mother's tissue. This African Trinidadian woman, the Duvet twin, coupled with an African man had, for all practical purposes, a Caucasian baby. I thought Oscar'd be elated. I know. I know. It is not politically correct anymore to wish for a pure white race, but that's what I guess Oscar and I had secretly hoped for originally."

"Get real," I mumbled. "I'm sure that baby was a fluke of nature. An albino." I knew from Kia Mutota's notes this much but I wanted him to tell me more.

"No. It was not an albino. It seems that Oscar and William knew what I didn't know. Even though William swore to me that he didn't find it out until much later."

"Find out what?"

"That the potion the Dogons gave them, if used in the right combinations, which only the Delecartes knew, would render all the melanin recessive."

"Okay. I didn't take Genetics 101," I said, tired of holding the damn taser up.

"In other words, thanks to the Dogons' knowledge, the Delecartes could make a white baby."

I dropped the taser. It tumbled and landed upright, which is more than I can say for my stomach. I bent down and picked it up and slipped it into my purse which was slung over my shoulder. This man was not the "they" trying to kill me. I needed something to do while I processed this.

Up until this moment I hadn't believed this was really true. I wanted to believe that Dr. Mutota and the Duvets were a bunch of paranoid nuts running around crying wolf. "You can't be serious. You mean they could make a white baby no matter the race of the parents? Every time?"

"I'm serious, yes. That is correct. Except it would be in the next generation, the offspring of the people taking the treatment."

"It still doesn't make sense. Then why wasn't Oscar Delecarte elated?"

"That I'm not sure of. All I know is that if I'm correct about what happened next, I set off a chain of events that caused Oscar to make sure all the twins had fatal accidents."

"I don't believe you. You're lying. If the twins' kids were going to be white babies, why kill them? Isn't that what you just said Oscar wanted? Proof that his formula worked so that he could make this all-white race? And to be famous on top of that?"

"You would think he'd be elated. But he wasn't. He vowed me to secrecy. I don't know why he didn't want it revealed. But trying to find out is why William got himself killed."

"Listen," Dr. Gerstner interrupted, "I would love for you two to ponder this philosophically, but if Wallace doesn't leave now the both of you might actually have an eternity to ponder it together."

I truly liked this woman. I said, still pursuing Dr. Gramm, "So William and his brother did this to all the twins?"

"Heavens, no. Are you listening to me at all, young woman? William Delecarte found out about the Duvet baby from Kenneth Lawson. Oscar didn't tell him. He knew William would have been furious.

"Kenneth confronted William after someone attempted to cause his brother, Keith, to have an 'accident' by slipping pills in his drink. Both of the brothers knew something was wrong even before this. They'd fallen ill gradually and had been seeing a doctor. William Delecarte didn't even know they were given injections in the Gemini study. Oscar did it behind his back. William would have never permitted the twins to be exposed to any experiments."

"But," I protested, "Kenneth must have known. My understanding was the twins in the study were given rings. Gemini rings. I know for a fact that Kenneth Lawson wore one of those rings. So why didn't William know that? He obviously knew more about Kenneth than I did."

"You're right. But if I remember correctly, Oscar claimed he gave those boys their rings so they wouldn't feel left out when other children, who were getting the injections, showed up at their lab when the boys were kids.

"William Delecarte was one of the most naive men I've ever known. So it's conceivable to me he believed Oscar when he told him that the twins weren't involved in the experiments."

"And so you're telling me Kenneth was sick and William didn't know it and couldn't have found out? After all, he was a doctor. I'd think he had connections."

"On the days Kenneth was ill, he merely stayed out of William's sight. As for another doctor telling William, Kenneth used his Christian name, Saul, to seek medical treatment so William wouldn't find out he was sick. He didn't want to worry the old man. Kenneth had been taking some totally useless injections from a quack doctor in Seattle.

"William called me after Kenneth confronted him about the Duvet women's illness. Somehow the remaining Duvet twin had tracked Kenneth down and filled his head with suspicions. William denied them to Kenneth, but then he called me.

"William demanded to know if Oscar had injected the boys all those years ago as a part of our study without telling him. I hated to admit I knew, but I did. So I told him the truth.

"The two boys didn't even know until William confessed to Kenneth that they'd been a part of the study. Kenneth was furious and quit his job at William's laboratory, thinking William knew about the injections and the resulting illness all along. Kenneth had been working for William since his parents had their fatal accident."

"Working for him? So what did William care if Kenneth was mad at him?"

"You certainly know very little to be suspected of killing two people. It's simple. William Delecarte loved those boys. He'd abandoned any active role in the research soon after we started using twins. Kenneth and Keith didn't know that, of course. They had no idea why or when the Delecartes fell out with each other.

"They also never knew William financed both their educations and found the family that adopted them to make sure they had a good home. He paid for everything for those children."

"You've lost me," I said, pulling a box over and sitting down. I motioned them to sit too. I was tired, frustrated and getting more than a little confused.

"You're a smart woman. After Kenneth confronted him, William was furious with Oscar. He immediately started investigating his brother, when it occurred to him that signs the Dogon elder had described to them were appearing. William told me that he believed this a signal of something yet to come. It was during this time the Dogons believed changes on the earth were going to begin taking place. The Dogons' ceremony, called the Sigui, was last performed in 1969. And according to William, if the signs for the ceremony weren't present in 1998, the world would have hell to pay by the year 2000."

"What signs?"

"I'm not sure of all of them, but they were supposed to come before a time when, the Dogons said, the world would know the meaning of the two Genesis stories in the Bible. Before the millennium."

"The two Genesis stories?" Here it was again. "You still didn't tell me what signs." I was beginning to like this old man too. He'd not said I was a smart *black* woman.

"New stars and planets in the solar systems. New discoveries related to carbon, the basis of our life-form, and new discoveries that would spin Darwin's theory of evolution on its axis."

I studied his face. I wondered if he noticed the shadow that sailed across mine when he mentioned carbon. I wondered if that meant they all knew about the diamond. I didn't want to question him further about this.

But I had to ask the question that poked at the back of my mind. Who was funding Oscar Delecarte now and what was he up to?

CHAPTER THIRTY-SEVEN

But before I could ask, bullets poked themselves into the bodies of Dr. Gramm and Dr. Gerstner and had them dancing around the cement floor like puppets on a string. I crawled on all fours toward the warehouse entrance. I couldn't figure where the shower rained down from. I thought about the taser, but whoever was shooting was more than fifteen feet away. Plus, I didn't even know if it would actually work.

Dr. Gramm and Dr. Gerstner lay almost on top of each other wearing red, gory outfits. Now lovers together eternally.

I crouched down behind a wall of crates. A thought attacked my mind like a meat cleaver. Evidently Shihan Ted and Shihan Scott hadn't got my message, so there would be no cavalry. Where was the old Dogon when I needed him? Like he could help, even if he were real. But someone knew where I was.

Jeff Samuels. He was the only one who knew. Goddamn it. How stupid could I be?

There was a time for self-flagellation, but now wasn't that time. I crawled my ass out the door and sprinted for the car. A barrage of bullets pounded the ground behind my heels, whipping up mini-tornadoes of dust. I ran for the car and dived for the door handle. A bullet zoomed and hit me in the shoulder. The force of it dropped me like a brick. Colorful dots jumped in my eyes while I attempted to crawl the rest of the way to the car.

A blur came toward me. My shoulder hurt like hell and my thoughts crushed together. The dusty vision got closer. It was Jeff. With a gun. Fire blazed from the end. He was shooting at me.

No. He was running and shooting over my head. I turned and glimpsed two men shooting back at him. When he reached the car he dived on top of me as a hail of bullets ricocheted and hit Dr. Gerstner's car a few feet away.

The car exploded, spewing metal and offering a momentary cloud cover as Jeff picked me up and shoved me onto the seat of his car. He got in and gunned the engine. In seconds everything was a blur. And I had my second blackout without alcohol.

♊

When I woke we were back at his place in the country. He opened the door for me and got out. I could see a light on inside the house. No other cars were in sight. I grabbed his arm. "Someone's in there," I said, panicked.

♊

No one was inside. Jeff had a timer on his lights. He helped me to the couch, made me some sleepy time tea and placed wet towels on my forehead. Slowly the tea did its work. Down, down into another kind of haze I fell, where the Dogon's face from my dream could haunt me freely.

When I opened my eyes again, it was night. A macabre darkness engulfed the candlelit room. Jeff sat watching me. I rubbed my eyes, allowing time for my pupils to adjust to the room's light.

"Are you feeling any better now?" Jeff asked, coming over and rubbing my forehead. "I was worried about you."

I looked at my shoulder. He'd dressed my wound. It still smarted.

"You ought to be worried about yourself," I said. "It seems people who're around me are dropping faster than rain. I think I need to do something about it but I swear I don't know what. Maybe it's time to go to the police. I'm not sure what to say but I can't keep protecting Kenneth. I didn't kill him or anyone else, so I have nothing to hide. Not anymore."

"Are you sure you have nothing to hide? Somebody thinks Kenneth Lawson gave you or told you something? Whoever it is, is not going to stop until they get what they want from you. Maybe if you tell me what it is I can protect you."

I stared at him. Was he trying to trick me into telling him about the diamond? Or could it be he knew about it but didn't know where it was? I grimaced and attempted to sit up. "I don't think—"

"Shhhhhh," Jeff said, his head tilted. He'd been listening and looking toward the window. The screen door was locked but the outer door was open.

In a split second he blew out the candles.

I let out a little shriek. Jeff didn't make a sound.

"What did you do that for?" I gasped.

"Shhhhh," he said again, and I felt his hand come up to cover my mouth.

I wanted to say something but then I heard a sound coming from outside the screen door. A faint sound. I didn't recognize it at first and then it swelled up like it might have been inside my body. Wheezing. The wheezing I'd heard on the phone.

The door crashed in. A flared light burst into the room. I could see shadows rushing forward.

Jeff moved away in a swish. I heard grunts, groans and crashing all around me. I heard Jeff yell out, a solar-plexus cry. A flurry of movement beside me. I heard someone else scream out. A man, but not Jeff.

I jumped to my feet. A hand crashed into my stomach. I stumbled backward against the wall.

"Don't kill her. Take her down and then get the hell out of here," an unfamiliar male voice roared.

I felt a huge hand go around my neck in a chokehold.

There is no fucking way all my money for martial arts lessons is going to waste. I actually thought that thought before I stepped in with my right foot. I grabbed him by both lapels and shoved my foot into his stomach. I dropped down on my back, throwing him over my head while still holding on to him. I felt the weight of his huge body coming upward with my momentum. His momentum pulled me back over on top of him. While squatting on his chest, I reached down and drove both thumbs into his eyes. Without slowing I executed an open-hand technique to his windpipe.

The person began sputtering. Coughing. I struck again, this time using a V hand strike.

Crash. Still coughing, the attacker grabbed my arm. I jumped up off his chest and grabbed his wrist with my right hand, twisted it and flipped him over on his stomach. I placed my right foot on the floor and pulled his arm up against my bent knee, dislocating his shoulder and breaking his elbow.

He screamed.

Before I made my way in the direction of the door, I kicked him in the back of his head with my heel, driving his face into the floor. Now, that's what I call kicking them to the curb!

I heard Jeff yelling to me, "Get out now. *Now.*"

Others had entered the room. Fighting sounds pounded as if from loudspeakers at a ball game. I couldn't see anything.

"Jeff," I yelled.

"Get out now. Right fucking now if you care about me at all."

His words stabbed me in the heart. Jeff Samuels had cursed. Oh shit. I ran outside to the car.

I dived behind the wheel of the Volvo, waiting for Jeff to follow. A bullet whizzed past my head and the windshield imploded. I covered my face instinctually. I screamed and peeped up long enough to see the glass flying into my face as I revved the engine. For a split second I weighed whether I should go back inside. Then it occurred to me that they were after me. If I left, maybe they'd leave Jeff alone and follow me. I speeded off, honking the horn loudly.

As I drove I couldn't feel the shards of glass embedded in my cheeks and chin. The pain in my face and shoulder was nothing compared to the pain in my heart. My hands did not leave the wheel and I was doing at least ninety miles per hour. I thought stupidly, you might get a ticket, as though it really mattered at this point.

Then I heard it. An explosion. Gigantic flames leaped so high into the air I could see them in my rearview mirror. My foot jerked in a convulsion on the brake. I couldn't stop the car.

Finally, I managed to stop. The house had to be engulfed in flames; I could see the hot yellow glow beyond the bank of trees. Tears streamed down my face. I started the car and pulled off at a normal speed. It was a few minutes before sirens filled the air.

I prayed to be lifted over the houses like the kid on the bicycle in my favorite movie, *E.T.* Because now I knew exactly how *E.T.* felt. What I wanted more than anything was to go home.

♊

Where could I go? The police were after me. All the men in my life were either dead or missing. Carol, my only friend, shot. I didn't want to involve anyone else until I could think. The only leads I had, dead. I needed some rest. I knew that. I needed to think this out and rest. The only person I knew that no one could connect to me was the Prof.

♊

I drove without much thought back to the Red Light Cafe, which stayed open until 4 A.M. I prayed the Prof would be there, not that I knew what the hell I was going to tell him about his car. It might be full of bullets. Whatever. I had no place else to go.

♊

The Prof was still waiting for me. "Don't sweat the car. You can crash at my house."

He lived in a small duplex in Little Five Points. If ever there was a place the cops wouldn't search, it was here. The hippies of the seventies lived here in droves. Only now, they were mixed with the punk rockers.

I lay down on the futon. You cannot sink down on one. Even when I'd had one, I'd wondered if sleeping on the fucking floor wouldn't be the same.

The Prof gave me prescription painkillers, doctored my face and ordered me to sleep. He'd observed he'd never been shot before but it looked like whoever cleaned me up knew more than the basics.

I agreed. Jeff Samuels had cleaned my grazed shoulder like an old country doctor before making me drink the tea. He'd had a first aid kit. My mind drifted, carried on a wave of drug-effected thoughts.

What if he is dead? Dead because of me? I do care for him. I love him. I thought that thought, even if it made me feel like I was betraying Kenneth.

But if I did love Jeff, why in the world would my last conscious thought be, He could have staged all of this to gain my trust again.

At least, I could say men had to go to great extremes to trick me. Uh-huh, Patricia Conley didn't just fall for the first okey-doke tale men had to tell.

CHAPTER THIRTY-EIGHT

When the sun hit my face, so did the pain. It might've been a shoulder graze but it sure hurt. I got up and tried showering with one hand. It was hard as hell to get that color shit out of my hair. I looked worse than a swamp dog.

I slipped on the man's clothes the Prof had laid out for me. The little nicks on my face reminded me of shaving, which brought me to the razor. Damn. The police were looking for me.

I phoned Carol's hospital room. No answer. I looked up her parents' number in the phone book and called them. I couldn't even remember where I'd written their number down before I left the hospital.

Carol answered.

"Hey, how are you? How are you feeling?" I asked her.

"Better than you. What in hell is going on? The word is they're snooping around the paper, asking questions. You would not believe the people who are claiming to be your friend. Defending you too. Amazing, huh? That fucking detective keeps calling me asking have I heard from you. And today this woman detective called. She's a piece of work, I tell you. Maybe you should turn yourself in. You didn't do anything. They say they only want to talk.

"Wait. Before we hang up . . . I hate to remind you but I picked up Kenneth Lawson's ashes for you. They're here whenever you're ready. We better hang up. Tracers, you know."

"Don't. I need to talk to someone I can trust."

"Quickly. What do you need me to do?"

"Nothing. I want to say thanks. And Carol . . . "

"Yes?"

"I . . . I—"

"We're friends, right? Speaking of friends, you know who is not a fucking cop?"

"Thanks, Carol. I know. Jeff Samuels. I'll call you later."

Ashes. Kenneth Lawson or Saul Bernard was now ashes in an urn. I couldn't accept it. I *would* not accept Kenneth was dead.

Don't dwell on it. You've got things to do. You're in deep shit. And whoever is doing this has got to pay. Not only for what's happened to you but what has happened to Kenneth, the other twins, the doctors and to Jeff. The thoughts made tears well up. Oh my God. Jeff and my fucking cat. But I didn't have time to waste. I wasn't stopping until someone went down with me.

I stared at the phone. Did they have enough time to trace the call? Shit, for all I knew they probably monitored this phone. Damn it. I'd forgotten that the Prof had been in trouble with the feds—or maybe he was working for them. *Shit.*

I looked around. He was gone. No note. I pulled on the Braves cap he'd left on the futon and let myself out, locking the door. I hoped he had his key with him. I walked down to the corner and called a cab.

This damn time I would rent a car. But how? If I did that I couldn't use a false name; they'd want my driver's license even if I paid cash. Damn. I caught the cab to Ira's place.

We huddled in the back. I told him what had been happening.

"I've got a plan, Ira. I've been thinking. Dr. Gramm told me that this Oscar Delecarte had found new funding. Who would fund him, is my thought. Then it occurred to me. You could find out through the Anti-Defamation League. If there's any funding going on about how to create a white man, in essence a white race, who would be doing it but—"

"The eugenics folk or the Aryan Nation people. You are a genius," he said.

I smiled. I wasn't a black genius to Ira. I was just a genius.

"That's the ticket. Can you check that out for me? See who is funding Delecarte? If we find that out, then that might lead us to what he's up to."

"I'll do it right away. And you? Vill you rest?"

"No. I'm going to see that material scientist. I phoned on my way over from a pay phone and made an appointment earlier. There's only one problem. I need to rent a car."

"I can do that for you."

"That's very kind, Ira, but you can't. You need a driver's license to rent a car."

"I said I didn't own a car. I didn't say I didn't have a driver's license," he said, smiling. "When I go out of town, I drive. I can have a car delivered here in no time. You vait here," he continued, heading for the phone book.

He was a wonderful man and a good friend. For someone who felt so alone all my life, I managed to have two good friends right under my nose. Sometimes a person cannot see the forest for the trees.

I'd broken all the stereotypes. I have a white girl friend, I thought, a good Jewish friend and I had or have at least one or maybe even two wonderful black men who love me. Or loved me. Damn. Life has its surprises.

When he returned from the phone he said, "I'll take you for the car, and then I'm going over to the League's offices. I'll meet you back here later on. I'll be here until five. Then you can go home with me tonight."

"Thanks, Ira," I said, wishing I could hug him. He hugged me and I awkwardly put my hands up like I was going to hug him back, but never made the contact. One step at a time, I thought. One step at a time. And when this is over, I'm carrying my ass to AA.

We picked up the car, and after I dropped Ira off, I drove to the cemetery and retrieved the diamond, careful that no one followed me and staying out of sight of police.

The company NVA was in Norcross, in an area filled with research facilities. I hadn't even known it was there. They analyzed space dust for NASA.

"Hello. You must be Miss Conley. I'm Dr. Phillip Bradley. My friends at Georgia Tech tell me you have an interesting diamond. May I take a look?"

"Sure. Thank you for seeing me on such short notice. But I'm sort of pressed for time." I handed him the diamond.

"This shouldn't take long," he said. "Follow me."

The room was off-white. Three machines I had never seen before sat on separate white tables. There were three large computers beside each one of the tables.

One of the machines in a room we passed had smoke billowing out of it. There was a man sitting in front with goggle-type glasses.

"Is that machine on fire?" I asked, feeling stupid as I said it, since if it were they'd certainly be panicked.

251

your back,' and left. I figured, better to be safe. So I used our code."

"Good. I'm glad you did. Ira. You will not believe what I found out about the diamond."

"And you vill not believe vhere Delecarte's funding came from. But you go first."

"Inside the diamond is something organic. The doctor says it's a molecular compound that is being held under tremendous finite pressure. It is less than a tenth of a nanometer, whatever that is. In other words, it is extremely small. But he thinks it's either some living matter, possibly amino acids, or maybe antimatter. He doesn't know. He says it could have a carbon base but unlike a diamond, which is inorganic, this is organic. The only thing he knows that's similar is the element discovered a few years ago in the Mars rock, which they are still analyzing. But he thinks this is even more significant than that."

"I have never heard of such a thing."

"Neither had he. However, he says it's possibly from out in space."

"Outer space. Like the Mars rock?"

"Yes, Ira, outer space," I said. "The thing is, the Dogons' mythology includes what they describe as our origin. Their description sounds a lot like the idea that we were formed from volcanic activity or in some pool of water after this seed came to earth. But the bottom line is, the Dogons believe our ancestors were spacemen too. So if I put this with what I know—well, this gets more and more unbelievable by the second."

"Did he, your scientist, find any of this believable?"

"Yes. He was 'damn near fascinated to death.' Wanted to keep the diamond. I told him I couldn't leave it yet but I would bring it back if I could. I'm sure he had no idea that it's caused so much death."

"My God, Patricia. What vill you do with it?"

"I don't know yet. What about you? Who's pumping the money?"

"We know who it is. And the League is ready to expose this group. I told them about vhat ve'd learned and they believe this is an attempt on Delecarte's part to make a master vhite race. They had actually heard rumors about some new method being researched but could not confirm this. They are one hundred percent behind you."

"Who is it?"

"At first it looked like it vas the original funders of the Delecartes. The Carnegie Institute and the Kellogg Foundation both vere originally established by eugenic-oriented benefactors and funded the Delecartes in their earlier efforts. The Delecartes had been avid supporters of Sir

Cyril Burt, a prominent British psychologist who proclaimed the largely genetic basis for intelligence."

"I know the name. It was on the list of books Kenneth Lawson had checked out."

"But only Oscar Delecarte, not William, spoke out recently against Leon Kamin and John Horgan, who were denouncing the genetic superiority of the white race. Oscar's a big supporter of the journal titled *The Mankind Quarterly Review*. He even offered the fellow who recently authored *The Bell Curve* a job in his lab."

"So what was William's take on all this?"

"It seems in later years, William Delecarte believed vhat he and his brother had been doing to be wrong. William apparently thought the things they found could be used to better mankind and bring us all together in some vay, not separate us. Dr. Gramm sided with Villiam in the end. William even considered publishing the names of prominent scientists who sit on the *Quarterly*'s board. William was doing research on his colleagues, whom he believed to be undermining the integrity of science, vhen he was found dead."

"That makes sense. Dr. Gramm said William ran across some data that led him to believe his brother had not only started up their research again but was now generously funded. But how do you know this?" I asked.

"Because Villiam Delecarte had contacted the Anti-Defamation office about what steps he needed to take to uncover a racist project. But at that time he did not disclose it vas his own brother."

"So who is funding Oscar now?"

"We think the Pioneer Fund. They've funded projects for years. They funded most of the researchers cited in *The Bell Curve* at one time or another. According to an *ABC World News* story, their mailbox service in Manhattan is their official address. Sources claim the fund to be behind Proposition 187 in California. Jesse Helms, Thomas Ellis, Oliver North, even a former Waffen SS officer in the Fourteenth Gallican division in the Ukraine. Not to mention ties to the aerospace program, the CIA and Rockwell International, the company that vas connected to the National Reconnaissance Office complex in northern Virginia, which was apparently being built vithout the knowledge of the Congressional Budget Office, the Senate Intelligence Committee or anyone else in Congress. Ve're confirming it now. Either vay, the League would like to go public with this."

"Of course," I said, half hearing him. Something was nagging me but I didn't know what it could be. "Okay, so you've got these guys doing research. But what are they doing exactly?"

"It seems like your suspicions are true. They are trying to create an all-white race."

"Well, if that's the case, do you know what the biggest irony is, Ira? It appears the Africans gave them the means."

CHAPTER FORTY

By the time Ira and I got over the shock of this information that confirmed all our fears, the Cyclorama was closing its doors. I gave Ira the envelope with the key inside, so that he could get the letters the monk said Kai had left in the post office box for her sons. He hugged me and left to continue checking things out.

I walked to the car and decided to call for my messages. I took out change and went to the phone booth. It is as near a fatal mistake as you can make and still live.

"Ms. Patricia Conley, this is Oscar Delecarte. I'm sure you know who I am by now, since my people tell me that loose-lip Gramm talked to you before we could stop him. We have a proposition for you.

"Oh, don't fret. We're not worried about you going to the police. They do not tend to believe murderers. Remember you're a suspect, my dear. After we understood just how much of a problem you were going to become, we decided to help the police find the murder weapon you used. Razors are so sharp don't you think? And jealousy. Well, most crimes are crimes of passion. As you people say, you had to do something about that slut taking your man away. How dare she.

"Believe it. We've covered all the bases. There is no tap on your phone and once you've picked up this message your tape will be replaced. You're on your own. You have eight hours to get my gifts to me. If I don't see you, we cannot exchange our gifts.

257

"Bring me the diamond and the document and I will give you two gifts in return. Two of your friends stopped by to chat. Your boyfriend, you know the one—and, surprise, surprise—your old friend Carol. Don't think we're insensitive heathens like your people, we have thought to give you proper time to adjust to this news. In case you don't know, we are playing hardball. Call 555-9406. It's a pay phone number; someone will have instructions for you. Good day."

I couldn't move.

With my fingers shaking I dialed Carol's parents' home. Her mother answered and said Carol had already left to meet me. And, she added, "I want you to know we tried to stop her from going but she said you needed her. It was insensitive of you to even ask her when you knew she needed to be resting."

I hung up, wanting to scream, but instead dialed the number Delecarte had given me. A wheezing voice answered, "Yeah," and I dropped the phone. I recognized that wheeze. The Wheezer at Claudette Duvet's when she phoned me and the same wheezer bursting into Jeff's mountain cabin. Oh my God. Fumbling with the receiver and cord, I picked it up and put it to my ear. My entire body convulsed. Jeff. It must be Jeff they have with Carol.

"Within six hours," the Wheezer said, "I want you to go by this place. They will have a cell phone in your name, waiting for you, that cannot be traced. Wait for us to call you. Have the diamond and the document. Be ready to come to us. Oh. Be sure you have plenty of gas."

I didn't say a word. I couldn't.

Then the Wheezer laughed and added, "Hey, I forgot to tell you. Your friend is burned up like a crisp piece of bacon. And if you don't want your little Hymie friend to end up like him, you'll do what we say and talk to nobody."

Was Jeff burned? Were they taking care of him? Keeping him alive? I was on my own. I stood there. Not moving. Not breathing. Nightmare on Elm Street didn't mean shit. What was I going to do? Tears streamed down my face. Motherfucker.

I sat down on a cement bench. Kenneth Lawson. Carol? Jeff Samuels may all still be alive. Damn. I should have asked to speak to Jeff. To Carol? To make sure they were all right. But what if Jeff's already dead? Carol could be too. Jeff Samuels—still alive.

The thought hit me like a bullet in my gut. How is it that someone could kill and hurt all these people—all to make a *white man*. I might die before this is over, I thought, but not before I drop somebody else's ass.

♊

I climbed in the rented Toyota. It was red. Floridians say never rent a red car. It's bad luck. Damn if they don't know what they're talking about. Shit. I lay my head on the steering wheel, not thinking or trying to figure out what to do.

Tapping on my window. I looked up. I wiped my eyes. It couldn't be. It was the old black man. How? "How did you get here?" I asked, seeing him standing outside the car.

"Please, come with me," he said, moving swiftly away from the car.

I had no time to argue with him.

"Really," I pleaded, "there is something I must do." Then it dawned on me; he wanted the ring. I couldn't give him the ring. Not now. The ring was the price I had to pay to get my family back. The only family I'd ever had in this world. Hell, no. I was keeping the ring.

"Look," I said, getting out of the car and following behind him so I could talk. "Listen to me. They have my friends. My friend, Carol, a woman who's just like a sister. I have to give them the diamond." I said it without thinking. A sister. Carol was like a sister to me now. Did I truly feel that? Gosh. *Gosh?* What was that about?

He kept walking and I followed him into the interior of the nearby park. He was headed to his lean-to now, near one of the park's gazebos. I followed.

"Why not let them kill me and get it over with before somebody else gets hurt? Why? Why not? I can't take any more of this. I can't. I can't."

♊

I whimpered. "I don't even believe you exist. You're a ghost. Not real. Oh God, if I'm going to lose my mind, let it be later."

"You must listen to me carefully. You have no choice. It is not the belief in the other world that makes it real—it just *is* real."

The old man sat in the spot before the fire altar.

He turned his gaze to me.

I was shaking all over.

He touched my hand gently.

I felt the warmth travel through my body and the shaking stopped.

"You, my sister, have a long road ahead. It is a difficult road. But you will save many lives. More than will be taken."

The words sprang in my head. A distant, unnamed memory. My

mind rewound to the day I spotted Kenneth holding hands across a table in a French restaurant with a woman who'd later have her wrists cut. Then Claudette Duvet's frantic phone call to me as I heard her die. Her photo in the newspaper. Later Dr. Kia Mutota's call. And then her body mangled before me, as I cried briefly while she bled onto the rail. Amazing, it had been only days since I knew I possessed a possibly priceless diamond with an organic material at its center.

And seconds before my life and world would change forever, but I didn't know this when I asked, "Can you tell me what's happening? What is all this about? God. I'm not ready for all this. Can you help me?"

"I have come many centuries, many life cycles, to be with you. To protect you," the old man said. "You are the key now. The legacy has been passed to you. Only you can return the primordial seed to the world now. I must ensure the harvest is a good one. This, the eighth harvest. In this seed, the beginning of time unlocked the secret to life. As in your Word, God, Amma, created both the female and the male from the womb of the sky and earth. In each seed lies the female and male equal.

"The primordial seed's feminine principle will lay dormant until it is time for the resurrection. The Ark of the Fox repressed the eighth articulation, therefore preventing the full force of the feminine principle on the earth.

"The eighth articulation will manifest during the ceremony of the next Sigui. Both twins must energize the diamond with their twin souls, before it is returned to the earth's core. The diamond contains the primordial seed. It must be returned before the preparation for the beginning of the ceremony in seven days.

"The force of the feminine energy must be unleashed through the ritual in order to save the world. As in all things as in the beginning, all things must come from the mother. We must go back to the time when we honor both souls of our beginnings.

"I have spoken in the void, in the primordial language. Let the last twin touch and energize his legacy and then return it to me."

"But I can't do that. And what if I can't get the diamond back from them? Maybe I could take a fake. Even if I could get the diamond back there is no Kenneth to touch it."

"It is too late for a fake. These people must be stopped on the physical plane. Fear not, only a mortal connected to the life force of my grandson can take the diamond from his hand. Do not worry. Do not be afraid. You were the person my grandson chose to be his wife. In the eyes of the Dogons you *are* his wife and must take up his responsibilities.

You are the regent now. Touch the fire and you may return in peace."

I remembered the dream. "I can't," I said, fear and terror rising in my throat like a slimy frog choking me.

"You must. Now. There is little time."

Tears streamed down my face. I couldn't do it. I was afraid of fire. I couldn't.

He sat with his eyes closed. Quiet.

I looked into the fire and there in the center was Grandma Dixon, smiling at me. I had so longed to touch her all these years. To feel her embrace once again. I decided. I flung both my arms into the searing fire to hold her and in that instant I did. I wept until I felt her arms come around me, unlike the last time I had seen her. The warmth engulfed me and then, satisfied, I pulled back.

I looked down at my arms and clothes. I was not burned. There was no fire. No old man. No lean-to. Nothing but me sitting out in the middle of the park in the dirt.

But in my mind I heard him say, "Please, go now. And remember, his mother died for this. Tell my grandson I will come to him but he must evoke his mother tongue and the names given to him and his brother at birth, Akwette and Akuette, while he holds the diamond in the palms of his hand. His name means 'to bow down before the shrine.' The shrine being the womb of the woman representing the Universe."

A cloud, Noxzema-jar blue, descended on me from above my head. I felt it like a wave coming over me in the ocean. I waited to drown.

CHAPTER FORTY-ONE

Had I been asleep again? I felt different inside, stronger, maybe even lighter, or maybe just protected. Or crazy?

Maybe I was truly losing my mind. Maybe this is what it's like to be insane, I thought. Either way, I was in the midst of this and it seemed I'd have to follow this path until I became sane again or fell completely off the edge.

I couldn't speak. My mind spun around like water in a sewage drain. This was way too much for me. This was the stuff science fiction was made of.

And, at that, I knew I at least maintained some of my associative skills as I heard the tune and words to a Grand Master Flash song—"Don't push me 'cause I'm close to the edge"—go off in my head.

Two hours had passed since they'd told me to pick up the cell phone. I drove to the rental office and picked it up. It was in my name.

♊

I phoned Ira. "I've been vorried about you. I know vhere Delecarte is but I still don't know vhere the people are who are funding him."

"Don't worry," I said. "He's already contacted me. I don't think it matters right now. Let me have the phone number. Sit tight, okay? I'll call you as soon as I can."

"You sound funny. Are you all right, Patricia?"

"Sure," I said, ending the call. The last thing I wanted was to get anyone else hurt. I would not tell him what I planned to do. I wanted to tell someone, but I was afraid if Ira knew he'd insist on helping me. And they'd already threatened to take his life.

Jeff Samuels? I'd not heard from him. He hadn't left a message on my machine. It hurt but this was not the time to focus on it. Even if he was burned he was still alive. Thank God. I had to fight somehow. Who the hell did Oscar Delecarte think he was messing with?

All of it was still incomprehensible. You know, like the experience of watching a movie and wondering how all that shit could be going down in one hour. Thinking to yourself that, that much crap never happens in real life.

And then you meet a family who has so many disastrous stories to tell about their lives, you want to get the hell away from them before a bomb, accidentally shot from a missile, falls on their damn house and your head in turn.

How could this be real? I thought. And really happening to me? This shit wasn't the same as making a decision to lead a more adventurous life and then skydiving on roller blades. This shit was real, kick-ass, stone-cold death.

♊

Whoever these people were, I could rip their throats out with my bare hands. I was tired of running. I needed a gun. A smoking gun. It was time for me to do what I do best.

I made a phone call to Shihan Scott at the television station. I needed a favor and I crossed my fingers that he wasn't still pissed at me. He didn't sound mad; he actually apologized for getting my message too late about the warehouse. He wanted to know what all the police brouhaha was about, and if he could help. Shihan Ted had been calling around trying to find me. I promised him I'd explain it in detail later. But right now I needed him.

I didn't mention how glad I was they hadn't shown up. And that I'd not put them in danger too. After he agreed to help me, I gave him instructions and then phoned Delecarte.

"Surprised to hear from me?" I asked Delecarte over the cell phone, focusing on keeping my voice mellow.

"No, Miss Conley," he said smugly. "We were about to phone you but you've saved us the trouble. I'm not surprised at all. I'm sure you people have some intelligence."

I could kick his ass right now. "Listen, I've got the diamond and the document. I'll bring them to you but on my terms. I'll meet you any place except your house. I would be too vulnerable there."

"Not your terms. You've been watching too much television, my dear, or you saw the movie, what was it called, *Ransom*? Now, that was clearly fictional. I have what you want. And as an orphan all your life, I'm sure you cannot afford the luxury of knowing you've killed the only two people who ever loved you. But if you insist, I'll hang up now and see that this nasty matter is taken care of immediately."

"No," I said, forcing myself to sound calm but firm while thinking, I have not been watching too much television, and, yes, I saw *Ransom* and it didn't seem fictional to me, motherfucker.

"I tell you what, Miss Conley. I'll give you an open invitation to my home. If you're not here, let's say, in two hours, it's a closed door."

"I don't want to come there. I refuse to come to your house," I said, beginning to get disheartened. Was this going to work or not?

"You're not that heathenish, are you? Turning down a polite and generous invitation. Fine. So be it."

"No. Wait. You win." Sucker. It was exactly what I'd wanted. That way I could control things better, and I was sure if he was telling the truth at all, that's probably where Jeff and Carol were. At least, I hoped so.

I put the diamond on my finger. I drove by Carol's and picked up the document.

On my way to Delecarte's house I stopped by the television station and picked up my package. The package was exactly where I'd asked Shihan Scott to leave it—with the security guard. It meant he was down with my game and would be there for me. I'd hoped he would come through.

Shihan Ted was right; Shihan Scott did love me even if I was a woman. In the car, I placed the document in the new briefcase Scott had left for me. And zoomed off to my destiny.

"Po: Seven is the number of vibrations
of the 'word' pursuing the formation of the seed;
eight is the number of elements
of this 'word' in the seed at germination."
—*The Pale Fox*

CHAPTER FORTY-TWO

I'd made up my mind. I'd exchange the document but not the diamond. The diamond didn't fucking be-
long to them. If what the old Dogon said was true, they couldn't do any-
thing without the diamond unless they had Kenneth's cooperation. And
Kenneth was dead. It hurt me to think it but the time for delusions was
over. Where was his body? This remained a mystery. No one had seen
or heard from Kenneth since he was in that alley.

It was hard for me to fathom that Delecarte was nuts enough to kid-
nap Jeff and Carol, and stage all this, in order to do the bidding of the
Aryan Nation or some other racist group. Some folk's balls are clearly in
their brains. They preferred to fuck themselves every time. Even if they
could rid themselves of all the nonwhites, then what? Science was always
fascinating to me. I'd met scientists over the years doing weird and funky
shit, but most of them had good intentions. Scientists were the last ideal-
ists. Always searching for a way to understand the world, to make it safer,
better, more livable. To find ways to help us live longer on the planet.
Even the scientists who discovered the atom did not picture the destruction the bomb would bring. It is the scientific community who keep
fighting with each other to maintain some ethics in what they do, while
the rest of us continue coughing down death in a myriad of ways without
a thought to what is right or wrong. In the end, it is the scientists who
bring us God's word, not preachers. Scientists let us know what God is

thinking. They help us understand what marvels God made. They encourage us that somewhere out there lies the key to our meager existence. We fall asleep at night knowing that these men and women are still on the job. Scientists are the only awakened people on the planet. They know firsthand that the power of God is beyond all of us.

While I drove, everything I'd heard earlier washed over me like a shower of mud. Heavy, foreboding and clinging. What in the name of God was a girl like me doing caring about a threat to a primordial seed? What was the world coming to? I didn't even believe in this crap. Maybe I just didn't want to believe.

My upper lip had begun to sweat and suddenly I felt like I was on fire. *The void. The void. The void,* echoed in my head, sounding like the little, bitty women who used to sing that whine-ass lullaby to Mothra, the Japanese monster. My knees trembled and I heard my stomach rumbling like a distant storm. I was pretty damn scared, but I was fucking madder.

"The four Nomma *anagonna* which came out of Amma are chiefs, 'rich.'
Chiefs because they are primordial ancestors; rich because they are
strengthened by their multiplication; powerful because they possess
Amma's 'word'; therefore, their name will be Ogo.

"Ogo wanted to get hold of the seeds created by Amma including the po,
the cornerstone of creation. In this way, he thought he could
take possession of the universe."
—*The Pale Fox*

CHAPTER FORTY-THREE

The Chattahoochee River skirted its way past the massive outer grounds. The ornamental trees bloomed large and vigorously, acting as an internal fence, guarding the perimeter of the oriental ponds and gardens of Delecarte's property.

A huge indoor fountain gurgled outside the oversized mansion with all the marks of modern technology. Satellite dishes up the wazoo. NASA would have been impressed with the setup.

Racist organizations had many arms and legs, political and religious, and even loyal militia. The money coffers were being siphoned by those they would one day have under their thumb, as sure as the old man breathed. Soon, all their organizations would join their heads, hands, bodies and arms, and like Lazarus in the Bible, attempt to rise up and walk. They were, after all, gods, or so they thought. I had no doubt they'd be disabled. All white people wouldn't buy this shit. There were more white people in the world who were decent than those who believed this crap. I knew this. I'd seen the evidence over the years. Yes, people said the race issues were getting worse. But like Grandma Dixon used to tell me, sometimes a sore's gonna look worse before it gets better. Gook and all kinds of ugly, vile, poisonous stuff has to flow out in the open before it'll heal. That's what I figured had been happening the last few years. The O.J. crap was there, but hey, I could remember the time when white people would have lynched O.J. on the first day and not a soul would have said a word

267

about it. The human race remembers what injustice from the inner core feels like, and I didn't think white people had forgotten any more than anyone else. No way. White people weren't stupid. They knew what lay ahead if the only enemy they were left with was themselves. They knew what they were capable of doing. But I refused to believe that whites were any different from blacks. In the end the good will triumph over the bad. Now where in the hell did those optimistic thoughts come from?

I rang the doorbell. A goon opened the door. I was thankful and surprised not to see any guards stationed on the outside.

The goon motioned me to come in with a gun, as though it were an extension of his hand.

Damn.

When the old man appeared I felt like I'd know him anywhere. A politician. In fact, in his younger days he could have run for senator or even president of the United States if he'd wanted to—and won.

"Ms. Conley," he said, smiling at me, extending a withered hand.

I eyed him. The old man would have been five-seven in his stocking feet, if his lankiness hadn't been long bent and drawn. A long nose and thin, lined lips centered his raisin-wrinkled pale white face. Not a *bad*-looking man, but he looked too old to make a man, even in a test tube.

"Dr. Delecarte," I said, smiling back, but not extending my hand to shake his. My armpits were sweating like hogs.

"Would you like some tea?" he said, turning and walking through the spacious hallway to his library.

Leatherbound books lined the walls. A huge ornate desk sat in the middle. Everything in the room looked expensive.

I considered the contrast, and wondered how this man got so greedy plus so fucking nuts. Dr. Bradley, the material scientist at NVA, seemed so warm, friendly and, more important, sane. He hadn't pressured me about leaving the diamond with him once I'd told him I couldn't. He merely gave me that forlorn look of regret and asked if I'd at least consider letting him examine it further. Dr. Bradley was the kind of scientist who could be trusted with new discoveries to do the ethical and right thing. There were many scientists like him.

Not like this slimeball. Irony. Here this man dealt with our origins, the beginning, the primordial essences of us all, and he was cold as the Ice Age itself.

He began pouring tea in two gold-rimmed china cups.

"I'm sorry," I said. "But I don't care for tea. What I would like is Jeff Samuels and Carol."

"Jeff Samuels? You mean Saul Bernard? Or, as you know him, Kenneth Lawson. And your white friend. I especially don't understand why a white woman would take up with a black woman. Burns me really. You people have taken so many liberties. Nevertheless, I'm a man of my word. They are both waiting for you downstairs in the basement."

I heard him but I couldn't believe it. It wouldn't compute. Kenneth Lawson? Alive? Kenneth is alive. My mind raced. I wanted to ask, What happened to Jeff? but now wasn't the time. If Kenneth is alive I must get to him. Oh my God. I had to act fast. "You think I'm going in your basement?"

"If you wish to see them you will. There is no trick to this. I need the diamond and the document. And then I'll be off."

"Before you're off," I said, thinking, You're already off in the fucking head, "would you mind filling in a few blanks for me? You know, because I'm so dense, genetically speaking. I don't think I quite understand all this. You certainly masterminded a coup."

Go ahead, fucker. Take the bait. I doubted he'd do it. Since he'd implied he didn't watch much television. Him explaining to me was nothing but TV drama. I'm always amazed when the crook takes precious getaway time to explain what he's done to his victim. I've never quite understood it or believed it, so I wished I'd thought up a backup plan. But I didn't have that much time.

"Sit, my dear young woman. I know it is through no fault of your own that you are of an inferior race. So I will give you the details. Hopefully you can get someone to explain them to you later."

Yes! He took the bait.

"You see, I was approached by a foundation that had come across some obscure mention about my earlier work in pigmentation research. And also my later forays in artificial insemination. I could have had the largest sperm bank ever. Were you aware that men could have babies in the peritoneum? I proposed that long ago. Nowadays the technology is already there. Dangerous, yes. But still quite possible. But I digress. You cannot imagine my surprise when the foundation asked me to scratch their back—and they'd scratch mine."

"Would you mind saying this in plain English?"

"You mean Ebonics? I'm afraid I can't speak that pig language."

I wanted to kick him in the face but instead I said, "Sir, English will do. I'm just not following you. And if somebody thinks they're so brilliant but they can't be understood. . . . Well I'm not so sure how—"

"No further. I see where you're going. And you're right. I should be able to break this down so that the common person and even the niggers can understand."

I flinched and bit my lower lip. He was asking for trouble.

Delecarte smiled and took a sip of tea. He knew he'd punched me in the gut with that one.

Then he continued, "I proceeded to examine what had gone wrong in my earlier experiments while doing their bidding. I was having no luck at all, and then by some miracle I got a phone call about one of the twins."

This man was rambling but maybe we could get something in the end. I crossed my legs and leaned my briefcase against the chair leg. My purse was lying on my lap, the strap on my shoulder, in case I needed the taser.

"Gramm had plenty of questions. But I assured Gramm I would help the poor twins. And as I pondered the answers for Gramm, it occurred to me what I was missing. I needed to have the original documents. That's when I went to my brother, William, and explained what was wrong with our original hypothesis.

"Poor William, mental deficiency had set in, I'm afraid, and he now believed our goals to save mankind were wrong. I went on without him."

"And then you had him killed?" I needed Delecarte to admit his murderous behavior out loud. Now. *Right now.*

"Don't be ridiculous. I'm not a murderer. My brother, poor, misguided soul, was killed during a terrible robbery. Anyway I accomplished it without him. I solved the puzzle and right here," he held up a valise, "is the results. I, my dear, can create a master white race to help restore order and discipline to the world."

I saw a gleam come in his eyes. He was mad as a fucking hatter. Okay, smart, but crazy as a coot.

"You tried to have me killed. In the car, your fools shot Carol. How were you going to get the diamond if I was dead?"

"No one was going to shoot you. Scare you, that's all. Don't misunderstand, my dear. Contrary to your belief, I am not a racist. This is not about race but who can best serve the world. I only want what is best for the world. We are just the best suited to rule."

I wanted to explain to him the mere fact that he thought whites superior to others made him a racist, but I didn't say it. Instead I said, "And what will you do with the people already here in the world who happen not to be white? You know, Asians, Jews, the natives of America, for instance? Kill us after you've made your Michael Jackson–cloned babies?"

"Of course not. Eventually you will die out, naturally. And the perfect order of the universe will be maintained through us. The original man on earth. And this is not cloning, my dear, this is selective reorganization."

"Okay, original man." Thinking, If you were the fucking original man, we'd all be dead by now. "But," I continued, "why kill all the twins?"

"I told you, I'm not a killer."

"Bullshit." Don't lose it, I said to myself. "I'm sorry. Why have the twins killed?"

"I did no such thing. Why would *I* kill them? They were dying one by one anyway. I'd seen the flaw in my original research. All of them were having to take injections of serotonin, estrogen and testosterone mixed to merely keep alive. In my first experiments, I had not thought about what would happen if they produced no more melanin as they aged. They were either going to die of aneurysms or deteriorate from Parkinson's disease or worse.

"Now, my dear," he said, slapping his knees and standing up, "I must be going. My plane awaits me. If you would please hand over the diamond and the document, I'll be off. I need the diamond to finance my initial getaway plans."

"I thought you wanted to destroy the diamond."

"Nonsense. I wished to sell it to the highest bidder, but I want to be in control. My present benefactors wanted the control. I decided, why share anything with them?"

"But I was under the impression you wanted the diamond to destroy it?"

"Are you repeating yourself, my dear? Tsk, tsk. We don't have any more time."

"How do I know Kenneth Lawson and Carol are really in the basement?"

"I give you my word."

"Huh. You *are* truly nuts." I was losing it. "So, let me ask you something. How did you know I would come alone? Not bring the cops? How did you know I wouldn't shoot you?"

"My dear, I live by a code of honor and I know that some of your people do too. Plus, I don't think you would risk your lover and friend's life. And there's always that terrible Jewish man."

I stopped in midthought. He still hadn't realized I had thought he was talking about holding Jeff, not Kenneth, when he'phoned me. "You can't get away with this. You know that, don't you?"

"You're wrong. If you have enough money you can get away with anything. I've changed my name. There is no more Dr. Oscar Delecarte, my dear. I have the papers waiting for me. Soon I'll be an after-thought. Gone and forgotten. I have a plane waiting to take me far, far away, to a land where the white man is still God."

"Wait," I said, ignoring that statement. Hell, he could stay *here* for that. I needed him to give me specific details about what he'd done. "What did you do to Kenneth Lawson? Did you have him shot?"

"Shot? Kenneth? Kenneth was family of sorts. Besides, he was going to die no matter what."

"You mean you knew your experiments would kill all the twins?"

"No. No, not until recently. By then it was too late. This could have all been avoided if your boyfriend had told me where the diamond was but he wouldn't. I'd arranged to buy the diamond through a third party from Keith. He was always a touch greedier than Kenneth. Then after their adoptive parents died in that dreadful accident, I don't think Keith cared about anything anymore. He probably would have *given* me the diamond. But then Kenneth stopped him from selling it by taking the diamond from his possession.

"I would have come after you sooner, but to be honest, knowing that African mumbo jumbo, I didn't think Kenneth would give you or any-one else the diamond. Then sitting here one night, still not able to lo-cate the whereabouts of the diamond, I realized the Dogons were matriarchal and you could very well have it.

"I'd tried to keep Kenneth alive until he felt up to telling me. Oh, did I mention he's in a medically induced coma? I'm sort of the Dr. Kevorkian of experimental science."

"Did you shoot Kenneth or did you have him shot?"

"Heavens, no. I suppose some black heathen shot the poor fellow in a robbery attempt. I believe that's what the news said at one point. I think they even implicated you. He and his friend, Claudette. Tsk, tsk. I'm glad you only killed her and not Kenneth. I needed him alive. After all, he was my ultimate insurance. If anyone got the diamond or the doc-ument, I had the upper hand."

"You're nothing but scum, Delecarte!" I screamed. I wanted to calm down. I needed a confession. Here he was still trying to implicate me in Claudette Duvet's murder to the end. The scumbag.

"Look at you? All your composure is gone, my dear. That is not good for your blood pressure. You know Negroids must watch out for blood pressure. One of the many differences in our races."

I wasn't going to get out of here with him alive. I could see that now. I was going to have to pick that poker up and smash his fucking head in.

And then it hit me. A memory from the void: Violence would never, could never be an option.

"I won't keep toying with you," he continued, smiling. "It's uncivilized."

"I want to see Kenneth and Carol before you get the ring. To make sure they're okay."

"Listen, Miss Conley, please don't make me use this. Be ladylike and hand over the ring."

He'd pulled out a gun. He pointed it at my head.

"Oh, I see. You're the bastion of civil discourse. Somebody better teach you what *civil* is." Suppose they were dying while we were up here fucking around. Maybe I should give him the ring? What could he do? Eat it?

He called out, "Get in here. I have to leave now and she's giving me trouble."

I expected to hear men running. Guns poked into my side. But nothing.

"What is going on?" he said to himself.

I knew damn well he wasn't asking me.

"Mack, Gary. Get in here," he yelled, his voice losing its composure. No sounds.

He looked panicked. "Get over there," he said, waving the gun at me wildly. "Take the ring off and toss it to me. Now. Then slide the briefcase to me. I'm not playing. I will shoot. I'm a desperate man, Miss Conley. There are people waiting with money for me and right now you're holding me up."

"You don't get it, do you? I'm a journalist. A black journalist. Not only that, I'm a damn good journalist." For the first time in a while, I could understand the relevance, in a society where you are still measured by your skin color, in reiterating your identification with your blackness. Particularly when it's clear your humanity, dignity and mental status are being called into question merely because of your color.

"I don't care who you are. Toss me the goddamn ring."

"My, my. Such uncivilized language from such a superior genetic pool. What do you want with the ring?"

"I'm ditching this foundation, Miss Conley. I can sell my work to the highest bidder. I can have both power and money that way. How much do you think I could get? Billions? Who wouldn't want the primordial seed? The feminine aspect of our beings? The missing half?

"Sure, the research would pay a lot. But I need more—backup, nest

273

egg, like all men my age. A legacy. Insurance. The ring is very valuable. I know what's inside the ring. The primordial seed. Our other half. What the Dogons call *po* and *po pilu*. Do you know how much men would pay to have a piece of the rock from Mars? Compared to this—that rock is sand.

"And, of course, I need the document so no one else can follow the strains of my work. Everyone associated with my experiments are either dead or dying. Now quit fucking with me."

"Sir, I'm not—what was that word? I can't say it. I hate bleeps in my speech." This was as good as it was going to get. I could see that it was over. I was wasting time now. His cultured facade had deteriorated to the profane. I wasn't the only one who could curse.

"Anyway," I said, smiling, "you've heard from Dr. Oscar Delecarte, who has been doing research for, possibly, the Humankind Fund, the Pioneer Fund and some other eugenics-based foundations in genetic engineering and has unknowingly exposed his plot to create a superior white race and sell it to the highest bidder. Of course, he had to kill a lot of people to keep this under wraps until he was ready to make the grand announcement. I'm sure the genetically superior doctor would like to speak with you now. Wouldn't you, Dr. Delecarte?"

I pulled the tiny wireless transmitter and the camera recorder out of the hole in the briefcase into full view, happy that Shihan Scott had kept up with the latest technology. They could conceal an audio feed and transmitter in almost anything nowadays. And even happier that WXIG TV was the sister station to *The Atlanta Guardian*. Scott and his crew and possibly others were outside right now.

"As in so many cases," I said, "like the Rodney King incident," I continued, smiling toward the window, "videos can talk in words and pictures."

"What kind of trick are you pulling here? Do you really think I'm going to let you leave here with that video, you little nigger?"

"Oh, my. The *N* word again. I don't have to leave. See," I said, pointing to the television station's initials on the side of the camera. "It's a live feed. One of only six telephoto lenses trained on your brilliant self right now through those huge windows, Dr. Brother Man. Come on in, guys. You can get better angles if you're in the room with me."

Bursting through the doors, print and TV journalists buzzed around the genius like bees riled up on a beehive.

Delecarte dropped his gun, as police, their guns drawn, pushed journalists out of the way. The boys in blue wanted to talk to the great geneticist first.

Ira, whom I instructed Scott to bring along with his camera crew, shoved through the crowd clapping.

Two ambulance crews, along with Ira, escorted me down into the basement.

It was set up like a mini-hospital. Kenneth Lawson lay in a hospital bed, a saline-type drip hooked into his arm. I hurled my purse to the floor and raced over attempting to lift Kenneth. The gunshot wound was bandaged, but blood trickled out of his nose and ears. The paramedics pulled me from him.

Ira held me up. It registered that another team of medics checked Carol.

In a few seconds the paramedics signaled me to come back over. "He's weak. We've got to get him to a hospital fast. The 'copter is on the way."

I wept. I whispered in his ear, words I'd not said aloud to anyone in my life, "I love you. Oh my God, I love you, Kenneth Lawson. I love you, Saul Bernard. I love you, Akwette."

I thought I saw his eyelashes flicker. I squeezed his hand. Guilt twisted my heart.

A paramedic touched my arm. Carol had been untied and now stood with me, unharmed. Ira took me by my arms and escorted me up the stairs. Carol, her shoulder still in a sling, walked behind us, carrying my purse.

When I climbed into the waiting Medivac helicopter with Kenneth, and held tightly to his hand, the diamond was on my finger. I felt so tired. I couldn't see Kenneth's face for the tears in my eyes.

At the hospital I waited outside while a team of doctors attended him. Carol walked up and wiped my face with Ira's handkerchief, then dabbed her own eyes. I could hear her sniffling, even as my own sobs escaped my lips. It was clear to me now. The wheezer was telling me the truth. Jeff Samuels had burned up in the house. He was dead. But Kenneth was alive. I wanted to scream as the guilt of what I'd done pressed on my chest. I wanted them both to live. The pain ripped through my heart. Kenneth was dying and I was alone again. But then I looked up. Carol was wiping my tears away allowing hers to flow freely down her face. Silently, I said, *my sister*. I glanced over at Ira and my mind whispered *my family*. It was clear to me now. We were going to have to get past this race thing in this world. And who better to do it than us, black folk? Otherwise, we ran the risk of judging people by the color of *their* skin. Which meant we all might as well be turned back to dust.

Ira walked over and hugged me as if he heard my thoughts. He handed me two envelopes. One read: "From Kai to Akuette" and the other read: "From Kai to Akwette." My hands trembled as I held them. I would read it to Kenneth as soon as I could. He had a right to know his mother's thoughts first. I couldn't bring myself to read words so personal. A mother's words to her son. At that moment it made me miss the mother I never knew even more. I wished she'd left me a letter someplace to explain her walking off and leaving me. Maybe whatever was in this letter would answer any questions Kenneth had harbored all this time.

When I was allowed in the room with Kenneth, I broke down. I hugged his body to mine.

He opened his eyes slightly. His parched lips moved. "Please," he whispered.

"What did he say?" I screamed, afraid to trust I'd heard him. "What is he saying?" I looked from Ira to Carol, panicked, grief-stricken. All the hurt suffocating me. Hot air pumping into my nose like a blast furnace.

I leaned near his mouth, trying to be calm, "Yes," I whispered. Squeezing his hand tightly. "Yes, dear Kenneth," I said, hearing myself and wondering how I could feel such loss when he was still here in the flesh.

Carol and Ira left the room whispering to me they'd leave us alone.

I knelt beside the bed. "Sweetheart, don't talk. I have a letter here from your mother. Would you like me to read it?"

His head moved slowly but I knew he was signaling yes. I began to read, wiping my eyes as I spoke.

"My beloved son. Sacred is the day and night of our lives. We the seeds of the beginning. I know you will understand the sacrifice I had to make. Only my seeds can know the pain it caused me to leave you in the flesh without seeing you into your manhood. This is difficult for me but I am sure I will not live too much longer.

"Years ago, just before your birth, I saw my mother and father tortured and murdered. I saw the diamond cut off my father's hand and taken away by a few men from a nearby village. Overseeing all this was Oscar Delecarte. The Ark of the Fox, to our people. The evil one from the west.

"I hurt so badly knowing that you and your brother had come from his lineage. But I knew in each seed is the duality of man. You were his twin brother's sons.

"He, William Delecarte, loved me, but knew that to fight his brother was impossible. Poor William never knew

276

that his brother killed my parents and I never told him. I never let William touch me again after witnessing the death of my parents at the hand of his own blood. And I'm sure he will die not knowing what happened between us.

"But I made sure I avenged our family, as I was the only regent. I came with the Delecartes to America, not to be with William, but to find a way to take back the diamond. When you and your brother were only five years old, I stole the diamond out of Oscar's safe. At first nothing happened. Oscar knew that William would not let him harm me. So he waited.

"I read the oracle and knew the hour of my death. I would die at Oscar's hand. I went to Father Fred and asked him to keep a watchful ear for my sons and to give you both the diamond on your thirty-fifth birthday. That is the time I knew you would have realized the wisdom of our people. Yes, you both were the same in your physical mantle, even to your birthmarks. My father told me your birthmark would be an omen of your unique destiny. You, my son, Akwette, would be our regent and keep your brother's twin soul on the true path. As initiates, I was sure your grandfather's spirit would be with you both, so that you would know to return the diamond energized twofold by you and your brother's twin spirits for the great time of the final Sigui. The time when the primordial seed, the po, and the po pilu, would be understood once again. When the true genesis of the world would be revealed. The time of the full eighth articulation.

"If you are reading this history, then I have moved into the spirit world as I foresaw. And I am sure that Oscar has made it appear that I died of an accident. But trust me, my son, it is murder. Please know my sons, Akwette and Akuette, that I am always with you. My heart will always beat in your heart.

"Your mother, Kai."

Now I understood the actions of William Delecarte against his brother. He had known these were his sons, even if he didn't know what his brother had done to their mother.

Kenneth opened his eyes. "The ring," he gasped.

I held it up and then placed it in his hands. "I love you, Akwette," I whispered.

"I love you too, wife," he whispered back, offering me a slight smile. He choked out, "My heart will always beat in your heart."

I could hear the rattling like a snake uncoiling in his throat.

He squeezed the diamond, and with a powerful singsong voice began an incantation. It was as though he had no wound in his chest. His color returned to his face and the rubbery look of his skin vanished.

I imagined he was healing himself and I let the tears flow freely. I was so sure he was coming back to me.

Then I heard the incantation double. I looked up and saw in the corner his twin, then a beautiful black woman, and finally the old man, all joining him in the incantation. Elongated gourds surrounded the old man.

The room filled with sound. I feared Carol and Ira or the nurses would come rushing into the room and interrupt. Then the silence closed around my ears like a clamp. I smelled roses. I looked down to speak to Kenneth and he lay quiet and still. I quickly looked to the corner and only the old man stood, holding the diamond and smiling at me. Then he too was gone.

I screamed the wailing sound of women all over the world. My mind flashed images of the two other people I'd loved and lost—Jeff and Grandma Dixon. Both dissolved before my eyes in less than a second.

"Please, please don't leave me. I can't take it," I begged. "Please, oh God, please don't let him leave me. Oh no. Oh no. Oh no." I could hear myself echoing "Oh no" over and over, while the emergency monitor shrilled in the background.

Carol and Ira raced into the room and wrestled me away.

I pulled at the sheets, Kenneth's body, the bed, anything I could get my hands on, just to hold on as they wrestled me from the bed. I needed to hold on to the one person who would have loved me no matter what.

A flurry of doctors and nurses rushed into the room screaming, "Code Blue!"

It was too late. There was nothing they could do. Now Kenneth Lawson or Saul or Akwette was gone forever. And once again I was alone.

CHAPTER FORTY-FOUR

It had been only three days and I still could not sip soup. There's a fable about a dog holding a bone in his mouth who, upon gazing into the water, spots what he thinks is a bigger bone and drops the bone he has, ending up with nothing. What he sees is only a reflection. There I was with two men finally loving me, and in my effort to save one I lost the other. Of course, there were differences but in the end one thing was clear—I lost. I had not known loss until this. I'd thought I knew it. But this was so deep my body felt as though my very flesh rotted on my bones. I could barely lift the spoon to my mouth.

It didn't matter to me about the diamond being returned or their spirits at rest. I was empty. Empty and abandoned. Empty and alone.

Akwette's, or Kenneth Lawson's, face spun in my eyes like a spiral with each breath. I had begun grieving over Kenneth-Akwette the day I'd seen his brother's body, not knowing for sure it was him. But now, I'd lost him forever.

I sat on the couch in Carol's living room staring at the television. It droned on and on but it didn't matter, I couldn't hear it. Carol had turned it to mute in the morning before she left. For some reason she thought the animated pictures might spring life into me.

I'd not taken any calls. I'd explained to her that in the end Jeff Samuels had died protecting me. She was working on finding out what had happened and where the remains of his body, if any, had been taken. According to the police, the house had been destroyed by the fire and explosion. They were still investigating.

The Prof had contacted Carol at the paper twice to let me know he was thinking of me and had gotten his car back.

Scott and Ted had sent me bunches of flowers to add to the trillion flowers other people whom I didn't even know cared about me had sent.

I could never get over this. I still refused to look at the two urns with the ashes of Kenneth and his twin on Carol's mantel. I now thought of them by their given names: Akwette and Akuette. I waited for instructions from a Dogon scholar Carol had located for me as to what to do with the ashes.

I balked at going back to work. My journalism days were over. I hated the media. I hated television. I hated news of any kind. But today I was being forced to go back.

John Biggers had called my boss. He'd read how I'd exposed the awful, diabolical scheme to make a white man, and he, along with the Anti-Defamation League, was actually footing for a dinner and an award in my honor.

First, though, he wanted to see me at his offices. He wanted me to go with him to Washington today and cover the awarding of his first contract. My boss's words exactly: "He wants a first-rate journalist to cover this."

Ordinarily I would have felt wonderful. But right now I didn't feel anything but pain. The paper was most generous when it came to giving people time off to grieve. I knew that this had to be important to them to even ask me. One thing I can say about newspapers, they are like families. They might dog you out and even curse you out, but nobody else better mess with you.

I dressed and started out the door. I stopped and went back for my new cell phone, compliments of Delecarte. Until somebody asked me for it back. I stuck it in my purse. And then on an impulse I checked to make sure the taser was still there. From now on I was zapping any fool who messed with me. I was in no mood to take any crap. Washington could be as dangerous as Atlanta.

I finally had my car back. I had also been cleared of any suspicion in the deaths of Kenneth Lawson and Claudette Duvet. And now old Oscar Delecarte was on the hot seat. The police were still trying to identify and round up his goon squad.

I drove toward Marietta, Cobb County, where the real hub of new money and business sits in Atlanta. When I pulled up to Biggers's complex, I was impressed. He had a big fancy new lab with all high-tech shit in it.

As I rode up in the elevator to the tenth floor, it struck me odd that I'd been allowed to come right up. That's what celebrity-journalist status could do for me, huh? When I'd interviewed Biggers before, it had taken me almost two hours to see him and I had an appointment.

Biggers was sitting at the head of his Oriental conference table. The entire room was like stepping into China.

"Howdy. Howdy," he said, reminding me of Jeff Samuels. I cut the pain off. Soon other journalists pushed and shoved into his conference room along with me. Cameras flashed and mikes squealed as Biggers sprinkled around that colorful good-old-boy charm.

The press conference was short and sweet.

Biggers had gotten the contract for three Southern states, Georgia, Florida and South Carolina, to begin immunizing children right away. He was very happy and had already set in motion plans to immunize the Third World countries' children for free at a much later date. Georgia's immunization program would be first. Everyone involved was excited.

When all the other people had cleared out Biggers invited me back to his office. "Come on in. Have a seat," he said in his best Texas drawl. "Little lady, we're going to have a jumping good time in Washington on this hot firecracker day."

"Mr. Biggers, I really appreciate all you're doing for me."

"Now, little lassie, don't fret none. By the by, call me John."

I grimaced. If he called me one more freaking animal I wasn't so sure I could keep this up.

"You are a smart little lamb. And an asset to our community. I know your people would be proud. You know what? I think I'm gonna see if you can't get to meet old Bill while we're up in Washington."

I bit my lip. This is important, Conley; don't go off. So you're a darn slew of ranch animals. So what? "Bill?" I asked.

"You know, *Bill.* That's the one."

I hesitated. Sat up and forward in the chair.

"No mind. I trust you want your career to go places, a journalist like yourself. I tell you what I'm gonna do." He picked up the phone. "Get me Bill on the saddle," he said, smiling at me while he barked into the receiver.

Only minutes passed before the phone rang. I marveled. He'd made one call and Bill Clinton, the president of the United States, had called him back in seconds. Damn. He was more powerful than I thought.

He'd said very little to President Clinton, other than enough collo-quialism to choke a horse. Biggers was notorious for doing business only with Southerners. All his management were Southerners. NEVER TRUST A MAN WHO WAS BORN IN THE NORTH was cross-stitched in a frame over his desk. Almost everyone in his office came from Texas, Kentucky, Tennessee, the Deep South—anywhere other than the North. A Southern drawl was a prerequisite for employment. I still hadn't quite figured out why he liked me. Okay. So maybe I had a slight drawl.

"Done," he said, rubbing his palms together. "My men will see to it that you get to sit a spell with him while we're there. I'm gonna be too busy for that old Arkansas boy myself. I don't really like him much. Too damn touchy-feely for me. And I never trust a man that seems too honest."

I sat stunned. I was going to meet Bill Clinton. I know. People have lots to say about Clinton. But the one thing I know for sure, the man is damn brilliant. And I respect that in a person. Also, I wasn't so sure he wasn't just too damn honest. I'd speculated that's the real reason he's not liked. People don't really like the truth. Or maybe Clinton just cares too damn much. Now, if he could fake caring and not give a shit, people would feel safer. It's what they're used to. Bullshit and more bullshit. But an introduction right now, today, was not what I had in my mind. Not in my state of mind. Okay. Okay. I calmed myself. So go with the flow, little chicken.

"Sit and rest your duds, filly. Drink some cappuccino," he said, pointing to the machine behind his desk, "until it's time to take off. Hey, by the way, I heard a rumor that some dude gave you a hell of a diamond. You know, I'm in the diamond trade. Can I take a gander?"

"I'm afraid I don't have it anymore," I said, wishing he'd change the subject. "Actually, I didn't know you were in the diamond trade. You must be into everything." So many businesses bought up other businesses these days. It wasn't inconceivable that one person could own everything in the U.S. Now, that's scary.

"Right, little chickie, I *am* in the diamond trade. Big diamond collector, trader, seller. You name it. I'm the DeBeers of the South, if you get my drift. What'd you do with the stone? Hock it? You didn't go and sell your engagement ring, now did you?"

I really didn't want to discuss this, but he had no way of knowing how painful this was for me. "I just don't have it. But no, I didn't sell it."

"You sure you don't have it? Not anywhere? Did you sell it to one of your friends?"

"Yes. But no, I didn't sell it. I don't have it, that's all." I was getting annoyed. The questioning seemed inappropriate and out of line. How did he know about the diamond? The diamond was not mentioned in the news articles. But I suppose power people can know whatever they want to know in this country. And when there is anything of value floating around, they know it.

His phone rang and he answered it. Talked for a few minutes. Smiled, chuckled and hung up happy as a bird dog in a chicken coop.

"No mind. I'm sure you don't have it anymore," he said, smiling and excusing himself. "I've got to see a man about a horse before we can ride off into the sunset. Give me about half an hour or so."

His last words persisted as I sat fidgeting in his office. *I'm sure you don't have it anymore.* Why was he suddenly so sure I didn't have it anymore? No one knew what had happened to the diamond except me.

A journalist dies hard. I checked out the papers on his desk. What else did I have to do?

The first was a report from a research scientist titled "Induction of Meiosis." I flipped through the pages of the introduction. It might as well have been written in French. But one paragraph caught my eye.

> What does this mean in lay terms? Once the process of induction of meiosis is solved it will not be out of the question to have a cell fertilize itself. Males will be able to fertilize males and females will fertilize females. In the case of females, since they have no Y chromosome, they will reproduce females. But males will be able to reproduce both the male and female.

I put it down. What did that mean, exactly? I saw a note to someone about China. I picked up a thick red folder and opened it, still pondering what I'd just read.

I read the page twice. Slow comprehension seized me. Biggers had promised China immunizations first. Tomorrow, in fact. China? *China?* Why would he immunize China first? That wasn't what he'd said at the press conference. And there were enormous profit projections here.

I saw Oscar Delecarte's greedy face. Reran the scene in my mind for the millionth time. Saw him say his brother was killed in a robbery. Saw the pain pierce his face for an instant. They were twins. Twins. What if he didn't kill his twin? He'd said he'd scratched the foundation's back and they scratched his. What did he mean by that? What itch did the foundation have that his building a white man wouldn't have scratched?

Maybe the foundation killed those people. Maybe *they* thought Oscar Delecarte would expose their findings before they were ready. I'd read a piece in *Scientific American* on the price of silence. I could see the subtitle in my mind's eye: DOES PROFIT-MINDED SECRECY RETARD SCIENTIFIC PROGRESS?

The Dogon's voice sounded in my head: *In a world based on color sometimes you must be color blind to see the true problem. Look beyond your fears, your own stereotypes, your own vision of the world for the truth. Catch the world in the diamond's prism, where all facets are as old as time primordial.*

Yes, Delecarte wanted the diamond but he sure as shit hadn't acted like he knew anything about destroying it. So why had there been someone trying to destroy the diamond? Who else could have known about the diamond? Of course—the foundation. They probably needed money to fund some more *Bell Curve* shit.

I flipped open my cell phone and dialed the Prof.

"Hi, it's me, Patricia Conley."

"Man, I love what you did to my car."

"What?"

"I'm shitting you. I'm getting it fixed. What can I do for you, friend? Are you all right?"

"Yes. I need a favor."

"What kind of favor?"

"I need you to check out a foundation for me."

"What foundation?"

"I need to know if John Biggers or any of his companies have anything to do with any medical research anywhere. Not the immunization projects but other stuff. And I need it as soon as possible. Can you do that?"

"Yep. Where do you want me to call you?"

"555-8821. It's a cellular number and I've only got a half-hour at the most."

"Amma judged that Ogo's deeds were seriously upsetting
the order of things, and he put all that he had created
back inside the female seed of the *po pilu*,
which he placed to the south."
—*The Pale Fox*

CHAPTER FORTY-FIVE

I was too nervous to sit still. I began rifling through Biggers's desk drawers. The center drawer had keys, an exercise rope, a Swiss Army knife and some Skittles. I found nothing to link him to Delecarte. One drawer was locked. I fumbled with the key ring. Found a tiny key. Inserted it. Opened the drawer. Shit. A gun. I closed the drawer quickly and locked it. Okay. So he has a gun. This is crime-ridden city. It's for protection, I'm sure.

But the China thing nagged me. It just didn't fit. I almost knocked an expensive crystal figurine over when the phone rang in my pocket.

"Hey. Your boy is busy. He is also a big backer of the Aryan White Resistance. Not only was he a part of the funding of that build-a-white-man stuff Delecarte was researching, he practically financed most of the funds Delecarte had in the last thirty years. He owned Oscar Delecarte."

I stopped breathing.

The Prof was inside the private documents of the Pioneer Foundation and its ilk. He was right. The Dogon was right. I'd missed the forest while checking out the trees.

"Check this out," the Prof continued. "Guess what your boy commissioned Delecarte to do, my friend?"

My body trembled as I listened, my adrenaline pumping like a speed skater. What I was hearing was incredible. I knew researchers had long known that the embryo destined to become a boy starts out as a girl. In

285

the first weeks all mammal embryos start forming the basic female structures—the uterus, vagina and fallopian tubes. It is not until thirty-five to forty days that the male shit starts.

Last year, a doctor, I think his name was Weis, had published in the journal *Science* that they'd found the master switch, MIS, which removes the female parts of the original embryo. I remember laughing and saying it sounded like he'd literally opened up a can of worms. Now what I heard was not so funny.

"Apparently," the Prof continued, "this foundation paid Dr. Oscar Delecarte big money to unravel not only which master switch did that, but to show them how to make it do it all the time. This information was also a part of Delecarte's original forays into genetics after being with the Dogons.

"In other words, Dr. Delecarte didn't just know how to make a future world filled with white people. He knew how to make a world filled with *men*."

"My God," I said.

"Even if this could be done," he continued, "I don't think geneticists would do it. Would they?"

"I'm not so sure. There was a report done by an ethics think tank in the eighties; something like over sixty percent of U.S. geneticists would go along with the parents' wishes if they could choose the sex of their child. But if this is true, people wouldn't—wait a minute—shit. I've got it. It's the immunizations. That's it. When their offspring had babies they'd all be males. White males at that. No matter the ethnic makeup of the parents."

"Okay, let's say it began happening. . . ." the Prof said, more to himself than to me.

"Yes," I said, my mind spinning. "But what would he do then? You have to have women to have more babies. So what the hell is he thinking?"

The Prof interrupted. "Hold it. I believe I see where he's going with this. Hmm. It appears he's got another research team working on cloning. Maybe he thinks if you can clone men, you don't need women."

"Yes, but—"

"Holy shit."

"What is it?" I asked, terrified that he could have read something that made him react even more alarmed.

"He has another team in Switzerland working on making babies using artificial insemination and fake wombs. I can't believe this. It's something about breaking through the meiosis problem. Whatever that is."

I heard him but I didn't want to. Could anybody be so stupid? So fucking nuts? Then it hit me. Meiosis. Men producing men. Could that happen? No way. "Listen," I said, my mind speeding back, "if somebody had told us twenty years ago that they'd be able to make women into men and vice versa, would we have believed it? Or five years ago that scientists would make blood interchangeable, erasing the need to type it before a transfusion? Or only two years ago that there were over eight solar systems in the Milky Way and more are found each day? Or that you could transplant one portion of a brain into a different brain and have that animal and yes, even eventually person, act like the host? Or that one day in the not-too-distant future we could all be twins whenever we wanted to be?" Twins? *Twins*. There it was again.

Of course, the answer to all my questions was no. Some people wouldn't believe it. But that wouldn't mean it wasn't true. God. There are people who still think we staged the moon walk, for Godsake. "What's the name of this study in Switzerland?" I asked.

"Gemini Rising," the Prof said in a whisper.

There was no time to decide whether Biggers's research teams were milking him for money by selling him a pipe dream, or actually onto something.

"God, Prof, they must be stopped."

"But how?" he said.

I noticed he was still whispering like he didn't even want to hear himself saying any of this aloud. Neither did I, but it was too late for denial. "I don't know how, but we must do something," I said. "Let me think. I've got to call my editor. I'll call you back."

CHAPTER FORTY-SIX

I dialed the number. The phone rang a thousand times. There is no such thing as calling the newspaper quickly.

Shit.

John Biggers's door opened. "My private jet awaits, little chickie," Biggers said, coming in with a cigarette hanging from his lips.

At first he attributed my look to the cigarette. He removed it from his mouth and held it up to me. "I've got to patronize my own business investments, don't I, little filly?"

"I'm sorry," I said, "but something's come up." I stood and put my purse on my shoulder. "I've got to go by the paper before I can leave." I looked at the desk drawer. If there was trouble, could I get the key, open the drawer and grab the gun before he got to me?

He followed my eyes to the drawer. Shifted them quickly to the desktop.

Damn. I'd left the red folder open. "I tell you what, I'll meet you at the airport."

He smiled.

I thought he didn't notice. He thinks I'm stupid, so he doesn't think I could possibly put this together. I walked past him to the door. I turned to thank him, to let him know how much I appreciated everything. Distract him from thinking. And that's when I felt it. Motherfucker. I spun around.

288

He held a gun on me. Another gun, not the one in the drawer. Two men swung the door open wider and stepped inside.

"You figured it out, didn't you, old gal? I can see it on your face like makeup. See, I don't underestimate you like that imp Delecarte. Hell, if you weren't smart as shit you wouldn't be around.

"We men"—he pointed to himself and the other two men—"we've done everything we could to get rid of you jigs—not to mention the women. And up until now we've failed. Well, thanks to some primitive monkey tribe, we know how to get rid of your asses finally. And none too soon. Now be real good and put the purse down on the floor."

Two more men entered the room. One, the same guy I'd seen at Delecarte's, snatched my phone from my hand and switched it off. Then he threw it in the trash.

I sat my purse down. Outnumbered.

"Now hand the ring over," Biggers demanded, stretching out his wiggling fingers to me.

"You were the one all along," I said. "You had the twins killed and Dr. Delecarte's brother, William. The poor fool didn't even know it."

"Now you're cooking barbecue, little calf. See, we're not as stupid as you gals think we are. Are we, now?"

"So why didn't you take the diamond from me before?"

"We wanted to stay out of this. Delecarte was after you. We let it play out. Of course, our framing you didn't hurt none. Delecarte actually believed you killed the Duvet woman. We thought that would help us isolate you so we could keep track of where the diamond was. We didn't know until you unraveled the conspiracy that the diamond had any more value than money. We had foolishly dismissed the fact that Delecarte believed it was magic or some crap.

"See, after Delecarte's death, we reviewed our surveillance tapes. That's when I knew the diamond had some other value. You know the tape, you and the doc in the warehouse with the old broad."

"So you want the money from the diamond? But why? You're rich. Why kill all these people? Risk everything for the diamond?" Stupid question. Greed, I thought quickly. But I was wrong. Dead wrong.

"I don't want the damn diamond. The thing needs to be destroyed if it might tamper with the way we plan to have things back in order in the world. See, my dear, I'm not a racist. This was never about race. Sure, it would be easy if it were only us, the pure white man, but I'm a bigger man than that. Man, my chickie. *Man. Men.* And believe me, we don't need any primordial feminine seed on the scene."

289

I started to question this, but then his words seeped inside my brain. "What do you mean *after* Delecarte's death?" This man was crazier than Delecarte ever hoped to be.

"Didn't you hear? Dr. Oscar Delecarte, renowned scientist, now disgraced and shunned, killed himself this morning with a gunshot to the head."

"You killed him, didn't you? But why? He was *working* for *you*."

"He was running out on us. To the highest bidder, my ass. I set that phony foundation up personally years ago when I was working freelance with the CIA, and not him or anybody else was going to destroy it."

"But how were you going to use the diamond? I destroyed the document. Without Delecarte you don't know what to do to make what's inside the diamond work."

"You're right. We don't want it to work. We're going to crack that sucker open so that damn primordial seed is never unleashed."

"Why destroy it?" I asked as I heard the old Dogon in my head: *If the diamond is cracked open before the Sigui, it will explode and destroy the world.* "Look, you don't know what you're doing," I warned. "If you crack the diamond open we'll all die. That diamond is like a time bomb. It's being held under pressure and if opened it'll explode. Only the Dogons can release what's inside that diamond without destroying the world."

"As sure as geese fly south, we're opening it. We have what we need, honey dumpling. See, we don't want what's inside the diamond. And I don't give a hooting owl's fanny about the Dogons."

My mind was slow on the uptake. He was going to open the diamond with his ignorant ass no matter what I said. At least I could stall. Maybe find out exactly why I'm going to die. And why Kenneth and all the twins really had to die. "So why kill all the twins? And William Delecarte?"

"The twins were in our way. So were their adoptive parents. I couldn't take the risk that William had shared his revelations about the twins being in the study with their adoptive parents. Fire is swift, painful and reliable.

"We couldn't let anyone know what Delecarte had been doing in the past. It's politically incorrect, trying to make some white babies. It would throw too much suspicion on us. Who would give us an immunization contract then? Nobody. Then when we realized the fool was actually planning to run out on us, we needed to clean the chicken coop."

"What about his brother?"

"A chicken that won't lay eggs gets eaten."

"But—"

"I think that's enough information for somebody that's so distraught over her lover, she's going to jump out of a twenty-story building, don't you?"

"One more thing," I said, stalling for time. "How do you plan to pull this off?" I knew. "My God. That's why you're going to China, isn't it? You want to immunize all the children with whatever it is you have that turns off the switch to make girls."

"Goddamn, I told him you were a smart fish. Too bad you swallowed the bait."

"No wonder they're paying you a fortune. You bastard. How could you do something like this? Do you know how much disruption and chaos this could cause in the end? To fill the world with nothing but men? Shit, you'd destroy each other in a fucking week. Then what?"

"I'm counting on most of them doing just that. Those of us remaining will have the power to reproduce ourselves, thanks to the Dogons. Did you know your people had the secret to the problem of cell division and fertilizing your own cells? And we can thank Oscar Delecarte, of course, for introducing my new team of scientists to their work. See, we're not worried about anything now."

"But you don't have the diamond. It's gone." I knew it and I was glad the Dogon had taken it with him. Maybe I wasn't safe. But the world was.

"Wrong. The diamond is on its way back here and we're destroying it as planned. Now, shut up. Get her out of here, will you?"

"Wait." I needed more time. Time for what? To live. "Someone else knows I'm here." I meant the Prof. But what diamond was Biggers talking about? Why did he think the diamond was on the way here? The diamond had gone back with the old Dogon. Hadn't it?

"Yes. We're going to take care of the Prof as soon as we're done with your little flight. Everybody will understand if a has-been computer hacker gets depressed. What does he do? Kills himself. Not too hard to believe. No one will connect him to you or us."

"Your goons," I said, pointing to the four men, "Delecarte was calling to them to help him get rid of me that day, wasn't he?"

"Damn girl, you're good. And you're lucky. Now you can take your own life. After all you've been through, no one will be surprised. But stalling is only wasting my time. And you. You don't have any time left."

The two goons started dragging me. I knew it was useless. He'd never even spoken to Bill Clinton. Actually, on second thought, I bet he had. That way he had an alibi. If there's any questions, I thought, he can claim he'd even made arrangements for me to meet with Clinton. That would prove he would be as shocked as anyone that I'd taken my life. This motherfucker would get away clean if I didn't do something and quick.

"Did you shoot Kenneth Lawson?"

"He did," Biggers said, pointing to one of the goons.

"Why? Why shoot him since you were making all the other twins look like suicides or accidents?"

"Thanks to that damn bitch Duvet, Kenneth Lawson found out too much about our operation. Your precious Kenneth didn't want to go inside the restaurant, so he was supposed to meet Claudette Duvet in the alley. I think he was concerned you might see him. What he didn't know and neither did we was that Duvet had also invited Keith Lawson to meet her at Le Chef. Keith and Kenneth had fallen out over the diamond. Keith had been in Seattle drowning himself in booze.

"Duvet found out that Oscar Delecarte engineered the murders of the Lawsons' mother and grandparents years before to keep the diamond. I'm speculating that William Delecarte found a way to inform Duvet after he couldn't locate the Lawson twins just before his unfortunate death. I knew if Duvet told the Lawsons, it would reunite them, and vengeance would become their collective motivation. Everything I'd worked for would be in jeopardy if that happened. Up until that point all the twins had been doing was trying to figure out all they could about their mysterious illness.

"So it turned out all of them needed to be eliminated and quickly. Both the brothers and Duvet all dying accidentally wouldn't work, not here in Atlanta, so we planned something more believable for Kenneth.

"A shooting was the perfect solution. He'd been in Atlanta long enough to make enemies, if push came to shove. You know Atlanta—a black man gets shot by another black man, what's the big deal? No news there. Then Keith, so distraught over his estranged twin's death, jumps off a bridge or something. What's the news? Just another black man saving the taxpayers money for more jails."

Now I understood. That had not been Kenneth holding hands with Duvet but his brother Keith. That scene I'd witnessed had had nothing to do with love or intimacy, only empathy and past betrayals.

"Your Kenneth was waiting for the woman in the alley in your car. Anyway," Biggers said, "my man decided what the hell, shoot Kenneth in the alley. Rob him and make it look like a botched carjacking. Then take care of the other two later."

He pointed out the man I recognized now from his labored breathing to be the Wheezer. And for a split second I wondered how he got out of the house fire at Jeff's.

"My man had just shot Kenneth in the chest, when a vagrant came into the alley. The fool ran out of the alley so he wouldn't be seen."

The Wheezer said, "What did you want me to do? Stay? Be identified as the shooter? Do I look like a carjacker to you?" he asked, grinning at me.

"No, you look like a blimp," I volunteered, wishing I could grab his balls.

"Shut up, you two cows," Biggers said, glaring at the man. "Let me finish, so we can get on with this. We knew Keith Lawson and Duvet pulled Kenneth from the car. I suppose they were taking him to a hospital. My men ran all of them off the road."

"So how did Claudette Duvet get away?"

"Duvet jumped from the car and ran. The Lawsons weren't in any shape to run. So my boy here took care of business.

"Neither one of the Lawsons had the diamond on them so we decided maybe Keith had hidden it somewhere. Keith died on us while we injected him with some concoction Delecarte had given us that he said would make a person tell the truth. I think the shit killed him instead. Delecarte could be such an idiot.

"And, of course, your Kenneth, well, he was not in a talking mood. So we took him to Delecarte to nurse him back to health until we could locate the diamond or make him sing. No matter what happened we knew he'd make good insurance.

"Duvet went home to get her stuff and go underground. She probably would have gotten away if she hadn't taken the time to phone that bitch friend of hers at the CDC."

I realized in that moment it *was* me Claudette Duvet had phoned when I'd heard his men bursting into the room to kill her, not Dr. Mutota at the CDC.

Biggers talked on. "We then got rid of Duvet and made it look like a suicide attempt. Later we revised our plan on account of you. Actually, it was perfect. You killed her and tried to make it look like a suicide. Women are so deceitful."

"You're an idiot. No one believed I killed Claudette Duvet. No one. They didn't have any real evidence."

Biggers smiled. "Want to bet? See, when the police found Claudette Duvet's body, there was a razor but it only had *her* prints on it. I'm not a genius for naught. I sent my men over to help the police find the real murder weapon. The idea was that you'd slit her wrists and planted that razor in her hands to throw the police off your trail. But you'd ditched the real murder weapon in the trash in an alley. It was simple. We got

Kenneth Lawson's razor from your house and planted it in that alley. Then we phoned the police from a pay phone with an anonymous tip. The rest is history. If we hadn't sacrificed Delecarte, your ass would be in jail this minute, little chickie. The funny thing is, when we did it, we just wanted you out of the way because we thought you were beginning to snoop a news story out of this," he continued, seeming to enjoy hearing himself describe his own brilliance.

"Then Delecarte finally had his own clever moment," Biggers said, frowning as though attributing something to Delecarte robbed him of his glory. "He suggested we act like Kenneth Lawson was dead, since the boys were identical twins, and see who would surface with the diamond. In the meantime, we got busy tracing Keith's steps to see if he'd hidden it back in Seattle.

"You were actually the last person on our list who might have the diamond, since we thought, shit, Kenneth wouldn't entrust the only thing he had in life worth a good goddamn to a woman. Obviously, we were wrong. But we had an ace in the hole, like all good poker players, and that paid off. You, my filly. And the rest, of course, is history."

I assumed he meant kidnapping Carol and I said, "You're a lowlife—"

The Wheezer stuck a gun in my ribs. And now I was mad.

"Let's move," the Wheezer said.

The black one shoved me.

I whispered, "Brother, what the fuck are you doing here? I'm your sistah, remember?"

I could see he didn't remember shit, as he pushed me out the door. They led me into a stairwell and we started climbing steps.

My mind was back in the dojo.

> *The shihans demand Mukuso, silent prayer. We are in seiza, sitting knee position, eyes closed, body straight but relaxed, completely still. Then the call for the precepts.* Dojo kun.
> *I jump up: Be humble and confident with others.*
> *Joined shouts. One by one, I hear the precepts echoing in my mind.*
> *Access every threatening situation as if your life depends on it.*
> *Do not overreact or panic.*
> *Avoid confrontation if possible; act only in self-defense.*
> *Believe in yourself, the truth and your faith.*
> *My faith. My faith? I do have faith. Faith in God.*

I am shocked by the revelation from my soul. We're up on the twentieth floor in an area that is under construction. Four idiots plus me. We're all huffing and puffing. I might die, but somebody is going to get their ass kicked first.

"Does it take this many of you to screw in a lightbulb? No damn wonder you want to get rid of women," I said.

The Wheezer one-stepped over into me. He was one of those white guys who has puke on his breath. He leaned over and kissed me on the mouth while two others held my arms behind me.

I spit at him.

"If you know what's good for you, you'll keep your filthy mouth shut or I'll screw you, all right."

He bent over laughing with his fat ass.

The others laughed with him.

I glared at the brother.

He looked away.

"In fact," the Wheezer said, unbuckling his belt, "that's a good idea. Why throw good pussy out the window. Let's see how many of us it takes to screw a black bitch."

The brother stepped forward. "Man. This shit is not necessary."

"Fuck off," the Wheezer said. "You don't have to screw her. I'm sure you've had all the black bitches you can count, starting with your mama."

This was my chance. This was one of those white men who only spent business hours with black folk. If he'd been a little more liberal, he would have known this man was over forty and he came from the school where bitches didn't fly and saying "your mama" was a prayer for him to whip your ass.

Wheezer didn't even know it was coming. The other two relaxed their hands on me for a second to try to reach out to hold the black guy, who for all practical purposes I will call the Bull, since he damn sure was charging his partner.

Kiai! I yelled in my head. Because my plan was to whip all their asses. Nobody on this earth was ever going to rape me again. I'd pull a Thelma and Louise first and jump off the fucking building. But I figured even they should have turned that fucking car around and rammed into the men's asses instead of sailing over into a canyon to die. If I was going to die, it would be the first time in life I could say I wasn't alone.

I rocked back and forth attempting a *ginga*, the beginning movement of Capoeira, the African-Brazilian martial art.

I broke loose at the moment they realized the Wheezer had pulled out a knife to go along with his gun.

I spun over on both hands and let my feet make direct contact with the Wheezer's knife hand. The knife skidded across the floor while my ankles closed around his neck and brought him reeling away from the brother in a face-forward fall.

I flipped up over on my right hand and caught the other hard-head behind me off guard, because my foot was already up-side his fucking head before he could pull out his weapon of choice. He fell hard to the floor.

I jumped up into the air, spun around and gave the Wheezer, now coming for me, a spinning back kick to the left side of his head. This toppled him as his pants slid down.

The Wheezer skirted toward his knife. I didn't have to worry about him because the brother, whether he wanted to or not, now had *my* back.

I dropped quickly down on my hands and let my legs grab the one now pointing a gun at me around the neck and spun him over onto his back with a thud. I stomped his penis hard and he folded over like a paper napkin.

I heard sirens as the black guy unloaded his gun into the Wheezer. Only, the Wheezer had a spare gun and they both collapsed. Now it was just me and one man standing.

I could see him weighing—me, the sirens and how much money Biggers was paying his ass. To his credit the measly paycheck won. He raced down the steps and left me the fuck alone.

I dragged myself up. Pain seared through my body. I didn't start this shit. But I knew who did. I was about to finish it. I picked up one of the guns.

♊

I stumbled my way down the stairwell. I peeped out on the fifteenth floor. Everything was quiet. Obviously it was a soundproof building and nobody knew I'd almost been raped and murdered.

I tried straightening up my clothes and hair but it was useless. I hobbled down the hall. I pointed the gun right in Biggers's assistant's face. "I have an appointment; don't bother announcing me. Unless red is your color."

I opened the door. He thought it was his assistant. His smile froze. "What the fuck?" He scrambled for his drawer.

"Don't even think about it, motherfucker," I said, pointing the gun at his head.

"Where are my men?"

"Hell, I don't keep them in my pocket. Maybe you should pay them fair wages, though. The work of killing folk shouldn't come cheap."

"Lookie here, filly. If I were you I would cut my losses and haul ass."

"That's exactly what I intend to do. If I'm not mistaken, this gun can cut some mighty star-studded holes in a body. Am I right?"

"You're wrong. I'm sure my assistant is getting the guards right now."

"Is that a fact?" I opened the door. "Excuse me, Miss. I hate to interrupt your crying but how much is he paying you?"

She looked up, startled and scared shitless. In a wee voice she said, "Thirty thousand dollars."

"Oh, then I don't suppose you'll be calling any security guards, since if I hear you, I will shoot your little ass. Got that."

"Yes. Yes, ma'am," she said, scurrying under her desk.

"Respect. All I want is a little respect," I said, turning around to Biggers. And damn if Aretha Franklin's voice didn't ring in my ear.

While Aretha was singing, *All I want is a little respect, just a little bit*, in that split second Biggers made his move.

I smiled my most charming smile. "Don't let your fingers do the walking to that gun, big horse. If you'd like to keep them, that is."

A dark wave descended over me. I wished I'd had the diamond. I'd smash it in his face. All this shit over nothing. Goddamn it, when will we learn? We do not control the fucking Universe. I sat down, still holding the gun on him.

"I know we can work this out," he said, still sounding confident. "I have money. Lots of money."

You prick. "Shut up. I'm thinking." I wasn't thinking, though. I was tired and pissed off. This motherfucker had taken the only two men who'd ever loved me away, and here he sat in this office. If he went to trial, shit, he might only have to pay a fine. That is, if he were found guilty at all. The haves take care of the real money people. That scenario made my decision.

I raised the gun. "I'm going to help you out, Biggers. You know, like you wanted to help me." I started walking toward him. "It'll be so sad for your wife. You do have a wife, don't you? Well, no mind, your loved ones will know you sat right here in this fucking room, on the brink of making billions of dollars, and you, stupid shit donkey ass, shot yourself with your own fucking gun. Take it out of the drawer now and place it on the desk in front of you, mule face. I know that's what you have in that locked drawer, hog filly."

He fumbled with the drawer and finally took the gun out, sweat belying his calm look.

"Careful now. Don't try anything stupid," I said. "It'll be a hell of a lot easier to die instantly than for me to pump all these bullets in your ass, don't you agree? What kind of gun is that you have there?"

"A Luger. You're making a mistake," he said, smirking at me. "I'll give you millions."

"No. No, you won't," I shouted. "I don't want millions, hog-face. You made your mistake when you killed Kenneth Lawson and Jeff Samuels."

"What? Jeff Samuels?" He smiled.

"You heard me. Jeff Samuels."

"You're slipping up, little filly. You hooked me up with Jeff yourself, remember? I thought to myself at the time, now wasn't that nice of that old gal? Hooking me up with a great jock like him."

"I did no such thing."

"Sure, you did. He introduced himself and said you sent him over. I even phoned you or had my gal phone, to thank you. See, I'm a man of etiquette."

I recalled the phone message on the day after I saw Kenneth Lawson with Claudette Duvet. *Thanks for the intro to your friend, little filly. He's a damn good old boy. And from my home state, too.*

That message seemed like a lifetime ago. I hadn't understood it then. But now I did. I'd been set up. Damn.

Wait, I thought, this is probably one of Biggers's sick tricks. Jeff Samuels wasn't from Texas.

"Yeah. I don't believe you," I said. "Jeff Samuels is from Kentucky." But my thoughts raced even as I said it. That would explain Jeff's living above his means. And then, the photo of him hobnobbing with Biggers, playing golf, planted itself in my mind's eye. Was Biggers telling the truth? Why believe him? Biggers was a horse-trotting liar.

"Yeah. Well, if you'd done your homework when you did the profile on me, instead of relying on other news articles and their sources, you would have possibly known that. You journalists have gotten so lazy. You don't dig, just scratch. You're a bunch of fucking chickens, that's all. See, I'm from Kentucky by way of Texas, little lamb. Now, how did I know it would end like this?" Biggers continued, smiling. "You and he against each other. You black men and women just can't get along, now can you?"

"What do you mean he and I against each other? For your information, Jeff died trying to save me. You ought to know that. Your own men killed him."

Biggers grinned. "So you're not so smart after all. No one killed Jeff.

He wanted you backed up against a wall so you'd be easier to handle. He also wanted your trust, even though it didn't matter."

"You're lying."

"Ask him. He's standing right behind you."

"Do you think I'd fall for that? I watch television, see movies—where the hell do you think I've been? Sitting inside the fucking *Bell Curve*?"

"He's there, all right. Right behind you. Holding a gun on you as of . . . " He checked his Rolex. "Well, never mind. What does it matter what time you die?"

I knew it was true. I could feel him. I turned around slowly in disbelief. I wanted to shoot my damn self.

Jeff Samuels stood there holding a gun. His head bandaged.

"What the hell is she talking about, old fellow?" Biggers said. "Does she think I would kill my own damn partner? The reason we were willing to merely get rid of you today, little filly, and not sweat you until you told us where the ring was hidden is because Jeff has the ring."

"Partner?" I whispered, staring at Jeff in horror. "Jeff? *You* think Jeff has the ring?" Damn, had Jeff switched the ring out at some point? He couldn't have. The old Dogon would have known the real thing. But maybe that was a figment of my imagination. My cognitive mind had resisted what I'd witnessed in the hospital. There was still a part of me that believed I'd made up the old man. But then, if so, what did happen to the ring? I sure as hell didn't have it. Did Jeff Samuels pull some *Mission Impossible* illusion on me at the hospital? Damn.

"Patricia," Jeff said. "Let me explain. First you need to put the gun down."

"Hell no. Shoot me, goddamn it," I shrieked, aiming at Jeff. "You might as well shoot me now. Because I will not leave this room until either I'm dead, or you two are dead. And tell me, motherfucker, do you have that diamond?"

"Please, Patricia," he said, "put the gun down and step away from him."

I bit my lip. The tears filling my eyes were going to make hitting either one of them difficult, but I was going to try it.

"Don't pick that gun up," Jeff said to Biggers.

Then to me, "Could you please trust me?" Jeff pleaded. "Put the gun down, Patricia. You don't want to do anything foolish here. Believe me, I have it under control. There is no diamond."

My shihans taught me that when someone is about to do something stupid, you can smell his odor rise and his aura expand. My nose twitched and I lunged into a handstand and flipped into the air.

299

John Biggers picked up his gun and fired at my back. He missed. The bullet whizzed past me.

Jeff Samuels dived to the floor, shooting as he rolled in my direction.

He hit John Biggers in the chest. At the same instant I heard Jeff groan. He fell on top of me, so I couldn't really see, but I knew now he was hit too, in his right shoulder.

I pushed out from under him and snatched his gun. I pointed it at Biggers. Biggers's gun lay inches from him. He was holding his chest, gasping for air.

Jeff rolled over, begging, "For God's sake, don't do that. You'll go to prison. I'm telling you." He stumbled up, gripping his wound. "Trust me, Patricia. Put the gun down."

"It'll be you and me then, asshole. In prison, together."

He held his left hand out to me.

Biggers eyed his gun even though he was bleeding badly.

It was now or never. Fuck it. I aimed. I squeezed the trigger. The bullet zoomed through the air and hit the wall far to Biggers's right.

I turned around and handed Jeff the gun. Fuck this. Violence was not the way.

Biggers made a leap for his gun and fired again. He obviously didn't give a shit about the way.

The bullet hit Jeff and spun him around.

Biggers yelled in pain and his Luger tumbled on the floor.

I scrambled for the gun and pointed it once again at Biggers. "Say adios, motherfucker." Then the words from the void pulled at me as I heard the old Dogon say, *Violence is not the way.*

Biggers was trying to get his Luger off the floor. I yanked up my purse, which was still on the floor, and pulled out the taser gun. Stepped back and fired it.

Biggers convulsed immediately. I yelled for the assistant to call the police and I ran around to Biggers and pulled his hands behind his back. Blood spurted from a gaping wound, but I knew the taser thing didn't last that long and I couldn't take any chances. I tied his hands with the exercise jump rope I'd seen in the drawer.

"You know this rope might come in handy in the federal pen. Don't you think? Exercise is the key to long life. And just think, Biggers, in prison I bet you'll even experience the ecstasy of being a woman."

I could hear sirens and this time I hoped they were really coming to this building. I sat down on the floor beside Jeff and lifted his head gently onto my lap.

"Are you hurt bad?" I asked, holding back tears.

"I've been worse." He reached up, grimacing, and touched my face. "I love you, Patricia Conley. You're one hell of a woman."

"Yeah, well, where the hell have you been? I love you too," I said, and then smiled. Irony. Shit. He'd passed out.

CHAPTER FORTY-SEVEN

Jeff, Carol, Ira and I had our celebration along with our new friend, the Prof. It felt wonderful and I real- ized I had the family I'd longed for all along. In my friends. The people who cared about me. Sometimes you can search for something so hard you fumble all over it. I felt lucky I'd come to understand what a true family was—not always biological parents, not even biological siblings, but those who cared for, nurtured and loved you.

Jeff and Carol made up, once she found out he was doing an under-cover investigation on Biggers's organization for his family, the CIA. Jeff had lied to Biggers about having the ring to get him off me. What he didn't count on was Biggers still thinking he needed to kill me in order to tie up his loose ends. Jeff hadn't known what Biggers knew: that I'd figured the entire mess out.

It turned out Jeff had approached me to get to Biggers, who was an ex-CIA informant. He'd been following Biggers's diamond trade and money-laundering schemes for a long time.

When he read about me in *Greater Loafing*, he figured I'd be his in to meet Biggers. He introduced himself to me. Made sure he was seen in my company and then approached Biggers as one of my friends, who'd recommended him. Biggers accepted him after the CIA put out a false alarm indicating Biggers was going to be investigated by the Justice De-partment for discriminatory practices. Biggers didn't have any minorities working for him and none on his management team. There were several lawsuits pending against some of Biggers's companies based on discriminatory hiring practices that would have cost him a pretty penny.

Then when Jeff heard about the diamond issue with Keith Lawson through Biggers's staff, Jeff suspected Kenneth or Keith Lawson had stolen the diamond from somewhere.

Jeff explained, "Claudette Duvet surfaced and at first we thought she was in on the theft, so we followed her for a while. She gave us the slip the day she arranged to meet Kenneth and Keith at the restaurant. Evidently, she'd made contact with Keith and he'd just flown into Atlanta that day. Kenneth waited for Duvet's meeting in the back of the restaurant because he didn't want you to see him. Kenneth was not aware Claudette had his brother inside the restaurant, since Duvet knew they'd been feuding. She'd planned to use Keith as backup pressure on Kenneth for him to believe the conspiracy theory she held."

It turned out Jeff had wrongly decided Kenneth Lawson had approached me for the same reason *he* had: the fact that he could get close to John Biggers because Biggers respected me. The CIA thought Kenneth wanted to sell the diamond to Biggers through the Delecartes, since they figured out Oscar was secretly negotiating to buy it through one of Biggers's brokers. Shows what happens when you're respected by scum. Go figure.

Biggers had financed the computer seminar where I'd met Kenneth. Jeff had been there watching him. Meeting me was strictly a coincidence for Kenneth, or an act of fate, if you believed.

Now, I'd agreed to testify before Congress that even though I believed genetic research was vital to our future, more restrictions needed to be placed on the sources of researchers' funding and their ultimate goals. And, of course, more policing of freaking nuts who happen to become geneticists.

Jeff and I talked about the implications of what had happened and the future problems lurking around the corner regarding ethics. It was clear to both of us: Man's desire for power and perfection would one day kill us all.

"So what did the Dogon elder tell you would have happened had they destroyed the diamond?" Jeff asked me.

He couldn't quite believe the Dogon elder had appeared to me. His explanation was that under stress, we create many illusions to help us. Only Carol accepted that an old black man helped me do this. As for the ring, Jeff thought I still had it someplace for safekeeping.

I knew better as I repeated to Jeff the old Dogon's words: "The world would have exploded if they'd cracked the diamond open. There is a special moment when the diamond can be opened. It is not yet time for the joining of the eighth articulation, when the primordial seeds will be one again. The time of the Sigui."

With or without this happening, I still believed that, if given a choice, no one in their right mind would want the world without the people of color or the glorious women. The problem is, there are too many people on earth not in their right mind.

CHAPTER FORTY-EIGHT

"Patricia, I love you."

Jeff repeated this refrain every day since the ordeal had ended. His wounds were healing and he'd been reassigned. He wanted to get married.

It was funny. Now I didn't feel so pressured to settle down. Have a family. I'd witnessed a new part of myself and I wanted to get to know more about it.

"Hey, we can have a long-distance relationship. People do it," I said. I needed time to heal myself. To explore that other side of me. I'd neglected myself too long, while longing for a family. Maybe I'd been waiting to exhale in my own way. Not about hang-ups with men so much but my own spiritual self.

"Okay. Long distance," he said. "You still call the shots."

"Tonight, guess what I'm going to do?" I said.

"What?"

"Let you cook dinner for me."

"Hey," Jeff said, "I've already been doing all the cooking in this relationship."

"And that's why I don't want to break tradition. What about it? My place at seven?"

"Seven it is."

We kissed.

"I've got something for you for our dinner tonight," Jeff said. "It's in the car." He went to his rented car and came back with a basket. "Here."

"What is it?"

"Something to keep you company while I'm gone. A little champagne."

"I told you," I said, feeling a tinge of anger, "I'm going to AA now."

He smiled and shook his head from side to side. "I know that."

I bit my lip. Alcoholism can give you a one-track mind. He wasn't offering me alcohol to keep me company. Something else.

I took the basket and lifted the lid.

A kitten the color of champagne.

Before I went to bed that night, alone, the doorbell rang. I walked slowly to the door and looked out. There was no one there. I was about to close it when the Dogon appeared with the ring on his pointer, which had supposedly been cut off.

CHAPTER FORTY-NINE

We talked into the night. He answered my questions patiently.

"What about all the problems in the world?"

"Yes, there are problems in the world, but the Universe is in perfect order. Amma created it in perfect order from the beginning when there was only the Word."

"Why are dual births important?

"We are all twins. All androgynous beings. We have the two souls, both male and female. Both shadow and real."

"What about homosexuals?"

"We all have male and female. There is no such thing in reality. As long as the people allow spirit to lead the body and not body to lead the spirit, it does not matter. We all deserve to love the spirits of others, no matter the body they have chosen. We are all one."

"But what of sin?"

"We are all doing what we can within the frame of our own spirals. The Creator is in control and the Universe is in perfect order. Our task is to rid ourselves of imperfection."

"Will we be punished?"

"Are you not already punished? The natural laws of the Universe render us subject to cause-and-effect relationships. We are continually returning to rectify any misunderstandings or misdeeds on the Arc."

"Will the world get better?"

"If the people come to understand and carry out their role in it. Still, they do not control the Universe. They are merely the caretakers."

"Are we only carbon, matter, DNA, RNA?"

"We are all things in the Universe. We are water first. Our beginnings, in your words, came from the germination of the primordial seed."

"Are there others out there?"

"We are the others. There are many worlds and many beings. There are fourteen worlds and fourteen heavens. We are only one. But we are told that the Nommo will come again. A certain star in the sky will signal the resurrection. This will be soon."

"Will the races ever get along?"

"When people can accept that the separation is of their own creation. The Creator and we are one. In the face of each is the face of many."

"Will men and women ever truly love each other?"

"When they love themselves. All Ogo's future attempts will be to look for and take back his lost female twin—or yet, his female soul—a loss due to his pride, his revolt and his initiatives. Which brings us to the eighth articulation: for it is the seed of the female po pilu which, by its spinning about, will complete Amma's creative work."

♊

The eighth articulation: In the beginning, after Ogo lost his twin, the female was three, the male four. When the primordial seed is released at the time of the Sigui, the male and female will both be four once again. Twinness. Love. Equality. Peace. Compassion.

♊

Does that mean what I think it means? Is that why under certain circumstances and pressures we, both men and women, behave in exactly the same way? Is that why power and money cause us to lose our love for one another? Is that why we don't know ourselves and become so critical of others no matter whether they are men or women? Is it why we betray both men and women? Why we emasculate, circumcise and mutilate boys and girls?

The Dogon answered.

"Some men and women are with honor and others without. Some men and women are with understanding and others without. Some men and women are with balance and others without. Some men and women acquire wisdom and others do not. That which we know to be male and female are mainly all variations of one principle in two formed bodies. The masculine principle. The masculine soul.

"There is no true female spirit in its fullness on the earth yet. Yes, there are bodies that manifest in female form. But that is all there is. All the life force presently functioning is that of the masculine principle; the feminine has been suppressed. The complete female is yet to come. Thus the complete human evolution. It is so.

"When the feminine principle returns we will once again be perfect, whole beings. It is the time of the resurrection. The return. Some call it the return of light. The Christos principle. It is the eighth articulation. *The joining of the primordial seeds.*"

EPILOGUE

I knew I would never see the world the same again. In less than two weeks my entire life and world had altered itself. It was alien to me to think in the abstract, metaphysical world of the Dogons, but on a gut level I wanted to understand it. And if I suspended my conscious thoughts I could even possibly believe it.

I wanted to laugh. According to the Dogons, we are all the same. If it were true, then I was finally one of the *boys*. And to prove it I went back to join the Dojo with a humble heart and bowed head. I understood what my shihans had been trying to teach me all along—those are the truly manly ways. We are not alone. And then I remembered reading:

The eighth articulation of the Word will be in the sex, the reproductive organ, that will permit the adult to give birth to a new being.

THE TRUE GEMINI RISING

Gemini, the twins, Castor and Pollux, is one of duality, interchange and
as the first of the "human signs," of oncoming education, culture, civilization.
Gemini attends to the needs of mankind by inculcating the special sense,
largely by means of its chief instrument, genetic redistribution.
When two or three people are thus related, finding themselves brought
into contact with each other from day to day, the need of interchange of ideas
and of commodity are urgently felt.

♊

There it was. Twins. Twins. We are all twins.
Dual beings both female and male equally.

Acknowledgments

I tried to kill myself once: After reading this you'll know why I didn't go through with it—too many suicide notes. I'm like the old woman who lived in the shoe. I've got so many family members, friends and, let's not forget, ex-husbands, I don't know what to do. Now, if they'll all buy a book, I'll be on my way to huge sales numbers.

I wouldn't have a book without Denise Stinson, the ruler of all agents. Without her I'd be unpublished and locked up somewhere crazy. She is the alter ego of Patricia Conley, a woman who knows what a woman has to do. She believed in me before I even had a book. And if there is ever a movie please consider her for the leading part, okay, maybe a walk-on role.

I want to say to Mary Ann Naples, who believed I could turn that outline into a book before I did, I'm forever grateful. You're an editor who understands that black people have the answers to big questions too. Not only did you teach me how to say "fabulous" with flair, but your editing talents and constant encouragement are what I needed to see me through this work. I don't take for granted that you also let me cry on your shoulder. And to Carlene Bauer, who let me whine and fuss, you're so wonderful, may the editor's mantle fall on your shoulders as quickly as it fell on that incredible past assistant of Mary Ann's, Laurie Chittenden. A huge thanks to Victoria Meyer, the publicity director who made me feel so special. Cheers to the copy editors, Philip R. Metcalf, Karen Richardson, and Gypsy da Silva. And a hug to all the marketing/art people who struggled to come up with a plan for my sales. Thanks to all of you for making my dream of publishing a suspense thriller materialize in the real world.

And thanks to my ex Thomas Mueed, who taught me "What a Woman's Gotta Do" by drumming into my head that "A man's gotta do what a man's gotta do." Tommy, you'll always be my best friend. And to Paul and Michael, my other ex's, thanks for being there when I needed you. I'd also like to thank all the other men I've known, you know who you are—and forget the tabloids. I love telling it all myself, remember.

Thanks to Charlene Shucker, my sister, who stayed up nights reading this book alternating between "take that out" and "I love this." And also to my brother Ira who not only let me borrow his name but his wife. Thanks to Pat Carr for being there to talk ugly to me whenever I was whining that I really couldn't write, who chased down the pages when they got caught in the wind and who was the first to tell me after reading this manuscript, "this is it!"

Now for other firsts: Thanks to my freshman year English teacher at North Carolina Central University, Linda Hodge, an avant-garde woman living in a barn, for telling me I was a writer. Where are you? And to my roommate, Jean Farmer Butterfield for taking my work to Miss Hodge, when I should have been in class but was asleep instead. Thanks to my other sister Deborah Winfrey and other brother Robert Winfrey who were the first people to cry over something I wrote and who also gave me love, support, use of a computer and a place to stay whenever I needed it. To Dothula Baron Butler for letting me live with her so I could write on a porch and watch birds. And to my sister Dorothy Oliver for letting me bunk in her house, reading everything I wrote and loving me no matter what, even after I talked her into selling her house and moving to Italy. I'm glad you're back in the United States. To the North Carolina Arts Council for making me the first African American to ever win their fiction fellowship, which gave me the idea that maybe I was truly a writer. Hugs to my brother Mel White who believed in my writing enough to let me stay with him for months rent free.

Support to die for: Thanks to Jennifer Erickson, Monica Giles, Tina Howard, Valarie Boyd, Brenda Yarbrough, Brooke Stephens, Angela Benson, Barbara Neely, Sabina Evarts, Joan Broerman, Pam Walker, Alice Lovelace, JoAnn Fox, Lavern Davis, Louise Pulliam, Kay Pinkney, Calvin and Teresa Stovall, Toia Taylor, Anita Richmond-

Bunkley and Cristina and Joe Kessler for cheering me on. To my early readers, Awa of The Shrine of the Black Madonna, Andrea Dorsey and Mike Sussman. And my friend and the top travel agent in the Universe, Janice Camp, who sees to it I travel happy.

And for a lifetime of cheering, thanks to my best friends, Linda and Keith Turner (the same Linda, I'm buying a car for with my first million) and Glenda Bigelow Payne, Carolyn Jordan and Levones Kendall Rhodes (who all still let me call to cry in the middle of the night). And thanks to all my sister- and brother-in-laws.

To people who made my life richer and easier: My cousins and their families, Ed and Annie Carol Walker, Lula Jane and Connie Hooker and Olene and Bernice Pulliam. My Aunt Loretta and Aunt Pearl Lee and their families. My friends Lavern and Bobby Jones, Ethel Rouse and her family in Baltimore, the Taylors in Winston-Salem, Butch and Elaine Davis in Jersey, Brenda S. Poteat, Brenda Tinnin, Ed and Myrna Hughes, David and Ada Gilman, Lucy Parker and family, Ola Mae Reese, Minnie Dickerson and family, the Snells in Fayetteville, the Alley-Barnes in Seattle, the Richardses in Savannah, the Thompsons (all three families), the Ebenezer Christian Church, Ms. Bryant, Paul Evans and family, the Leaths, Zack Wall, the Sharps, Aunt Vivian and Uncle Jack Shoffner, my cousins Marilyn (Lynn) Coleman and Cornbread, Stephanie and Janelle Godbolt, Edward Skeeter Harmon and his family, my uncles Algie and Richard Coleman, Aunt Evelyn and the other Harmons and all the Tilghmans. To my cousins Constance Glascow, Dorian Mendezvaz, William Tilghman and my Aunt Lucile Mendezvaz, who taught me you can change your life whenever you want. Also a thanks to my present in-laws, Louise Pelton and family (who love me even though they've never seen me). All my family of the entire White/Coleman clan, my Burlington, Winston-Salem, Baltimore and Camden, New Jersey, friends. And thanks to my mentors, Aunty May Kyi, Ernestine Mitchner and Mabel Jessup, and my teachers in Burlington.

You who went beyond the call of duty as supporters: thanks to Cynthia Tucker for putting on the most expensive, sophisticated book party ever held in Atlanta for a children's book. Thanks to Rosemary Pinson, Aunt Audrey White, Sarah Brooks and Amelia Tucker Shaw for selling all those children's books. To Harold Underdown and Ann Rubin who kept me going. And to Kathy Tucker, Lisa Fedie and the gang at Albert Whitman Hobbit Hall—you're the best. And to the Mutotas, who've vowed to throw me an unprecedented adult book party and who always let me rant and rave.

A special thanks to John Walter and Jan, and Ron Martin, Izell Booker, Julie Santos and all you *Atlanta Journal and Constitution* newspaper folk who supported my writing career to the end. And to Bob in payroll and your mate Michael, I love you both. I can't forget you either, Bette Harrison, for just giving me money. Thanks to Marilyn and Iris in the cafeteria for caring about my health. To my old colleagues at Alamance and Forsyth Mental Health Centers, I love you.

Thanks to the money people and miscellaneous: my love to Angela Shelf Medearis (the most prolific children's book author I know) and her husband the author, Mike, and to the greatest Pulitzer Prize–winning cartoonist in the world, Mike Luckovich, for the three of you believing in my talent enough to actually loan me money to survive this writing business. And to Inland Mortgage, which has been decent enough to wait until I got money. And thanks to Mary Britton and Lee Army Malcolm and her family for being the kind of neighbors that would let me hide out from the storm. Family and friends, if you looked for your name and it wasn't here, it's because I'm saving it for the next book. Not to worry.

And to the Simon & Schuster Sales Force: without you I will surely be lost. Thank you! Thank you! Thank you!

A book like this one requires a lot of research and input from people who know a lot more than I do. Let me thank the charming Ms. Genevieve Calame Griaule in Paris, France, the daughter of famed anthropologist Marcel Griaule, who opened the eyes of the world to the Dogons; Nii Sowa Laye, a Dogon Elder of the Gah people of Ghana, whom I'm proud to claim as a friend; the gracious monks of the Monastery of Holy Spirit; Dr. John Bradley of the NVA Research facility and the kindest material scientist in the world; Detective Michael B. Griffin, a hard-working twelve-year veteran of the Atlanta Homicide Division; Maggie Hartley, CDC, scientist administrator extraordinaire; Dr. Marc Goldstein, author of *The Couples Guide to Fertility*, published by Doubleday, and Professor of Urology at Cornell University Medical Center and Director for Male Reproductive Medicine and Microsurgery at the New York Hospital–Cornell Medical Center, who happens to be someone who really cares; Mike Burnette, a friendly gemologist with Shane Company Diamond Importers; Dr. Toni Miles, a phenomenal geneticist at Penn State University; the brilliant Dewey Brown, Chief Investigator, and one-of-a-kind Lori Campbell, Chief Forensic Technician, at Dekalb Medical Examiners Office. Bruce Sterling, author of *The Hacker Crackdown*, a must-read book; the great Shihan Dave Young of the Dave Young Karate School in Norcross, Georgia; Dr. Richard Hansen, a fantastic internist; Chuck Baker, a sharp-as-a-razor, Producer and Director, GPTV; good guy Randy Moreland, MARTA; and samaritan, Deirdre LaPin for the contact with Genevieve Griaule. And to Gilia and Bryony Angell, the twins with the identical cowlicks—thank you for sharing.

Things to look for when you come to the Atlanta area: when you're hungry, Suzie's Cafe, The Flying Biscuit, and The Red Light Cafe. Try Delectables for a delightful gourmet lunch, and the Varsity for hot-dogs. And for lively Jamaican cuisine, Bridgetown Grill. And if you're wise, The Monastery of the Holy Spirit in Conyers, and if you're smart, the Spectrum Bookstore in Clarkston. For outdoors try Clayton County College's pond. To tour a real newpaper do *The Atlanta Journal and Constitution*. And for the greatest show on earth, The Cyclorama—don't miss it. For a stone-cold fun picnic visit the Oakland Cemetery. And why not toast with that wine. You know the one.

Things that aren't here anymore: The Dekalb Medical Office has a brand new, technologically superior building, so don't try to ID any bodies in the one described in this book. It's gone. I made up some of the streets too so don't use this book as a map. You'll be lost.

And remember this book is a work of fiction so don't try to figure out who the people are or fit the situation to real stuff. In other words, as Patricia Conley would say, "Don't start no mess and there won't be none."

About the Author

Evelyn Coleman is the author of six well-received and award-winning children's books. She has written for such publications as *The Atlanta Journal-Constitution, Essence, Black Enterprise, Jive* magazine, *Utne Reader* and *The Quarterly Black Review.* She lives in Atlanta, Georgia. This is her first novel.

Visit Evelyn Coleman's web page at:
http://www.mindspring.com/~evelyncoleman